DISCOUNT

DISCOUNT

A NOVEL

CASEY GRAY

THE OVERLOOK PRESS
NEW YORK, NY

This edition first published in hardcover in the United States in 2015
by The Overlook Press, Peter Mayer Publishers, Inc.

141 Wooster Street
New York, NY 10012
www.overlookpress.com

For bulk and special sales, please contact sales@overlookny.com,
or write us at the address above.

Cataloging-in-Publication Data is available from the Library of Congress

Book design and type formatting by Bernard Schleifer
Manufactured in the United States of America
ISBN: 978-1-4683-0730-6

FIRST EDITION
1 3 5 7 9 10 8 6 4 2

For my father, David Gray,
who works like a mule and
gives like an orchard

Superstore

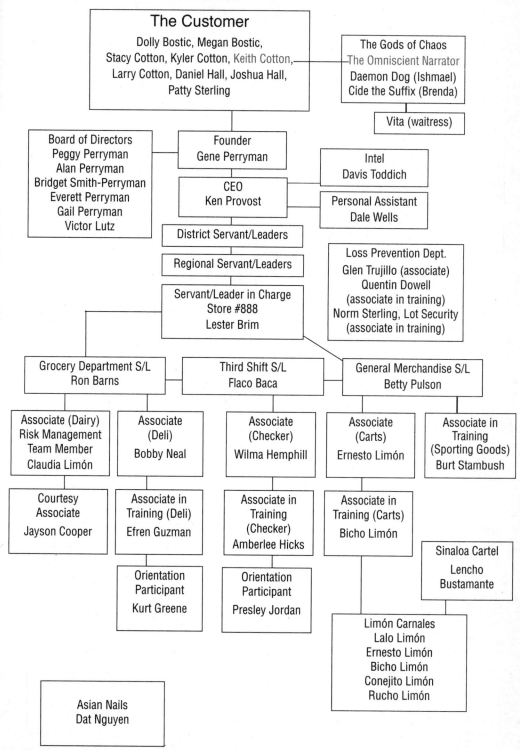

The Customer
Dolly Bostic, Megan Bostic,
Stacy Cotton, Kyler Cotton, Keith Cotton,
Larry Cotton, Daniel Hall, Joshua Hall,
Patty Sterling

The Gods of Chaos
The Omniscient Narrator
Daemon Dog (Ishmael)
Cide the Suffix (Brenda)

Vita (waitress)

Board of Directors
Peggy Perryman
Alan Perryman
Bridget Smith-Perryman
Everett Perryman
Gail Perryman
Victor Lutz

Founder
Gene Perryman

CEO
Ken Provost

Intel
Davis Toddich

Personal Assistant
Dale Wells

District Servant/Leaders

Regional Servant/Leaders

Servant/Leader in Charge
Store #888
Lester Brim

Loss Prevention Dept.
Glen Trujillo (associate)
Quentin Dowell
(associate in training)
Norm Sterling, Lot Security
(associate in training)

Grocery Department S/L
Ron Barns

Third Shift S/L
Flaco Baca

General Merchandise S/L
Betty Pulson

Associate (Dairy)
Risk Management
Team Member
Claudia Limón

Associate (Deli)
Bobby Neal

Associate (Checker)
Wilma Hemphill

Associate (Carts)
Ernesto Limón

Associate in Training (Sporting Goods)
Burt Stambush

Courtesy Associate
Jayson Cooper

Associate in Training (Deli)
Efren Guzman

Associate in Training (Checker)
Amberlee Hicks

Associate in Training (Carts)
Bicho Limón

Sinaloa Cartel
Lencho Bustamante

Orientation Participant
Kurt Greene

Orientation Participant
Presley Jordan

Limón Carnales
Lalo Limón
Ernesto Limón
Bicho Limón
Conejito Limón
Rucho Limón

Asian Nails
Dat Nguyen

Let flow the purest blood,
give from your own veins,
to blend with many bloods
and thus his cult sustain

—SOR JUANA INÉS DE LA CRUZ

DISCOUNT

1.
Wanting/Not-Having

6:39 AM

THE BLANKETS HAVE BEEN KICKED TO THE FLOOR AND CLAUDIA IS lying under the sheet, rolling like a white gypsum dunefield. The slope of her hip makes Ernesto sick with the disease of wanting and not having, which manifests itself physically in his stomach, in his throat, and in every single follicle.

Conejito is occupying the other bed in the pay-by-the-week hotel room, sprawled like he has been splatted there from a great height, and emitting a phlegmy, gurgling snore that no twelve-year-old boy should produce. Most mornings, Ernesto's third-shift sleep schedule makes the bed arrangements easy. Claudia's Superstore shift starts at 7:00 a.m., and he usually gets off work just in time to crawl into her warm, slightly damp empty spot to sleep.

He takes off his Superstore vest and his work shirt and tosses them onto the pile. He opens the minifridge, slams it closed when the sour-rot funk wafts into his nostrils, and kicks his shoes into the corner of the mauve room.

Claudia rolls over and hugs a pillow.

Conejito emits a congested snort and sticks two and a half tattooed fingers into his belly button.

Ernesto removes the last Pop-Tart from its foil and steps onto the balcony to wait. He smokes a Newport between bites and leans against

a blue-green rail pocked with the soot of hundreds of mushed cigarettes. The motel swimming pool in the breaking light, square and old
and stagnant, reminds him of his grandmother's waterbed. She
watched all of the kids while their parents worked in the summers, and
when she got overwhelmed, she put them in the bed and made them
take a nap. Abuela Limón hadn't been able to get in or out of the waterbed for years, but she was also unable to get rid of it. It was the bed
she shared with her husband. When her back got bad, she moved into
the kids' room and slept on one of the old sharp-cornered, metal-
framed singles they bought for three dollars at a government auction.
Gradually, the clothes, magazines, radio, humidifier—anything that indicated the presence of a living inhabitant—migrated across the hall
with her. The old bedroom became her tabernacle, with tobacco
stained wallpaper and a holographic picture of Christ writhing on the
cross or blessing the children, depending on the angle. An entire gen-
eration of cousins—Ernesto, Claudia, Bicho (then known as Emiliano),
and Lalo—shared her waterbed, which seemed enormous, even with
all of them on it. Conejito (who has been called Conejito for as long as
Ernesto can remember, even though his given name is Mark) slept in
a playpen in the living room.

They were still small enough to lie across it like sardines in a can
and passed the time making waves. Claudia would say, *Make little waves*,
and they would synchronize very tight, quick movements which created
ripples beneath them. Then Claudia would say, *Make big waves*, and they
would sync into a rolling, languid flop.

A large wave jarred a tiny fart out of one of them, and they fell into
hysterical laughter. The harder they tried not to laugh, the harder it was
not to laugh. Bicho was laughing the loudest. While they were trying to
hold it in, he was trying to force it out.

Abuela Limón didn't get angry when they misbehaved; she got tired,
more and more tired with each dropped cereal bowl that needed mopping and each scream-inducing pinch. Her weight pooled at her waist
and her ankles, and without a wig, her scalp was visible through wispy,
matte-black hairs. She took seven painful steps toward a dresser top covered by old photographs of a handsome man and asked the children if
they knew who he was.

All of them knew who he was.

Bueno, Abuelo Limón. When I was pregnant with your mother, Emilianito—a car he was working on fell onto him and he died. June fourteenth, 1971.

Was he nice?

Yes, he was very nice.

Then how come he's never smiling?

He was always *smiling. But he hated having his picture taken. He loved cartoons and he was good with numbers and machines. He was from Chihuahua City and he loved mole sauce, but he said I could never make it the way he remembered. He would sop it off of his plate and tell me that he loved me for trying. He was clever! He knew the way to keep me making him mole sauce, which is a real process. Always mischief, always dirty fingernails, like a little boy.*

Was he a army man?

The Marines, Abuela Limón said. She held out a portrait of him in his dress blues for the children to see, and Ernesto remembers swallowing a giggle at the sight of his grandfather's faggy white hat.

Did he kill people?

Yes, he killed many many bad people.

What did the bad people do? Ernesto remembers asking.

Close your eyes and try to remember every person you've ever seen. Every single one. Start with the ones you love: your mothers and fathers and brothers and sisters. Think of me. Think of your aunts and uncles and all of your cousins. Think of each other. Think of all the kids in your school: your friends, the teachers, every person in the neighborhood, even the ones you've never talked to, all of them with their own lives. Think about all the people you met and walked right by when we went to the fair. Close your eyes! Try to imagine them. The boy at the McDonald's register when I bought you all Happy Meals. Everyone in line. The little girls who ride their bikes through the neighborhood. Every face you've ever seen. Imagine that someone killed them and piled their bodies on top of each other like trash. And that that wasn't even all of them. That that wasn't even close to all of them.

Then she lit a candle with a very long match and said, *When this is burning, Abuelo Limón sees everything that you do. He sees down from heaven, through this picture, right into this bedroom. So cállate.* The Young and the Restless *is on.*

When she left the room they all laid still and quiet across the stagnant bed, except for Bicho who sat on the padded frame, staring at the picture and the burning candle through Coke-bottle glasses. Those black black eyes in that black-and-white photograph . . . It wasn't hard to believe that they saw you.

Lay down, Bicho Ojos, Claudia said. They all giggled, and Emiliano's name changed forever.

Bicho stared deeper into the photograph.

What are you doing? one of them asked.

If he can see us, maybe we can see him, Bicho said. Claudia stole his glasses from his head and put them on. She looked into the picture and said, *I don't see heaven, but I see the future. I'm a famous singer. Ernesto owns the record company. Lalo plays for the Dallas Cowboys. And Bicho Ojos is dead.* They laughed and Bicho let go of a scream that Ernesto can still remember the exact pitch of, one that sent gusts of cold wind and dried leaves through his veins. Abuela Limón threw her slipper at the door, as she often did when she was too tired to yell or walk, and Claudia gave the glasses back.

When they awoke, to the smell of smoke, Bicho was holding the photograph over the flame. At seven years old, Bicho was banished from Abuela Limón's home and was not allowed to come back under any circumstances. He did not return until she died seven years later.

Claudia joins Ernesto on the balcony, drinking from a two-liter bottle of pineapple soda. "You can have the bed. I'm sorry I slept in."

"You're going to be late for work."

"I'm calling in today. It's too pretty to be locked in a dairy cooler."

"How do you get away with it?"

"I've got a picture of the manager's dick on my phone."

"So you're going to lock yourself in that hot room and smoke glass all day?"

"No. Just every once in a while now. I want it to be fun again."

"It will always feel good, but it won't ever be fun again," Ernesto says. He gives her the rest of his cigarette.

"Are you sure you don't mind us staying with you for a while?"

"You're family."

"It's too crazy for Conejito over there right now. He's getting so big that Tom is like, I don't know, trying to show him who's boss before he outgrows him, or something. Like he's training an elephant. Ron put me on the risk management team. Fifty cents more an hour, so I'll be able to help out more."

"The Superstore doesn't pay you if you don't clock in."

"Lencho will give me some money."

"Don't take anything from killers."

"You take money from him."

"I make money *for* him."

"He writes me beautiful letters in Spanish. He says he wants to take care of me."

"Risk management team? I'm going to lay down while it's still cool enough sleep."

Conejito jogs past them, down the stairs and through the gate. The sun has just cleared the jagged peaks of the Organ Mountains. When he plops himself into the pool, the waves rise and glint in the orange sunshine.

6:46 A.M.

Ken Provost and Kun He follow the setter's fringed tail through the green switchgrass.

"Welcome to Perryman Prairie, Mr. He. *This* is why I named my first daughter Dawn."

"There is a lot of sun rising in Oklahoma. It deserves a capital D."

When Ken blows his whistle, the setter returns and stands at attention in a patch of dewy clover. "Management perfected, Mr. He. She smells things we don't, knows things we don't, so we follow her. All the while, we are in complete control. Our voices mean food and water. Shelter. Reprimand. We follow and we lead at the same time. It's why we spend a lot of time at our Superstores talking to folks: cus-

tomers and associates. I've got a round of Southwest visits planned
today."

"This impresses me, Mr. Provost. Even if we never see a pheasant."

"Please, call me Mr. Ken. It's what my associates call me. Or just
Ken, if you like. She'll find 'em. Sometimes they just roost where they're
released for a while. The transplant takes something out of them. Kind
of like jet lag. I hope it's not too early for you. Superstore executives pre-
fer hunting to golf."

"Sleep is the only luxury that men like us can't afford, Ken."

"Respect is complicated here. Tied to humility. Fluid. We need to
see our presidential candidates eat the chicken wings. Our founder, Mr.
Gene, understood that. Understood *folks*. 'Why is the ocean king of a
hundred streams? Because it lies below them.'"

"Americans are famous for their humility," Mr. He says.

"I had this property stocked with fifteen hundred Chinese ringnecks
Thursday. We might walk up on all of them at once."

"I'll know them when I see them. I'm what you call a country boy,
Mr. Provost. From the Sichuan Basin flatlands. Does that surprise you?"

"No, Mr. He, I can tell by the way you walk through the brush."

"I was a child during the famine. My father occasionally trapped a
pheasant in kochia weeds like these, and we ate it in secret while our
neighbors starved to death." A horsefly lands on Mr. He's neck and he
resists the undignified urge to slap it away.

Ken wipes his brow with a blue bandana and tucks it under his
safety-orange cap. He whistles for the dog and walks towards the shade
under a line of hackberry trees. "My mother used to talk about people
starving in China when I gave her grief about eating my broccoli."

The setter slows her trot and enters into her point, packed with potential energy like a drawn crossbow.

"There's probably a heap of them right around here." Ken follows the
dog's nose to a hen roosting in the pigweeds. "Okay, just like I showed you.
I'm going to kick her up. Don't pull the trigger until you have a safe shot."
Ken rustles the grass around the bird with his boot. When the hen remains
static, he gives it a gentle kick and it takes lazy flight. Ken hears Mr. He's
gun fire twice behind him while he watches the hen dart unharmed into
the tree line. "That's okay, Mr. He. It isn't easy to hit a bird in the air."

Mr. He bends the gun at the elbow and inserts two more shells. He takes one shot at the ground, then another. He discharges the shells and tucks four dead birds into his vest.

"We usually let them fly. It's more sporting."

"I don't like sports, Mr. Ken. I like meat."

2.
Orientation

"WELCOME TO THE SUPERSTORE FAMILY ORIENTATION. I'M BETTY and I'll be one of your Servant/Leaders here. I'm here to serve you, and I'm here to lead you. That's what that means. Follow me through the swinging doors that say 'Associates Only.' That's you now. Officially. You are being paid for this time.

"This storage area is designated for layaway items. Lot of bicycles and swamp coolers back here this time of year. That African-American gentleman in the snazzy suit is Mr. Brim, the Servant/Leader in charge of this whole store. He's just finishing up the morning meeting. You don't have to do the Superstore cheer at the end, but you really should. If you know it. It's real easy."

"Does everybody come to the meetings?"

"No, not everybody attends. We rotate. Somebody's got to run the store. Twenty-four hours a day, seven days a week, three hundred and sixty-four and a half days a year."

"When does it close?"

"Christmas day from twelve noon to twelve midnight."

"Why the different-colored vests?"

"The regular associates wear blue vests. Sporting Goods associates wear khaki vests. Deli don't wear vests. They wear white polo shirts and black pants. Lawn and Garden wears green. The AS/Ls (Assistant Servant /Leaders) wear red vests. They are technically Servant/Leaders in training, so if someone with a red vest asks you to do something, you do it. And the real Servant/Leaders don't have to wear vests. We're the ones wearing ties or dressed for business like me if they're a girl. One of you might find yourself wearing a tie if you work hard enough. I've been with the company for just five and a half years: sixteen months as cashier, twenty-one as a TL (Team Leader), one year as a AS/L, and going on eighteen months as a S/L. It's pretty sweet. They pay you good and you get to wear dressy clothes to work, so, you know, that means you don't have to throw trash and do crap like that. You can make someone else do it. And you don't got to be here for a long time because there's no such thing as seniority, just who does their job best. It don't really matter if you're Mexican or black or didn't finish high school because you had two kids, or what."

Betty joins the associates gathered around Mr. Brim in the company cheer: "My name is Betty, and it's my Superstore! I'm the reason it is super for!"

"We'll be here for almost eight hours, minus two fifteen-minute breaks and an hour for lunch. We're going to go over a lot today. Like really a lot. Don't feel bad if your head feels like a marshmallow after we're done. But if you walk out of here remembering anything, you need to remember the three principles Eugene Perryman founded this company on in 1963: 1) exceed customer goals; 2) respect; and 3) strive for greatness. A manager might ask you to repeat them at some point. They are extremely important. Sear them into your brain. If you forget them, they're painted on the wall in the breakroom, on the backs of the name tags, company letterhead, your paychecks: 1) exceed customer goals; 2) respect; and 3) strive for greatness.

"This is the Personnel Office. Have a seat at the round table we got here. Right in front of the glossy folder with your name on it. Inside you'll find three slightly smaller file folders called My Health, My Money, and My Goals. Put those down. Put the pens down. If you like filling out forms, they'll be plenty of that later on. Don't you worry. Okay, here goes my little spiel. My name is Betty. Did I say that already? Like I said, you're going to get a lot thrown at you today. I might say some things twice. I might say a lot of things twice, but the second time it might be a little different than the first. So it's important to listen, even if I say things twice. Take in as much as you can. When I went through my orientation, my goodness, they were throwing so much at us. I got home and I looked at my daughter and I couldn't remember her name for, like, ten seconds. For real. I was like, quit spitting on your sister... Crystal! We spend more time orientating our associates than most places because Mr. Gene understood that good associates are the ones who really make it happen. You are the face of the most successful company in the world. You are the ones who directly engage the customer, and you have the most impact on the customer's overall shopping experience. Here at the Superstore, we value everyone. We listen. Lots of the best ideas come from just regular associates like you.

"Okay, let's get started. Let me start by saying congratulations on joining the Superstore family. You are now a part of a very large family. We are the number one employer in New Mexico, and we are committed to growth. Each person in this room represents sixteen people who wish they were sitting where you are. That's right. That's a lot of people who want the jobs you got. So you are all very special people. Give yourselves a round of applause. Yea! Excitement, people! That's what I'm talking about! Why does everybody want to work at the Superstore? Well, one good reason is that the Superstore is about doing. We learn by proving and we prove by doing. Maybe you weren't good in school. I wasn't. Once I discovered boys, the teachers couldn't keep my attention. Well, this isn't a school of learning. It's a school of doing. We'll show you everything you need to do. You do it. And the people who do it best will rise to the top. The man in charge of this store, Mr. Lester Brim, runs an operation that grosses up to two million dollars a week. A week! He drives a Suburban with four TVs in it. They don't bring guys from Harvard in to do that job. He started out on night maintenance eighteen years ago, when he was twenty. Those jobs belong to you if you work hard enough. Here everybody's equal. We're not distinguished by race, or stuff like that, or education. We're only distinguished by who works the hardest. Mr. Brim is African American for example, if you haven't noticed.

"Notice we have round tables around here. That's a message the Knights of the Round Table used to symbolize equality. No head or foot. In fact, you'll find that all the tables in the associates-only sections of the store are round. That's not a coincidence; it's symbolism. It's no accident that we call ourselves associates, either. Associates work together. Nobody works *for* anybody. We do however have a flowchart. This chart explains the flow of our family. We here at the Superstore want to make sure information flows like a stream: both ways."

"Streams don't flow two ways."

"Some streams do flow both ways sometimes. Sometimes a shallow current flows one way and a deep current flows the other. It has something to do with the moon. But obviously this is not a real stream. It goes like this. How many of you play cards? Think of it like this. It goes:

Board of Directors
CEO
President
Vice President
Servant/Leader
Assistant Servant/Leader
Supervisor
Team Leader

And after that you're just a regular associate. And we're all associates. But anyway, that's like the card's value: the nine, or the A, or the two, or the jack it has on it. This other column is the card's suit:

Company
Division
Region
District
Branch
Store
Shift
Team

"And the customer is trump. They're the boss of everybody. Before you say anything, I realize that that's too many suits. Try to think beyond the literal. That's what's real. It's kind of confusing, but you'll learn the game pretty fast. Those computers along the wall are for CBLs. That's computer-based learning. You'll be doing plenty of that after the videos and the tour. Don't let me forget this is only your first day. I know it's a lot of initials and jargon to keep straight. If you don't understand something, just ask. Please. That's why I'm here. And we're not going to get out of here any faster without any questions. It just means I got to talk more. We've all got to be here until at least one thirty. No matter what. That's how long the manual says it takes."

"Those tables are square."

"Desks aren't tables. Desks are for one person to sit at and tables are for a bunch of people to sit at. It doesn't make sense to have round desks."

"There are a bunch of chairs around that big desk."

"All right, most, or a whole lot of the tables are round. The tables in the breakroom are round."

"Not the smokers' breakroom."

"Okay, not the smokers' breakroom. Listen people, a thing that's symbolism doesn't have to happen all the time. Just the gesture is symbolic. Okay. And you shouldn't smoke, anyway. It's a horrible way to die.

"Moving on. Okay, that call sheet by the red phone is coded for different emergencies: bombs, active shooters, lost children, severe weather, and media. You'll find one in the Personnel Office and by every red phone. There's a red phone in each of the departments. It's for associates only. It's got access to the intercom and the home office. We'll show you how to use that on the tour.

"Okay, let's get to know each other a little bit. Why don't you stand up and introduce yourselves. Tell us what department you'll be working in and a mnemonic device. That means something to help remember you by. Something besides where you're from or how old you are. Just a little or a quick thing. It can be anything. I'll start it off: My name is Betty Pulson. I'm a Servant/Leader. And me and my husband like to spend our free time riding our Honda Gold Wing luxury motorcycle. And all our other time paying it off."

"My name is Efren. I will work with the deli meats and cheeses. I have seven daughters."

"Wow! Seven girls," Betty says. "How many bathrooms?"

"One," Efren says.

"I bet there's bloodshed."

"No, they're not those kinds of girls," Efren says.

"I grew up with four sisters," Betty says. "We *were* them kind of girls. I got curling iron scars all on me. Dished a couple out too. You, with the hair?"

"My name is Norm. I'm going to be on third-shift lot security. I got one daughter."

"Sorry. I need something else, Norm."

"What do you mean?"

"Well, seven daughters we're going to remember. One daughter? We're never going to remember that."

"Her name is Patty. She's sixteen. She's a straight-A student."

"That doesn't help. Something about you."

"I write country music songs."

"That's fantastic. Do you ever perform?"

"No, I don't like to play them in front of people."

"Do other people ever play the songs you write?"

"No, I don't like other people to sing my songs."

"Well, you're never going to get famous that way. Okay. Dang, you're tall. What's your name."

"My name is Quentin. I'm a plainclothes LPO, so I won't be walking around with a badge and a can of pepper spray advertising it like Norm here. I'm gonna be watching the store dressed like your average Super-store customer, trying my best to be inconspicuous. My last job was at a maximum-security prison, so this shit is like nothing. And, I hate basket-ball, before you even ask."

"I don't know how you talk in the prison, but here at the Superstore we don't cuss."

"I'm sorry."

"And if you think this job is S-H-I-T, maybe you're in the wrong place."

"I didn't mean the job was S-H-I-T. That word just slipped out. I'm sorry. My last job—it was part of the language. I'm sorry."

"It's the first day, so I won't give you an official coaching, but under normal circumstances I would give you an official coaching for a discourse policy violation. There's a copy of the *Official Associate Discourse Policy*

Handbook in each of your packets. If I was you, I'd read it. There's lots of ways to get fired in there."

"My name is Presley. I want to get tattoos all over my whole body. Like ink where all the skin is. I'm from here. I'm going to be a cashier. I got three kids."

"Okay," Betty says. "Everywhere?"

"Like even all on my face and eyelids and stuff," Presley says. "I want to paint the whole thing."

"Like makeup tattooed all on your face? I seen a bunch of girls here do that."

"No, like leopard spots or scales everywhere. Or my organs diagrammed all over me like a textbook. And maybe some drawings I've done."

"We've had to readjust our tattoo policy here at the Superstore in recent years. Used to be no visible tattoos at all. But so many people have them now. You'll see people here with tattoos on their necks and hands a lot. I don't judge people. I got one myself. Don't ask me what or where it is. But I'm afraid we still draw a line before scales."

"What about leopard spots?"

"Them too. They'll scare the kids."

"My kids don't judge people," Presley says.

"Honey, do you ever think about what that'll look like in thirty years? An old lady with leopard spots."

"I don't look at stuff that way," Presley says.

"I'm just saying, you're a pretty girl. Please, before you say anything, do not agree or disagree. In fact it's best we moved on. We're going to take a CBL on what's appropriate to comment on and what's not after lunch. But you should all know that commenting on someone's personal appearance isn't okay. Now if you want to compliment someone on a new hairdo, you could. I mean, if it's all in a good-natured compliment sort of way. But I personally, if I were you, I would avoid that can of worms all together. Especially if you're a man."

"What about you?" Betty asks.

"My name is Kurt. No kids. I'm married, but my wife is a bisexual, so we have sort of a progressive relationship."

"Okay, that's not appropriate, Kurt."

"I'm sorry. There's just so much hate and prejudice out there right now. If this work environment is going to be hostile to my wife's sexual orientation, you should let me know so I can call my lawyer."

"I can assure you that the Superstore is not prejudiced against anyone's personal orientations."

"Well, what do you call that?"

"Maybe this was partly my fault for allowing the tattoo conversation to take place: they're things, on your body. Looking at the parts of each others' bodies. I'm certain there's something against that in the *Associate Discourse Policy*. I'm coaching myself up. I'm taking it as a learning opportunity. We're hardest on ourselves. That's what we do here. I'm coaching myself up, and I'm coaching you up. There is stuff we don't talk about here. Do you know what I'm talking about? Bedroom stuff. Not because of any prejudice on our part. But because it's just not polite. We don't talk about bedroom stuff, and we don't talk about money. Everyone in this room was assigned a wage based on several factors, including job description, experience, and other stuff. Talking about that stuff hurts feelings. Now, where are you going to work, Kurt?"

"The dairy, I guess."

"Okay, I don't think anyone's going to have any trouble remembering that one. Next."

"Mi nombre es Fatima. Voy a limpiar la tienda. Vivo con mi novio," Fatima says. "The Virgin appeared to me when I was a child. I have Magic."

"All right, cool," Betty says. "But we can't really get into Jesus here. Again, the CBLs will go over the *Official Associate Discourse Policy* later. You can't preach openly while you are on the clock. Or in the breakroom. I'm a Christian myself. But I guess some people aren't. So, you know, litigious society and all that. 'Litigious' means you like to sue people all the time. Will someone ask her what she does in her free time?" Betty asks.

Efren translates the question and her answer: "She said 'roller skates,' but I can't tell if she's serious."

"Well, I bet that's quite a sight. If she's serious." Betty nods at the young man wearing Coke-bottle glasses and a rattail. She notices for the first time the barely visible tattoos beneath his thick, black buzz cut—the cursive on his neck.

"They call me Bicho. I'm going to bring the carts in. I'm from here. I don't got no kids yet."

"Can you give us a mnemonic device?" Betty asks.

"I don't know," Bicho says.

"Just something to remember you by. It can be anything, just something you like, or something you like to do."

"I don't know."

"Well, what do you like to do?"

"I don't know."

"You can't name one thing you like to do?"

"Just kick it, I guess."

"What does 'bicho' mean?"

"Bug. Like bug eyes. Because of these glasses."

"Bug eyes?"

"Don't call me Bug Eyes."

"I guess it sounds better in Spanish. This is Bicho everybody. He's going to bring the carts in and he likes to 'kick it'"

A tall woman with skin like an orange peel says, "I'm Amberlee. I'm the one who was disfigured by severe burns over eighty percent of my body."

"Okay. All right. Any kids, Amberlee?" Betty asks.

"No. But it should be easy to remember all the burns."

"Okay."

"I'm sorry. Should I have said something else? I just thought it would be silly to say anything else. Let's be honest, you're not going to refer to me as the lady who collects panda figurines."

"That's fine. There's no wrong answer. Is there another thing you wanted to say? I was just trying to learn a little more about you. Do you collect pandas?"

"No, but I breed pugs," Amberlee says. "My mom won't even come over to my house because she says she can't stand to hear them all breathing. But I like it. To hear them breathing all loud all the time."

"Dogs are great. That's great. I have two cockers. You, sir."

"My name is Burt. I just lost three hundred pounds. I'm going to be working in Sporting Goods."

"Good for you. That's amazing!" Betty says.

"Not really," Burt says. "I had the surgery."

"Wow. Still. Anything else?"

"I'm a transfer from Deming, so I've already done this crap before."

"Well then," Betty says. "You'll remember we have a couple of videos to watch."

●   ●   ●

"Okay, let's see who was paying attention to the first video. Who can tell me something about Eugene Perryman?" Betty asks.

"He won the homecoming king elections all four years of high school," Amberlee says.

"That's right! Great! He is the only person in Oklahoma high school history to do that. He was always very charismatic. His positive energy is what built this place."

"He drove his same old truck even after he turned into a billionaire," Norm says.

"Great!" Betty says.

"He started the first Superstore in his hometown of Broken Arrow, Oklahoma," Efren says.

"Okay, great, what else?"

"During World War Two, Mr. Gene killed thousands of innocent people," Kurt says.

Burt groans.

"What do you think those bombs do when they land? Ever heard of Operation Rolling Thunder?"

"I've heard of Pearl Harbor," Burt says.

"Does anyone want to clarify Mr. Perryman's service record?" Betty asks.

"He was a navy pilot in World War Two. Also, he is awarded many medals for his service," Efren says.

"Okay, that's great. This guy really did pay attention," Betty says.

Efren continues, "The video says that Mr. Perryman is the American dream and all the American dreams are achieved through perseverance and teamwork. And he does not discover, but understands better than all of the people, that in a free market you can compensate for lower profit margin with volume. And so he lowers the prices for all of the people by eliminating extra expenses and creating the most efficient supply chains and businesses in the history."

"Wow! That's great stuff, Efren. This guy's on it. He even brought something to write with. If you're interested in the American dream, you should read Mr. Perryman's biography. There are always a few copies floating around the breakroom. Spanish and English ones. It's inspirational. I'm impressed. I like the ones like you that come over here and seem real interested in being American."

• • •

"Any questions on this video? No. Okay. It's very important to lift parcels in the green zone, close to the body. This job can be hard on your back. Okay, this next one is important. Listen up."

• • •

"If—God forbid—we do have an active-shooter scenario, don't be a hero," Betty says. "Stay out of the open. Run to the exits and get as far away as possible."

"What about Norm and me? Can we be a hero?" Quentin asks.

"LPOs secure and cover and let the police do their jobs."

"But we're Loss Prevention Officers. We're kind of like the police of the Superstore."

"The manual says that, 'Loss Prevention Officers may engage in verbal restraint only. In regard to aggressive subjects who pose a viable physical threat to customers and/or associates, LPOs are to phone police immediately and engage them in a passively responsive posture at their own risk.'"

"You'll have to pay me a little more to passively respond to a man with a gun," says Quentin.

"What does that even mean?" Norm asks.

"It means nobody can sue us if someone gets hurt," Betty says.

Burt, the man with deflated jowls, asks, "What if we're working behind the Sporting Goods counter, hypothetically, and we have an active-shooter scenario. And let's say, hypothetically, that we have the keys to all the gun cabinets and access to thousands of rounds of ammunition. If we have a clean kill shot, could we take out the active shooter?"

"I think that definitely, according to the manual, you shouldn't ever discharge a weapon in the Superstore under any circumstances," Betty says.

"What if an active shooter comes in actively targeting children," Burt asks. "Just decides to shoot all the children in the store in the head or something? People are sick. I mean, is there any plausible scenario where it might be acceptable to use deadly force?"

"That's not going to happen."

"That's easy to say. Some sicko just shot up a middle school on Wednesday. I watched them carry the little body bags out on the news. Stuff happens all the time that's hard to imagine."

"You've got a better chance of being struck by lightning."

"People always say that—with the lightning. Forty miles away, in Juárez, narcos sew faces to soccer balls. They kill entire families—kids and pets and all—routinely. They've got torture houses where they're slicing people's backs open with box cutters as we speak. You think the world can't go to hell like that here? We're no better than them."

Efren does the sign of the cross.

"Officially: you're not allowed to shoot anyone for any reason. And that's not going to happen."

"You never know what's going to happen. It might not be that. I'm just asking if under extremely improbable and terrible conditions we could use deadly force."

"No. Those aren't my rules. They're the Superstore's. Unofficially, I say, if some unthinkable scenario presents itself, do what you got to do."

"I'm not sure I follow."

"The manual, this entire orientation, is about what we're obliged to say," Betty says.

"It's no fair that he gets access to a gun and I don't," Quentin says.

"Bottom line: do not shoot anyone. I can't emphasize that enough. Let's move on to the next video."

• • •

"If the people around you aren't following lock-out/tag-out or temping procedures, it's your job to tell a S/L. We've got to watch out for each other. Because it's never the guy jerking around on the pallet jack that gets hurt; it's the person who's just doing their job like they're supposed to. Okay. And you may think it's cool to fudge the hot holding logs, or the cold holding logs, but what if a customer gets sick? Dies? A little kid dies? It happens. Old people and little kids are usually the ones that die the most. Food is very dangerous. And every time we have to send someone to the doctor for a work-related injury it costs the store ten grand. That comes out of our annual bonus, okay. When the store does good, we all do good. So follow lock-out/tag-out. And make sure everyone around you follows lock-out/tag-out. If your supervisor isn't following lock-out/tag-out procedures, he's wrong. Coach him up. If *he* gives you any grief, tell an S/L, and if he gives you grief, tell someone even higher up. But he should thank you for coaching him up. At least that's the kind of person we try to hire for leadership positions. If I'm doing something wrong, coach me up. I'll thank you. I might even nominate you for a commendation metal. That's what kind of Servant/Leader I am. This next video just came down from corporate. They're dead serious about this now."

· · ·

"Any questions? You deserve to be paid for every minute you work here at the Superstore. And you must take all of your breaks, even if we're real busy. Two fifteens and a hour every time you work more than six hours. It's the law. Say a manager asks you to clock out before cleaning up so that he can make his payroll budget for the week—don't, because not only will he get in trouble, you'll get in trouble. You could even be fired. It's against the rules to work for free. You get paid for every minute of work you do here at the Superstore. And you get all of the breaks mandated by state and federal labor laws. That's our official policy.

"Which brings me to another type of stealing: time stealing. That means sitting around talking to your friends, horse play, text messaging. We want you to have fun at work. But have fun doing work at work. We got a saying here: 'You got time to lean, you got time to clean.' Take your breaks, take your lunch, but when you're on the clock, do something. Grab a rag and clean up. Sweep. Find something to do. There is always something. Always."

· · ·

"Questions? Okeydokey. Next video."

. . .

"If you come upon any ethical concerns—you catch someone stealing or acting inappropriately—call the Superstore Ethics Hotline. There's no place for that here. Here everyone is ethical all the time."

. . .

"How'd you like the health and wellness video? Just a few ideas in there about living a healthier lifestyle. Our Superstore wellness program has recently added a mental health 1-800 number. You can call them with any problems you're having. Any at all. They don't even ask for your name."

"They can cross-check the number from the caller ID with the associate records database. I got a buddy that works in the S.L.I.C.E. division," Quentin says.

"Don't worry about that," Betty says. "It's pretty anonymous."

. . .

"Any questions on the employee-theft video? It's Superstore policy to prosecute every associate theft to the full extent of the law in absolutely every circumstance. So, you know, like the person in the video got four years. Quentin, do they want to go to prison?"

"No ma'am."

"If we turn someone in for stealing, what do we get?" asks Bicho.

"You get a commendation medal," Betty says. "Like this little happy face pin on my blouse. Get three and we buy you one share of Superstore stock. Who knows how much that could be worth. A lot of people think, 'Wow, the Superstore is so big how could it possibly get any bigger?' Well, let me tell you, we're getting into real estate, banking, health care, medicine. There are no limits."

"Is everyone with a smiley face pin a rat?" Bicho asks.

"Look, this store belongs to all of us. If we work hard, and the company prospers, and we're honest, and we're prudent—that means careful—then we will prosper with it, especially the ones who bought the stock.

"You might get away with it once or twice or three times. But I promise, if you steal, you will get caught eventually. There are cameras that cover every inch of the store and little microphones everywhere that hear everything. We're even watching the watchers. Mr. Brim fired a department S/L a few months ago for stealing an energy drink. One of the associates under him turned him in. And now that associate has his S/L job. There is a strict zero-tolerance policy. Because who are they really stealing from?"

"Us," Efren says.

"That's right," Betty says. "Every time someone is injured on the job because of carelessness, or steals, it comes out of our shared annual bonus. It comes out of our stock prices if we are wise enough to buy in. I'm glad he's gone. And me and him were good friends. But he stole that drink from me. And do you think that's the first thing he ever took?"

* * *

"Let's say union dues are three thousand dollars a year and you've been paying them for fifteen years. This represents the red line that plunges down here. Let's say you invested that same money in Superstore stock fifteen years ago. Look at this black line. And for every dollar you invest, the Superstore will invest fifteen cents. That's better than any bank will do for you. There's a cashier at the other Superstore on highway seventy who's sitting on a half a million dollars of stock. It's split six times since she bought it. That's a nice little chunk of RV money.

"A union is a company that takes your money, basically. What they do is talk to us on behalf of you. We speak for ourselves here. We don't need a union because here you can come directly to us with any grievance you have at all. We want to hear what you have to say, and we'll listen. We can't guarantee we can accommodate you, but a union can't guarantee anything, either. When you can speak for yourself, it's stupid to pay someone to do it for you. All you have to do is call anyone on the flowchart, all the way to CEO Ken Provost (Mr. Ken). You might get his secretary, and he might take a while to get back to you. He's got more employees than anybody in the whole world. And he might even not get back to you at all, directly. But the point is someone will get back to you on his behalf, for sure. Not just a secretary, someone who speaks for him. But really the most effective way to rectify a problem is to follow the flow-chart."

"Has anybody you've known ever actually spoken to this Mr. Ken?" Presley asks.

"I've seen him in this store three times since I've worked here. That's a lot if you figure he's got over six thousand stores. He's the biggest executive in the world and knows Jayson, one of the special boys who does takebacks, by name.

"Don't you wear name tags?" Presley asks.

"Well, I bet he would remember his name, even without it," Betty says. "But the flowchart is still the most effective way to handle most problems. So don't call the CEO to ask for the day off to go to the race with your buddies. But you could technically call him if you wanted."

"Could I call Mr. Ken and tell him I think his anti-body-art policy is prejudiced against my personal creativity?" Presley asks.

"You could. I wouldn't use that tone with him."

"Ugh! If I quit now, you still got to pay me for watching your videos, right? One of your own videos said it."

"You can pick up your first and last Superstore check at the courtesy desk on Thursday."

"Good luck, people. Enjoy the rest of your lives in this shit steam." Presley slams the door behind her, knocking an autographed poster of company founder Gene Perryman off-kilter.

"You know what's wrong with a lot of young people? I feel old saying it, even though I'm only thirty-nine plus six—it sounds better than forty-five, but a lot of young people have got this strange thing, like they deserve their own reality show that pays a million dollars where everybody just cares about them and wants to know what they're doing all the time just 'cause they're so special. I'm sorry, it just really makes me mad. Like I'm some kind of a sucker for working for a living and not stabbing ink into my face. It is a privilege to be a part of this company. The Superstore is about working hard, pride in working hard. And it's about bringing things to people, putting things in their grasp, things they couldn't have before. I know it sounds hokey, but we're making America a better place. Indi-vidually in our own little way, and together in a great big way. I know it's a lot to soak in. Why don't you take your hour for lunch. Meet back here for the tour at 11:22."

10:22 A.M.

Presley's mother sighs at her daughter breast-feeding in the passenger seat. "Christ, put a blanket over it. That bloody heart tattoo is warping his mind. You're going to turn him into an axe murder."

Presley has an anatomically correct heart tattooed into the skin over her real heart. She wants to look like a health-class poster and has talked about illustrating her lungs and her entire circulatory and reproductive systems.

The Blazer's AC unit blows a paltry stream of air into the hot vehicle, just cool enough to bother turning it on.

"I think it's great they hired a burn victim. I'm just saying, if it's really just about 'scaring the kids,' why is she allowed to work there? You should see her. I don't think she has eyelids. I didn't see her blink. Maybe she blinked. I didn't pay that close attention. I didn't want to stare, you know. But believe me, she'll scare more kids than I could with scale tattoos, devil horns, and a bobbed tongue. I can't work at a place like that. That's not where I belong."

Two men in a raised cosmetic truck hover over Presley and her mother at the light. The passenger reaches over the driver to honk and give Presley the thumbs-up. The driver hides his face under a baseball cap. Presley turns to the men and squeezes a dribble of milk from her nipple. The passenger's woo-hoo pierces all the rolled up windows between them.

"Why would you do that? That sicko is probably going to go home and do it to himself thinking about that."

"Men always forget what they're for."

"That's what they're for? To give some sicko his jollies?" Presley's mother pulls into the Arby's drive-through. "It's not discrimination. You could choose not to do that to yourself. You don't even have those tattoos yet."

"They make me feel different. Alive."

"Everyone is alive, stupid. Everyone is different."

• • •

The screens are fastened to the steel lattice that stretches across the Superstore ceiling. They hang exactly eight and two-thirds feet in the air, a height determined by the world's foremost retail layout guru to be just above the shoppers' fields of conscious vision. Superstore commercials play on these screens in a constant loop, at subtle decibel levels that don't distract customer attention, but permeate it. The screen in the fast-food restaurant is playing fifteen-second clips of music videos. Every one hundred and twenty-five seconds a comforting female voice says, "Visit the Superstore music section for big savings on your favorite artists." The sequence of videos seems random to Kurt: a gold-toothed rapper, to a country music sex symbol, to another county music sex symbol, to Bon Jovi, to a platinum-toothed rapper. But the sequence is controlled by a computer program operating at the home office in Broken Arrow. The Chart Matrix Program calculates the units sold in each and every Superstore nationwide. Each time an album passes a fifty-thousand-unit threshold, the computer increases the frequency of its fifteen second "tease" in the Chart Matrix Program's system.

Kurt is happy that once he orders his dozen chicken nuggets, fries, and large Dr Pepper. He never *has* to come back—not to shop, not to work. It's a joke. His mother needs to be taught a lesson. She spent his entire childhood telling him that his potential was limitless. When he took a placement test entering middle school, she told him that his IQ score was in the high one eighties and the highest ever recorded in the district. She let him walk around believing that for two years, inserting the score into conversations with kids and adults alike the way one might insert one's scrotum into the punch. He was smarter than you, whoever the hell you happened to be, and this had been quantified. Because the curriculum wasn't as easy as his supposed IQ indicated it should have been, he decided that the curriculum was retarded. He developed an air of boredom and superiority, neglecting his studies completely in favor of learning obscure words and facts that he could use to remind people that he was the smartest person in any room he happened to enter. Then, in the eighth grade, as Mrs. Peña explained the physics of orbits, he told her that she was being "pedantic," and then promptly asked her if she knew what pedantic even meant. When she sent him into the hall he told her (told the class, really), "My mind is a sailboat. And this classroom is a fish tank," which was a line he remembers crafting hours before class and feeling pretty good about. He entertained the thought that the entire student body might adopt the phrase as a battle cry. That they might start writing it on their jean jackets and carving it into the desks, and that some version of it might make a pretty good title when they wrote his biography: *My Mind is a Sailboat; My Mind is a Sailboat, and this Classroom is a Fish Tank; My Mind is a Sailboat: this Classroom is a Fish Tank; Sailing in a Fish Tank; The Fish Tank Seas.* After school Mrs. Peña explained to him, gently but with apparent glee, that according to the records, which she retrieved from the office for him to see with his own two eyes, his true IQ score was 111. She assured him that he was still "pretty smart," but that a career in particle physics (which was the cool-sounding thing he was telling people he wanted to "get into" that month) was probably not feasible. Then she just looked at him, like it was taking all of her strength not to ask him if he knew what "feasible" meant.

When he confronted his mother, she denied it. Then she admitted it. She petitioned to have Mrs. Peña fired, which got around the school and basically publicly de-pantsed him, exposing him as an aggrandizing liar, even though he had never knowingly lied about anything. Middle school had been hell for him even before this happened—his condescending barbs were never much of a defense against a well-timed "fag" or a punch in the dick. But they made him feel better, and hopeful that eventually the neanderthalic torturers who finger-bang girls and carry pocket knives would line up to kiss his ass and beg for a job. When the lie was exposed, that solace dissolved, and all that was left was a chubby, weak boy: smart, but not exceptionally so; talented, but not exceptionally so, one of billions. Unique, but none the less ordinary and abundant and fleeting like a snowflake. Kurt's mother justified the fib by telling him that she didn't want him walking around thinking that he was anything less than the smartest boy in the world, which he was, in his own way. And now she wants him to work at the Superstore loading milk into a slide. She thinks that's where he belongs.

The insidious fifteen-second pop music clip won't be so easy to shake. It's repeated six times since he got in line. It's the new ambient noise of his consciousness: *Let me know if you like what you see/if you like what you see come and stay with me tonight.* He tries to remember another song, any other song—*"Radar Love," "Happy Birthday," "Fanfare for the Common Man"*—but he can't. *Advertising is pressing at every orifice. It's like high water looking for cracks to seep through,* thinks Kurt. A hulking woman with cornrows and a patient voice walks a flustered, acne-ravaged girl through the keys on the register.

"Can I change that Dr Pepper to a strawberry shake?" Kurt asks.

"Sure you can. Don't worry. This is good. You got to learn how to do this. Now push the button with the milkshake on it."

"Do you have malted shakes?"

"Yes we do. It's twenty-five cents more."

"Never mind."

"Are you sure?"

"I don't want to be any trouble."

"That's okay. She's got to learn this anyway sometime."

"Okay."

"Which kind of sauce do you want?"

"All of the sauces."

"A dozen only comes with two sauces. It's ten cents for every extra sauce."

"Sure. What the hell."

"Shyanna! We need the manager code to void!"

An associate named Wilma Hemphill is standing behind Kurt in line. The top of her brain thinks, *If I can't shit and eat before my fifteen minutes is up I'm going to kill myself,* while the bottom of her brain chooses lunch.

It's so much better to be a customer, thinks Kurt. *Trump. Don't these people realize that you only have one life to live, a set amount of time to breathe and be aware and exist. Who could feed their time into this shredder? God. If you think of life as time, this shit is a massacre. If murder is just stealing some of the time someone has left, it's a time holocaust. The circumstances that led to my existence were miraculous. If my great-great-grandfather hadn't survived his war wounds, if my father had pulled out in time, if my particular sperm lost the race, I might have been some different combination, or I might have never even been at all. And much farther back, to the protoplasm and the naked savages, to the formation of the universe itself: an inhabitable planet. Water, sun, life. I'm a cosmic miracle.*

Kurt the Cosmic Miracle dips each of his nuggets into all four sauces: barbecue, sweet-and-sour, honey-mustard, and ranch. He cleans up the van by stuffing fast-food bags into other fast-food bags. He turns the music up until the factory speakers start to crackle. The piercing guitar solo twists his face into a knot. *Does it make me gay if Led Zeppelin gives me a hard-on?*

• • •

Wilma Hemphill returns to her post at register seventeen feeling lighter on her feet and less hungry, but still very tired. Her eyes are slow to focus, and it feels like a damp, musty towel has been draped over her brain.

"Twenty-four minutes," Cruz says. "Did you fall asleep in there?"

"If that toilet seat was five degrees warmer, I might have."

"You're not the only person in the world with pressing bodily functions. This isn't Sunday morning with the funny pages after a big breakfast and three cups of coffee. Now I got to do my break in six minutes."

"I said I was sorry. The motherfucker in front of me at McDonald's took all day."

"You ate?"

"Just go. Unless you want to spend your six minutes tearing me a new asshole. You can have my whole second break." She enters a pleasant state of exhausted delirium wherein the usually rote mechanics of entering codes, validating checks, and deactivating antitheft devices requires her entire brain. She has so thoroughly mastered each and every aspect of her job that it usually requires very little frontal lobe activity at all, which is the worst, because this leaves a significant portion of her mind to obsess about the time that is passing, and to drift into daydreams that are almost always nearly as boring as scanning items and counting out change. She imagines sitting on her new porch and watching the sprinkler sway over the yard, changing the dust to mud. She sometimes daydreams about *Dancing with the Stars*, not appearing on the show, just watching it in an oversize T-shirt and house shoes. Occasionally she actually daydreams about cashiering, the very thing she is currently doing. The same line 17. The same store 888. Only the customers and time of day are different. The result is a miserable, reverberating boredom that slows time down to a torpid crawl.

In her present state, her mind is entirely devoted to the keystrokes and the bar codes at hand. She becomes a very tiny black hole, a tear in the fabric of the universe. Time slips and falls right through her until Ron Barns' Tommy Hilfiger cologne yanks her out of her zone. She can smell him behind her, can feel his eyes on her, but she does not turn around.

Ron is astonished by the I.P.H. number displayed at the bottom right corner of her screen. Thirteen-hundred and eighty-eight items per hour is unheard of, the equivalent of a three-minute mile. "How are you doing that?" he asks.

"I'm just doing it," Wilma says.

"Breaks are fifteen minutes long," Ron says.

"I told her I was sorry. I was having a feminine problem."

"You ladies think that works every time."

"I had to go to the bathroom."

"Did you have to eat too? Was that the feminine problem you were having?"

Wilma turns to look at Cruz three registers down. Her look asks, *why?* Cruz's look says, *Some minutes seem like hours and some hours seem like days. Some hours seem like minutes and some minutes seem like seconds. We have a fucking clock. With a big hand and a little hand, or digits and a colon. To keep it all from dissolving like a packet of Splenda.*

11:22 A.M.

"All right gang, gather around," Betty says. "Fatima, Amberlee, Efren, Bicho, Norm, and Burt. Five out of seven back from lunch. No more tattooed lady (thank God). And no more swinging weirdo (thank God). That ain't bad, believe it or not. Go ahead and forget them. Forget their names. Forget their mnemonic devices. Forget everything about them. Make new room in your memory banks. You're going to need it. One thing you'll notice around here is a lot of new faces all the time. Of course we got a lot of people who have been here for years and years, but a big percentage don't last two weeks. Not everybody can cut it here. It gets confusing as heck. You just start to get to know someone and then they're gone and you probably aren't going to see them again. And you turn around and there are new faces to replace them. That's why you each now have your own personal Superstore name tag. Inside the white envelope in your folders you'll find your new Superstore associate discount credit card. Ten percent off everything. Call the number to activate it. Mine's a god-send those last three days before my paycheck.

"Listen carefully. Efren, please translate: you are the only one who can use this discount card. You can't lend it to your sister or your daughter to get her stuff. I have had to fire a lot of people personally for misusing this card.

"It's time for the grand tour. Stick together. Don't touch anything yet. This room we've been in all morning is the Personnel Office. We do a lot here. The file cabinets lining the back wall are marked: Medical, Professional, and Personal. But we're getting ahead of ourselves. This is where we have our meetings. And this is everyone's office. None of the S/Ls have our own office, not even Mr. Brim.

"The computers are a little old, but they work. The SMART system does everything. You can get on the computers to check your hours worked for the week. Every time a customer buys a can of beans, the SMART system orders another can of beans. It dictates every step in the production line from the field to the cash register. It calculates, follows, and records every purchase in every Superstore constantly, every hour worked by every associate, every store cost down to the last paper clip. At the time it was built it was the second-biggest database in the world, second only to the U.S. government. After the tour, you come back here and finish as many CBLs as you can before one thirty, then you can spend a little time getting acquainted with your work stations.

"Follow me. Okay, this is layaway. It's very important that we never ever block these garage doors with anything. About twice a month we are FLOWed. And about twice a month we FLOW. I forget what the letters stand for, but that's when the managers from the store across town come here to monitor our quality. They audit our safety kits and temperature logs and everything. And we go to their store to monitor theirs. If they see that door blocked with a forklift or a crate, it's bad. Through the doors is DSA 3. That's dry storage area three. It's where we keep the impulse-buy items: the breath mints and celebrity magazines and stuff you didn't mean to buy.

"It's a narrow hallway here, so get back out of the way of the fork-lifts. It's sort of maritime rules—the larger vessel has the right of way. Maritime means ocean.

"These are the dry food shelves. They go all the way up to the ceiling. Pretty much everything that's dry that you can eat is here. The shelves accordion together because it's a better use of space. The button on the right makes them move right and the button on the left make them move left. The button in the middle stops it. There's also this automatic kick stop that extends three inches past the bottom and shuts it off before it crushes you. But that don't work if you're climbing all the way up there like King Kong looking for some merchandise you're too lazy to get the lift for. All accidents are preventable. Each trip to the hospital costs the Superstore profit-sharing plan fifty thousand dollars. So be careful. That money comes out of our money.

"This is the bailer, for boxes. And this is the trash chute. Get some-one to help you lift the big gray cans. And help each other, people. That's how we do it here. Don't be showing off and hurt your back. There's a trash chute back here in dry grocery, one in merchandise, and one special medical waste receptacle in the pharmacy. They have to count and doc-ument each pill they throw away. Don't worry. None of you are going to be anywhere near there.

"This metal room is the dairy cooler. Where's Claudia?" Betty asks a man steering a pallet jack.

"Sick."

"Sick of working for a living? We got a cure for that. Right now we're walking down Action Alley. It's the main thoroughfare through the store. Thoroughfare means just like a main roadway or something. Think of it as the store's aorta. That's the big artery that runs through the middle of your body. A whole bunch of little veins spring off it. We place all our hottest deals here. Toaster oven, under twenty bucks. Fluorescent beach towel, under four bucks. Feel that thing. Plush. Where else are you going to find a deal like that?

"Here's the checking stations. Amberlee, you'll be working up front here. If you need anything, just ask Wilma. She's the African-American lady with the yellow highlights. She's kind of a celebrity around here. She's had the highest I.P.H. rating in the district for fifteen straight months. She'll know how to fix any problem I can imagine you having.

"This is the deli. Efren, your new home. You got your meat display cases here, your slicers. The cold salad case. Deep fryer. Rotisserie oven. Notice the poles with the red stripes around the store. They're the Superstore fire stations. There you'll find an extinguisher and a silent alarm that will alert management. The poles with the orange arrows pointing down are spill stations. You'll find rubber gloves, a medical face mask and gown, disinfectant, Super Solvent, and sterile wipes. There's also orange safety cones you put up and leave up for thirty minutes after you clean up any wet spill.

"This is the meat cooler. Be very careful in here, the floor is usually wet. It's cold, obviously. You got your rubber floors, hose, shelves, meat, raw chickens. A drain in the center of the floor for all the little bits and meat juice to wash into. Let's not stay here any longer than we have to, okay?"

3.
The Difference Between
Lines and Arrows

A HARD RIGHT TURN DUMPS THE OPEN TUB OF SWEET-AND-SOUR-sauce onto Kurt's leg. The slow-flow viscosity makes for an easy spit-finger clean up.

He rolls through a stop sign and parks by the motel pool. A large man bursts out of the water, tossing a young girl high in the air. She squeals like a bottle rocket and splashes into the water a few feet away. A swimming pool full of children swarm the man, begging for a turn. *This sound is music,* thinks Kurt, switching off the radio. *All splashing and laughing. You can hear the weather.* Kurt can't stop watching, even though he realizes fully that a thirty-two-year-old gringo sitting alone in a dank van with no windows watching the children play must look more than suspicious. He has never been at all impressed by the physical feats of athletes. But for the first time, watching this giant man tossing gleaming child after gleaming child, he understands how someone else could be.

A young girl in a purple bathing suit leads her little sister wide around Kurt's van. *Why can't I just sit here and watch the kids play?* He tilts his mirror to spy on a very pregnant teenage girl taking a mental picture of his license plate. *I wish I could just step out of the van and say: "Listen folks, my interest in watching your children play is completely platonic. I know that vans are creepy, windowless vans in particular. I'm just here to buy weed." Probably not a good idea to say that out loud. Just get out and walk upstairs. Go. Do it confidently. Don't seem suspicious. Why do I feel so suspicious? It makes me suspicious.* Kurt emerges from the stale, fried smells of the van into the smells of pool chemicals and summer. A fat twelve-year-old boy with tattoos across his fingers and belly runs past him, cursing the hot pavement underfoot. His wet tracks evaporate behind him like deleting letters.

The motel surrounds the pool like a stadium. Almost everyone who isn't at work is basking on the balcony or in the water. Even the late shifters, who usually sleep through this part of the day, are sitting on coolers and sipping beers.

Kurt knocks politely and is invited into the upper-deck motel room by a young man with jet-black hair growing in symmetrical splotches on his chest and back. A blunt is smoldering on top of a soda can. There's no reasonable place to sit, in Kurt's estimation. It's clear from the toaster oven and the hot plate on top of the minifridge that the young man has been living here for a while.

Ernesto is sitting on one of the unmade beds, and Claudia is lying across the other bed like she has been squeezed out of a tube. The thin, doubled-over pillow meets her fat cheek like cleavage. The crease is repeated in various locations as Kurt's eyes move down her body.

Ernesto tears just enough attention away from the video game he is playing to acknowledge his presence. "You wanna hit that blunt?"

I wish they sold this shit at the Superstore, thinks Kurt, letting a plume of blue smoke slide out of his mouth before sucking it back into the bottom of his lungs. His lifetime Superstore ban is already forgotten. *At least there I wouldn't have to sit around until the cashier feels like getting off her ass and ringing me up.* Kurt has been through several dealers during his lifetime, and they've all had this same requisite field test. They get you high and then sit around sizing you up. Kurt feels like an undercover cop. He feels like he looks like an undercover cop, particularly his hair, a military-style fade he's had since he was eleven. He wonders if Ernesto or the girl lying half conscious on the bed can feel him feeling like a cop. Does he smoke weed like a cop? *At least the Superstore respects the customer. The customer is God there. If I buy a sack of corn meal at the Superstore I don't have to go home and weigh it again on my own scale to make sure it weighs what they say it does. How come when*

I buy groceries I have all the power, and when I buy drugs they have all the power?

There is something off about the girl on the bed: glassy eyes, a disturbing undertone to her skin. "Are you okay?" Kurt asks. She does not respond. Her eyes stay fixed on some invisible mark nine inches east of the TV screen. *I could carve a more realistic girl out of a bar of soap*, he thinks.

"You can sit on the bed. She won't bite," Ernesto says.

"That's okay," Kurt says.

"Do you want me to tell her to get up?"

"No, she looks more than comfortable."

Ernesto doesn't take his eyes off the digital zombies he is killing. The sound is all the way up, death groans and machine gun fire.

"Is she okay? She looks not okay," Kurt says.

"Claudia," Ernesto says.

"Huh."

"What's your name?"

"Ernesto."

"What's my name?"

"Ernesto."

"See? She's fine."

The fat twelve-year-old boy who ran by Kurt moments ago walks through the door, dripping onto the carpet. Kurt glances at the tattoos on his hands and belly, but he doesn't read them. To read them would require looking directly at the boy, which seems like a terrible idea for reasons he is too high to explain to himself. It's not that he is intimidated by the boy, who is still soft and underdeveloped somehow, despite his size, and gives off a pleasant enough vibration. He is compelled to look away from the boy for the same reason that that very morning he had found himself compelled to look away from the stray wiener dog dodging traffic on El Paseo. He recalls the boy being launched in the pool. As the heaviest of the kids the man threw, he didn't get very far, but he can still hear the high-pitched joy in the sound he made.

"Quit dripping on my floor, Conejito. Look at your fucking belly button, güey. You could hide your fucking wallet in there," Ernesto says.

Claudia stands up and walks to the bathroom. A fluorescent green beach towel flies out the door into Conejito's face. He walks outside, dragging the towel across his back.

"So . . ." Kurt says.

"What's up with you?" Ernesto asks, taking one hand off of the controller just long enough to bring the blunt to his lips.

"I spent all morning at a fucking Superstore orientation. My mom's friend from church set it up with her son. I figure what the hell. Infiltrate. Maybe start a union or a lawsuit."

"Me and Claudia work at the Superstore. She goes in when she feels like it."

"How?"

"I've got a manager's dick on my phone. Do you want to see it? It's hilarious."

"Put that shit away," Ernesto says.

"There's your lawsuit," Kurt says.

"I don't know," Claudia says. "He's kind of sweet."

"I think the manager, or leader of the servants or whatever, is going to fire me. I mentioned a lawsuit in the orientation, so I think she's talking it over with the lawyers first."

"How'd you fuck up in an orientation?" Claudia asks.

"I told her that my wife is a bisexual and that we have an open relationship," he says.

"What the fuck brought that up?" Claudia asks.

"She asked us to say something about ourselves," Kurt says.

"And you said that?" Claudia asks. "What the hell is wrong with you?"

"I want them to fire me. I'm going to get litigious," Kurt says. "I'm going to sue them,"

"I know what it means. *You* got two women?" Claudia asks, though she already knows the answer. She doubts that this dumpy man in a black, dandruff-dusted Planet Hollywood T-shirt could find one woman willing to have sex with him for free, much less a wife and women on the side.

"No, but I'm willing to fight for people's right to live their lives any way they want. They can't discriminate against you for anything," Kurt says. "Do you know four of the top ten richest people in America are related to Gene Perryman?"

"So they got so much money that they're just going to give some to you?" Claudia asks.

"I'm hoping they'll settle just to keep it out of the press. I'm not greedy. A hundred grand, five hundred grand, whatever."

"Good luck with that rachety bullshit. Did you read your contract?"

"Of course."

"Do you know what a forced arbitration clause is?"

Kurt takes another puff of the blunt. "I'm high. I went to college."

"It means if you sue, you can't go to court. The dispute is settled by a third-party arbitrator, but who do you think picks the arbitrator? Who do you think pays him?"

"Fuck it," Kurt says. "I'm half an hour late, anyway."

"Manny got his fucking foot crushed off by a forklift last year and they only gave him twenty thousand. What do you think your bullshit is worth to nickel and diming motherfuckers like these? I didn't go to college, but I know what I fucking sign."

"They make you pee in a fucking cup. I couldn't even stand the orientation. It was like being stoned to death with popcorn kernels."

"How'd you pass the piss test?" Claudia asks.

"Well," Kurt says, clearly pleased to be asked. "You need clean urine, a thermometer, tape (I suggest anything but duct), a motel-size shampoo bottle, and two portable hot beverage. . ."

Living voices break through the digital zombies, urgent Spanish cries from the balcony. Kurt peeks through the closed blinds to witness a mad scramble from the balcony to the pool. He follows all the eyes to the pink smudge in the water and the crimson brushstroke on the pavement. Blood soaks through the fluorescent yellow beach towel that the young mother has wrapped around her daughter's head. The man stands dripping on the pavement, a safe distance from the commotion. He lights a cigarette, takes one deep drag, and extinguishes it on the crucifix tattooed on his chest. He puts one out on the tiger's eye. On the demented clown. On his mother's name. He goes through the rest of the pack. He does not spare his own nipples. Nobody stops him. Nobody but Kurt even looks.

12:26 P.M.

A big part of Ron's job as an S/L is just walking around. He roams the grocery section of the store looking for sellouts and checking the meat and cheese coolers for sloppy conditioning. The products that expire first must be constantly moved to the front.

Two days ago Ron sent a regrettable image to Claudia's in-box, and the message hasn't been returned. They had been corresponding for months online. Initially they chatted about her new position as a member of the risk management team, a position Ron eventually nominated her for, but soon the correspondence grew more intimate. Usually, when Ron finds himself talking to beautiful women, the words that leave his mouth are all in the service of impressing them. But over the Internet, conversing between screens, he was compelled to reveal the weakest, lamest parts of himself, the parts of himself that he had taken great lengths to hide from beautiful women his entire life. He wrote about the way his voice fluctuates with the flowchart, how he can hear it getting higher in tone and more sycophantic whenever he talks to an associate who outranks him, like a waiter's voice. He wrote about how much he despises all the people in the world who are exactly like him. Her responses were always poorly spelled and loaded with emoticons, but he sensed a unique and profound intelligence in them. She seemed wise, as if she had lived more in twenty years than he had in thirty-eight. He told her she was beautiful, using the most poignant and demonstrative words he could bring himself to type into the keyboard. She told him that he was sweet, and that his words had made her heart feel like a ten-pound sack of flour in her chest. When he told her that he loved her, she told him that she loved him too, but qualified it with a lot of extra words that he has willfully expunged from his memory.

Two days ago, Claudia sent him a picture of her new tattoo, a five-point star deep enough on her pubis bone to reveal a hint of jet-black pubic hair. He liked her body. It was both soft and dense. It sloped and curved like a wave. He imagined the springy feel of it under his hand and responded with a picture of the erection it caused. *It's something Troy would do,* he thought as he pushed send. Troy the Deli Manager at the West Side store. Troy his friend. Troy who was always getting laid. Troy who women knew what they were getting into with, and got into it anyway. *It could be all over the store by now,* thinks Ron. *They'll lock me away.*

It's worse than it sounds. The regrettable image is of Ron's erect penis coming through the window of his daughter's dollhouse like the arm of Kong reaching for Ann Darrow. It dwarfs the refrigerator and has knocked the miniature place settings and turkey off the table. A plastic family lies scattered around it, nonplussed, their clumsily painted, circular eyes astonished in context. He thought it would be funny, and he desperately wanted to introduce some element of levity into his potentially creepy gesture. And there was of course the added bonus that the scale would make his average penis seem humongous. It was perfect. After three gin and tonics, it seemed like the single funniest thing he had ever done. He wants to tell Troy in person. He wants Troy to see him talking with his hands, the hilarious expression on his face. And he wants Troy to be slightly-to-very drunk and/or stoned if possible. But Troy is a busy man. Ron has invited him for beers, offered to buy him dinner. The more he thinks about it, the more it seems like Troy is the only person in the world he can tell, who will get it, how funny it is. *You always have to hit Troy up a few times before he gets back to you. That's just the way he is,* he thinks in refrain to each new text message he sends.

An indignant customer approaches him to complain about the wait at the registers. He's got a thirty-minute drive home and his ice cream is already melting. It's unsanitary! Ron apologizes profusely. *I stuck my cock in my daughter's dollhouse,* he thinks. The longer Troy doesn't call back to laugh with him, the creepier Ron feels.

1:31 P.M.

The care Dat uses when pushing the cuticle back makes Stacy swoon. This is why Stacy has her nails done professionally, the hand touching. It's not particularly romantic or clinical, just a nice comfortable place in the middle. Her skin is raw-steak red and peeling off in sheets. She needs soothing. Her husband rubbed aloe on her sunburn twice, but it wasn't enough. He complained the whole time. She wanted him to do it while she was lying naked and facedown on the bed. She wanted to be sandwiched between the cool-soft comfort of the bed and the cool-slick comfort of the aloe lotion. But Larry said he didn't want "this crap" all over the bedspread, so they had to do it in the bathroom, under the harsh light, while her nipples were cold and bare and not pressed against the quality sheets, into the sublime softness of her memory-foam mattress. *I make that bed every morning, Jesus. I wash the sheets and the bedspread. And he just sort of smeared it on, like a little kid being forced to finger paint.*

"Do you mind if I ask you how old you are..." She feigns looking at his name tag, "...Dat?" The name has rattled around her head like a loose bolt since he first took her hand five months ago. *Dat. Dat... DatDatDat-DatDatDat. It's like a snare drum. You could pace your life to it. Dat. Dat's funny. Dat's hilarious. Dat's all folks. Could you pass me Dat syrup?* It takes her mind off of her tortured skin.

"Seventeen," Dat says.

"Oh my." In her mind, Stacy is sitting in a room, staring at a television in the corner. She feels no responsibility for the debauchery on the screen. In fact, she would love to complain to the programmer, whoever that is. The TV in the corner examines a body so different from her husband's: thin and hairless, with poking hipbones—an appeal so opposite: innocent and eager. *His idea of spicing things up wouldn't be imitating Internet porn, like Larry.* Dat's brown body twists on the screen. *Jesus, please turn the channel. I don't see a remote or a knob. Or turn it off. Fine. But he's the only thing in this room to stare at.*

"How old did you think I was?" Dat speaks with the flat American accent of a sitcom teenager.

"It's so hard to tell with Asians. Maybe twenty-six."

"Really? You thought I could be twenty-six?"

"I just assume you all look younger than you are." *Jesus, please forgive me. I'm fine. I'm a hundred miles away from doing anything wrong. This is innocent. Money for service. There's my wedding ring right in front of his face.* "Seventeen! That's about the youngest I thought you could possibly be."

"I'm tall for my age."

"Yeah, you sure are. And for, you know... Anyway, I'm terrible at telling people's ages."

"There's a trick."

"Yeah?"

"The hands." Dat loves hands. Especially ladies' hands. The way a well-manicured fingernail can extend a finger into abstraction, turn a line into an arrow. Dat even likes this hand: its rolling paper skin and its big, wormy veins.

"Oh, yeah?"

"I can tell exactly how old someone is by their hands."

"Exactly?"

"Within a year or two."

"Still, that's pretty good. How old am I?"

Dat rubs the pads of his thumbs gently over Stacy's cuticles to judge the elasticity in her skin. He notes the thick, blue vein weaving through the delicate bones. *Forty-two.* "Thirty-six."

"Hah! You're four years off. I'm not going to tell you if it's older or younger." She steps out of the bare room of her mind, the one lit by a lecherous television—

"It doesn't work all the time," Dat says.

—into the Times Square of her mind, with layers of lecherous monitors and billboards and street criers screaming about the same unspeakable thing: the hairless Asian boy, the tent-pole hip bones, what she imagines, based on racial stereotypes, is an adorable and tiny penis. *Please Jesus. Just talk back. Tell me what to do? Cut the evil out like a surgeon. Fill it with something holy.* The lotion made the burning go away, but not forever. Here in his hands, all she can think is: *Dat. Dat. Dat. Dat.... DatDatDatDatDatDatDatDatDatDatDat.* Her nails are drying, a good excuse to blow an amber ringlet of hair playfully out of her eyes, to toss that hair back with a jerk of the neck, to give Dat a look that pleads with him to draw that pesky red ringlet out of her eyes and behind her ear. *Gently please, with one finger that passes over the slope of my ear and makes me feel squishy.*

Dat does not dare help Stacy with the ringlet of hair. She thinks, *What if I told him it was okay? What if I just asked him? Jesus, why did I think that despicable thought? You made me. What do you have to say for yourself?* "You're getting a big tip," Stacy says.

"Thank you, but the Superstore doesn't allow us to accept gratuity," Dat says.

"How does that work? Are you a Superstore employee?"

"We rent this space inside the store from them, so they pretty much have a say-so in everything. What we charge, our hours. But, technically, I guess this is my Aunt Ling's nail shop."

"Well then I don't see how my gratitude is any of their business."

"Thank you, but I really can't accept it."

"Nonsense."

"I can't. They treat it like stealing. I'm sorry. I just really can't. They could terminate my aunt's lease."

"How will they know?"

"The same way they know if you're stealing."

"How's that?"

"They watch us."

"I hate this place. I just can't keep away. Ya'll got everything here—and so cheap."

4.
Loss Prevention

2:13 P.M.

"IT'S YOUR FIRST DAY, BIG DADDY. SLOW YOUR ROLL," GLEN SAYS, sizing up his new partner in one word: asshole. The Loss Prevention Office is a converted maintenance closet, and now Glen has to share it with eight monitors, eight digital recording devices, two chairs, a locked steel cabinet, and this arrogant giant, whose elbow has already touched him twice without an "excuse me."

Quentin doesn't like something about the way the old lady on monitor seven is walking, with intense purpose but no direction. Trying too hard to act casual. "If there's one thing you learn working in the prison, it's how to size people up quick. Sometimes it's life or death. There's something about that one. Baggy clothes. Floppy hat to hide her face from the cameras. Possible crotch walker."

"Crotch walker?" Glen asks.

"She looks like she's had a couple of kids. You'd be surprised what they can put up there."

"This isn't a prison."

"I can spot 'em," Quentin says. "She's not just perusing the merchandise. She's looking up, watching us watch her. She's checking for blind spots in our camera view. Who the hell looks up? Why, unless you're doing something wrong? I bet you she steals something. Check the other cameras for a partner."

"No way. I can see it too. She's definitely going to steal something. I can see it in her hip rotation," Glen says.

"Your mother's hip rotation," Quentin says. "Switch to camera sixty-four... Sixty-five... There, look. She's going to steal that."

"Oh my God, she's going to hide that surge protector in her pussy hole, no she's just going to turn it over and see how many volts it is."

"She's looking up at the cameras for our blind spots."

"So because you look up, you're a thief?"

"Not necessarily," Quentin says. "But it's a reason to be suspicious. Sometimes you just get a hunch. I'm going into the field."

"Be fucking positive before you approach. You just can't go around shaking down customers like prisoners. If you approach them and you're wrong, you're fired. And bring me back some sour candy."

"What kind?"

"The most hard-core, nut-twisting, sourest fucking candy they sell."

"Give me two dollars."

"Don't you believe in karma?"

"Fuck no, I believe in Jesus Christ." Quentin puts on what he calls his stalking glasses. They wrap around his eyes and reflect an opaque spectrum of colors. He has to duck his head slightly to get under the doorway.

Glen hands him two dollars. "Then bring me change. And the receipt. Always keep your receipts. All of 'em. Forever."

· · ·

Dolly buys two cases of Bud Light because the tall man is staring at her, and she wants him to think that there is a group of people waiting for her back at the RV. For the first time in years, Dolly is worried about being raped. She's seen him in three different aisles now, watching her. He's wearing a blue track suit and sunglasses that look like a blade. The man is very very tall, *seven foot at least,* thinks Dolly. She is taking mental notes in case she has to describe him to the police. *White. Early thirties. A big man, but not a powerful build. Soft. Short brown hair. Wrap-around sunglasses with reflective orange lenses. No distinguishing scars. No visible tattoos. Big head, even for a giant. Real serious look on his face.* His head is so far above her own that it feels like she's being tailed by a police chopper.

Dolly's cart wheel stops squeaking and the tall man's polyurethane pants stop swooshing. There he is, half a row down, picking up the top-shelf items like a giraffe. He has an obscene dog chew toy and a bottle of moisturizer in his cart. In Dolly's cart, there are phosphorescent green and orange beach towels, a power strip, beer, rain-scented candles, and heavy-duty trash bags. She can't look at him. She stands with her back to the tall man and waits to hear the swooshing pants fade into another aisle.

• • •

On monitor six, section four, Glen watches Quentin watching the old lady. *As inconspicuous as a hurricane,* he thinks. The old lady reminds him of his dead grandma, the one that loved midget wrestling and drank Dimetapp by the bottle. Glen smells his fingers again. *Goddamn Doritos.* He's washed his hands twice since breakfast but they still smell like cool ranch.

• • •

Dolly tries on a pair of pink flip-flops. The tall man is in the young boys clothing section peering over the racks. With his eyes hidden behind opaque sunglasses, Dolly can't tell if he's looking at her or past her. She thinks, *He could follow me to the RV. Who would be able to stop him? Look at the size of his hands. It's going to hurt.* She is afraid to look, but she feels his gaze in housewares and in electronics. *I hope he doesn't do it with a knife.* She imagines the way a knife might feel going into the loose flesh of her gut and being pulled back out. She feels the tall man behind her somewhere, slitting her throat, imagines the blood spraying the man standing in front of her. The associate's blank smile doesn't change. Skin hangs like a deflated raft over his face, making a more genuine smile seem impossible. His name tag says Burt. He asks, "How can I help you?"

"I want a gun and some bullets," Dolly says.

"What kind?" Burt asks.

"I suppose the cheapest kind will do."

"This single shot twelve gauge is only eight-eight ninety-five."

"That's fine."

"What kind of shells do you want?"

"Whatever kind—you know—come with it."

"There are different kinds of shells for different things. They have different spread and different velocity. It's about the way you mix the shot and the powder: a few big shots and lots of powder like buckshot, a lot of little shots and not much powder for small foul and skeet. If you're hunting duck it's someplace in the middle. What will you be using it for?"

"To shoot any son of a bitch that comes in my RV."

"Double aught buck. You won't even have to aim," Burt says.

"And it's on sale! I'll take two boxes. Can I pay for all of this here?"

"Sure."

Burt shoots her trash bags with a laser and "$3.99" appears on the computer screen.

"And I need three big bags of ice—for the beer. I'm having a big party."

"Alrighty."

"So, where's a good place to eat in this town?" Dolly asks. "We're from Kansas."

"Do you like Mexican food?"

"Love it. My husband just can't handle the hot stuff," Dolly says.

"Then don't eat any until you get back to Kansas. I like the Golden Corral. It's on Telshor next to the bank. That will be one hundred forty-four dollars and forty-four cents. How do you like that?"

"Is that one of those family-style places? Can I slide my card now?"

"Yup. All you can eat everything."

"Lovely."

"The ice is in a freezer by the door. Show your receipt to the greeter there."

"Thank you."

"Have a nice day."

"You do the same." Dolly turns around and there he is, staring at the portable propane grills and the bug repellant. *Let's see how you like it, you bastard.* She pushes her cart right up to him and he retreats into a bog of crisp, fluorescent light.

• • •

They're like two flies crawling across the monitors thinks Glen as he watches the old lady stalking Quentin now. *A fly on a monitor, consider that perspective: a frozen pond of light. And all that static charging you up! And a thousand eyes to see it with!* Glen bites into a piece of nicotine gum and scratches his balls discreetly through his trousers. *God bless you ma'am. I like your style. People should be more interchangeable. That's the way a more sophisticated society would work. My good grandma is dead and I want a new one.* When Quentin is looking at the razors, Dolly is looking at the deodorant. When he is looking at the car fresheners, she is looking at the car batteries.

The itch is back, and Glen realizes that with Quentin out of the office, he's the only one in the whole place not being watched. His hand goes under the boxer shorts, down to the slimy crevice between his scrotum and his fat thigh.

I am an agile mosquito, thinks Glen. With the click of a button, camera forty-four zooms into Quentin's face. You notice his skull before you notice his face. Every bone in his body seems like an exaggeration. The forehead bone juts far over the eyes, and his cheekbones look like elbows. Camera forty-six follows Dolly as she grabs three bags of ice from the freezer and presents her receipt to the old man at the door.

Glen smells his fingers. *Balls and Doritos.*

•   •   •

A beam of sunlight breaks the gray clouds, speckling Dolly's face through the loosely woven straws of her sun hat. Her metal shopping cart vibrates every time it hits an imperfection in the blacktop. When her hands start to tingle, she wonders if she's having a heart attack. *It would be so romantic if it happened now.* Dolly lights the rain-scented candle. The rain outside begins to patter gently on the windowpane, and everything feels like a sign.

She opens the windows, then pulls a shotgun shell out of the box and bites it like a gold nugget. *Make yourself breakfast. Make yourself breakfast. Make yourself breakfast.* She puts a ten-pound bag of ice over Cal's face, another over his chest, and another over his legs and feet. She covers Cal and the ice bags with the phosphorescent towels. *All you can eat everything. Family style.* But she doesn't know how to get the Neon off the hitch and, with her one-eyed depth perception, couldn't drive this city-bus-sized RV to the Golden Corral without putting innocent lives in jeopardy. She cracks two eggs over a black skillet. There's a sizzle when she mashes the turkey-sausage patties flat with her spatula.

If Cal were alive he would say, *"Breakfast? It's almost four in the afternoon."*

"I don't care what time it is. Breakfast always comes first," Dolly says, and thinks, *You're saying it to yourself now. If you acknowledge that, you're not crazy.*

Dolly opens a room-temperature can of Bud Light and contemplates the custom frontier conversion package. She made fun of Cal when he said he wanted to "see the country at his own leisure, without departure times." Did he read that in a brochure? But when the salesman talked him into the forty-five-hundred-dollar conversion package, she tried her best to like it. After forty years of marriage, she could tell that the RV, its faux log cabin interior in particular, had become a throbbing emotional artery, off-limits to even gentle teasing. When he brought people aboard they chanted obligatory compliments as Cal pointed out each custom feature along his grand tour, down to the Native American light switch covers: *"These symbols burned into the wood mean warrior in Chippewa. We bought them from a real Indian in Arizona."* He jettisoned more than one friend who he felt was not effusive enough in his praise. *And there you are dead on the couch,* thinks Dolly. "You were right about one thing. Composite woods have come a long way in the past twenty years. You can't hardly tell it's fake."

• • •

"Don't feel bad," Glen says.

Quentin fills the LP office with elbows. "Why would I feel bad? I had I hunch. I checked it out. I didn't engage. Isn't that what we do?"

"Where's my candy?"

"Here." Quentin hands Glen a bag of sugar-dusted worms, his change, and the receipt.

"Thanks," Glen says. "I know you think you got this job down already, but let me hip you to a little veteran Superstore LPO inside information: there's not shit in here worth stealing."

"You're crazy. We got fucking everything here: iPods and video games and shit."

"What are those iPods and video games going to be worth to you in ten years? Hell, three years, one year. It's all shit you're going to have to replace and replace and replace. Every year they take more steel out of the mowers, more petrol out of the plastic, put more high-fructose corn syrup in the juice. Do you know who makes this shit? Communists. You think Chinese communists give a fuck about craftsmanship? Fuck no, man. They just want their bowl of rice or whatever pittance they pay those fucking people. You think they're up all night worrying about a high heel coming unglued on some fat American wedding day? If it doesn't sell, we throw that shit away, millions of dollars worth of merchandise a year, tons of edible food, usable medicine."

"What the hell are we supposed to do then?"

"Watch the money first. Millions of dollars will change hands in this store on an average week. Watch the money first: managers, checkers, money counters, returns, everybody that touches the money. They'll rob this store blind if they feel like we're not watching. Most of that goes on at the return counter. People will pick up receipts in the parking lot, come in and find the item in the store and return it for the cash. Watch the time clock second. The fucking associates will start taking thirty-minute shit breaks on the clock, disappear for hours while they're punched in. If they see one person getting away with that, best believe you got a big fucking problem on your hands, hundreds of thousands in wasted man hours. I'm not saying don't watch the merchandise, just don't be thinking that this job is all about stopping old ladies from walking out of the store with surge protectors up their pussies. The money is most important. The clock is second. The merchandise is third. Of course we're out fucking numbered. We can't watch it all. So make sure everyone feels watched, always, that's the most important thing. Presence. And if you hear the words "union" or "organize" call corporate right away. I don't care if they're talking about organizing their closet. There it is: your real training. The orientation is just a bunch of legal shit they have to say so that they can say they said it."

"Where are the microphones?"

"Microphones?"

"In the orientation they said there were microphones all over this place."

"There aren't any," Glen says, laughing at Quentin. "But it doesn't hurt people to think there are. Impressions are all we got. These LPO badges we show to people—you think they mean anything?"

"You know what would be fucking awesome?" Quentin asks. "If we were pit bosses in Vegas. Watching all the high-roller tables real close for cheats. And we see something fishy then we take 'em to the back and our mafia boss tells us to fuck 'em up like that movie."

"Yeah, that would be badass," Glen says, and means it. He hones camera sixty-four in on a young boy crying as he tries on a pair of shoes. His mother smacks him lightly across the face.

Glen has been writing a screenplay for four and a half years. It's about an alien prophet who comes to a small desert community very much like Las Cruces. The prophet brainwashes its inhabitants by using advanced technology to perform what people take to be miracles. The aliens separate the converted population into breeding zones for optimal genetic structure and force them to procreate at alarming rates: one zone for the intellectuals, one for the physically adept warrior class, and another for the ditch diggers. When two people from separate breeding zones fall in love, even a vast alien conspiracy cannot keep them apart. From there, even Glen will admit that it turns into a Zombie movie when, suddenly and inexplicably, the converts' eyes emit strange green light and they begin to eat the nonbelievers. The film ends in a violent standoff at a store very much like the Superstore (though of course it's not called the Superstore for legal reasons). The few that have managed to avoid the grasp of the prophet arm themselves with the wares of the store and kill the attacking horde in creative and often comical fashion, with garden tools, George Foreman Grills, and bombs made out of fertilizer and baby bottles.

Often, Glen practices his craft by giving dialogue to the silent figures on the security monitor:

"I want to buy my shoes at the mall!"

"You don't buy your shoes. I buy your shoes. Now pick a pair."

"But I don't want to buy my shoes from here. I want to buy my shoes from the mall."

"Say that shit one more time, see what happens."

Quentin interrupts: "Can we take home some of the old iPods and shit they throw away? I wouldn't mind having it."

"Absolutely not. One of the biggest parts of this job is going to be making sure all the shit is shot with the computer gun, accounted for in the SMART system, and expunged according to protocol."

"I don't see why not."

"If we give the shit away, who the fuck is going to buy it. The Superstore is like the earth: its fate is our fate, but our fate isn't its."

5:28 P.M.

Ernesto hooks the U-Haul carriage to the ball hitch. "Make sure the signal lights are connected, güey. We don't want to get pulled over for that shit." He connects the dangling plug from the car to the dangling plug from the trailer. "Get in and pump the breaks. Turn signals. The other one. Bueno. Ándele Pues."

"What's wrong with him?" Ernesto asks, indicating towards Bicho, who is sitting still in the middle of the empty backseat.

Lalo laughs. "So fucking much, güey."

"What's wrong with his eyes?" Ernesto asks.

"What do you mean, 'What's wrong with his eyes?' He's blind as a fucking bat," Lalo says.

"Not that, I mean his pupils." Bicho's pupils are fully dilated. Looking through the thick lenses of his glasses is like looking down into two half-empty cups of black coffee.

"They always look like that when he's trying hard to see," Lalo says, lighting the half-spent blunt and passing it back to Bicho.

Ernesto inches the car forward until he feels the ball hitch catch the socket.

"What's in the trailer?" Bicho asks.

"An atomic bomb," Ernesto says.

"Really?" Bicho asks.

"No," Lalo says.

"The Ark of the Covenant. The last living unicorn." Ernesto steps lightly on the brake to estimate the weight of the trailer and calculates a safe stopping distance from the moseying RV in front of them. For a while, they don't say anything. Lalo scans the roadside for IEDs and clenches his butt cheeks at the sight of a freshly dead coyote. Bicho holds a blurry fingertip up to the bulbous right lens of his glasses. He has never been able to see the distinct and delicate swirl of his own fingerprint, and tries to imagine it.

Lalo turns the knob on the nine-speakered sound system until Ernesto can feel the bass vibrating in the steering wheel. Ernesto turns the system off.

"Why, güey?"

"I can't concentrate."

Ernesto exits off of I-10.

"We bumped this shit in the Abrams," Lalo says, fingering the Glock 19 through his jeans. "It doesn't get more serious than that."

Ernesto pulls into a gas station parking lot surrounded by a vast industrial cattle ranch. "Why would you bring bug eyes?"

"I needed somebody with sense and somebody with balls," Lalo says.

Bicho runs his finger over his forehead and uses the grease to draw a picture of a Tyrannosaurus on the inside of the rear passenger window. Ernesto exits the car and walks towards the station. "Take the car. I'll get a ride home."

"Where are you going?" Lalo calls. "We'll talk about it in the car."

"No fucking way."

Lalo exits through the passenger door and walks around the vehicle and the trailer three times. He doesn't check the hitch or the brake lights; he just walks around it like he has forgotten where he's going, then gets into the driver's seat. Ernesto imagines his cousins rolling the car and the trailer off the highway into the desert, the contents of the trailer strewn about the brush. The cops arrive on the scene. He sees Bicho dissolving into psychosis, grabbing the revolver under the seat and shooting at anything that moves. He sees cartel-style retribution, gory wounds in their disconnected bodies. Stark faces. He would be the one who left them to it.

Ernesto returns to the car and shoos Lalo out of the driver's seat. "Don't you think I'd like to be high right now?"

"Here, güey," Lalo says.

"Not now. Save the roach for me."

"It might burn your fingers," Lalo says.

"Does the whole world smell like an inflatable pool toy to you guys?" Bicho asks. "Does everything smell like water wings, or is it just me?"

Ernesto stares through the windshield at the industrial ranch surrounding the gas station: thousands of cows and millions of pounds of hamburger, jostling in insufficient space, churning their shit with their hooves in the hot sun. He remembers something disturbing his seventh-grade science teacher told him, that when you smell something, microscopic particles of that very thing are attaching to olfactory receptors in the nose. So anytime we smell something, a part of that thing is entering us. He looks at the tiny houses spotting the horizon and wonders how long you have to live in shit before you stop smelling it.

"Don't be a pussy, güey," Lalo says. "Easy Money."

"If I have to be a criminal, I shouldn't have to push carts and wear a name tag. For this much money, I should be driving cabbages."

"Just drive, fool," Lalo says. "Vámanos."

"What's really in the trailer?" Bicho asks.

"For the last nine months we've been picking up trailers and driving them to El Paso. Every fucking time, you ask what's in it."

"Because you never tell me," Bicho says.

"We don't know, güey," Lalo says. "Lencho tells Rucho what he wants him to know. Rucho tells us what he wants us to know."

"Don't you want to know?" Bicho asks.

"We're driving it south. What do you think it is?" Ernesto says.

"Let's look," Bicho says.

"See," Ernesto says. "If I wasn't here to tell you how stupid that idea is, you two would probably do it."

"We could just look," Lalo says.

"We don't even have the key to the padlock," Ernesto says.

"We have bolt cutters," Lalo says.

"What happens when we deliver it unlocked?"

"We'll buy a new lock," Lalo says.

"Who do you think has a key to *this* lock? The one on the trailer now. What happens when they try to stick it in the new lock? What do you think your life means to them?"

"I just want to know what's inside. I wasn't going to take nothing," Bicho says.

"We're driving it south. Only one thing gets smuggled *into* México," Ernesto says.

"What?" Bicho asks.

"If you don't know, I'm not going to tell you. We're just going to drop it off and go."

"Just another day at the office," Bicho says.

"Why did you say that?" Ernesto asks.

"What?"

"If this was a movie, and three guys were driving a suspicious package, and they had guns... Picture it, all of them driving down the highway all high, laughing like fucking idiots, and then one of them says some goddamn thing like, 'Just another day at the office.' What do you think might happen immediately after that? A diarrhea fire hose sprayed into a propeller. If we were in a movie, our life expectancies would be about two seconds after those words left your mouth."

"This isn't a movie," Bicho says.

"Are you sure about that, güey?" Ernesto asks. "Are you sure we aren't just the figments of someone else's imagination? Maybe this is a movie and we're the bad guys who die ten at a time, whose deaths don't mean a fucking thing."

They take a byroad past the old Asarco smelter.

"I'll never understand why they put their name on it," Ernesto says.

"What?" Lalo asks.

"The smelter. You've got this twenty-story cigarette sticking up in the air, poisoning everybody, and you print your name right there on it. Put your name on billboards. Put your name on pens and Little League jerseys. Leave the fucking smelter blank."

They squeeze down the narrow street. The men under the hood of the green Pontiac, the old woman sweeping the sidewalk, and all the patrons of Rico's Taco Cart turn to watch them pass. A very young boy in electric-blue basketball sneakers sees them coming and types something into a phone. The turn down the gravel alley is tricky, and Ernesto has to swing into the wrong lane to clear it. They are at the very bottom of America, close enough to wave at the citizens of Ciudad Juárez across the river.

The trailer starts to jostle and Ernesto slows the car to a speed that just barely registers on the needle. Cinderblock walls and corrugated steel line both sides of the gravel path and display a surprising lack of graffiti, only overlapping patches of slightly different-colored paints. Each man is trapped inside of his own panic. Ernesto imagines Bicho getting out of the car, all sudden movements and inappropriate questions. Gunfire. He prepares himself to leave him there. Drive away.

"So this guy Lencho fucks Claudia?" Bicho asks.

"No," Lalo says. "She met him at Rucho's one time. She texts him dirty pictures, and he writes her love poems and gives her money."

"How much do you think he would give me for a picture of my verga?" Bicho asks. "Do you think he would write a poem about it?"

"I don't know about a poem," Lalo says. "Maybe a good joke."

"Will you two shut up and concentrate," Ernesto says. "This is serious."

"Lighten up, Primo," says Lalo. "You don't want to go into something like this snarling. Human energy is real. It vibrates."

Ernesto only thinks about the thing he hates thinking about the most under extreme stress. It is as if the significant forces of his brain dedicated to guarding it are called to action someplace else, leaving it to tear the bars off its cage and escape. When he and his cousin Claudia were both fifteen and drunk on schnapps, they had sex. She asked him to fuck her like it was a small favor, like she was asking a stranger for change of a dollar or directions. He laughed, and then she asked again, like she was asking if she could copy his homework. When he told her it wasn't funny, she taunted him. The exact words escape him, but he remembers that they made him feel the way he felt when his mother made him wear that goddamn Eeyore sweatshirt to school. He tried to kiss her, but she wouldn't meet him. He fumbled, and she helped him find it. She winced and made one pained sound when he entered her. She turned her head to the side and clamped her eyes shut. She laid there, as inanimate as a wet towel, enduring it. Profound sadness and shame fried every synapse inside of him. He stopped and rolled next to her on the bed. He didn't talk right away. He let her stare off. She was naked and beautiful, like a sin committed and a prayer answered. After a while, he put his fingertips on her wrist and asked her if she was all right. And all she said was, "Thank you for stopping. They usually don't."

At the end of the alley, a small motor drags a corrugated steel gate open. They pull the car and the trailer onto the smooth driveway and four overmuscled pit bulls surround the car.

Lencho steps onto the concrete porch in pointed boots. He's wearing a white snakeskin cowboy hat and sucking a giant fountain soda through a straw. He gives them a surprisingly friendly smile and wave that only Ernesto returns.

"Stay here," Ernesto says. He tries to ignore the dogs' muzzles clamoring for his crotch and butthole as he unhitches the trailer. Bicho laughs hard at the sight.

Lencho laughs too. When the trailer and the wires are disconnected, he goes back inside the house.

Ernesto turns the car around and steers it fast down the alleyway. Unburdened of its load, it rolls lithely over the gravel.

"Friendly dogs," Bicho says, still laughing.

"Do you want some information that will get you killed, güey?" Ernesto asks. "This knowledge is worth millions to someone, but it's worthless to you. It's less than worthless. In fact, just knowing it will make your life worth less than nothing."

"No," Bicho says. "I don't want it."

"Quit fucking with him," Lalo says.

"That house is the end of a tunnel," Ernesto says.

"How do you know that?" Lalo asks.

"The same way I know what's in that trailer."

"Where does the tunnel go?" Bicho asks.

"All the way under the river, güey."

7:11 P.M.

Mass shootings are to the Sporting Goods Department what Super Bowls are to the Deli Department, what Thanksgivings are to the Cold

Grocery Department, and what Christmases are to the Toy Department. On Wednesday, a disturbed high school junior named Peter Vaughn walked into his former middle school with an AR-15, a Glock 17, and a Ruger SR-22 Rimfire pistol. He was able to kill fourteen children, three teachers, and a security guard before the police cornered him in the cafeteria dish pit. It took him three shots to kill himself, and enough time, one can assume, for him to watch his own blood circle the drain in the concrete floor.

The push for stricter gun legislation in the wake of the shooting has left the Superstore ammunition shelves bare, save a few boxes of 12 gauge and 410 shotgun shells, and a few scattered boxes of 30-30 cartridges. All of the defensive rounds—the .223s, .9 mms, 45s, .22 longs, and the 7.62 x 39 mms—flew off the shelves within hours of the tragedy.

Burt Stambush has spent the afternoon deflecting angry questions and accusations about the lack of ammunition from customers. When the handheld SMART system device indicated a load of ammunition on the truck manifest, he alerted his Gulf War buddy, Rucho Limón, via text. It is a small favor, and one that was hard to refuse after Rucho represented him for free, and got his DUI thrown out on a technicality.

A white man in his early thirties approaches Burt at the counter. There are three men and two women behind him, all wearing hats pulled down to their eyebrows. "Your friend says it came in," he says.

"Where is he?" Burt asks.

"At the office. He says 'thank you.'" The man buys three boxes of Tulammo 7.62 x 39, the twenty-four-hour maximum. The three men behind him in line buy the same. The two women each buy three boxes of Winchester .223 Remington PXD1 Defender 60 Grain rounds. They all pay in cash.

"What was that?" Burt texts Rucho.

"Perfectly Legal. They'll be back in 24hrs for 9s and 45s."

7:24 P.M.

"I can't believe that bitch ratted me out. I'm just going to walk the fuck in that Superstore like nothing ever happened," Wilma Hemphill says.

"Good plan." Even when Tony Hemphill is drinking he can't build anything less than a perfect deck. The sturdy pine structure stands in sharp contrast to the decomposing trailer it's attached to. His right hand hammers. His left hand smokes a cigarette and drinks a bottle of sweet wine.

"I'm never cussing again, ever. Not even at home. Fuck. That was the last time," Wilma says.

"Good for you. I don't like cursing," Tony says, hammering.

"If I violate that discourse policy one more time they'll fire my butt for sure."

Tony takes a sip and wipes his forehead with a dirty rag.

"If I do get fired, are we going to be all right?" Wilma asks.

"Yes."

"For how long?"

"Just long enough."

Wilma says, "I'm so—shoot—tired. Who can sleep when the sun is up? And Josiah's always needing something." The child waddles after a friendly brindle pit bull named Daisy in the small strip of dusty yard between trailers. Daisy darts just outside of Josiah's grasp, then rolls over at his feet and squirms in the warm dust. Wilma contemplates all that her eighteen-month-old grandson isn't hearing: cars roving, Daisy panting, faraway TV sets, his own high-pitched squealing. Wilma's bra cuts into her back fat, making her feel like a balloon twisted into the shape of a woman. It is one of many small pains in her body. To fix one would only call attention to another.

"What if we lose our insurance?" Wilma asks.

"It's already gone."

"What did you do that for?"

"It wasn't a decision."

"What if one of us gets sick, Tony?"

"We live like real people. Like our ancestors."

"Great, we'll live in teepees and use every single part of the buffalo. I hope your Medicine Man takes Medicaid, mother—shoot!" She sits on the top step of the deck. Tony hands her the bottle. She takes a deep drink and rubs her hand over her grandson's tight black curls, the only distinctly African feature she has passed down to him. The purple mountains are useless to Wilma, warts on the skin of the earth. The sloshing colors of the desert sky are boring. She doesn't feel like this all the time. "What if we get sick, Tony? What if Wes gets sick? What if Sai gets sick?"

"There's no such thing as insurance," he says.

5.
La Misa Votiva

THE LIMÓN FAMILY ARE THEIR OWN GANG, AND THEIR COLOR IS blue. Their color is blue because they love the Dallas Cowboys, and they love the Dallas Cowboys because the Dallas Cowboys wear blue. Most of the origins and reasons have been lost to the unwritten history of the neighborhood. Only colors and symbols remain. They are worn and waved, tattooed into skin, sprayed onto walls and Dumpsters, and written inside the bathroom stalls at the Carl's Jr. and the Diamond Shamrock in Sharpie. They are crossed out and written over. They are inverted and broken. Threats, declarations, and violations are coded in their lines. Respect and disrespect. They are corpseless graveyards, monuments to the dead, with spray-painted flowers and epitaphs. They are hidden inside the elaborate paños sent home from prison, like the images of the balloon-tittied Aztec Goddess and the Blessed Virgin of Guadalupe tacked on the wall that Ernesto and Bicho are leaning against.

Keg beer twitches with the baseline inside blue plastic cups. Much of the family resemblance is manufactured: the same blue jerseys, the same impossibly white tennis shoes, and the same haircut for almost all the boys: shaved with a rattail at the base of the skull. Take all that away and Ernesto and Bicho don't look much alike at all. Ernesto is tall and thin, with putty-brown skin and thickets of jet-black hair on his body. His chin juts out and his head tilts back, which gives the impression that he is staring down his nose through invisible bifocals. Bicho is short and pudgy with hairless skin the color of gold paint that has been faded by the sun. Chunky, tortoiseshell glasses cast his brown eyes outward, like lanterns, and would probably seem more at home on a kindergarten teacher than on a head adorned with gang tattoos. He doesn't cock his head back arrogantly the way Ernesto does. And while Ernesto's gait is confident and flamboyant, Bicho's is a shackled shuffle.

"Conejito's Misa is a joke," Bicho says. "They beat my ass in. Gangster Bar Mitzvah."

"It's all fucking dumb," Ernesto says. "We should just have an orientation, like the Superstore. Make folders and shit. Show videos. I'm not joking."

Conejito runs elbows first through the crowd and vomits Hawaiian Punch and vodka into a square, rubber trash can. Someone hands him another drink.

"He doesn't even have hair under his arms yet," Ernesto says.

Conejito staggers to where Bicho and Ernesto are standing and shows them his new Cowboys jacket, a gift from Uncle Rucho.

"Give me that," Ernesto says.

"No!"

"I'm going to put it in the car so you don't vomit on it. It's still hot outside."

Conejito goes limp and lets Ernesto peel the jacket off of his arm.

"Don't lose it," Conejito says.

"Other arm. Come on, champ. Give me your cup, güey" Ernesto takes Conejito's cup and gulps it down.

"Hey!"

"Pace yourself. It's not even dark yet."

"Are you ready to meet la bruja, güey?" Bicho asks. "She makes herself cry blood and you have to lick her tears."

"Man, I'm ona kick that bitch in the pussy," Conejito says.

7:59 P.M.

The setting sun casts sheets of marmalade light through the blinds. Dolly doesn't bother to open or close them all the way. *There's only a parking lot.* She runs her fingers down the fake logs on the wall and thinks, *bump, bump, bump.* The ice on Cal is melting, leaving dark watermarks on the bright fluorescent beach towels. Dolly removes the towels and the ice and arranges his wet, gray hair, combing it to the side. She dumps what's left of the ice into the stainless steel sink and turns the air conditioning up as high as it will go. The two Duo Therm AC units churn cold air with a dull hum.

You were right about the salt. I didn't have to put it on everything. Dolly hears this sentence in Cal's voice, the slow country voice of a cartoon hound dog, but Cal's mouth stays as open and still as a tree hallow. Skin is draped over the face like a tablecloth, the muscles and tendons that sculpt the face into expressions—disconnected.

When she woke up this morning and saw his slack face, her initial reactions were rote, a result of thirty-three years of nursing experience that allowed her to bypass emotion and do the job. She checked for a pulse, then wrote down the time on a piece of paper. And then there was no more job to do. If it had been a stranger, she would have performed the requisite attempt at resuscitation. But he was too far dead. There was no mistaking it. Massive heart attack was her diagnosis. Sometime during the night. No need to beat his chest. She kissed his cold lips. She did not blow into his mouth.

She is a light sleeper. If he would have groaned in pain, or called out to her in the night, she could have helped him. Saved him maybe. She was fully trained to do so. When his heart trouble got serious they bought a defibrillator. She even managed to get her hands on an adrenaline shot, the kind delivered directly to the heart. But they sit useless in a box at the back of the RV. There was no emergency then and there is no emergency now—just a long stretch of time in front of her that seems completely inconsequential.

I should call 911, thinks Dolly. But how can she, knowing what she knows about what they do to dead bodies. The last twenty-seven years of Dolly's career were spent as a forensic nurse. She watched them pull faces over skulls like sweaters, remove the tops of skulls like a hubcaps. She has been handed countless livers and hearts to weigh. After six years working the ER, she couldn't stand watching the lights go out anymore. But once the lights were out, she was not afraid of the dark. The dead didn't bother her, the dying did, and she can't help thinking that Cal dying in his sleep was one last act of willful kindness.

She picks up the phone and puts it down again.

She wraps a fake Navajo blanket around her shoulders and thinks about the day she lost her left eye to a large shard of glass. The pain wiped out the panic. She can feel her eyelid splitting apart again, like something zipped up tight coming undone. She remembers how it felt to have her eyeball pinned still like a golf ball nailed to a wall. The memory of the pain is located in the same place that the actual pain was: her left eye. She wonders if the memory of pain is worse than actual pain because actual pain only happens once. Every second of the accident is remembered with crystalline definition: Cal drifting the motorcycle into the left lane, gently accelerating to pass a sky-blue minivan, a bored-looking preteen girl with dirty blond hair and bangs teased out like a tumbleweed rolling a toy car across the inside of a dirty window. And then the girl's father decided to come into their lane. He didn't see them, but the girl did. There was time for her to say something, but she didn't. She just stared with her dumb mouth agape as the van nudged their motorcycle. It was just enough to make Cal lose control. And then wild tumbling. And then stillness and incredible pain, skin grated by the pavement well down into the meat. Dolly's realization that she was alive, and that she could move. And then the glass in her eye. She didn't scream, and remembers thinking to herself, *why aren't I screaming?* Then Cal lying still on the pavement. His limbs sprawled willy-nilly like the last four matches inside the box. Immediately, the pain in her eye was forgotten and she had her hand down his pants, around his testicles, threatening to squeeze like hell if he closed his eyes, even to blink. *Now what? No more Cal to make pain irrelevant.*

You know what, this cabin could use a fireplace. I could build it out of ceramic stones, set up a small propane tank.

Dolly stares at his still, open mouth as if she expects it to move. She scoops shards of melting ice into a jelly glass and douses them in Canadian Club. "I'm not crazy if I know what's real and what's not."

What's a cabin without a fireplace?

"This isn't a real cabin," Dolly says.

I used to play cowboys and Indians in a refrigerator box, and in my imagination the cabin I was shooting out of looked just like this. But with a fireplace.

"It's silly! It's a silly goddamn thing! Mounted fish on the wall. Who are you kidding? You don't fish."

Why do you crap on everything?

"I'm going to sell this goddamn thing and buy a condo as soon as we get back to Kansas. When *I* get back to Kansas. One where someone else does all the yard work."

Don't you even joke about that. It's the only thing I ever created.

"What am I going to do? I can't drive this thing."

You're conveniently incompetent.

"I just fixed my fourth drink, and I have no depth perception."

You couldn't program the VCR either. Remember when we started dating and you couldn't put gas in the car. I pumped your gas for two years.

"It's fun when you're young, seeing what you can make boys do for you." Dolly moves up into the captain's chair and stares at a panel of mysterious buttons. *The steering wheel is like a goddamn hula hoop,* she thinks to herself. The parking lot is laid out before her, not in two dimensions, or three, but some fractioned number between. The relative size of an object as it moves towards or away from her is her only indication of depth. She's not impaired enough or foolish enough to actually drive the RV, but she can't help thinking about it the same way certain people are compelled to entertain thoughts of jamming their hands into grinding garbage disposals. She imagines taking out a park bench full of people with a reckless right-hand turn, cars bouncing off of the RV and exploding into flames, children in strollers and on tricycles strewn across the windshield like dead bugs. "I'm going to call Meg."

Don't tell her. Not yet. She's all alone in that house at night. Nobody is there for her.

"If I call her tonight, she won't be able to sleep. And she might do something stupid like drive right out here in the middle of the night when all the drunks and killers and tired truck drivers are on the road."

Let her sleep. She has to drive a long way in the morning. Driving tired is just as dangerous as driving drunk.

"I saw that *60 Minutes*. I'll call in the morning before she gets off to work."

Why tell her at all?

"Are you crazy?" Dolly asks.

You're asking me if I'm crazy? That's rich.

"I hope to Christ Meg can drive this thing."

Why go anywhere? Do you think the settlers who trekked across the desert would have moved from this oasis? Food. Water. Clothes. Fire. Every kind of tool you can think of. Everything you need is right across the parking lot.

"I know that you're dead. Your mouth isn't moving. Your voice is my imagination. I am perfectly sane. I just wanted to say that out loud again."

You're the only person who ever knew me. Dolly can't imagine Cal ever actually saying anything like this while he was alive, but these words came to her, and the line between hearing and thinking was blurry.

8:35 P.M.

The sugar bowl is shaped like a rooster. A ceramic frog sits on the edge of the sink, holding a scrub brush in its mouth, and a magnetized, corpse-less protestant cross is stuck to the refrigerator. It seems to Norm like a sitcom-set version of the house he grew up in. He whisks the batter and butters the hot pan.

"God, what's with you and pancakes for dinner?" Patty asks.

"Pancakes don't stop being delicious after ten a.m. You got to stop living by their rules." When the edges start to bubble, Norm executes the flip. The cute brown circle makes him smile. "It's breakfast time for me." He is wearing a starched white shirt, a badge, and snug black pants. His belt is equipped with pepper spray, a two-way radio, and a very large flashlight. "You see how much I love you? I'm doing graveyard lot security at the damn Superstore. Do you know what I hated most in the world when I was your age: security guards. I mean cops—you hate cops, but you need them. You respect them. Security guards . . . Shit."

"Poor you," Patty says. When Norm was arrested for a DWI two years ago, he lost his good hazardous material transport job. Soon after they had to move out of their nice three-bedroom, two-and-a-half-bath ranch home with a pool and in with Norm's mother, Patty's grandmother.

Part of Patty's reaction to these events was to wholeheartedly embrace the ideals of the Republican Party. Last year her youth group became a minor cause célèbre for right-wing pundit Patton Treadeau when several members, herself included, were suspended from school for stuffing brochures with pictures of aborted fetuses and bible verses on them into classmates' lockers. "You know, Dad, reconstituted dairy fat is like the worst stuff in the world for your heart," she says.

"Do you want one or not?" Norm asks.

"Sure."

When Patty slouches down on her stool, Norm considers giving her a lecture on posture. *All that effort you put into being a teenage girl. You have to have the right clothes, the right hair, the right plastic gardening shoes. I understand that I don't understand. But it's all for nothing without good posture. It says so much about a person, where they are in the world, what they have, how they feel. Confidence. Hair. Faces. Pupils. Posture. Products. We're constantly projecting something. We can't not project something.* He decides not to say any of it out loud. Everything he says to her lately is taken the worst possible way.

"Is there syrup?" Patty asks.

"Half a bottle in the fridge," Norm says.

"Thank God." Patty slaps the counter with her palm and the orange cat scurries off. "Have you been using my hair products again?"

"What are you talking about?"

"Why does your hair smell like apricots?"

Norm holds a white-gold lock to his nose and says, "My hair smells like cigarettes."

"I buy my stuff at the salon with my own money. It's not the cheap Superstore stuff."

"What's with the third degree here. I said I haven't been using it."

"You didn't say that, actually."

"Sweet Pea..."

"It looks especially lush is all I'm saying."

"I'll take that as a compliment, I guess."

"Take it how you want."

"I'll take it as a compliment then. Pert Plus works just as good. It's conditioner and shampoo in one. It trims a few minutes off my shower time."

"What gets me is how you lie to my face."

"You should be on your knees thanking me for that angelic head of hair of yours. It's the genes, Sweat Pea. This stuff don't come in a bottle. Look at this." Norm whips his white-gold hair around and lets it cascade over his face like a woman in a shampoo commercial. It was an easy way to make her laugh as a child, and it still gets her every time.

"They let you have that hair at the Superstore?" Patty asks, laughing.

"They want me to cut it, but I'm going to make them ask a couple more times."

"You should cut it. You look like a roadie for Bon Jovi."

"You know, Sweat Pea, jealously is an ugly thing," Norm says, pouring his hair over his face in that shampoo commercial way and making Patty laugh again. "Enjoy it while you can."

"Don't fall asleep at the wheel, Dad."

"Don't think you have to worry about that. I haven't been able to sleep more than an hour at a stretch for a week."

"It's not how long you fall asleep at the wheel, idiot."

"You're smarter than me, Sweat Pea. There's no doubt about it. And that fact makes me proud every single day. But that's no reason to call your dad an idiot. I may not have gotten straight As in school like you, but I know a lot that you don't. I know some things I hope you never have to learn. I was a class-four long-haul truck driver for eight years. I know how to drive a quarter-ton pickup truck around a parking lot at six miles an hour."

The barely perceptible quiver in his tone makes Patty feel sorry. "You're not an idiot, Dad. You're smart. You're just hapless. And you do have a truly stunning head of hair."

"Why thank you," Norm says, pouring his hair over his face.

"Please don't do that again."

9:11 P.M.

The space-age memory foam mattress conforms to the shape of Stacy's ass when she sits on it. She pinches the lip of loose flesh hanging over her pants and asks her husband if he still loves her.

"Of course," he says, smearing aloe lotion onto her naked back.

"Even though I'm disgusting?"

"Stop with that. You're beautiful."

"Can you really rub it in?"

"What do you mean? I am rubbing."

"You're smearing, Larry. Really rub it in there."

Larry's hands used to be smarter. They knew exactly where to go and how hard to touch. There was a time when he could dance without looking like an idiot. Now he doesn't bother with music, even in the car. It's talk radio or books on tape. She used to laugh at the way he positioned himself diagonally behind her in pre-algebra, lusting after a glimpse of side boob through the loose armholes in her T-shirt. And now here she is naked from the waist up on the bed, and he's smearing lotion on her back like herbs on a raw turkey, watching the television over her right shoulder. She imagines herself back at the nail salon inside the Superstore. She imagines her hands in Dat's, the way he gently submerged her fingertips in the solution. They were like jumper cables. Dat's face has been on her mind. She transposes it over every Asian face she sees. Secretly, she used to think they all looked the same. Now they all look like him, the same delicate crease in the corner of the eyes, skin the color of well-steeped tea with a dash of milk. She has never had a particular attraction to Asian men. Earlier today, curiosity grabbed her and she actually had to thumb through her high school yearbook to recall if she had gone to school with any. There were eleven in her 1990 graduating class. *Jesus, I have never looked over a balcony that I haven't imagined myself jumping off of. Sometimes I imagine that I am falling and sometimes I imagine that I am watching myself fall. But that doesn't mean I would ever actually jump. I know. He's too young, and I'm too old and too fat.* She is repulsed by her image in the dresser mirror: sitting hunched head over knees on the bed, a ridge of fat hanging over her slacks, burned skin, red nipples in the pasty-white triangle shadows of her swimsuit top. *Jesus is God and God is love, right? If love is what you are, why is love blind and cruel and probably retarded? How can you be love and perfect at the same time? Why can't it always be like it was, feel like it did, when the lyrics of every cheesy power ballad seemed ten times better than Shakespeare?*

"Why does the TV have to jump five thousand decibels when the commercials come on?" Larry asks. "Will you turn it down? My hands are too slimy to touch the remote."

"I'm never going out in the sun again. What's it those Muslim women wear?" Stacy asks.

"This insurance jingle makes me want to heat up a hanger on the stove and poke my eardrums out. I whistled it all day yesterday."

"I could get as fat and saggy as I want. You could only see my eyes. Would you still love me?"

"Of course," Larry says. The dead skin on his wife's peeling back mixes with the aloe and the grime to form tiny dust-gray balls that stick to his hands like sesame seeds. Patton Treadeau's bulbous head floats in the center of the television screen over his wife's right shoulder. Treadeau's flailing indignation appeals to Larry, and to Stacy, though to a lesser extent. The world *is* breaking; that's for sure. The program segment is dedicated to an activist judge who has overturned the conviction of a child rapist because of a legal technicality. The words "activist judge," "child rapist," and "legal technicality" have been emphasized and repeated numerous times throughout the broadcast.

"I'm not saying that I hope that judge's child gets raped, because that would bring me down to her level. But if her child were to get raped, you could see the justice in it," Larry says.

"Let's pray," Stacy says.

"Right now?" Larry is trying to rub one slimy hand clean against the other.

"Yes."

"For what?"

"For Kyler and Keith."

"Don't you want me to finish putting this crap on?"

"After."

"I'm almost done."

"Come on. It's night out. This world is wicked and desperate and Kyler and Keith are out there in it."

Stacy and Larry kneel at the foot of the bed. They ask God to bring their children home safely tonight, to protect them from molesters and school shooters—to keep them chaste and drug free. They plead with

God that he might keep the real evil and tragedy of the world at a safe distance, an arrangement of pixels on a screen. They pray that their children will keep God in their lives and the lessons of Christ in the centers of their hearts, that they won't be corrupted by secular culture: the TV, the music, or the bounty of filth on the Internet. They pray for the troops, that God may keep them out of harm's way, and that their bullets and missiles find the terrorists and kill them. And they pray for the innocent civilians caught in the crossfire, who only want freedom, who have lost limbs and family members, and must live in constant fear.

• • •

Kyler manages to look dramatic under the insipid fluorescent lights of the Superstore food court. There she is: gently chewing her straw, trying to make eye contact with any man who looks older than twenty-one.

The way she drinks her milkshake, thinks Patty. *She acts like there's a camera pointed on her at all times.* Patty doesn't drink herself, but agreed to help Kyler buy the alcohol for the party because nothing builds friendships in high school like mischief.

Kyler dips a nugget into the red sauce.

"Am I the only one who thinks it's weird that these shakes never melt?" Patty asks. "They just turn into a nasty pink sea foam at the bottom of the cup. Wait, why don't you just get Linda's sister to buy it for you. She always does."

"That's not fun. I can get a guy to buy it for us in two seconds," Kyler says. "I do this all the time."

"Don't choose anyone scary."

"What about that aging douche with the fauxhawk?"

"Ugh, stranger danger."

"You're not helping."

The last thing Patty wants to be is the girl in the story who's not helping. She imagines all her actions as a part of Kyler's narrative. She can see Kyler later tonight, Stoli Vanil and Coke in hand, telling the story of how she flirted with a guy at the Superstore to get the alcohol for the party. *"Patty was totally not helping. She was totally scared the whole time."* All of them hanging on her every word, laughing when she laughs.

"That guy can't be too creepy. He's got a kid with him," Kyler says.

"What do you want me to do?" Patty asks.

"Try not to look so... I don't know."

*   *   *

It doesn't take a very thorough inspection of Daniel's cart to surmise he's shopping for a camping trip: electric lantern, beef jerky, and an inflatable mattress. His eleven-year-old son, Joshua, is making a show of lugging the safety-orange quarter-barrel drink cooler through the aisles after him. He pretends the cooler is filled with depleted uranium, which he learned in science class is very, very heavy. He holds his breath until his face turns red and fake strains until his eyes water.

"Quit screwing around, Josh. Pick out a flashlight."

"I want that one."

"Under ten dollars."

"Then I want this one."

"No."

"Why not?"

"It's a toy."

"Its a skull."

"It's a toy skull."

"It's from that pirate movie. The mouth opens up and a light comes out."

"Get a grown-up flashlight for crying out loud. We're going camping."

*   *   *

Glen writes dialogue in his head for the figures on the security monitor:

Dad, I like this girl at school.

I guess it is about that time. You kids are growing up so fast.

I just don't know how to tell her how I feel.

Well, how do you feel?

I like her kind of a lot. I'm always thinking of things I'm afraid to say to her. I see her face all the time in my head.

Well, why don't you tell her that?

I can't tell her that. She'll think I'm a psycho.

Then pretend you don't give a shit about her. They love that. I'm going to buy this flashlight.

On monitor 6C, two young girls approach the man and his son. It's hard for Glen to imagine what they have to talk about. *Maybe they're related, and just running into each other at the Superstore?* The cock of the pretty one's hip says differently. *What the fuck is going on here?* He's heard stories from LPOs at other stores about prostitutes trolling the aisles. Ray, an LPO buddy of his from Los Lunas, says the cops caught a seventeen-year-old girl there picking up tricks in Home Furnishings and turning them in an RV in the parking lot. It has become a phenomenon in Albuquerque. Ask a savvy cab driver to take you to the prostitutes late at night and he'll drop you off at the local Superstore.

I've never seen any, thinks Glen. But how could he know? *Half the people in the store are dressed like prostitutes in the summer.* He stares at the monitors and wonders how many times it's gone on right under his nose.

· · ·

"You got one of those new phones." Kyler says

"Yeah," Daniel says.

"Awesome! Do you think I could I could try it out?"

"Do you need a ride somewhere, or something?" Daniel asks.

"No, I just never seen one." Kyler grabs the phone from Daniel's petrified hand. "I'm programming my name under 'Tim.' You don't know any other Tims, do you?"

"Josh, go pick us out a folding chair," says Daniel.

"Any one I want?" asks Josh.

"One of the canvas ones with the drink holders that folds into four posts."

"I saw one with an ottoman that folds out."

"No ottoman. Just drink holders."

"Is there a price range?"

"No."

"Is Aunt Val going to sit in it?"

"What the heck does that have to do with anything?"

"I was wondering if I had to take weight limit into consideration, but I didn't want to be rude about it."

"Just go."

Joshua takes the scenic route towards the folding chairs, through electronics. A grown man is already playing with the display console. Joshua would kill both of his pet lizards for five minutes alone with the newest Zombie Slaughter installment.

He likes the grown man's hair, a gel-slicked fauxhawk.

"You want to play?" the grown-up asks.

"Thanks," Joshua says.

"It's pretty fucking sick," the grown-up says.

When Joshua thinks about the number of times he uses the words fuck and shit and ass and pussy in a day, not to mention the number of times he hears them on the playground and in the cafeteria, he has to laugh. At the same time grown-ups are cussing around each other but not when there are kids around, kids are cussing around each other but not when the grown-ups are around. It's like the only time they don't cuss is when they're in the same room. He loves it when one of the adults breaks through the fucking bullshit. "This shit is fucking awesome," Joshua says. He sees the grown-up with hair like a dorsal fin's smile reflected in the Plexiglas game case.

"You know, I have some burned copies for sale," the grown-up says.

"Of ZS4?" He's heard of this. And wouldn't it be great to tell his friends that he got it from some stranger in the Superstore. It would be like he had bought drugs or something.

"Ten bucks for one. Three for twenty. You can sell the extras to your friends. Make some money."

"Fuck. I only have five dollars on me."

"Are you fucking kidding?"

"I can get it from my fucking Dad."

"You can't tell him what it's for. You're not stupid right? You know I could get in a lot of fucking trouble."

"I'm not even fucking allowed to have ZS4. I'm not going to tell him shit."

"Meet me in the bathroom in fifteen minutes."

• • •

The tingle has left the piece of nicotine gum tucked into Glen's cheek. He scans the monitors. The show rarely changes, just a bunch of people milling around the Superstore, going about their lives. It's up to him to add the content. He wonders what's inside the child's head as she stares into the tropical fish tanks, and what kind of life the middle-aged man buying a cart full of Hungry-Man dinners and K-Y Jelly is going home to. He wonders about the hipster pacing around the bathroom. But his eyes keep coming back to monitor 6C, where Kyler and Patty are still talking to Daniel.

· · ·

The man with dorsal fin hair waits in the handicapped stall, testing the blue arch of his 50,000 volt Taser and trying to talk himself into something horrible. *I can't be more evil than a hurricane, than the God who made us both. I guess I deserve the worst fate of all. I deserve to be executed, tortured, raped in prison. I say that sometimes because it sounds good, but I don't know. I don't know if I believe that anybody deserves anything. I guess if clean-living people deserve to be healthy, then retards and cripples and kids with cancer all deserve what they got. I say nobody deserves anything, good or bad. Nobody deserves to live to a certain age. Nobody deserves to be healthy or free or punished. Or loved. Or hated. Punishing me is just as ridiculous as punishing a hurricane, or an earthquake, or any other force of nature.*

· · ·

Glen locks the Loss Prevention Office behind him. He's not a giant, like Quentin, but he is built with the kind of hard, ambiguous fat that might be muscle. In the smooth concrete hallways of the back corridor, he is the only one without a smock or a name tag, but they all know who he is. He's undercover, wearing faded blue jeans and a T-shirt with the words "Old Navy" and an American flag printed on it. Even the innocent conversations dissolve when he passes by them. He enters the sales floor ("the show," management calls it) through the double doors behind the bathroom accessories and quickly blends into the fray. He is halfway down Action Alley when he feels a sudden and pressing urge to urinate.

· · ·

"What's all this?" Joshua asks, pointing to the booze in his father's shopping cart.

"It's for a surprise party. You can't tell anybody about it," Daniel says.

"Who is having a surprise party?"

"People I know. You can't tell anyone. It will ruin everything."

"I won't tell."

"I trust you."

"Was it those girls? How do you know them?"

"It's for their parents. They're throwing them a surprise anniversary party and they need someone to buy the alcohol. You've got to keep this a secret. Especially don't tell your mom. She always blows it."

"Can I have some money?" Some gut instinct tells him to skip the pitch he's prepared in his head and just ask.

Daniel gives him twenty dollars. "Don't tell *anyone*."

Surprise party for their parents? Joshua is shocked by his father's gullibility. *I'm only eleven and I know that's fucking bullshit.*

*   *   *

Patty tucks herself between two full-size SUVs. Her eyes bounce between Kyler's face and her father's white security truck. It is currently snaking through the rows at a safe distance, but it is headed towards them, and it will be here soon.

"What are you doing?" Kyler asks.

"I don't want them to see us."

"God, hiding like a freak isn't helping. Just act normal."

Patty wants to ask Kyler what it's like to be beautiful and coveted, but she can't. *It's an impossible question to answer seriously without looking like some kind of stuck-up bitch. And I'll come off like some sort of lez.* It seems to Patty that her own life has been a massive effort to draw people to her. She asks people about their problems, laughs when she's supposed to, does all the group work, lets people copy and never tells. Somehow she has politicked her way into the Kyler Cotton-Stephanie Welsh-Abigail Gomez-Kelly Cabañes inner circle without the benefit of beauty, upper-middle-class parents, or a particularly good sense of humor. Meanwhile, Kyler doesn't have to do any work to draw people in. In fact, it's all she can do to keep them away. *She's like one of those Hollywood clubs that keep the ugly, boring people clamoring behind a velvet rope, and I'm like the Applebee's offering free appetizer coupons to get anyone in the door,* thinks Patty.

"Is that camper made out of logs?" Kyler asks.

"Where is this guy?" Patty asks. The headlights of her father's truck are getting closer.

"He's coming."

"Why do you think he's doing this?"

"God, you don't know anything."

"I wish I had your body."

"I'd trade my ass for your hair in a heartbeat."

"Ass trumps hair. Everyone knows that."

"Where is this guy?" Patty prays as she imagines her father stepping out of the security truck. His tight, black pants are even smaller in her imagination, his gut rounder, his eyes redder, his teeth browner. In contrast, his hair is even more beautiful, glowing and rising from his head as if he were underwater. Then he hugs her and calls her his daughter, right in front of Kyler. The only words to the prayer are God, please, and no.

"There he is," Kyler says.

"Thank God." Patty runs to Daniel's cart and drags it in between the SUVs.

"Be cool," Daniel says. "There's a security truck driving around somewhere."

"How much do we owe you?" Patty asks.

"Don't worry about it," Daniel says. "How old are you guys? Eighteen. You're in college. I remember college. It wasn't *that* long ago."

"Sixteen actually, and we're going to pay you," Patty says.

"Jesus Christ! Where are you going to drink this stuff?"

"You can take the money or not, but you're not coming anywhere with us."

"Hold on, *you* talked to *me*! You don't have to make me out as some kind of pervert. One minute I'm a nice guy doing you a favor and the next I'm some kind of pervert. I never said I wanted to go anywhere with you! I never said that!" Daniel says loud enough for the hidden camera crew. "I just wanted to make sure you were going to drink this someplace safe. To be honest, I'm having second thoughts about the whole thing."

"Don't fuck this up, Patty," Kyler says. "How much is it?"

"Sixty-four dollars," Daniel says.

"We have forty," Kyler says.

"Oh my God, this was the worst idea I've ever had," Daniel says. "I almost did it. It was like being carried down a mountain in an avalanche. I'm just going to give all of this booze to the first homeless person I see."

The twirling lights of Norm's security truck fall on the scene in metronomic flashes of yellow. A man on the balls of his feet is pushing a shopping cart away from Patty and a friend of hers that he hasn't met. His daughter's face flashes in the yellow light like a highway warning: *Bridge out! Do not get out of that truck. Do not embarrass me.*

She turns her back to him. *She is embarrassed of me, sure, but that's normal for a teenager.* Suddenly he is embarrassed of himself. The friend with Patty is stylish and beautiful. How can he step out of the truck in the lowliest of uniforms? He fantasizes about opportunities for heroics in his new job: stopping a sexual assault in the parking lot, saving a child from an abductor, taking a bullet, receiving a medal. But that might never happen. He might just drive around this parking lot for years, without ever having the opportunity to make her proud.

He puts the truck back in gear and continues his promenade. *I have to write a song about this feeling,* he thinks to himself.

• • •

Glen's yellow stream froths at the bottom of the urinal. He is slightly startled by a flush inside the stall. A tall man with hair like the ridge of an angry coyote walks through his peripheral field of vision and leaves without washing his hands.

Glen gives his penis a wag. *The older I get, the longer it drips.* He flings a few more drops onto the porcelain. *Zip.* He actually has to remember to zip his pants up now. The circuit in his brain that used to do it automatically was destroyed sometime during his stoner years. He washes his hands thoroughly before leaving the restroom.

• • •

The bathroom is empty. Josh whispers "Hello," and peaks under each stall in case the man is standing on one of the toilets. It was kind of a miracle, the way he just met that guy selling burned games. His dad gave him the money without any questions. It seemed like God was aligning the fates to do him a personal favor. It would really suck if nothing were to come of it. He was going to buy three games and sell two of them, mark them up a couple hundred percent, still well under retail. And he was going to use that money to buy Gears of War, all on his own. He checks the baby changing table, just because it would be the perfect place to hide your burned video game stash. He thinks about how many awesome things almost happen to him. He almost got to kiss Julie Hota once. They were in the same room and the lights were out. All he had to do was grab her and kiss her. And now this. He thinks, *I guess some things have to almost happen a few times before they really happen.*

9:56 P.M.

"Where is Conejito?" Ernesto asks.

"Getting his verga sucked," Bicho says.

"I guess there's an upside to growing up fast. Pass la mota, fool," Ernesto says.

The Limón Carnales is a subsidiary of a larger gang of distributors in town, which is a subsidiary of an even larger cartel of traffickers over the border, which is itself the subsidiary of an even larger production syndicate protected by a brutal but effective guerrilla militia and propped up by a charismatic dictator and a very poor nation. The family in America sprung from the very fruitful Estevan and Juana Limón, who immigrated to Las Cruces from Mexico City and settled on the far east side of town in the nineteen forties. When Juana was pregnant with her seventh child, a car Estevan was working on fell off the jack and crushed him to death. It began as an anti-gang: the Limón Carnales, six brothers who didn't suffer disrespect, keeping out the gangs and their bullshit. Not all the Limóns became gangsters, and for that matter not all members of the Limón Carnales are related. Many are just kids from the neighborhood. They consider themselves a necessary force engaged in necessary evils—justified and wholesome compared to the greater evil that is all around them.

Young Conejito walks out of the garage with a broad grin on his face.

The young girl, Elena, stays behind on the couch and waits for the Limón Carnales to finish whooping it up. They slap him on the back and punch him hard on the shoulder. She pulls a blanket up under her nose. Uncle Rucho yells, "Viva México, hijos de la chingada!"

Someone ties a blue rag around Conejito's eyes. He feels Rucho's square hands firm on his shoulders, guiding him and holding him up. His legs feel like eels. He hears the flimsy scrape of a sliding metal door. Smells aluminum. Feels the wind disappear and knows without seeing that he is inside of something. Pink light saturates the blindfold. They tell him to kneel, and when he does he can feel the nylon fibers of the carpet sample through his jeans.

A few nights ago Ernesto laid out for Conejito exactly what would happen during La Misa. He was having trouble sleeping. His cousin Bicho had been filling him with stories for weeks about what the initiation would entail: that he would have to drink a shot glass full of somebody's blood, that a bruja with white eyes would draw some of his blood with a sacred blade, that San Malverde would manifest in his spirit form, that it would take over his body and make him speak in tongues. It always changed. The idea Bicho put in his head that scared him the most was that he might have to kill someone. But Ernesto told him everything while they were playing video games. He told him that since Bicho, they don't jump you in any more. Before Bicho, the jump-ins had been like a professional wrestling performance, with pulled kicks and brotherly slugs to the shoulders and torso. It looked worse on the Internet and prison closed circuit than it actually was. But Bicho, without his glasses, swung elbows and fists at the clamoring blurs, and only made the Limón Carnales put more weight into their feet when he was finally brought to the ground. They stomped well past the requisite thirteen seconds, until he stopped kicking at them wildly, stopped grabbing at their ankles, and couldn't put his hands up to protect himself. He suffered a major concussion, two broken hands, and lost all of the respect earned doing it the hard way when he cried. Lalo created a different initiation out of cheesy narco movies, sporadic visits to St. Genevieve's, and a Wikipedia page. The ceremony is ridiculous in Ernesto's estimation, but aren't all ceremonies ridiculous at first? He imagines the first Penitentes, flogging themselves in the desert.

Ernesto's words are now a comforting ring in Conejito's memory, *First, they're going to get some hood rat to fuck you or suck you or something to make sure you're not a fag. Then they're going to blindfold you and take you to the shed. Then Lalo is going to talk like Denzel Washington and shit. You know how serious that bitch likes to talk.*

Lalo delivers La Misa's homily: "I know you can't see, Conejito, so let me paint a picture for you. You're inside the shrine of Jesús Malverde, the place you knew before as the locked shed behind Victor's house. Me and el Instrumento de San Malverde are in the shed with you. Outside you got about thirty fools trying to look in one small doorway. You are kneeling before our patron San Malverde, who sits in judgment. We are all vouching for you. You will share in our respect, and in the responsibility of defending that respect. We stand against rats and bitches and devil worshippers. We protect our family and our place. We got a lot of rules, but we only got four commandments: don't be a rata; don't be a maricón; don't be a politician; and if they kill one of ours, we kill three of theirs."

After Lalo is done talking like Denzel Washington and shit, he's gonna be talking about this fucking statue seeing into your heart. The saints. Jesus. All that old lady bullshit.

"San Malverde, this boy is ready to do battle with the forces of evil in Jesus' name. We ask you to pray for him, and that if you should accept him, you look after him."

Then they're going to let you feel the revolver, so you know it's real. They'll put the bullet in your hand. You won't be able to see it, but when you feel it in your hand, you'll know what it is. Make the sign of the cross with it. Then they put the bullet in a pocket and spin the chambers. They'll tell you there is a bullet in the gun. That's bullshit. There is no bullet. They are very careful about that. Everybody without a blindfold on will see there's no bullet in the gun. Don't worry. All of it is only nothing.

Conejito hears the chambers spin and lock into place. Lalo says, "Right behind you, el Instrumento de San Malverde is pointing a gun at your head. He is your family and he doesn't want to kill you. There is a bullet in one of six chambers. It is already decided which one. In front of you is the shrine of San Malverde, and he can see deep inside your heart. If he chooses you, you will be under his care."

They pray. Each man in the shed absolves el Instrumento de San Malverde, who is pointing the gun at Conejito's head, from any responsibility. Conejito can feel the man standing behind him. He can feel exactly how tall he is. The man asks, "Do you accept it?" Conejito recognizes the high, tense voice as Bicho's, and fear bolts through his body. He hears Ernesto's voice again in his head, *It will feel like there must be a bullet in the gun, but don't worry, there isn't.* He feels it drawing an imaginary line through the back of his head. He doesn't understand what he has been asked, but he answers, "Yes." A click. Someone behind him yells, "Órale!" They remove the blindfold. Conejito finds himself face-to-face with the shrine of Jesus Malverde, a black-haired statue with olive skin and a black mustache. Heavy glaze is chipping away from his ears and nose. The pink light is emanating from a lamp made out of a white plastic planting pot, with holes drilled into floral patterns and filled with plastic jewels.

"He has decided you should live. Make your offering," Lalo says.

Conejito lights a twenty dollar bill and lets it burn in the dish at the altar.

Then they make you burn twenty dollars. Don't ask me what the fuck that is about.

10:20 P.M.

At the Pancake Alley on Motel Boulevard, the smell of bacon frying overwhelms everything, even the cigarettes. Stacy and Larry's son, Keith, has painted his lips and eyes black and is bemoaning the state of the world to his friends. "It's like, made to keep us unhappy. A conspiracy. I got a PlayStation 2 for my birthday a couple of years ago. And I was so fucking happy. It was really the shit, you know. The world was round, not all boxy like the PS1. I couldn't believe it. I practically came in my fucking pants as soon as I peeled back the paper. It was like, how could it get any better than this? I remember thinking that to myself. My friends and me stayed up all night high on Mountain Dew playing it. And then this fucking PlayStation 3. I go to the Superstore with my mom one day and watch all the kids gathered around it in the game aisle playing the sample one they had. You couldn't even get on it to try it out. And then just like that my PlayStation 2 became a piece of shit. Like, here's the thing I can't stop thinking about: if there wasn't this new thing, or even if I didn't know about this new thing, I would have been perfectly happy with my old thing. And can you imagine if I could get in a time machine and give my PS2 to a kid playing an original Nintendo or an Atari? They would freak the hell out. They would play it until they had a seizure and then sell the technology to NASA or the government for a billion dollars. And now it's practically worthless. And it's like I'm the only one who it bothers. And I can't stop thinking about how everything is like that: computers, cell phones, shoes, clothes, books, musical contraptions, music itself. Records to eight tracks to tapes to CD to iPods. Reel-to-Reel projectors to VCRs to DVD to Blu-Ray to who knows what's next. All buried on top of each other. It's like there is always something to come along and make what we love worthless. That was the first time I thought about killing myself."

"We should be writing this shit down in the manifesto," says Brenda, the girl with blue-green hair.

"Fuck that, we should be making this into a movie," says Ish, the giant pink-haired Aztec boy eating french toast.

"We should be born again. Baptize ourselves. Not in Jesus, in something else," says Keith. "We should change our names."

Brenda asks, "Is there any way to live without becoming a total cliché?"

• • •

"Patty fucked everything up," Kyler says to the small huddle of drunk teenagers passing a joint. "He had already bought the booze. He wasn't even going to make us pay for it."

"There are people here I don't know," Patty calls to Kyler from outside the huddle, a safe distance from the intoxicating smoke.

"Relax," Kyler says. "It's my birthday party and you're totally stressing me out."

Patty thinks, *Your birthday isn't for two weeks*, but she doesn't dare say it out loud. Kyler carries a commanding presence and surrounds herself with friends who respect her authority. "I'm sorry," Patty says. "But there are cholos here."

"You are so racist," Kyler says.

"This is my grandmother's house. Help me keep an eye on it, okay. Where's your brother?" Patty asks. She has a fantasy that she can save Keith from the negative freaks and marry him. This would make her Kyler's almost real sister, and Larry and Stacy would be her new parents. She would be invited every time they went to the lake, not just sometimes.

"Probably at Pancake Alley living out his goth phase," Kyler says. "This house is perfect. There's not a lot of expensive stuff to break. Don't get me wrong. You know what I mean. I like it. It's not too fancy. I feel like I can put my feet up on the coffee table. I never feel like that at home."

"Help me put the quilts someplace safe," Patty says.

"How long does the medicine usually put her out?"

"Like ten hours."

"You're sure she won't wake up."

"On this stuff? No way."

"When does your dad get back?"

"Usually between seven and eight."

"You're so lucky." Kyler examines the ceramic leprechaun collection and Precious Moments figurines in the display case. "You know what we should have bought: black lights! Can you imagine how fucking creepy your grandmother's old lady shit would look in the black light."

Patty is deeply embarrassed by her grandmother's house, where she has lived since her father lost his hazmat trucking job. Everything about it, from the lighthouse paintings to the shag carpet, seems wrong to Patty. The wooden frame around the TV set makes her want to die. *Who has wood on their TV anymore?* She feels like apologizing to everyone at the party, especially Kyler and the three people she doesn't know.

Recently she has found that she likes the same music as Kyler, the same movies, roots for the same reality TV contestants. She used to hate herself for pretending to like what Kyler liked, but now she seems to genuinely like it. This terrible feeling in her stomach, could it be the mixture of wine and Sprite she concocted? She takes a sip and pours it into the sink. It's not a good night for her to try getting drunk for the first time. There is nobody to take care of her or her grandmother's house. Her friends are obliterated, carrying their heads around on wet-noodle necks and slurring their words. *If I get drunk, who will make sure nobody gets raped?*

"What in the fuck is this shit?" Kyler asks, indicating towards a Mason Jar full of pallid gray sludge.

"Bacon grease. My grandma saves it," Patty says.

Kyler sticks her fingers down her throat and vomits onto the dishes in the kitchen sink.

"Oh my God," Patty says.

"That is the grossest shit I have ever seen. Get it away from me or I'll barf again, I swear to God!"

"Are you okay?"

"No! Jesus! Who does that? Keeps bacon grease in a glass jar?"

· · ·

"I'm so worried I could pull my hair out," Stacy says, sitting up in the bed. *Jesus, watch over them.*

"They're fine," Larry says.

"Then where are they? Why is my call going straight to voice mail? I have the most terrible feeling."

"It embarrasses them when you call so much."

"I have a horrid feeling. I can't explain. It's motherly."

"They're okay. I promise." Resigned to the fact that Stacy will not let him sleep until she's heard her children's' voices, Larry turns on the television. He cues the Astros game on the DVR. "Remember when there was nothing on after midnight? When things used to stop."

"How the hell could you promise that? You have no idea!"

"They're teenagers. They're not going to pick up the phone every time you call."

"They could at least return my texts. I feel sick to my stomach. If something happened to one of them, would we deserve it like the judge who freed the child rapist?"

"Why do you do this?"

"Do you think our kids are on drugs?"

"They're good kids, Stacy."

Stacy hates him when he talks this way, a stone wall of ignorant reassurance, telling her what she wants to hear. *Like it's his job is to find the words that will calm me down and say them to me.*

"This isn't the first time you've had a *really bad feeling* like this, and it's always been fine," Larry says. "Do you think it's easy reassuring you all the time? You look at me like I'm the stewardess and the plane is smoking."

"This time is different."

"It's not the first time you've said that either."

"You're worried too. We should pray again."

"If you're not going to let me sleep, I'm going to my office."

Larry hasn't been able to look at pornography with any peace of mind since last Thursday's *Dateline*. That certainly doesn't mean he hasn't been able to look at pornography. His penis is chafing, despite his obsessive "moisturizing." But this particular *Dateline* took most of the joy out of it. They did a story on a young kid who looked up a few "Playboy type" images on the Internet and wound up, through a series of malfeasances on the part of some very technically savvy pedophiles, unknowingly transporting files attached to child pornography. His computer became what the throaty female news anchor called 'A Zombie,' completely under the secret control of child pornographers. The doughy high school senior, who had band geek coming out of his ears, seemed comically unprepared for prison. In order to avoid a possible life sentence, he was forced into a plea agreement that required him to register as a sex offender for life. *They could be underage. They could be slaves. There could be someone off camera with a gun to their heads. Who knows who makes this shit? Who even thinks about it? That's exactly the kind of thing that would happen to me,* thinks Larry. He has never wittingly visited any child pornography sites, but who could be sure each and every girl was at least eighteen. He is counting on the personal integrity of pornographers for that. And it wouldn't be too hard for a hacker to worm into his three-year-old security software. He doesn't know how to download a song or navigate a chat room. His interest in computers is purely sexual. He clicks on gutterhos.com. A very large black woman smokes a cigarette with her vagina, inhales and exhales smoke somehow. *Oh my God. Does her vagina have lungs?* The white cameraman wears a white lab coat and carries a clipboard. He says, "The scientific question of the day: can a pussy cough?" Larry is routed to a screen asking for his credit card information. *Isn't that always the way. Just before the answer.*

10:45 P.M.

Dolly is swaddled in four sweatshirts and three pairs of sweatpants. Two of the sweatshirts have hoods, which she has pulled over her head. Her husband insisted on two industrial air conditioners for the RV. One would have probably done the trick, but they were going to be crossing the desert, and he didn't think he could enjoy himself fully while sweating. *It certainly is coming in handy,* thinks Dolly. The digital thermostat on the log wall says sixty degrees Fahrenheit.

She decides to take the gun out of the box. She lays it on the foldaway kitchen table and slides the Styrofoam brick out of its cardboard sleeve. She cuts through the cello tape with a steak knife and removes the top half of the Styrofoam packing brick. She cuts the plastic ties and lifts it to her shoulder. *There is a lovely balance to the thing,* she thinks, teetering it between her hands. *A nice cold to the steel. A nice smell to the cold of the steel.*

Be careful, Cal says.

"It's not even loaded." Dolly is disturbed by the fact that she has continued talking to her dead husband, but she is comforted by her disturbance: *how could an insane woman be disturbed by her own insanity?* she thinks. She says, "I bet they got enough Dimetapp in there to put me to sleep."

Watch yourself crossing the parking lot.

"This gun changes everything." *What if I propped him up in the captain's chair, turned on the reading light, pulled his hat down over his eyes? A man in here with me. The bad guys would think I wasn't alone. Bad idea. That's a bad crazy idea. I know I'm not crazy because I know that's a bad idea.*

10:48 P.M.

They are deep in the desert, with a trunk full of guns, drinking beers and teaching young Conejito how to shoot. The stellar canopy is brilliant. In town, light pollution fuzzes up the sky. The stars seem two dimensional, freckles on the back of a shoulder. On the other side of the mountains, the sky is deep. The parsecs between heavenly bodies are perceivable.

Conejito turns the pistol sideways and unloads it into a cactus.

"Who taught you to shoot like a fucking nigger," Lalo says. "Cup this hand. Build the castle with your sight: even on both sides."

"That's not how Chow Yun-Fat shoots."

"You're holding a weapon, not a prop," Lalo says. "Don't jerk the trigger. Squeeze. Let's do some dry fire drill until you get the hang of it."

"I just want to shoot," Conejito says

Bicho shoots the AR-15 at a mountain.

Lalo lays down on the hood of the truck and for the first time looks up. The universe is spinning, and not just because he is drunk. The vastness of a sky like this causes a certain type of vertigo, like peeking over a ledge from a great height.

Bicho follows a jackrabbit into the brush with the AR-15. Puffs of desert kick up just behind it.

"Viva los conejitos!" cheers Conejito.

This cheer for the shifty rabbit is so childlike that it makes Lalo Limón's eyes wet. He says, "Stop shooting and look up. I said look up to the sky, güey."

"Simón. There is a really fucking lot of them," Conejito says.

"Let's pray a rosary for all our dead people," Lalo says.

Bicho shoots at the stars and says, "It's gonna take those slugs a hundred years to get there."

"They're never getting there. It's like trying to hit a falcon with a handful of dust," Lalo says.

"I thought this little bitch was going to piss himself tonight," Bicho says.

"I wasn't even scared," Conejito says. "Ernesto told me there was no bullet in the gun."

"There was a fucking bullet in the gun!" At this point, after a boy had been through it, said his prayer, made his offering, and proven his worth, Lalo would usually admit the truth, that there was no bullet in the gun. They're not lunatics. The boy would be in on the joke, and he would get to watch the next kid kneel in front of the shrine. It's all ruined now. It never meant anything. All he can do is lie retroactively, go back and try to interject meaning into something that now has no meaning. "There was a bullet in the gun," Lalo says again.

11:18 P.M.

Dolly is excited and saddened by the sight of a woman at least as old as herself still working at this late hour. There is something spooky about her face, like it is the remnant from a bad dream she forgot as soon as she opened her eyes. Her immediate reaction is to walk towards her. As a child, Dolly took all the fun out of a neighborhood game called Bloody Mary by spinning in a circle while chanting "Bloody Mary" three times every night at midnight for a week without incident.

"Do you know where I can find cough syrup?" Dolly asks, though she assumes the woman doesn't speak English.

Fatima smiles.

Dolly mimes the act of coughing and drinking from a bottle.

Fatima laughs.

"No. I'm not drunk, honey. I'm looking for the cough medicine."

"Lo siento, Señora."

Dolly blurts, "My husband is dead, and I still hear him talking." It feels good to tell this to a woman she doesn't know at all, a woman who doesn't speak English. There is none of the requisite explaining. Still, there is recognition and understanding in the woman's face, a face that seems to Dolly fifteen years younger up close. A bridge of brown freckles arches across the woman's nose, barely perceptible in the context of her brown skin. Her brown eyes are awake and empathetic.

Dolly is smiling cordially, but a deep hurt shines through the cracks. Fatima can see it burning under the surface. It manifests to Fatima as literal light, the light of a green-orange demonic fire. "Limpia," Fatima says. "Usted tiene una muy mala vibra."

"I'm sorry. I don't speak Spanish," Dolly says.

Fatima takes a small brass crucifix from her pocket and presses it into Dolly's hand. She takes a small pouch tied to a black shoestring from around her neck and passes it over Dolly's body, including the soles of her feet, as she chants her icaro. She produces a splash of holy water from a small bottle hidden in her fist.

"Am I supposed to give you money now?" Dolly asks.

6.
The Minutes

12:50 A.M.

THE THUMBNAIL ICON ON LARRY'S DESKTOP IS A TINY, STOP-ACTION movie of a woman with a dick in her mouth. A woman's bodiless head is fellating a man's bodiless dick in two alternating pictures: one where the shaft is visible and one where it isn't. Every time he deletes the icon, it multiplies. When curiosity overtakes him, he clicks. Pornographic web pages fan across the screen like a solitaire victory, naked women asking for credit card numbers. He jerks the cord out of the wall and prays to Jesus that after he waits sixty seconds and plugs it back in, everything will return to normal.

12:51 A.M.

Wilma wakes in a panic. Her hands are gripped at ten and two on the wheel, and by virtue of some miracle she is still driving down I-25 in the center of her own lane. She loops off the highway and parks in the associate section of the lot, ten rows from the store. The air is dry and thin in the high desert, and cool this time of night. She recalls the moon in the sky last night as she was walking into work: slightly creepy, not full or blood orange or anything, just slightly creepy in a way and for a reason she can't explain. *This moon is almost friendly compared to it*, she thinks. She walks on painful feet towards a gray door marked "ASSOCIATES ONLY" and hopes that she can slip in the back without Flaco seeing her.

The back of the Superstore is still a mystery to Wilma, an orchestra of buzzing halogen, unpleasant dins, and percussive crunching machines. There is a divide between the people who work in the front of the store and those who work in the back. It is a peaceful division, not nearly as tense as the divide between management and labor, or as acrimonious as the divide between shifts, but it's there. They segregate into their different camps at different round tables in the breakroom. There is the unsaid, sometimes said, resentment among the people who work in the back that the people in the front think they're better than they are. The people in the front point to the shit they have to eat. The customers have come to expect no less than every item they want or need available immediately and perpetually, twenty-four hours a day, seven days a week, at an astonishingly low price.

The door opens into a locker room full of heavy coats that opens into a dairy cooler. The temperature is kept at exactly thirty-eight degrees by four massive vents and an industrial air conditioner. Direct lighting is kept to a minimum after several peer-reviewed journals published articles on the oxidizing effect that fluorescent light has on dairy products. Three women load milk into the back of the case. Their breaths roll and merge in the air. Every time a customer opens the glass doors to buy a gallon of milk or a tub of sour cream, the sounds of the Superstore radiate inside. The conversations come in short bursts, the time necessary to open the cooler door, grab a jug of milk, and shut it.

—smelled my own finger and almost threw up—
        —Pero, la frente esta extraño—
                —ear-hustling me—
                        —fucking kids in the head—
—soak the beans in the crockpot—
                                —by ten thousand acre feet—
        —vende el cemento by the yard—
                        —sticky like a microwave burrito—

A woman squeezes the handle on a pallet jack, prompting the hiss of depressing hydraulics. The sound of the pallet hitting the floor is muffled by a tower of plastic and milk.

"Hey Risk Management, I'm bending at the waist. I'm lifting in the red zone."

"Fuck off, Linda," Claudia says.

"Oh no, I'm using the box cutter with the blade facing in."

Seeing Claudia so young with her tattooed, emoticon eyebrows and her bodacious form pressing through a formless coat makes Wilma feel like a thick-ankled, twelve-year-old girl again. She was the kind of girl who drew pictures of dragons all day until those tough and beautiful East Cleveland girls ridiculed her into tight jeans and fake hair.

"Do you want to see a picture of Ron's penis?" Claudia asks, opening her cell phone.

"Ron who?" Wilma asks.

"Ron Barns, the Servant/Leader in charge of grocery," Claudia says. A small crowd gathers around her. Wilma can tell by the way they are looking at her face and not the cell phone that they have all seen the image before. Her reaction is the show.

"Of course I do," Wilma says. "Whoa! Nice special effects!"

"I know. It looks like a train plowing through a wall."

"Is that a dollhouse?"

"I fucking hope so."

"Would you mind forwarding that to me? I need a raise."

"I couldn't do that to him."

"She's already on the risk management team," says one of the women in the huddle.

"Shut up! It's not even like that," Claudia says.

"I wonder what it says about this in the *Official Associate Discourse Policy Handbook*." Wilma is now six minutes late, but she is happy to have this once-in-a-blue-moon gossip for Cruz, a nice present to make up for horning in on her break. She passes from the cold dairy cooler into the ever-temperate Superstore. She contemplates sprinting to the clock, but that would only draw attention. Her eyes are peeled, hoping to see Flaco Baca before he sees her. *He's probably got thirty bean-eating motherfuckers lined up behind me who would work for half the money*, thinks Wilma as she swipes her badge through the clock.

Wilma increases the length of her stride, but not her pace, as she glides down Action Alley. She grabs two twenty-four-ounce energy drinks from the cooler by Cruz's register and pays for them with her Superstore discount credit card. "Que pasa, girl?" Wilma asks.

"Nada nada. It's kind of slow," Cruz says. "Y tú?"

"Shoot. It feels like I can't get all the way awake or all the way asleep."

"Maybe you should do the Superstore cheer. That shit always perks me up."

"Very funny," Wilma says.

"Those people that do it, that really do it all serious... Aye aye aye, I don't know about those people," Cruz says. "I mean, I do it, but I don't really do it. Maybe that's just me. I never been a fan of anything."

"All the future Servant/Leaders."

"I'd do any job here but that one. All those politics." Cruz takes out a spray bottle filled with blue liquid and wipes her spotless register station.

Wilma should get the hint, but she is sleep deprived and not functioning at full capacity. She says, "Shoot, give me a job where I tell someone else what to do. My feet hurt. Hey, did you see that picture of Ron's dick?"

It's no accident that Flaco Baca materializes out of thin air this way. Many of the Servant/Leaders try to cultivate omnipresent effects by sneaking up on people. *Holy fuck!* Wilma thinks at the sight of him. *Is ninjutsu part of the leadership training program?*

"You buy things on your time and sell them on my time, Wilma," Flaco says. "Buy your chips and your sodas before you clock in or after you clock out. We don't pay you to be standing in line, counting out change and having a conversation."

"It took two minutes," Wilma says.

"Our two minutes. I need you to train a new checker tonight. There's just one thing. She is differently abled."

"What?"

"It's just the new thing they're saying instead of disability."

"I can sign. My grandbaby is deaf."

"She's not deaf."

"What's her problem?

"It's not a problem. It's a difference."

"What's her difference?"

"She's got some burns on her body. Very very severe burns."

"What happened?"

"I'm not sure. If she wants to tell you, she'll tell you."

"Okay."

"I just wanted to make sure that you weren't going to stare. But don't be afraid to look at her either. Don't actively not look at her like she's gross, or anything."

"How much should I look at her?"

"Enough that she knows you're not afraid to look at her, but not so much that you look like you're gawking."

"How much is that?"

"A normal amount."

"What's a normal amount?"

"You know, just act natural. Did you say something about a picture of Ron's dick?"

"Yes," Cruz says. "Please go on."

1:14 A.M.

It is a new record: four minutes. Since 1:10 a.m. every shelf on aisle 9-C has remained fully stocked and perfectly conditioned, each and every box flush with the ledge of the shelf.

STOCKER #1: The cereal boxes look like a fucking parquet floor.

STOCKER #2: It's almost spooky to see it like this.

STOCKER #1: What if it stays like this forever? What if nobody buys nothing again?

STOCKER #3: Holy shit. How long has it been up, now?

STOCKER #2: Five minutes.

STOCKER #3: New record.

STOCKER #2: Fucking spooky, ain't it?

STOCKER #1: We were just saying that.

The stockers have never seen a shelf like this. Stocker #2 has been with the Superstore since 1994, and she's never seen a shelf like this, so still and full and perfect. Customers are constantly riffling though items like opossums. Until today, each of these stockers has spent a significant portion of their lives restocking the ravaged shelves of the Superstore, pulling the items to the front with the labels facing out, without hope that they could ever see their work completed, even for a moment.

Stocker #3: I had this dream. We were all building an igloo in the desert. A man in a truck was bringing us blocks of ice. The base was constantly melting before we could build the ceiling and we'd have to start all over. And the man kept bringing us more ice. And for some reason we couldn't build it out of anything else or ask any questions. And for some fucking reason the man driving the ice truck was Dr. Phil McGraw.

A mound of a woman with compression gauze holding the flesh onto her legs steers her motorized cart down the aisle.

STOCKER #3: There it goes. It was beautiful while it lasted.
STOCKER #2: There are people starving in this world. Look at that fat bitch and tell me she don't have anything to do with it.
STOCKER #2: Goddamnit. I should have taken a picture with my phone.

The woman molests an entire shelf of cereals trying to knock a box of Lucky Charms into the scooter with her walking stick.

STOCKER #3: It was never going to last forever.
STOCKER #2: New record.

7.
Having/Not-Wanting

1:27 A.M.

AMBERLEE FEELS SORRY FOR THE PEOPLE IN LINE WHO HAVE TO look at her. She feels sorry for her mother, who looks at Amberlee's old pictures many times a day to mourn the face her daughter had before the burns. It was not a striking face, but a good one, a dark, symmetrical face that bore the strong jaw and happy cheeks of her mother's side of family. Amberlee has tried hard to avoid having her picture taken since the disfigurement, relenting only occasionally for large group photos at weddings and family gatherings.

What she misses about her old face most is how much it said for her. Her brain sculpted the expressions out of muscle, fat, and skin. It bunched her cheeks up like dinner rolls and drafted meaningful lines in her lips and brow. She never had to try to do any of it. Her new face is taut and glossy pink, with raised bumps like a topographical map. She has to insert eye drops every few minutes because the eyelids the surgeons grafted don't shut all the way.

She often has to explain to people, 'that was a joke,' 'you hurt my feelings,' or 'I was being sarcastic,' explicit statements about what she is feeling that would have seemed ridiculous before her disfigurement. She still has hands to speak with, kind of: a thumb and four fingers on her right hand and a thumb and three semi-functional nubs on her left, but she feels self-conscious waving them around. They're not easy to look at either.

"It's best if you don't look at me until you get used to it," Amberlee says.

"I don't know what you mean," Wilma says.

"It's okay. It just seems like you're not sure where to look."

Fucking Flaco, thinks Wilma. "I'm just looking at you like I'd look at anybody," she says. *Three seconds. That's a normal amount to look at somebody. One apple. Two apple. Three apple. That felt long. That felt way too long. The next time you look at somebody normal, time it.*

"I appreciate you trying. I just want you to know that it's okay. Usually people get over it after a while. None of this feels like it's coming out right. If I had my own face, you'd see how friendly I mean it to sound."

"If it's fifty boxes of Jell-O, you got to scan each of the fifty boxes," Wilma says. "We don't just need to know how many boxes of Jell-O we're selling. We need to know how many boxes of *lime* Jell-O we're selling." *If Flaco hadn't said anything, I wouldn't be thinking about it so much. Trying not to think about it is only thinking about it in disguise. Think about something else.* The image of Ron's penis invading a dollhouse is cued in her imagination, temporarily scrambling all frontal lobe activity.

"I didn't mean to freak you out."

"You didn't freak me out. My grandchild is deaf."

"I'm not deaf. I'm disfigured."

"The trick to this job is just keeping your head down and plowing through it, not letting anything get you flustered." She cannot stop imagining Ron's dick. *This is worse. This is so much worse. But it does make looking at her easier, somehow.*

"Do you have a picture of your grandchild? I think black babies are the cutest," Amberlee says.

"I don't have one of those phones like that," Wilma says.

Amberlee, unsolicited, produces a picture of each of her six pugs, and of herself before the disfigurement on her iPhone. She has always come on strong, the kind of person who tries to fabricate friendships with copious amounts of personal information. "How's that energy drink treating you?"

"It's keeping my eyes open," Wilma says. She is examining every pixel of Ron's penis shot in her mind's eye: the disproportionately large gland, the angry vein, the way it slices slightly up and to the left. It will not leave her. *And I wanted someone to talk to.*

Incidental to the conversation, customers are moving through the line: swiping cards, counting change, and executing their ends of the cash register exchange by rote. They do not look at either of the women across the conveyor belt. They have a hard time looking at anything directly in fact, including the checks they are writing and the keypads on which they enter their codes.

Claudia comes through the line with pizza rolls and chocolate milk. Wilma is sure that if she was ever beautiful like that, she would have parlayed it into a happier life before it went away.

"Got any more texts from King Kong?" Wilma asks.

"That's not funny. I shouldn't have showed anybody. It's just not the kind of thing you can not show to people," Claudia says. "You have to promise not to tell anybody."

"Are you sure that's not funny?"

"I'm serious. I don't want him to get in trouble."

"He shouldn't be sending you stuff like that."

"Well, it wasn't totally out of the blue. I'm serious. Not a peep."

"I'm no snitch."

"What are you talking about?" Amberlee asks.

"Can she see it?" Wilma asks Claudia.

"Don't tell anyone," Claudia says.

"Okay"

The women crowd around Claudia's cell phone with shoulders touching. Claudia and Wilma are energized again by Amberlee's gasping, laughing reaction to the picture.

"Is that your boyfriend?" Amberlee asks. "He'g going to fucking kill you with that thing."

"Not exactly," Claudia says.

"That was Ron Barns, S/L in charge of grocery. Try not to laugh next time you see him," Wilma whispers into the hole where Amberlee's ear used to be.

"Don't worry, I've got a pretty decent poker face."

2:06 A.M.

Inside the Pancake Alley's bathroom, Keith washes the black makeup off of his face and rearranges his hair. He pushes his smoky, black clothes to the bottom of his backpack, changes into blue jeans and a Florida State

T-shirt, douses himself in cologne, looks in the mirror, and thinks, *Jesus, like a normal fucking person again. So normal it's scary.*

Black streaks and fingerprints cover the sink and the soap dispenser. He decides to clean up a bit, but despite his extensive use of paper towels, the bathroom is still smirched with black smudges when he walks out of it.

Brenda, who is now calling herself "Cide the Suffix," and Ish, who is now calling himself "Daemon Dog," share a laugh at Keith.

"What are you, some kind of counterculture superhero?" Cide the Suffix asks. "Black metal corpse by night and Abercrombie and Fitch douche by day?"

"Do you want a ride home or not?"

"It's really hard to take you seriously when you're dressed like that," the Daemon Dog says.

"Keith looks like a preppy date rapist," Cide the Suffix says.

"Totally. Keith looks like one of those guys who takes you to his Mustang to listen to his subwoofer, then doesn't take no for an answer," Daemon Dog says.

"I thought you were going to call me the Omniscient Narrator."

"Not when you're dressed like that," says the Daemon Dog.

"Unlike you fuckers, I'm not starving for attention. I want to be invisible. Right now, I'm wearing camouflage."

"You're a poser, Keith," Daemon Dog says.

"Maybe I like changing into different people."

"It's not that easy," Daemon Dog says.

"Actually, it kind of is."

"If he came home dressed like a freak mommy and daddy might take away his car," Cide the Suffix says. "I love you, Keith, but you're a total poser."

"Fine, I'm a poser. But how can you believe in authenticity? I thought you were nihilists. Fuck authenticity. Authenticity is so twentieth century."

2:27 A.M.

Why can't you take the hint? The fellating icon is back on the screen, right next to the TurboTax icon. Larry has combed every FAQ regarding his brand and model of computer and found nothing definitive on fellating computer viruses that won't go away. *Go away you crazy bitch! I have a family!* He remembers Debbie Pointer, a shy girl with good tits and bad acne, how she wouldn't leave him alone after he fucked her. She wrote him long, strange letters and followed him home from college once, to Denver, ten and a half hours away. He clears his cookies, erases the file, and pushes control-alt-delete.

A window pops up on the screen warning Larry that his computer's security has been compromised. It offers to perform a free virus scan. He gives it permission before he wonders if this is the right thing to do.

2:30 A.M.

Cierto que este es el trabajo de un hombre maduro, thinks Fatima as she cuts a log of feces in half with a wire hanger. The other cleaners speak in Guatemalan Spanish of the days before the Superstore's green initiative, when all the trash went in the same place and the toilets could flush a kitchen sink. She wishes now was then.

She thinks about the way the gringos look down their noses at the Mexicans, and the way the Mexicans look down their noses at the Guatemalans. She thinks about how nice it would be if the good people of El Salvador would come here and cut her shit in half.

Fatima rolls the trash can out the door and down the hallway and imagines roller skating down the sales floor, gliding on the flat, groutless tile. Several times God has spoken to her on the glimmering parquet floor of a roller disco, that kinetic cathedral, under those magnificent lights twirling like gears without axles. She hears her favorite ABBA song in full stereo as she imagines tear-assing down the aisles with her arms spread. She is a short woman with short, thick appendages, but in her daydream her arms reach across the aisle into both shelves, knocking the merchandise to the floor as she glides by. If only the wheels were on her feet and not on the trash can she is pushing.

She pauses by the bakery display to admire the cakes. She wishes she had a reason to push her trash can around the counter and into the bakery itself, into the heart of the smell of hundreds of rising loaves.

She could watch the cake decorator with meringue hair work for hours. She burned her first fifteen-minute break gazing into the display case, and can distinguish her favorite decorator's work immediately by its beautifully looped letters and perfectly piped corners. Even when the meringue-haired decorator is forced to conform to a customer's wishes—a man shooting a deer by a lake, a NASCAR race, a cartoon sponge kicking a soccer ball—she makes it spectacular. Fatima smiles, but the woman doesn't look up from the flat, white sheet cake she is decorating. The decorator's wrists are so thick that it's hard to imagine she can bend them. She moves her entire arm as she lays green icing across the sheet cake in fastidious loopity loops. Fatima wishes she could watch longer, but the biggest part of the job is looking busy. For Fatima, that means taking her time. If she's taking the trash out, she takes the scenic route through the pink icing and the smell of doughnuts frying. Her favorite thing to do is stock the maintenance closet because it's all reaching and not much bending, she doesn't have to scrub, and you can make it take all day if you do it right. You have to find something bearable to do, or they'll find something else for you to do.

"Puedo tirar tu basura?" Fatima asks.

The decorator with meringue hair says, "Sure."

Fatima lifts the bag of day-old muffins into her can and rolls it away. She is bothered by the decorator's response. Why did she address Fatima in English? She heard her speaking Spanish to the other cake decorators. Fatima is the first to admit that her power is not her own. It is only hers by virtue of her friendships with the dead. She converses regularly with uncannonized saints and spirits that could make this woman's skin molt, strike her blind, make her grandchildren retarded. She decides not to invoke them. Her own hurt feelings are not a good enough reason.

On the way to the trash compactor, Fatima contemplates the responsibility that comes with magic. She looks over her shoulder for a Servant/Leader, then stares at the segregated recycling bins. She hoists the large gray trash can to the mouth of the garbage chute and dumps it all inside. *Que la hace,* she thinks.

• • •

Dolly has been walking around the Superstore in a daze since the strange woman prayed over her. She's not sure if she is pushing the shopping cart, or if it is pulling her. And she's been putting things in it: dish rags, a cake pan, margarita glasses, several different salad gadgets (she's vowed to eat more salad), olive oil, cereal bars, and more ammo. She can still feel the drip of holy water hanging just over her right eyebrow. She needs to see the woman's real face again, to wash the ghost face away. It is hanging in her consciousness like a spider web, a thing that she can see but also see through.

2:41 A.M.

When Dayanand Sakaria, the Indian tech support operator, answers the phone, the voice on the other end of the line is an unfamiliar kind of desperate. He's used to dealing with people who can't retrieve their dissertations and regional managers whose entire systems are down, but the way this man whispers, "You've got to help me," sends a chill down Dayanand's spine.

"Okay, Mr. Cotton, I'm sorry but I see here that you did not purchase that additional IT support package and your one-year standard factory warranty has expired. You could go through our website or our automated phone system for free service, or you could renew your IT software service contract for one hundred and forty-nine dollars and ninety-nine cents."

"I just bought the thing. Has it been a year already?"

"I am very sorry, sir," Dayanand says. He has been trained to apologize profusely, regardless of personal fault. A training seminar asked him to memorize the fact that apologizing reduces lawsuits by eighty percent, though a source for this was not cited.

"Fine. If this is what it takes to talk to a person these days," whispers Larry, then reads a series of numbers from his card.

"Fine, sir. What seems to be the problem?"

"What's your name?"

"Jeff, sir," Dayanand says.

"Do you have a sense of humor, Jeff?"

"Does this have something to do with the computer problem, sir?"

"Oh yes, Jeff. I wish it didn't, but it does."

"In that case, I have an excellent sense of humor, sir."

"I saw this thing on TV about zombie computers. Is that real? There's this chick giving head on my computer that won't go away."

"Sir?"

"It's one of the icons. I tried deleting her from every drive."

"Click on 'My Computer' at the top left of your screen."

"Your left or my left?"

"Your left."

"That was a joke, Jeff. I thought you said you had a sense of humor. My computer has herpes."

"Which antiviral and spyware programs are you running, sir?"

"My son does all that."

"Can I speak to him?"

"Were you listening? There is a woman giving head on the computer screen. I'm going to have to blame him for this if you can't help me."

"Are you logged out of Windows? Try 'revert.'" Dayanand believes that computers should be taken away from some people the way a pair of sharp scissors might be taken away from a child or a mentally impaired adult. The hardest part of his job is speaking without contempt, and after thousands of hours of training, it's hard to detect any variance at all in his voice. He speaks like a computer navigation system. This mode of communication serves him well at work, but recently he has begun to speak this way at home, to his mother, and to his wife and children.

"Revert is gray," Larry says.

"Click on 'open search,'" Dayanand says.

"Is that under something?"

There is a knock at Larry's locked office door. He warns Dayanand to stay quiet.

"Guess who's home," Stacy says through the door. "Why is this locked?"

"I told you they were fine. Did Kyler text you back?"

"No, but she might have just forgotten her charger again," Stacy says. "Don't you want to come out here and say something to Keith? I think we need to talk about taking the Mustang away."

"I can't let my friends drive drunk, Dad. I might have saved their lives," Keith says through the door.

"I can't do this right now, honey. I am on the phone with a client."

"It's three in the morning," Stacy says.

"It's a vendor. Indonesia time. Keith, buddy, come close to the door. What are you doing scaring your mother like that?"

"I was the designated driver. Some of them lived all the way out in Radium Springs." He wants to tell them that his sister isn't really in Lubbock visiting Texas Tech, that she's at a party. That would solve the problem temporarily, but it would undermine the mutually beneficial parental nondisclosure agreement that took them years to finesse.

"You could have called," Stacy says. "This is not okay. He's hours past curfew."

"You always tell me not to talk on the phone when I'm driving. Make up your minds."

"Okay, bud, relax. That sounds reasonable, hon," Larry says through the door. "At least he's not drunk. Let's talk about it in the morning after we've simmered down."

"Can we get back to your computer-related problem, please sir?" Dayanand asks. His calls are constantly timed and critiqued. His efficiency rating is negatively impacted by drawn-out, costly calls like this one.

"Absolutely. Are you kidding? If you could just tell me a button to push so that when my daughter uses the computer tomorrow morning there isn't a woman with a dick in her mouth on the screen, that would be great. We could skip this whole conversation," Larry says, struggling not to raise his voice.

"I apologize, sir. I respect that this is a sensitive issue. So there is an unacceptable icon on your computer that won't go away?" Dyanand asks.

"This poor kid on *Dateline* had downloaded some fairly innocent booby show kind of stuff, and completely unbeknownst to him, his computer had been highjacked by all sorts of sickos and used to transmit child pornography. Do you think that's what happened?"

"I'm sorry to say anything is possible when you don't keep your defense software updated. Have you found the 'Open Search' option?"

"Hold on. I had to unplug it just in case she came in. It's starting up again. It takes a couple of minutes. Listen, between us, Jeff, I swear to

God in heaven that I only looked at straight, very straight, very regular-guy-type porno."

"I would recommend using the Virus Sweeper 7.1 program available for free from the website."

"After it happened, this little box came up that said my computer had been infected with a virus and it asked me for permission to mine my system, so I went ahead and gave it."

"You should never do that."

"Maybe I got one of these zombie computers they're talking about."

"Do you bank online?"

"Yes."

"You might want to contact your bank to make sure there hasn't been any irregular activity. Check your credit."

"I got this crazy woman that won't go away. She gave me a virus, and now she's screwing with my money. I thought that's why people masturbate to Internet porn, so they don't have to deal with this crap."

"I think that Virus Sweeper 7.1 is a good first thing to try," Dayanand says.

"I'm not some sicko, everybody looks at this stuff."

"Not everybody looks at this stuff," Dayanand says.

"I got the one guy that doesn't look at porn? Are you kidding me, Jeff?"

"I'm very sorry, sir. I was just stating the fact that not every single man in the world does."

"That's okay. I wish I never looked at it. It's bottomless. It's like doing it with my wife isn't any fun anymore because she's not three nineteen-year-old girls."

"I would download Virus Sweeper 7.1 and see if that takes care of the problem, sir."

"So that's it, download Virus Sweeper 7.1? What if that doesn't work?"

"You could take it into one of our service stations. It looks like we have one in your area."

"Are you crazy? There's no way I could ever talk to someone about this face-to-face."

"You could send it there."

"From my address?"

"They have seen it all before, I assure you. Can I be of any further assistance, sir?" Dayanand asks.

"So I pay a hundred and forty-nine ninety-nine and you tell me to download something I could have gotten for free? And this woman and this dick are still on the screen?"

"I am very sorry about that, sir. You can call back with further problems."

"Go fuck your mother, Jeff."

Dayanand is very lucky to have a cubicle by a second-story window. Right now, in the alley, a pack of feral dogs is tearing up a smaller, weaker animal, possibly a chicken, possibly a rat, possibly another dog, but sometimes a pretty girl passes by on her bike.

• • •

Kyler won't let Patty leave her sight, and Kyler is in no condition to leave the bathroom. She is sitting on Patty's grandma's shower chair, soaking wet and naked from the waist down.

"The party is over!" Patty yells through the door.

She hears one of them say, "Yo! There's a dead body in here! Never mind, she's alive."

"Don't touch her! I've got to go out there. I'll be right back," Patty says. There is a disturbing tenor to the laughing outside.

"Don't you dare leave me," Kyler says.

One of them yells, "George put his dick on her foot!" More laughing.

"Tell that fucking midget to get his genitals off her," Patty says through the door.

"That's not cool," says the voice behind the door. "They like to be called 'little people.'"

"Hey, it's Kelly. Let me in there. Is everything all right?"

"Go home, Kelly! Tell everyone to go home!" Patty says. The thought of Kelly Cabañes horning in on all this intimacy makes Patty furious. How could Kyler not be her best friend forever after this? How could she ever take a group of friends to the lake and leave her out again? "Everyone go home or I'm going to call the cops!" The laughing outside makes Patty's nervous center hum.

"Everyone is too drunk to drive," Kelly says through the door.

"Tell them to call their parents, or a cab." Patty hates drunk drivers. In her opinion, an apt punishment for drunk drivers would be some kind of public beating, and if the drunk driver kills a child or a parent, then death. The gruesome videos from Driver's Ed are still fresh in her mind, and she is willing to support any measure to make people comply.

"To be honest, if I kick them out, most of them are going to just drive," Kelly says.

"Take their keys. Aren't there any sober people who can drive?"

"No. I was counting on you to give me a ride home. Open the door. I got to pee."

"Pee in the yard. We're dealing with something in here."

"Is Kyler in there with you? Let me in. I'm her best friend."

You are not! thinks Patty, but she thinks better of saying it out loud. She says, "Everybody just needs to leave."

"I'm not leaving until I know everything is all right," Kelly says. "Kyler, can you hear me? Is everything all right?"

The light from Kyler's cell phone shines through the thin black fabric of her pants balled up on a mauve bath mat.

"Go away, Kelly!" calls Kyler through the door and a flow of tears and mucus.

Patty wraps a towel that she has warmed over the radiator around Kyler.

Kyler says, "It's funny how you can always tell an old lady's bathroom. I'm not sure if it's any one thing really. Besides the chair in the shower. It just feels old."

"Maybe it's the *Reader's Digest* with Carol Burnett on the cover.

"No, it's every single thing."

"What are we going to tell everybody."

"Nothing. Tell them I was puking my guts out."

"Do you want me to call your mom?"

"God no. She thinks I'm in Lubbock."

"Are you going to tell Rob?"

"I thought it stopped because of cross country."

Patty buries the bloody panties at the bottom of the wastebasket.

"It's gone. All I keep thinking is 'Thank God,'" Kyler says.

"I know you don't really feel that way."

"I need you to do something for me, Patty."

"What?"

"Can't you just say you'll do it?"

"I'll do it."

"Will you be the one to flush it?"

. . .

Scooter curls up on Larry's pillow. He has just been anointed with this monthly GuardX flea and tick killer. Warnings from the box bounce around in Stacy's mind: *Keep away from skin. If GuardX comes in contact with eyes, mouth, or skin, consult a physician immediately. If your pet experiences hyperactive breathing, bloody stool, mange, loss of balance or appetite, or extreme lethargy, consult a veterinarian immediately. Do not give GuardX to your cat! GuardX will kill your cat!* She should kick him off her husband's pillow, but he looks so cute: head down, eyes up. Such a happy little dog. And Larry's pillow is at the other end of a very wide mattress. "My little Scoot Scoot. I love you so much." Scooter's eyes follow the potato chips out of the bag, one into Momma's mouth and one into his own. He doesn't even bother to sit up and beg anymore.

4:15 A.M.

In Efren's opinion, a man is judged first by his teeth. It's no wonder Mr. Brim is the boss. His teeth are like jacklights. Lester Brim strides smiling across the sales floor, one of the few people in the store who seems fully awake. As always, he's forty-five minutes early to work.

Efren's own teeth aren't nearly as bright as Lester Brim's, but he has seen much worse. Bobby, the man training Efren on Deli protocol, has teeth the color of the snow that collects in wheel wells. The gums are a bad shade of pink and the incisor in the corner of his mouth has rotted down to nub. When Bobby extends his hand to shake, Efren notices a faded dollar sign is inked onto the web of flesh between his thumb and forefinger.

Bobby says, "New morning guy? Awesome. I was hoping they would send me a guy. Girls just don't want to work, bro. Especially if you get two of them together, they just talk and bitch and cause all kind of drama. Don't get me wrong, I'm not a faggot. Got to put a hair net and a beard net on before you set foot in the clean zone, bro." Bobby's hair net poofs from under his 'SUPERSTORE DELI' cap.

"I brought my own hair net," Efren says.

"We can't wear no vato hair nets. It's got to be one of these fucking poofy white hair nets they give us."

"Why?"

"And you got to wear a beard net."

"I don't have a beard."

"Your sideburns come past your earlobes."

"I have high earlobes."

"Forget your pride," Bobby says. "Jesus didn't have any pride at all, not the tiniest sliver. In this job someone's always telling you to eat shit and chew it with your mouth closed."

Efren puts on the puffy white hair net and looks at himself in the mirror by the slicer. *Parezco como un pinche quequi*, he thinks to himself. He puts on the beard net. It makes him look a claymation Santa Claus. "I should go wash my hands."

"Fuck it. That's what rubber gloves are for," Bobby says. "Mira, the almighty log book." Bobby opens the three-ring binder. There are fourteen pieces of paper inside, two representing each day of the week, one sheet for the openers and one sheet for the closers. Each page is broken down into once-a-day jobs, once-an-hour jobs, and once-every-half-hour jobs. Once-a-day jobs include throwaways, changing the fly traps, stocking the walk-ins, dumping the premade cold/wet salads into their bowls, and making the premade subs for the island cooler. Once-an-hour jobs include throwing trash, seasoning and cooking the rotisserie chickens, and dumping the meat bits and corn dogs in the hot holding case. Once-every-half-hour jobs include cleaning the slicers, wiping down the counter, and temping the food to make sure it's not in the 41°F to140°F danger zone, where bacteria thrives.

"Each time you do one of these things, you put your name by it. Only if you really do it. Those fucking bitches that close this place never do half the shit they sign for. Look at this," Bobby says, pointing into a closet full of boxes. "No XL gloves. Barely any cold/wet salad containers. This is filthy, just fucking filthy. Cocksucker motherfucker. How the hell do they get away with this? I swear, I hope every single one of the closers gets cancer."

"I know how it is," Efren says.

"Goddamnit," Bobby says. "Every one of those cold/wet salads is going to have to be rewrapped. But the first thing we do is throwaways. Every piece of food in the case that's opened up has a sticker on it with two dates: the date it was opened and the date it expires. Cheese gets twenty days to sell from the time it's opened; meat gets six. We got to throw any piece that's expired. It's still good, but if a S/L or LPO sees you eat it for lunch or sneak it in your pockets, you'll get fired. People have done it. That's all I'm saying. If they *see* you, you're fired. And they got cameras and microphones all up in this bitch."

• • •

Dolly will be the first to admit that she sometimes abuses free-taste policies, especially at the Superstore. She hates the Superstore for its hideous trade and environmental practices, and this small act of subversion makes her feel better about shopping here. She has already made her way through the top row of cured meats. "Could I taste this piece of pastrami with a piece of Havarti?"

"Sure," Bobby says, reaching into the cooler. He unwraps the piece of cheese, throws away the celluloid, and cuts one thin slice. "The Havarti is our highest-quality cheese in my opinion."

"Too milky," Dolly says.

"Well, most of our cheese is actually made out of milk."

"You don't say."

Dolly watches him reach deep into the transparent cooler to put the cheese back in its place. "Where could I buy one of those?"

"One of whats, ma'am?"

"The cooler."

"We've got coolers in sporting goods."

"No I mean this big clear cooler you keep the meat and cheese in."

"I have no idea. Some sort of supermarket supply store, probably.

But I've never seen one of those sold here. You thinking of opening your own deli?"

"What temperature do you keep this meat in here?" Dolly asks.

"Always below forty-one degrees," Bobby says. "It rots faster if it's any hotter."

Dolly is struck by the fact that the morgue where she worked as a forensic nurse recognized the same 'magic number' with regard to the holding temperature of corpses. *Why would it be any different,* she thinks. "Can I try the Cajun turkey?" she asks.

Bobby reaches into the cooler and removes the unopened Cajun turkey piece. At 8.99 a pound, it doesn't sell very fast. He opens the package with his carving knife. He creates a sticker with today's date, the thirteenth, and a throw-away date on the nineteenth. He places it on the slicer, cuts the two-inch rind off the end, throws it in the trash, then slices a piece and hands it to Dolly.

"This is our highest-quality turkey," Bobby says. "You see the striations in the meat. It's not all gelatinous like the blended stuff."

"Why didn't you tell me it was spicy?"

"I'm sorry." *It's called Cajun turkey, you cunt,* thinks Bobby.

5:12 A.M.

Larry has collected the magnets from the refrigerator and fastened them to the computer tower. He was hoping that they would result in some Eastern healing of the hard drive or destroy it completely, but they have done nothing. The lily pad screen saver is still up. The offending icon is still bobbing up and down.

Maybe she's in love with me, thinks Larry. *Her true love. Maybe I really crushed her when I clicked on the x in the corner of her screen, when I didn't choose to subscribe to her website after her sample video. Let's give her a thrill.* He imagines the two-dimensional head sliding up and down over his dick like an oil derrick.

Larry comes on a Kleenex and laments, *What did I just do? Now I'll never get rid of her.*

There are no people to talk to on his bank's emergency 800 number, just an automated voice offering to walk through his account information. He pushes buttons in response to questions and watches his penis retract back through the hole in his boxer shorts.

5:18 A.M.

Dolly is trying to believe in the healer. The mind is obviously very powerful. She has seen the benefits of faith as an ER nurse. And she has seen plenty of things she has a hard time explaining. Once she was helping a man die in his home. He was surrounded by five sons, four daughters-in-law, and all the grandchildren that were old enough to watch. He took his last breath the instant the priest placed the eucharist on his tongue, and you really could feel something palpable swirling through the room. But she has seen far more prosaic deaths, people who just turn off like switches, enough boring deaths to make the occasional spectacular one seem like an anomaly.

If she could just believe in the healer, maybe she could be healed. But she has been an open atheist and an ardent skeptic since middle school. *Heaven. Jesus. Latin women who heal with their blessings. I want to believe now more than I want to be right.*

The woman scanning Dolly's groceries is wearing a perfectly formed prosthetic nose. The skin surrounding the nose looks like ground beef wrapped in cellophane. Dolly wants to tell this woman that she has seen a lot, that she's not put off by her scars, but there is really no way to say it. She tries to give the woman a smile that gets the sentiment across. "How you doing tonight?" Dolly asks.

"It's my first day," Amberlee says.

"You wouldn't even know it," Dolly says.

"I'm smiling if you can't tell."

"I can tell."

Why can't these so-called religious healers heal that woman? If there is really some omnipotent God reaching his hand down, why can't he regenerate tissue? Why can't he wipe off scars? It's all migraine headaches and chronic pain. Conspicuous. Why stop just before the undeniable miracle?

When she steps through the sliding glass doors into the osmotic lights of the breaking sun, she thinks, *Still, maybe there is something to it. She wouldn't take any money, even when I tried to press it into her palm.* The metal shopping cart rumbles over the blacktop. Sunlight glints off of polished chrome and glossy paint. The world seems like it is suspended inside of a gigantic orange Jell-O mold along with chunks of various fruits. It stops the early morning shoppers in their tracks, people who are used to sunrises. She is glad she's alive to see it, and then she feels bad that she is glad to be alive to see it. She pushes the button on her keys. A flight of mechanical stairs extend from the log cabin RV. It takes her four trips to bring up the two portable swamp coolers and the other merchandise she purchased. She harkens back to the days when they sent a boy out to help an old lady with this kind of thing.

Dolly plugs in the mini swamp coolers, fills them with water, and points them at Cal. She sets the digital thermostat to forty-one degrees. She lays bags of ice over his body, puts on another two sweatshirts, and crawls into bed alone for the first time in forty years. She is grateful for the noise of the swamp coolers and the two industrial air conditioners because they drown out the noises in the parking lot. They even drown out the sounds that aren't there: Cal's raspy breathing, the small grunts he made when his back hurt, the annoying, sinus-clearing snort he made when his allergies acted up. She'd give anything to hear one last ripping Cal fart. She would laugh this time, like he always did after. She would not call him a pig and spray the Febreze at his face.

5:51 A.M.

When Larry decides to kill the computer, he begins the process by googling 'kill my computer.' Unfortunately, he can't just beat it with a hammer. Then would come the inevitable questions: *Why does the computer look like it's been beaten with a hammer? Are you crazy? My English portfolio is in there!*

The first hit is some sort of tech geek message board.

Flambustable112: my computer at work is a POS. Can someone help me to overlock and kill my computer in a not obvious
way so my cover plan gets me a new one? Do I need software
or just a tutorial? (6)

Larry is not sure he understands the question, much less the answers, which all have to do with technical-sounding procedures like scratching the bus lines under the motherboard and disabling the cooling system. He clicks the next link in the Google list. An anonymous poster poses a similar question: 'how do I kill my computer without anyone knowing?' The respondents write in gleefully violent terms, as if planning the perfect murder.

He is staring into the back of his tower. It makes so much sense, the way the pastel purple audio chord plugs into the pastel purple outlet, and the pastel green monitor jack into the pastel green outlet. It seems to him like this is where he should stay, outside the tower's walls, where everything is color coded and idiot proof. It looks like it will take three different screwdrivers just to get to the circuits. *I can do this. It's not like I'm trying to fix the darn thing, I'm trying to break it. What's the worst that can happen? I don't break it. Maybe I can do this,* he thinks.

He decides to take a break. He's still got about an hour and a half before anyone else in the house is awake. He creeps to the refrigerator, which looks strange with no magnets, or report cards, or pictures, like it belongs back in the store. He removes two Neapolitan ice cream sandwiches from the freezer. The first one he'll just scarf down. He won't be able to wait, and it will be too cold and styrofoamy. But the second one will be that perfect level of melted, just before it starts to drip. The sensitive nature of his front teeth forces him to bite with his lips.

This garage is insane, thinks Larry. His tool box is somewhere inside all the clutter. When Hanes boxer briefs went on sale eight pair for ten dollars, Stacy bought a lifetime's worth for Larry and Keith. The reserves have been vacuum sealed with her Deni Freshlock Turbo II Vacuum Sealer and stored in several plastic storage bins. The storage bins are a relic from the days when there was still some order to the garage, before old clothes began to grow on the heaps of barely used toys and gadgets like moss. *Never mind,* he thinks. *It's hopeless. There's got to be a way to break it without opening it.*

Larry returns to the office and types with sticky, ice-creamy fingers. Finally, something more his speed: a four-minute YouTube tutorial. It is a simple process: download a program that multiplies itself constantly until it overwhelms the computer's capacity like a cancer. After pausing and going back several times, he's able to get it to work. Black boxes filled with white gibberish fan out over the screen. He smiles and scrapes the ice-cream sandwich residue off the wrapper with his teeth.

6:21 A.M.

Ernesto and Conejito are playing the same game through different monitors.

The monitors are sitting back to back on the same square, folding card table. A cubicle built out of scrap pegboard divides the space between them. Ernesto has draped an old blanket over his half of the structure. He likes the dark, confined feeling he gets inside of it, like an astronaut in a cockpit or a horse in a trailer. He runs down a futuristic hallway with smooth pewter walls. As he approaches, the doors open like they are mouths and he is on the end of a fork. He switches to thermal vision and shoulders his plasma cannon.

"Lalo said there really was a bullet in that gun," Conejito says.

"Lalo's full of shit," Ernesto says.

"Bicho said there was a bullet in the gun, and he was holding it."

"Bicho's crazy. He told you there would be a witch who cried blood."

Conejito waits in an observation tower with his sniper's scope fixed on the heavily mined space rover. *Go ahead,* he thinks.

The outside light, passing through the holes in the pegboard, creates a perfect graph on Ernesto's face. When he takes the blunt from his lips and exhales, the beams manifest in the lavender smoke.

"Where are you? Don't be a little bitch." Ernesto is a voice inside a box and a blue avatar running in and out of Conejito's sniper scope. Conejito watches the smoke pass through the holes in the pegboard like cheese coming out of a grater. He wets his finger in his mouth and uses it to swab the bottom of a Cheeto bag for orange dust.

Ernesto puts his eye up to one of the holes in the pegboard and sees nothing distinguishable, just a lone pixel. When he pulls back he can just make out Conejito's bulbous silhouette tilting a two liter of pineapple soda to his lips. "It's no fun when you hide. Come out and get your ass blasted."

Claudia winces at the seventy-watt lightbulb. She walks to the bathroom and pees with the door open. "What are you all doing up this early?" she calls out from the toilet.

"We never went to bed," Conejito says.

"When I got home from work this little bitch was playing video games. He said he was having nightmares," Ernesto says.

"I dreamed of Jesus Malverde."

"San Malverde is an eight-dollar statue."

Claudia says, "You shouldn't talk like that about the saints, Ernesto. One day one of them might have a gun to your head. You want breakfast?"

Claudia drops some Totino's Pizza Rolls onto a metal tray and cranks the knob on the sticky toaster oven.

"Of all the bad stuff that really happens, it's all the bad stuff that could have happened that really fucks my shit up," Conejito says.

"When a boy was born in Sparta, they washed it in wine. Then they examined it. If it was weak they left it left it in the apothetae to die of exposure," Ernesto says.

"How could they tell it was weak before it could even talk or make a decision?" Conejito asks.

"I can see a bitch-made motherfucker from a mile away. It's all about how your head sits on your neck. They made them steal their food to develop stealth and kill slaves for practice."

"How do you know all that?" Conejito asks.

"I looked that shit up on Wikipedia after I saw that movie *300*," Ernesto says.

"They were a bunch of little-boy fuckers, I heard," Claudia says.

"They just fucked the little boys to show them who's boss," Ernesto says. "Do you know who's your daddy, gordito? Me, bitch."

Conejito laughs. He says, "If any man tried to Michael Jackson me I'd blow his fucking head off."

Claudia makes room for the pizza rolls among the clutter of wrappers, bottle caps, and makeshift ashtrays on the counter. "You wait for them to cool, Conejito."

"Their mothers wrote, 'Come home victorious or come home dead,' on all the shields," Ernesto says.

It's hard for Conejito to control himself around pizza rolls. He loves molten pizza gunk. He even loves the blister it leaves on the roof of his mouth: a full fluid sack and then a raw patch and lots of dead white skin for his tongue to play with. He pops the scalding pizza roll into his mouth and tries to blow it cool with short, pulsing breaths. Finally, he is able to work it into the grip of his teeth with his tongue, which is slightly more comfortable, until the molten pizza gunk begins to drip. He tilts the two liter of generic pineapple soda over his head. It glugs like a water cooler.

"What the fuck do you think you're doing?" Claudia asks.

"Trial by pizza roll," Ernesto says.

"My booty itches," Conejito says.

"You need to wash that shit," Claudia says, noting the folds of brown fat that seem to be choking her little brother. "And you need to run a rag or something through your creases. You stink."

"Chingao!" Ernesto yells, as the point of view of his nameless character is thrown into an erratic spin by a remote mine. There is a sharp crack inside the box, the rattle of some broken thing with a lot of parts.

"Be careful," Claudia says. "This shit is rent-to-own."

With Ernesto, there's always a point when the game stops being fun.

Conejito walks to the window to investigate the sound of heavy machinery in the courtyard. The sun is still rising but the show is over. The Jell-O oranges have given way to dusty blues. What comes into focus is the most senseless evil he has ever seen, including the time he saw his mother's boyfriend, Tom, kill his brown puppy with one steel-toed kick. He screams, "They're filling the pool with cement!"

Residents gather on the balconies overlooking the pool, buttoning work shirts with tooth brushes in their mouths and cream on their faces. They watch the men and the cement mixer filling the blue hole. The Plateau Inn was converted from a Best Western when all the chain hotels moved off Motel Boulevard and onto the far west side of town, closer to the new rash of strip malls, chain restaurants, and housing developments. The Days Inn became the New Meridian. The Motel 6 became the Oasis. The Red Roof Inn became the Sleep Well Inn. The IHOP became Pancake Alley. Without the corporations, the lawns have gone to shit and the paint is peeling away. The interiors are frozen in 1987. The alarm clocks have hands and the TVs have dials. The Plateau was the only place to keep a pool in operation, until today. And that's only because they had a certified pool maintenance professional living in the building who was paid in enchiladas and beers from the cooler and a measure of gratitude from his neighbors. He took up periodic collections to cover the cost of the chemicals. Their children were the rich kids on Motel Boulevard, envied by the kids down the street at the New Meridian, the Oasis, and those pobrecitos way down the street at Ben's Family Friendly.

Ernesto can't swim, doesn't see the point. But he thinks of the views he has enjoyed on its banks, especially when Claudia was oiled and sunbathing, when her waist and ribs were glinting.

"What kind of fuckhead fills a pool with cement?" Conejito asks, genuinely baffled by the idea.

"All because Jesus was tossing kids in the air," Claudia says. "I heard they're suing Mr. Lindy for three million,"

Ernesto says, "That fool ain't got three million. My car is better than his."

"He's got more money than Jesus does," Claudia says.

"But why did they fill the pool with cement?" Conejito asks, trying not to cry. "It doesn't make any fucking sense."

"Litigious." Ernesto snatches his neighbor's lawn chair and tosses it off the balcony into the wet cement. One of the workers lifts it out with his rake and curses in Spanish in the general vicinity of the balcony. When the worker bends down to re-smooth the mark in the cement, someone else from the balcony tosses a lamp in, someone else a VCR, someone else an empty bottle, and then a book, a toaster oven, and a clock radio. The workers take cover in the truck. And then a torrent of debris: broken toys, old cell phones, trash and assorted junk—embedded in the cement like fossils.

6:41 A.M.

Ron comes to work early every other Saturday for the Servant/Leader meetings. A lot of the most important conversations happen here in the breakroom over fast-food breakfast sandwiches and coffee before the meeting starts. He's disappointed that nobody important is here to hear his big news, just a few of the cake decorators and a couple of guys from seafood. He could have slept in, been at his best. This biweekly, forty-five-minute tick in his rigid sleep schedule puts his body off-kilter for days.

Finally, Lester Brim enters wearing his mint-green suit, microwaves his Jimmy Dean sausage sandwiches, and sits down next to Ron.

"I got a text from Cassy at the home office this morning," Ron says. "It just said, 'Be on top of it today. Something BIG,' with big in all caps. I called her, but she wouldn't say any more."

"How did she sound?" Lester asks.

"Excited. Like it really was big."

"Did you call Carlos at the east side store?"

"No."

"Good. Let that son of a bitch squirm. Do you think it's Donald again?"

"I don't know. A District S/L visit is big, but not all caps big. And she would've just told me straight out. I'm thinking it could be Mr. Ken, himself."

"Well, you know the drill. We gotta keep our buttholes tight," Lester says. "Say, on a totally unrelated topic. Is there any possible way that an employee has a picture of your penis on her cell phone?"

Ron laughs.

"I'm serious," Lester says. "I haven't actually seen the picture, and God knows I don't want to, but I've talked to people who have seen it."

"Very funny," Ron says. "Is there any way you could make some calls, see who's coming in?"

"Apparently there's no face in the picture. And there are some other disturbing aspects that I don't want to get into."

"Somebody sees a picture of a penis and assumes it's mine?"

"It could be baseless. Last year there were rumors I was giving it to Diane. You know what women are like when jealousy and ambition get mixed up together."

"Is this a joke? Are you filming this?"

"No, this isn't a joke."

"Sure it's not. What are these 'disturbing aspects?'"

"The penis is coming through a dollhouse window. Coming, not cuming. "

"You had me going there. That's funny, Lester." Ron is laughing as hard as he can bring himself to laugh.

"So it's not you?"

"You really had me going there. That's a good one. You almost got me."

6:52 A.M.

When is a computer really dead? wonders Larry, staring at a black screen littered with indecipherable white figures. He has eight minutes until Stacy wakes up. *Is it dead? What's its pulse?* He imagines his wife taking it into the repair center. The clerk is a scrawny man with tape in the middle of his glasses, a pocket protector, and a calculator on his watch. He says, "Ma'am, I'm sorry. Your computer was infected with a pornographically transmitted disease." Maybe she would take the kids along for some reason. He plugs them into the scenario. They have a pristine image of him, in his imagination.

He decides to go for the orifices. He gets one of the everyday case knives from the kitchen drawer and briefly contemplates eating another ice-cream sandwich. The programmed coffeemaker has just finished its tinkling. He makes himself a tall cup with lots of cream and sugar.

Six fifty-four. Six—now five—minutes until she's up. He is very tired, but he has the presence of mind to unplug the power strip before he jabs a metal knife into the holes. *If I were just slightly dumber, I could have died right there. It almost didn't cross my mind.* Larry jabs the knife in the disk drive and jimmies it around, trying to hit a vital organ.

Four minutes. He strikes the long grill lighter and holds the paperclip to the tip of its flame until it glows, then he jams it into every orifice he can find. The ideograms next to the orifices look like a headphone, a telephone, and a pitchfork. He smells melting plastic and considers it a good sign.

Three minutes. He plugs the power strip back in and restarts the computer. He hopes to see nothing on the screen. No indecipherable figures. Nothing salvageable at all. He will go to the Superstore today and buy a new computer. They're getting so cheap. *Hopefully, the kids will have their homework backed up someplace. If not, it will be a good lesson.* The computer whirs. The black screen turns blue. *Please God, just die.* A loading bar stretches across the bottom of the screen

Is this clock fast? Damn it. Larry tilts the tower on its back and pours hot coffee into every hole he can find. An arch flash sears a blue streak into his retinas. He feels like a tuning fork that has been struck with a sledge hammer, and then he slips out of consciousness.

• • •

Stacy wakes up one minute before her alarm is set to go off. In the master bathroom, she pees and slathers another coat of aloe onto all the parts of her sunburn that she can reach. After the last two nights, she is planning on doing some serious sleeping in. It's been so long since she's done this.

She returns to the bed, slightly sticky with aloe. Scooter is sleeping on Larry's pillow. His side of the bed is still firmly tucked. He's been falling asleep in front of the big TV in the media room more and more lately. He tells her she's being ridiculous when she takes it personally.

Stacy closes the satin curtains, crawls back into the bliss of contour-hugging memory foam, and falls back asleep.

8.
The Meeting

THE WEEKLY MANAGER MEETINGS AT STORE # 888 ARE HELD AT A round, folding table in the Personnel Office. The term 'office' isn't exactly correct. It's more a common meeting area for all associates, who congregate here to check their hours and take CBL lessons at the computers lining the walls. Mr. Gene believed that people with offices spend far too much time sitting in them. Alone. He wanted management out in the stores, among the people and the merchandise, generating new and better ideas and, even more importantly, listening for good ideas and stealing them from the competition whenever possible. Only the highest ranking Broken Arrow Home Office executives are allowed to have their own offices, but even they are not allowed to have doors. Not after, in 1978, early in the Superstore's rise, Mr. Gene declared famously, "I don't believe in doors when it comes to offices. They keep people out, and they keep people in." Even Mr. Gene's own office, the office of the greatest merchant who ever lived, was doorless and not much bigger than a maintenance closet. There were no toys or trinkets on the unimposing desk, a precarious particleboard thing assembled with only a hex key by Mr. Gene himself. He sat behind it in a cheaply made, faux-leather office chair. There was no diploma on the wall, though he did earn one from Oklahoma State, only two photographs hanging in two cheap frames. One was President Ronald Reagan presenting him with the Presidential Medal of Freedom, and the other was the cover of *Time* magazine, June 1990, which declared him the richest person in America. The paint was flat white and the light was hard fluorescent. Mr. Gene was amused by the confused looks on the faces of the world-shakers as they walked into the office of the most powerful merchant in history and negotiated the fates of nations and industries sitting on mismatched plastic lawn chair samples left behind by a vendor. The decor conveyed an important message: this is a man obsessed with the bottom line, a man at war with cost.

Of course there was only one Mr. Gene, and he's dead. But Servant/Leaders are expected to re-create themselves in his image as much as is humanly possible. They are evaluated and promoted based on how well they are able to live his way. His autobiography, *My American Way*, is not just read, but memorized, referenced, and quoted often. Laziness, waste, whining, being a "yes man" (changed in recent editions to "yes person"), and "getting too big for your britches" are mortal sins. The Servant/Leader class must prove to the people above them and the people below them on the Superstore flowchart that their britches fit just fine, that if anything they have room to grow. They must prove it by occasionally making fools of themselves for the associates' amusement, as Mr. Gene had famously done when, after the stock split for a tenth time, he honored a bet to the associates by riding down Main Street Broken Arrow on a donkey while wearing a pink tutu. Servant/Leaders are expected to exude the Superstore Spirit, give themselves over completely, to do the company cheer enthusiastically and without any hint of sarcasm. They must learn the company lexicon, replace soft words like "policies" with hard words like "beliefs." They must demonstrate that they are looking out for the best interests of the company, which means looking out for each and every associate, sure, but more importantly the organism that keeps each of their bellies full—not oligarchs casting willy-nilly decisions into a void. Everyone is in power and under power, from the top to the bottom. According to Mr. Gene, "The higher up you go, the more people you serve."

Mr. Gene's long-time secretary, Ms. Jan, a model of efficiency and organization, routinely dressed down Mr. Gene for leaving the light on when he stepped out of his office. "Waste is waste. I own part of this company too," she'd tell him, and they would exchange witting grins. Fifteen years after his death, the egalitarian corporate culture that Mr. Gene created is still the big idea. Superstore executives don't wear diamond-encrusted watches or pinstripes. They make a point of driving red pickup trucks in honor of "Ol' Red," the famous '71 Ford Mr. Gene continued to drive after becoming the richest man in the world. The Home Office suits are blue or black, single-breasted, tasteful but not expensive, and cut in traditional lines. Their offices are variants of Mr. Gene's own utilitarian work space. There are no themes or motifs. An executive associate who decided to "do" the office with a Southwest or Asian "flair," would be laughed right out of the state of Oklahoma.

As Mr. Gene stated on page 161 of his autobiography:

> "We ought to think of each dollar we spend on overhead as a dollar of cost passed on to the customer. Last year the king of Malaysia gave me a one-hundred-thousand-dollar Perazzi shotgun. Well, it was a very nice gift, to say the least. But you know I couldn't hit a quail with that gun to save my life. It was so pretty I think I was scared to shoot it. I'm not even sure it was meant to be shot, but I don't know what else a shotgun is good for. I ended up going back to the old shotgun my granddad gave me on my twelfth birthday. And that six-figure shotgun is just sitting on the mantel. It's pretty to look at, but not good for much else. And I'll tell you what, I wouldn't take ten hundred-thousand-dollar guns for that trusty old scuffed-up double barrel. I'm a pretty darn good shot with it. My point is, it's not about getting rich or showing off. It's about winning, not looking good while you do it."

Lester Brim, the man in charge of Superstore # 888, is dressed in a double-breasted suit made out of glossy, mint-green fabric. The broad cut of the shoulders and the wide lapels are meant to make his chest seem larger than it is and his stomach seem smaller by comparison. His eyeballs push though his eyelids like two crowning baby skulls, and his teeth gleam like radioactive alabaster against his black skin. The box suggests wearing the whitening strips a half hour a day for eight days, but Lester has been sleeping in them for the past twenty-one months because if a little is good, a lot is better. He has to pour the cold Dr Pepper from the machine into a coffee cup and microwave it for fifteen seconds before he can bear to drink it. Even the slightest cool breeze sends a painful chime through his skull, but Lester Brim smiles anyway. He even makes a point to smile in the meat freezer. His catch phrase, "Smile, work is supposed to be fun," has become a standing joke.

Lester has a chair, but he never sits in it. He stands in front of the round, particleboard table, sometimes promenading around it as he talks. "As always, we'll start the meeting with our big-ideas opening. Betty, go!"

"Fast lane the fluorescent beach towels. Put those suckers on Action Alley. They're really flying off the shelves. People can't walk by a three-dollar and ninety-nine-cent beach towel without putting one in their carts."

"Especially ones that glow," Lester Brim says. "They're hitting all the visual cues. That pallet is like a bug zapper. I'm certainly not calling our customers bugs."

"Wait a minute," Ron says. "That pallet is bringing a lot of traffic into ladies' shoes. This is flip-flop season for gosh sake!"

"I know you're just looking out for the best interest of Ladies' Footwear, and that's admirable," Lester says. "But like Mr. Gene says, 'We're Superstore people first, department people second.'"

Mr. Gene was always searching for ideas. And he didn't just open his ears and hope they would fall into his head. He looked you in the eye and wrote down what you had to say on a yellow legal pad with a ballpoint pen. Frank Morales, a meat wrapper from the days when meat was still wrapped at the store, became a famous allegory on "why to listen" in Superstore boardrooms and seminars for suggesting that the Superstore place a greeter at the front entrance to say hello and hand people carts. The idea was tested in five stores representing five variant demographics. A blinking metropolis of switchboard towers in the Superstore Control Room deciphered the SMART system sales data, and a homeschooled computer analyst with perfect SAT scores translated the data to the decision makers in the executive boardroom. They were selling more. Shrink had shrunk by four percent. Ten days after Frank Morales made the suggestion to Mr. Gene, there was an elderly person waiting behind the automatic glass doors at each and every Superstore. When the greeters presented customers with the deep, empty shopping carts, they took them without thinking and filled them without thinking. They came in for three things and bought twenty-five things, partly because of a primal compulsion to fill the empty cart, and partly because they could buy more than they could carry. It is impossible to calculate how much this idea meant to the company, even the homeschooled analyst couldn't say definitively. Many of the company's old-timers suggest that it was one of the ideas that helped launch the Superstore into the stratosphere. Mr. Gene liked to punctuate the anecdote by saying, "I never would have heard that idea if I was sitting at some desk chewing on a cigar."

"Flaco, what's your big idea?" Lester asks.

"We're over labor cost. Not getting enough out of these people." Flaco hands Lester Brim a folded piece of paper. He considers the sugar cookie with pink icing and sprinkles on the napkin before him. *I could divide this cookie in half, that half into fourths, the fourths into eighths, sixteenths, et cetera, et cetera. Over and over. Into a crumb. Into a cell. Into an atom. The atom was supposedly the smallest thing, until we split it. Then you got a new smallest thing. Split that, got a new smallest thing. You can't divide something into nothing. If it has mass and you split it in half, it still has to have some mass. We could just be scratching at how small things get, like we're scratching at space. The only limitations are telescopic and microscopic. We're somewhere on a line that stretches forever in two directions: divided infinity and multiplied infinity.*

The associates shuffle in and out of the office, completing CBL programs on proper hot holding temperatures and pallet-jack protocol, all the time pretending not to listen to the covey of green ties discussing their fates. The managers are speaking in their carrying voices. This meeting is meant to ring out.

"When people don't pull their weight, it has to be carried by someone else. I respect the people who are working their booties off too much to stand for that," Lester says.

"I haven't heard that word since the late nineties," Betty says.

"What word?" Lester asks.

"Booty."

"Please excuse my language." Lester smiles.

They laugh.

By decree of Lester Brim, all Servant/Leaders at Superstore #888 dress according to a weekly color scheme: blue Mondays, red Tuesdays, yellow Wednesdays, orange Thursdays, purple Fridays, green Saturdays, and salmon Sundays. For the men, at the very least, the tie must match the day's scheme. Ladies were expected to dress in the assigned color, or wear at least one piece of coinciding flair. Lester has entire suits coordinated to the days of the week. He is passionate about it because it was his idea. He's hoping to catch an upper executive's ear, get it implemented nationally. He believes his color scheme idea could achieve Frank Morales-level legendary status. *Yup,* thinks Lester, looking at the green ties and shirts surrounding the round table, *Like a team, or a gang, or an army.* He imagines a chanting sea of green ties at the Leadership Revival, and considers incorporating "facilitates team atmosphere" into the relevant skills section of his résumé.

Ron says, "Something big is happening today. Big rumblings. Mr. Ken Provost is visiting. We better be on our toes."

"Who told you that?" Betty asks.

"I got friends at HO. That's all I can tell you," Ron says.

"I just think we shouldn't be so quick to believe rumors," Betty says.

Lester says, "What do you suggest, Betty? That we don't do our best? We don't keep the store clean as a whistle? That we don't serve our customers well today. That we don't make sure the rotisserie is full, the endcaps are stocked, and the merchandise is properly conditioned? Which procedures should we fail to follow? Should we not follow the ten-foot rule today because nothing may happen? Because Ron could be wrong? Or should we do those things because we should do them anyway?"

"That's not what I meant," Betty says.

Lester says, "Everybody come up with your three best ideas and have them at the ready. Write them down. It's easy to draw a blank when one of those HO guys asks you a question. Review Mr. Gene's general principles with your associates. Make sure they can say them in English."

"I was just curious who told you. I know people there too. Of course we should do that every day." Betty is screaming at Ron in her mind: *Shut up squirrel! You're a squirrel! A squirrel is a rat! But it's got this bushy tail, so the same people who might scream or puke at a rat treat them like little puppy dogs! Don't even worry about them running all around them! Eat right next to them! Feed them on purpose! It's unbelievable! Just cause you got a fucking fluffy tail! And they call me crazy when I shake my keys at them!*

"We got to kick butt today, people. Work like Eugene Perryman's angel is looking over your shoulder," Lester says. "Is Jayson C working today?"

"Jayson C?" Ron asks.

"That real sweet kid who smiles all the time," Lester says.

"Still not sure who you're talking about," Ron says.

"Don't make me say it," Lester says.

"He's special," Betty says. "Differently abled in his brain. Mr. Brim knows his name."

"Oh, him."

"Call him in immediately. He's a nice touch," Lester says.

9.
Holding Temperatures

7:37 A.M.

"FUCKING NIGHT SHIFT. WHY DOES THIS SHIT ALWAYS HAPPEN when management has a hair up their ass?" Bobby says.

"What's wrong?" Efren asks.

"We're going to lose this whole case of food. I'm not sure how long it's been like this. We're going to have to throw all of it."

"What's the problem?"

"The cold case is in the danger zone," Bobby says. "Fifty-one degrees."

Efren bends to listen to the buzz of the cooling unit's motor. "It's the limit switch. I can fix it. All I need is the screwdriver."

"I'll call maintenance."

"I can fix with my fingers."

"That's okay, bro. I'll call maintenance."

"But it's warm. We can lose the whole cold holding case."

"My free advice: don't do anything that isn't your job."

7:40 A.M.

Dolly is startled awake when a bead of sweat runs from her left temple onto her left eyelash. She is terrified by her first waking thought: *Where's my gun?* The air conditioners and the swamp coolers are no longer buzzing. When she went to bed the world felt cool and slippery, like Jell-O right out of the refrigerator. The white noise was deafening.

The thermometer she inserted into Cal's mouth read forty degrees. Now her hair is dripping. The mercury is at eighty-three. Why does she feel inflatable? *Oh,* the five sweatshirts she is wearing. She removes them all at once and sits sweaty and naked from the waist up at the kitchen table. The lights don't work. The bags of ice that were resting on Cal's chest and legs are now empty plastic bags on top of a wet cadaver.

Thank God my cell phone is charged, she thinks.

This is the kind of thing that Cal would usually handle. The division of labor between Dolly and Cal was pretty old-school, though she has always been a staunch, second-wave feminist. Dolly handled the bills and Cal handled the lawn. Cal drove and Dolly decided where they were going.

She calls her brother, Scott, a master mechanic who lives in Lawrence, Kansas. She feels safe in the idea that he very rarely answers his cell phone. He was the last person she knew not to have one. It often sits for days unchecked, switched to a silent ringtone or completely out of battery juice. Waiting for him to call her back is the perfect excuse to do nothing, to wander around the Superstore where it is always cool, to buy more ice.

"What's wrong?"

"Since when do you answer your cell phone?"

"Is it dad?"

"The power in the RV is dead. The lights don't work. The AC and the fans stopped running. It's getting hot as the dickens."

"God, it's a fortune to tow those things. Is your RV a thirty-amp rig or a fifty?"

"I don't know."

"Are you sure you got the right adapter plugged in there?"

"I'm not plugged in anywhere. I'm in a Superstore parking lot in Las Cruces, New Mexico."

"Are you sure you have gas?"

"Oh, goddamnit. I'm so stupid." The needle is buried in the red.

Scott laughs. "Let me talk to Cal. I'm going to have to charge him six beers for my services. Idiot tax."

"He's dead."

"Oh, God. What do I say? I'm so sorry. I'm looking up the route. I can be there in twelve hours. What do I say, sissy?"

"I woke up and he was just a dead body there next to me." Dolly wipes the sweat off of her naked chest with a dishrag. Cal's body, in repose on the RV couch, is not sweating. *No heart pumping oxygen to the cells. Bacteria, alive in us already, just waiting to eat us up when the immune system shuts down.* She catches the first whiff of the death smell. She remembers the menthol salve they smeared under their noses to cover it when she was a forensic nurse. *Vicks VapoRub would do in a pinch.*

"How is Meg?"

"Could you call and tell her for me?"

"You haven't called her?"

"Please, Scotty. I'll be your slave for a year."

"You won't feel right about it later. God, I wish I knew what to say."

"It's hot in here. I feel like vomiting."

"Sissy, you need to go to the hospital."

"We pulled into the Superstore late Thursday night. I woke up in the morning, and I knew as soon as I touched his hand. Before I even opened my eyes."

"Thursday? Where is he?"

"Here in the RV with me. He died in his sleep. I wanted Meg to see him before the funeral home puts the suit and dead body makeup on him. I've been keeping him cold."

"Keeping him cold?"

"The air-conditioning units on this thing are really amazing. When there's gas. I hardly needed all the ice and the coolers I had plugged in. It's getting hot."

"Okay. Just relax, Sissy. I'll make all the phone calls. Just try to sit there and not worry about anything."

"Thank you."

"Is someone on their way?"

"No. You're the first person I called."

"We haven't spoken in almost three years."

"How Irish of us."

Skin like wet toilet paper, mouth agape, Cal looks like nothing so much as a dead body now. *Just a dead body,* Dolly thinks. *He's not smiling, or moving, or talking to me. He's just lying there like what he is. It's a miracle.* She imagines the curandera's face etched into a spiderweb and tries to believe in her magic. *Who are we to say it's all nothing, it's all nature and nurture and alive and dead? She refused to take my money, even when I pressed it into her hand.*

Dolly removes a few ice shards floating in the clear sack, holds them to her nipples, and thinks, *You can't feel hot with ice on your nipples. They're thermostats.*

When Dolly pulls back the curtains, it's like walking out of a cave. A man with a single transverse palmar crease is walking across the parking lot, wearing a blue Superstore smock and sweating through his collar. He looks through the window of the RV at Dolly, naked from the waist up. *Then why can't God heal the retarded?* she wonders. *Has that ever happened?* The boy gives her a cross-toothed, open-mouthed smile. *No use putting braces on a kid like that,* she thinks. She would give anything to be able to turn on the TV, for some distraction. She opens the window to the sounds of engines churning, metal carts jangling on the rugged blacktop, and a mother scolding her child in Spanish. *It's something. It's not nothing.*

· · ·

Jayson is excited to have seen boobs, but wishes the first live boobs he ever saw had not been those. Those were old enough to be his grandma's. Those had a flap of skin between them like the flap of skin between a thumb and a pointy finger. Those brown nipples were huge. And that woman was crying. He wanted the first real boobies to be Claudia's, on their wedding night, not an old woman in a bus made out of logs. Claudia helps him use the trash compactor and the cardboard bailer. Claudia tells him he's doing a good job. And Claudia is so pretty. So so pretty.

It is 7:54 in the morning. You can't swipe in more than five minutes early. That's a rule. Three drowsy associates lean on the wall with their smocks in their hands, while Jayson stands inches from the clock and stares at the digits.

When the last digit turns to five, Jayson claps and is first to swipe his card.

The image of the crying old woman and her breasts is expunged from his mind forever.

7:57 A.M.

Patty can't forget God's precious baby floating in the pink toilet water like a blanched plum, the way it spun into the tube when she flushed it. Down the pipes. Down into the place where all the flushing toilets lead, to mingle with pee and poop. *Was it a boy or a girl?*, wonders Patty. *We should have named it. We should have buried it.*

Kyler tries to roll onto her back, and Patty turns her gently onto her side again. She's been keeping vigil by the bed, watching the *Miss Congeniality* DVD and all the deleted scenes, rolling Kyler gently back onto her side all night long.

"What the fuck?" Kyler asks.

"If you sleep on your back, you could choke on your own vomit," Patty says.

"I'm not going to choke on vomit. I don't even like vomit."

"You can sleep on your side."

"Fuck that. Let's watch *Miss Congeniality*."

"Okay."

"Turn the sound down, please. My head is like a potato in a microwave that nobody poked holes in."

"I got you a big bottle of water. You should drink it."

"I'll totally pay for you to rent a steam cleaner."

"It's not your fault."

Kyler types a text message to her mom:

Y many kray msgs
i just woke up

• • •

Stacy hears the digitized chime from her sleep. The mobile phone on the nightstand flashes her daughter's picture and an ideogram that means "message received." She opens her left eye just wide enough to read the message and then drifts peacefully back into a dream about a plane crash. Even in the midst of her dream, she knows it's only a dream.

8:08 A.M.

"Ron said not to throw it away until the end of the shift. Sell as much of it as possible," Bobby says.

"What about the cold holding log," Efren asks. "We don't know how long this stuff has been hot."

"He said you should fill it out. Be creative."

"*He* said *I* should be creative?"

"Shit rolls downhill. This is how you move up the ladder. Play the game."

"But you're not my boss."

"Seniority, bro."

"Fine."

"They must have liked you. A level-three job right off the bat," Bobby says.

"Level three?" Efren asks.

"Cart pushers and Custodial is level one. That's where they put you if you got a criminal record or don't speak English. Checkers and Stockers is level two. Deli is level three, just like the cake decorators in Special Bakery, Sporting Goods, Electronics."

"Who's in the level above us?"

"In the store, only S/Ls, pharmaceutical, and automotive. And of course the optometrist. That guy gets so much pussy. You must have done good in the interview. It took me three and a half years to get up to here," Bobby says.

"My plan is to work hard and be a boss," Efren says.

"You got a green card?"

"My wife was American before she died."

"Your English is good enough. My advice is don't ask any wrong questions, and don't get any tattoos on your hands. They don't promote people with tattoos on their hands. I've thought a lot about taking this box cutter and just peeling mine off."

8:23 A.M.

Megan can't wrap her head around the fact that her dad is dead, even though she spent great effort imagining it as a child. She would cry in bed, trying to imagine what it might feel like. She was fascinated with the idea that her emotions were hers to control. All she had to do was cue the emotion with some sort of narrative. The grief narrative was always about her father dying. The circumstances she imagined weren't important: he had a heart attack or he choked on something. She was more interested in the kind of modesty he would have insisted on in a tombstone. She thought about delivering his eulogy, how she might slobber and blow snot into a handkerchief right there at the altar. Tucked into her bed, she would convince herself that everything was real and sob about it all until she felt like feeling something else. He would die someday. He would certainly die. And who can say when it's too early to mourn that fact?

Miles back, Megan had calculated that she was six hours away. But now she's barely doing forty, stuck behind an overloaded wrecker in the one-lane construction zone. She takes a drag off the cigarette resting in a dry coffee mug. She turns up the conservative radio talk show host because he makes her furious, and right now she would rather be furious than sad. Her dad is really dead. If she were to get sad right now, she's not sure when it would stop. *Those radio waves are passing through my body. Through. Nobody asked. War-dick spin doctors talking to us like children. They're going to give me a tumor.* She shifts the car into fifth gear when the construction clears. She remembers the day her father tried to teach her to drive a stick: *Put your foot on the brake. Depress the clutch with your left foot and depress the brake with your right. God help us. Now put the car into gear. Make sure the clutch is all the way depressed! Then stop crying and depress the clutch all the way—deep into the floor. Now put the car in first gear. There. I want you to very gradually give it some gas and— not yet! Wait! Very gradually release the clutch and give it gas until you feel the gears catch. You're thinking too much. You've got to feel it, give it over to a deeper part of your mind.* He gave up so quickly. Six years ago Megan bought an '86 Mercury Lynx for four hundred

dollars just so she could grind the shit out of the gears. She had attached so much metaphorical weight to the manual transmission that,
once she had mastered it, she felt a fundamental shift in her personal-
ity. She danced in public. She stopped letting people make her feel
bad for being over thirty and childless. She sent food back. She got
stoned and bored her friends with diatribes about how something as
seemingly insignificant as a manual transmission can really mean something in the life of a person.

Megan's cell phone rattles in the cup holder. "Hi, Mom." She tosses
her cigarette out the window.

"Did you talk to your uncle?" Dolly asks, her voice trembling.

"I did. I'm on my way. How are you?"

"Did he do a good job telling you?"

"What do you mean?"

"Did he do a good job? Was he a good person to hear it from?"

"He did fine."

"I'm so sorry. I should have been the one to tell you. I just couldn't
do it."

"Are you okay?"

"You know... How far away are you?" Dolly asks.

"A few hours."

"What about work?"

"For Christ's sake, don't worry about that."

"Well, I just want you to know that I'm okay. And I don't want you
to drive dangerously in order to get here faster."

"I'm going the speed limit."

"That doesn't mean you have to drive that fast. Especially if it's rain-
ing there. It rained here earlier."

"I'll be fine."

"The road is the most dangerous when it just starts to rain. It washes
the oils up and makes it dreadfully slick."

"The road is dry as a bone."

"Good, because I'm fine. You don't have to rush. How much is gas?"
Dolly asks.

"God, I forgot how far you can see in the desert once you get out of
the city. This rain cloud is just creeping across the distance. Big stripe of

gray." Megan wonders if it's the same cloud that rained on her mother earlier. How far can she see?

"Drive safe. I mean it. If you die too, I'm going to kill myself."

"Why would you say that?"

"I don't know! I'm so sorry. That was such a horrible horrible thing to say!"

"It's okay, Mom."

"No. It was horrible. I'm so sorry. I'm your mother. God, what's wrong with me? I'm so sorry, Babybear. This is why I had Uncle Scott tell you. What kind of mother would say something like that?"

"Is he still in the RV?"

Dolly hums the affirmative.

"You need to call somebody, or go someplace."

"Where? Who?"

"You worked in a morgue for twenty-seven years, Mom. Shouldn't *you* know who to call?"

"He was dead when I woke up, Babybear. Don't you think I would have done something?" Dolly had saved her husband's life twice before: on the Will Rogers Turnpike, at the scene of a gory motorcycle accident that left her with a glass eye, and again, six years ago. She nagged him into a colonoscopy that came back bad but operable. She thinks about the chunk of time between the motorcycle accident and the cancer. She thinks about the chunk of time between the colon cancer and now. *I never saved his life. We bought time. Spent time.*

"Keep it together. I'll be there soon."

"You don't know what they do with dead bodies. They take the organs out and weigh them. They pull your face over your skull," Dolly says.

"Mom, you're freaking me out. I'm going to call 911."

"Don't you dare. Those people have real lives to save. God, can you believe I said that? I'm so sorry."

"I'm hanging up, Mom. You're being weird. Are you sure you're okay?"

"Yes. I'm fine. Don't worry about me. Worry about the road."

"I'll be there soon."

"Well for God's sakes drive carefully!"

"I will."

"Promise."

"I promise."

"Well then hang up that damn phone. It's just as dangerous as driving drunk they say." When Dolly hangs up, she pictures her daughter
being crushed dead by a semi. Maybe she would die herself, of melan-
choly, like a zoo-kept panda. She chews a piece of yolk-soaked toast and
thinks, *Life is too short to use fake butter.*

The chile field looks like green moss on a dry, brown rock. The road
is gray and straight. The radio isn't taking Megan's mind off her father
anymore. Her attention is fixed on the pesky itch in the center of her
back. Rubbing herself against the smooth, vinyl seat just makes it worse,
teasing her with the thought of a fingernail. She imagines scratching her
back with the prickly bushes, the cacti, and all the hot, jagged rocks of
the desert. She's not sure if this makes her back itch more or less. If she
could only scratch. But both hands have a white-knuckled grip on the
wheel. The cruise control is set at ninety-four miles an hour. She passes
a white Lexus with "I LOVE YOU BITCH" spray-painted across all four
panels in rust-red letters.

Dolly is worried about how Cal will look when Megan gets there.
Will she even want to see him before they take him away? If she does,
Dolly certainly doesn't want her daughter to see Cal like this, his dead
face distorted into a spooky grin by a clear sack full of melting ice. She
empties the ice bags into the sink. She dabs his face dry with a fluorescent
beach towel, then combs his hair in the manner that she has always
wished he would comb it, to the side and not down the middle. She sniffs
him and contemplates putting him in something nicer than cutoff blue
jeans and a T-shirt. *It might be harder for Meg to see him all dressed up
and arranged. I should let her see how natural it is. It's his nicest T-shirt,*
brand new and purple with the words "Grand Canyon" written above an
orange-and-blue representation. *His color is changing.* Cal releases one
last rattled breath. "Thank you, Cal, for doing that before she gets here.
That was very considerate." She arranges his arms and legs into a position
that looks comfortable when she stands a couple feet back and squints
her eyes.

10:13 A.M.

Wilma has worked her way through each flavor of Rockstar Energy Drink: citrus, guava, pomegranate, and blue. The menthol in her cigarette opens her lungs and gives her a second wind. She feels almost lucid on the drive home from work. When she looks through the side window, the brush passes by like the serrated edge of a spinning saw. But when she stares at the brush through the windshield, everything seems so slow. A dark cloud is dangling just over the gentle molted slopes of the Robledo Mountains. The rain looks like falling smoke, and the smell of it overwhelms Wilma's burning cigarette. The broken yellow line blurs into a solid line and disappears under the hood of her Maxima. There are two holes behind the backseat where the subwoofers used to be, holes in the back doors where the six-by-nines were, and a hole in the dash where the CD deck used to be. She took the entire system out when the repo man put himself on her trail. They have a funny way of losing that kind of thing in the impound lot and saying it was never there. So she sings what she can remember of "The Longest Time" by Billy Joel in full throat.

The blood is finally moving out of her ankles. There are still pulsing pains in her knees and feet, but at least the pressure is gone. *Standing should be an Olympic sport,* thinks Wilma. *Endurance standing: seven hours a day, six days a week, for years and fucking years.*

There is just under five dollars in change in her secret money place: a tampon box at the back of the glove compartment. She keeps a few coins in the change tray as a diversionary tactic. Colorful fast-food signs are laid out before her on the drive home like birthday candles.

She slows down enough to annoy the drivers behind her. She needs time to process. Once she passes, she never goes back. Commercial images and jingles are jostling around the bottom of Wilma's brain like silt.

Sonic? She imagines biting into a hot, salty tater tot. Her spit glands begin to percolate, but she's not down with the roller-skating car hop shit. Waiting in your car for the food? *Do they expect me to tip them?* And the whole nostalgic white-America pull toward the fifties gives her the willies. Like it was all soda jerks and yes sir-no sir and niggers who knew their place. Give her a fucking drive-through; she hasn't slept since Wednesday night.

In Wilma's opinion, Taco Mexicana is the best Mexican restaurant in the city, which is saying something. They have lengua and cabeza and tripas on the menu, which she isn't brave enough to try, but their three-dollar, baby-thigh-size, carne asada burrito is her heart's desire right now. The meat has a special salty-citrusy grease. And they top it with god knows what deliciousness: cilantro, lime salsa and other homemade sauces. But in her present exhaustion, she needs corporate efficiency. Even minor annoyances seem unbearable, and last time the woman at the drive-through didn't speak English.

Arby's. She actually shudders at the thought. About once every two years she gets an inexplicable craving for Arby's, but it's only been about eight months since her last big beef and cheddar, not nearly long enough to forget the gray, slippery meat.

KFC has been effectively dead to her since Tony's cousin told her about the rat infestation.

McDonald's is serving breakfast for six more minutes. She doesn't care for the whole American breakfast palate. Bacon? Sure, put it on my cheeseburger. Ham? Yes please, between two pieces of bread. Eggs? No motherfucking way. She can't believe people actually eat them, with their wet chalk taste and their membranes. And she doesn't get pancakes at all, like regular cake but not quite as good. She does eat quite a bit of cereal, mostly at night.

A commercial for Subway's new Reuben sandwich comes to mind. It looks damn good, the golden bread and the hot pink middle, but she's never had a Reuben before, and she doesn't know what the fuck sauerkraut tastes like. *Something safe. Something I know will be good.*

She doesn't eat fish. Long John Silver's doesn't even register in her consciousness. It is filtered away with all the other things she sees but doesn't want or need right now, like the taekwondo studio, the billboard advertising a plaster-faced real-estate agent, and the fireworks stand. She tosses her cigarette into a soda can and realizes suddenly that she hasn't stopped singing "The Longest Time." Just the chorus at this point, over and over and over again. It feels like it's the only thing keeping her awake, like if she were to stop she might fall asleep behind the wheel and veer into the oncoming lane. And the thing is, she doesn't even like the song. She hates Billy Joel. She hates the way he charges her consciousness and sets up camp like fucking carpenter ants.

She's three-quarters of the way through fast-food row and running out of options. Whataburger is too rich for her blood. The yellow-and-red, A-frame Wienerschnitzel hut tops everything with a chili that looks a little too much like diarrhea to stomach, and the Taco Bell has a stronger, proven association with the condition. She settles on Jack in the Box and orders two ninety-nine-cent cheeseburgers with no onions, a large Dr Pepper, and a medium fry. She asks the very pregnant teenager at the window, "Do these cheeseburgers have onions?"

"Did you order them without onions?"

"Don't, '*Did you order it without onions,*' me like you people never fuck up an order. Let me tell you something, if I drive all the way home, finally take my shoes off, turn on the TV, kick my feet up, and bite into a fucking onion, I don't know what the fuck I'm gonna do."

"You could always pick it off."

"Everything that touches onion tastes like onion."

"There are no onions on these burgers, ma'am."

I hope your baby is defective, thinks Wilma as she drives away.

10:36 A.M.

The most important part of Jayson's job is seeming sweetly retarded. This part of the job requires no effort at all. He appears in two nationally broadcast Superstore commercials. In the one that plays on regular television, he has a speaking part. He stares into the camera. His hair has been arranged to seem more retarded by a team of professional hairdressers. His wide-set eyes squint behind thick glasses when he smiles and says, "The Superstore takes care of me by helping me take care of my self." The second commercial is televised on the closed-circuit Superstore station. Jayson appears in a faux newscast wherein a reporter extols the good that the Superstore is doing for the most special members of the community. The commercial plays every one hundred and twenty-four minutes in all 5,281 U.S. Superstores, on barely audible televisions placed eight and two-thirds feet in the air.

More than any other associate, Jayson is complimented on the job he is doing. Customers stop him to exclaim, 'You must know your way around this maze a lot better than I do!' But they rarely ask him where anything is. If you were to walk into the Superstore and ask for directions to, say, the foot powder, Jayson would grab your hand and walk you to it. He can't tell you where the foot powder is in the abstract, but he can lead you there by a sticky hand.

If Bicho had been born with an errant chromosome, he might have a cushy job like Jayson's. But the evidence of his damage is harder to see. So he pushes heavy carts in the hot sun and the rain, and people honk at him when he's not moving fast enough, people who would be scared to meet his glance if he weren't wearing a blue smock with the words "How can I be of assistance?" printed on the back. Bicho's gangster-ass tattoos strike instinctive fear like the markings of a poisonous snake. The thick, square, schoolmarm glasses and the band that stretches around the back of his neck make him slightly more menacing somehow. Incongruent. Off balance.

He's on his water break. There's plenty of free, cold tap water at the hydration station, but Bicho hates water. He asks Jayson where the cold Gatorade is. The thought that the Superstore does not sell cold Gatorade doesn't even cross his mind. Until now, everything he could ever imagine wanting has been sold here.

Jayson is putting a tub of sour cream back on the shelf. He knows he's supposed to put the cold stuff back first. The colder it is, the more first it has to be. What isn't cold, like the bamboo lamp and the hemorrhoid pads, can wait. He's afraid to grab Bicho's hand. They went to high school together. Jayson thinks Bicho is mean and cool.

"Come on," Jayson says.

On aisle six, Jayson replaces the dry beans and the shortening. He returns a bottle of hot sauce to aisle seven. He looks at the cart full of takebacks he's pushing and thinks about how cool it would be to stack carts up and push them like Bicho does. Everyone would see how strong he is. *No girl could do that job*, Jayson thinks. They turn back up aisle nine, past spaghetti sauce and eleven types of ranch dressing.

"Here," Jayson says, pointing to the powdered Gatorade.

"You make being a retard seem like some good drug, güey. Smoke some shit, get all smiley like you for twenty minutes. That shit would be bigger than crack," Bicho says.

Jayson screams "Claudia!" at the sight of her passing between the aisles. She throws her arms around him and kisses him on the cheek.

Claudia loves the way Jayson looks at her, the pure adoration, unmarred by lechery or suspicion. "Look, Jayson. You're on TV again," Claudia says, pointing at an image of him holding a stuffed red dog on the closed circuit monitor.

"I didn't let them put makeup on me," Jayson says.

"It's not real TV," Bicho tells Claudia.

"What is it, a fucking microwave?" Claudia asks.

"Where are you going?" Bicho asks.

"To smoke another cigarette and drink a peach tea."

"How do you two get to do whatever the fuck you want?"

"I have a picture of Ron's dick on my phone."

"Bullshit. Let me see it," Bicho says.

"Gay!" Jayson says.

When Claudia walks away, Bicho pinches Jayson's left tit hard enough to make him cry.

10:45 A.M.

Glen is in the cramped Loss Prevention Office writing dialogue for two women standing behind parallel shopping carts on monitor seven.

Hot today.

You said it.

How bout that PTA meeting?

Who does Becky Smitherson think she is?

I heard her husband is fooling around with the cheerleading coach.

That's terrible.

Eggs are up sixty-six cents.

Can you believe the price of everything?

Glen is holding the point of a pen to a blank page. Everything is coming out shit. *God, I have no idea what women talk about.*

Ron enters the Loss Prevention Office and sticks a wet pinky finger in Glen's right ear.

"What the fuck!"

"Don't be like that, baby," Ron says. "Anything good on TV?"

"The usual: bunch of motherfuckers wandering around the Superstore."

"I need to see the files on anybody named Limón."

"Why?"

"Come on, lover. I'll let you pee on me."

"Well, that's tempting."

"I just want to see them."

"I grew up in Chiva Town. Trust me. You don't want to fuck with the Limóns."

"Why?"

"There are some bad motherfuckers in that family. Let's just say some of their rap sheets are thick and disturbing."

"I got your thick and disturbing."

"Don't say I didn't warn you."

"Thanks sugar tits."

"You're welcome candy-corn cock," says Glen, and thinks about how he really would, if given the chance, love to piss on Ron's face.

10:49 A.M.

"He doesn't even know we're here," Keith says. He knows he's supposed to be here, but the psychic weight of his father so still on the hospital bed, the breathing tubes in his mouth, might break his back if he stays one more minute.

"Don't you want to be here when he wakes up?" Stacy asks. She is dressed in what she slept in: a faded pair of Larry's sweatpants with "BUM equipment" printed down one leg and an oversize T-shirt.

"I guess," Keith says, sobbing.

"He knows we're here," Stacy says.

"His eyes are closed."

"He can hear us."

"Maybe his eardrums work, but they're not connected to anything. If I die, put my body to use. If it makes you feel better, stuff me like a trophy, keep my body in the living room. Give me glass eyes and pose me any way you want."

"You're not going to die."

"Yes I am."

"He's not dead, Keith."

"He's kind of dead."

"There is no such thing as kind of dead."

"What are you talking about? Of course there is."

"Go wait in the waiting room, then." Stacy nibbles on her middle fingernail. She's always been curious about how her son would react in a grave situation. His life has been perfect so far in her estimation. She is disappointed, and she blames herself. Larry would have liked to have been harder on him, but she kept him tender and fragile by loving him too much when he cried.

She can't reach her daughter. It's her own fault, she figures. Who can blame Kyler for ignoring her calls and finally turning her phone off? Stacy would admit that she calls too much. When she does, it's usually to temporarily subdue the prevalent fear that her daughter is, at that very moment, being brutally raped and/or murdered. The idea surrounds her like a plastic bag wrapped tightly around the head, and it doesn't go away until she hears Kyler's voice.

It's true that cell phones give us more access, thinks Stacy. *But it's so easy now to push a button and make the ringing go away. You never thought about unplugging the old phones. You had to listen to them ring until they stopped.* Kyler's father is unconscious, a five on the Glasgow Coma Scale. They shocked his heart. His breathing stopped. The doctors warned her that if he lives, he will most likely never be the same. It's not the kind of message you can leave or text. *You can control your incoming ringtone: songs and Tarzan calls and babies cooing. Why can't I control the ringtone on the calls I make? Why can't I make her phone ring like a fire alarm?* Stacy considers the down side of Jesus living inside her head. He must have heard her thinking about the insurance money. *I realize you've seen some things you don't like. I don't like it any more than you do. If you could just scrub it out for me, Jesus. Cut it out with your holy scalpel. Take it away. I don't want a free will. Take it. If it's really mine, I'd like to give it away.*

Deb from church pokes her fat, sorrowful head around the door, rapping gently on the glass. "Hello," she says. "I brought Panera."

Does she have a fricking police scanner? thinks Stacy. It was just this morning that Keith found his dad sprawled out on the office floor, unresponsive. The paramedics lifted Larry off the cream-colored carpet and they all had to look at the rusty stain he left behind.

Deb is the go-to lady for congregation health news, a role she seems to relish too much for Stacy's taste. A screen in a corner of Stacy's mind is playing footage of Deb telling a small but rapt crowd of parishioners about how she hasn't left her husband's side in weeks, not to sleep, or eat, or shower, the way she wipes his bottom and feeds him like a baby. Of course she hasn't done any of this yet. It's all just happened, but she believes that this is how she'll act and how Deb will report it. She imagines the small crowd gasping and shedding tears of sympathy and respect. All the flowers and giant cards that everyone signs. It gives her a small thrill that makes her want to bash Deb's head against a sharp rock.

"It's bread and sandwiches and a few different kinds of soups," Deb says.

"Thank you," Stacy says. "That was thoughtful."

"You've mentioned before that you like Panera."

"I do."

"Then I won't tell you that their southwestern chicken panini has more grams of fat than a Big Mac. Of course you don't have to worry about that. You could tread water in a garden hose." When Deb From Church's son was in the hospital, she liked the visitors who added a little appropriate levity. They were a nice break from the ones that couldn't do anything but cry and radiate fear.

Stacy acknowledges the pale joke with a pursing of her lips, then nibbles gently on her thumbnail.

"You have to remember to eat. When Freddy was in the hospital they had to keep reminding me to eat. You got to keep your strength up for something like this. It's a physical effort too. A lot of people don't realize that."

"Thank you." *Do I seem sad enough?* wonders Stacy. *Why aren't I crying? I cried when Wendy's stopped serving pitas. Any time I drink more than five beers, I cry. I cry watching* ER *at least eighty percent of the time. Crying is nothing. It means nothing. This is past crying. This didn't hurt my feelings, Jesus, it decapitated them.*

"I'll go. I know you're probably not ready for visitors just yet. I just wanted to stop by and let you know I was praying for you."

"How'd you find out?"

"My daughter, Mindy, works in admin. She called. She's not really supposed to, but when it's a close friend, you know, there are exceptions."

"Thank you so much for the food," Stacy says.

"Do you have my number?" Deb asks. "This darn five-seven-five area code . . . I had to go through and change all the numbers in my phone. It took half a Sunday. I liked it when all of New Mexico was five-zero-five."

"Too many people with too many phones."

11:12 A.M.

Kyler is lying in bed, propped up by several pillows, afraid to move her throbbing head. Even tilting her head to drink from her water bottle is almost unbearable. Thinking hurts. *Miss Congeniality* is playing at a low volume on a small TV on the dresser. Sandra Bullock stumbles comically across the stage in high heels. If it were funnier, she might be forced to laugh, which would be agony.

Patty returns from her grandmother's medicine cabinet with a very large pill and petroleum jelly.

"Did you find anything?" Kyler asks.

"This," Patty says, holding the individually wrapped pill to Kyler's face so she doesn't have to move her head to see it. "It's for chronic cancer pain. It's probably pretty strong."

"If it didn't hurt to move, I would hug you so hard."

"I don't think you should take it unless it's like some kind of emergency."

"I feel like a tube of something that somebody stomped on."

"Wikipedia says this is a serious narcotic."

"Why did you get it out of your grandma's medicine cabinet and bring it here to show to me if you weren't going to give it to me?"

"What if you get addicted?"

"You know you're going to give it to me, so just give it to me. Please. My head hurts too bad to go through all the bullshit."

"Here." Patty puts the pill on the nightstand.

"Is that for a horse?" Kyler asks.

"You don't swallow it."

"How do I take it then?"

"You put it in your butthole."

"Goddamnit. Don't make me laugh," says Kyler.

"I'm not kidding."

"How can you take a pill with your ass? Does it crawl up to your stomach or something?"

"Hold it up there and it dissolves."

"It's real medicine, right? Not some hippie colon cleanse shit."

"It's pharmaceutical oxymorphone."

"From a drug store?"

"Yes."

"An American drug store?"

"It's a suppository. It dissolves."

"I've never put anything up my butthole before. Fuck, it hurts when I laugh."

"Put some of this on it first."

"Ugh. God. It's too weird. I can't."

"You're clenching. Relax."

"Do you promise this will make me feel better?"

"When my grandmother takes it she just sleeps real deep for a long time usually."

"Oh my God, that's exactly what I want."

"Turn over on your side. I'll help you."

They both laugh hysterically, Kyler while she gnashes her teeth and grinds her palms into her eyes.

11:30 A.M.

"The last thing in the world I want to be is creepy about this." Ron is sitting in front of a number two value meal, which he can't bring himself to eat.

"Why would you feel creepy?" Claudia dips a chicken nugget.

"I'm glad to hear that. I feel like that too. Like we're both adults. And professionals. And I want to assure you that this will have absolutely no bearing on your future with the Superstore. I think you have all the stuff. You're capable. You're smart and personable." Ron pauses and lowers his voice when two other Superstore associates sit within earshot. "I think you could be a superstar at this company. I really do. I just thought I should maybe buy you lunch, maybe clear the air. We have to work together. I don't want to avoid Cold Dairy because we might run into each other or anything. I'm in charge of the cold chain. Right now I'm feeling a lot of tension when I walk by you. Not like, anything weird. Just tension. Embarrassment, frankly. I'd like that to go away. That's why I thought it would be a good idea to just clear the air with a couple burgers. I really never thought I was the kind of guy that did that. God. I thought it would be funny. Can you believe that? I really did."

"It's okay," Claudia says.

"It was a very minor thing. We didn't even do anything. We didn't even kiss. A flirtation. No big deal. I'm not talking about the thing now. I'm talking about the stuff before the thing."

"What thing?"

"You could do me a favor by reaffirming to me that the thing wasn't something completely out of the blue. That there was something leading up to it. Some mutual cyberflirting for sure. I would even venture to say some mutual outright teasing on both our parts. Feelings on our parts, even. I had feelings for you is what I'm saying. Feelings that kept me up at night. For the sake of this whole Superstore organism we got here, let's just say I've forgotten them. What's important to me is that you feel comfortable in this work environment.

"Putting my thing through the thing. I thought it would be funny. I was drunk, and I thought it would make you laugh. I mean, we could certainly both see the correspondence heading in that direction. Not the final, specific direction (nobody could have seen that) but the general direction. I might have upped the ante so to speak, but that picture you sent me of your tattoo down there was something too. And I haven't shown it to anyone. I never will."

"I posted that picture to my page."

"All I'm saying is it's not like I sent you a picture of it out of left field. Right? There was a context. We both had feelings. We talked about things, you know. Things beyond sex. Most of the people I talk to, it's just banter. But it wasn't like that with us. I felt something. Most people out there in the world, they don't feel anything anymore. I even asked you if you wanted to see it. And I looked up the emoticon you replied with. It meant mischief."

"Ron, you know I have feelings for you. I told you so. We can just never act on them. You're married."

"Yes! Great. Of course. Thank you. I was starting to feel like I was delusional or crazy. Well, you did the right thing before it got too far. I appreciate that. I didn't have the will to stop it. I love my family. The truth is, I had no idea how weak I was until I met you. I'm sorry. I'm just trying hard not to be a creep here."

"I'm not getting that vibe at all." Claudia checks the time on her phone for the seventh time in five minutes.

"Good. A sort of spiritual counselor I have been seeing feels it's best if we don't speak. That's why I haven't really spoken to you when we cross paths. I don't want you to think it's personal. I wasn't trying to be cold or sore or anything."

"I haven't felt anything weird."

"Who knows. Who cares, even. I promise you I'm not going to be weird at all. You don't have to worry at all about a stalker-type scenario. That's not me at all. But I think it's really easy to try too hard not to be a creep. It's like walking across a three-foot-wide plank. It's easy when the plank's on the ground, but much much harder when the plank is a hundred stories in the air. And I feel like I'm on a plank a hundred stories in the air, like I'm trying so hard to do something perfectly easy and natural that I might fall to my death. You see what's happening now? This is why I haven't spoken to you. This is why. I've just spun a great big web of creepy."

"Ron, stop. What are you talking about?"

"I just wanted to clear the air and here I am polluting it. I just want you to know that I realize it was not a big deal and that we don't have to be weird around each other. I just wanted to cauterize, you know, the wound. I bought my daughter a new dollhouse. I'm gonna burn her old one in the backyard."

"What the fuck are you talking about?"

"The message I sent you."

"What message?"

"Are you kidding me? Don't do that to me. I did that to Lester earlier."

"Do what?"

"Do you know what I have to do now? I have to go over this whole awkward conversation over and over again in my head and obsess over how truly weird and creepy I was. I've got to, like, play it over and over in my head while I'm lying next to April trying to fall asleep tonight. I've got to relive every creepy word a million times."

"Ron. It's okay. I understand. It's really okay."

"You know—that's so fucking easy for you to say right now."

Ron decides not to tell her about his reoccurring dream. In it, they run towards each other through Action Alley. Their mouths collide with enough force to shatter all of their teeth into a gravel that they mix together with their writhing tongues.

11:51 A.M.

In the hospital, staring at her husband's rising and falling belly, Stacy is trying hard not to think about putting her hands in Dat's. It feels like the only possible relief, putting her hands in those delicate brown hands, holding them there while he gently pushes her cuticles back. She tries to stave it off by thinking about what Larry's hand looked like before they wrapped it in gauze: skin hanging like raw chicken fat, black fingernails. The current's entry point into his palm looked like like the bowl of an old pipe. It left a road map of burst capillaries down the right side of his body. She thinks about her own sunburn for the first time since she found him and rubs a piece of her own dead skin into a dust-gray ball between her fingers. For people who believe the way Stacy believes, there is no such thing as coincidence. *Is that the way it is? Someone ate a piece of your fruit and now we're all suffering to teach each other lessons?*

. . .

The blue line on the floor stretches from the bathroom to the waiting room and the red and green lines stretch God knows where. *I guess people are so disoriented here,* thinks Keith, only just now realizing how disoriented he himself is. The waiting room is a different kind of hell, one painted in a placid color and adorned with boilerplate landscape prints. There's too much quiet without the hissing tubes and beeping machines. In his father's hospital room, the smell of singed hair and burnt skin overwhelmed everything, even his thoughts. The guilt of not being in the room is worse than actually being in the room, which was bad enough. He has found a new level of unbearable that has rendered what he previously thought of as unbearable quaint.

He slouches down in an uncomfortable chair and sketches the oldest woman in the room. Old people are easy to draw. He lets the blue ballpoint pen fly wildly across the page, weaving the lines into a face.

He is careful with his glimpses, capturing her with the same careful tact he uses to look into Cide the Suffix's eyes. Cide the Suffix is the only person who could possibly fathom his poetry. When their AP English teacher—who thought she was cool because she had a nose ring—trashed his poem "Black Pussy" for being definitely sexist, probably racist, and absolutely terrible, Cide stood up for him, asserting that "black" in this case was referring to something metaphorical rather than racial, and reminding the teacher that she practically begged them to be provocative and gave them tacit approval to cuss. He thanked her after class and they got to talking. He explained that "pussy" didn't even mean pussy, really, and she said that she got that. She had blue-green hair, and he was wearing a well-patched letterman jacket. The other kids in the hallway all looked twice.

The old woman he is drawing opens her sandwich on her lap and eats it in a peculiar way: tomato first, then lettuce, then yellow cheese, then turkey, then bread—sucking on a mustard packet between bites.

Under the portrait he writes a note: "Black doesn't mix or blend to make new colors; it dominates—darkens. What can a color do when faced with black?"

Under the note he writes a poem:

Sterile air is the perfect breeding ground for death
"breed" and "death"
And sterility is the new fertility
Absence
            blankness
                        dead air
                            room

the old woman eats her sandwich in a curious manner
piece by piece
sucking bitter mustard
a dead or dying somebody somewhere
follow the green line on the floor
to your own breezeless, black coffin

He wonders if this tragedy has made him a better poet. Before today he was just a preppy kid with a Mustang and nothing other than the finite nature of everything to complain about.

"I'm going to the cafeteria. Can I get you a coffee or a soda or something to read?" Keith asks the woman.

"No thank you," the woman says.

Keith opens his sketchbook and reimagines the landscape on the wall, adding a monster to the lake and eager skinny-dippers rushing into to the water.

"I thought you were going to the cafeteria," the woman says.

"I'm not hungry now."

"You're a sweet boy."

Soon others will come to sit with him: aunts and uncles and friends—his remaining grandmother. But he would rather feel what he is feeling alone, or with this sweet woman who doesn't care to talk much. Keith picks up his laptop, his sketchbook, and his bag of pens and moves two seats down from Mustard Grandma, who offers him her nectarine.

• • •

Every few minutes or so Patty holds her finger under Kyler's nose to make sure that she's still breathing.

Patty flips the couch cushion over to hide a spilled beer, only to find a Lake Michigan–shaped bloodstain. She dabs it with a wet cloth and laundry detergent while she watches Dr. Phil eviscerate an unemployed thirty-eight-year-old man who plays video games online for sixteen hours a day. The studio audience erupts with cheers and laughter at Dr. Phil's homespun zinger. To Patty, Dr. Phil is common sense incarnate.

Kyler's phone flashes and plays a popular song. The word "MOM" appears on the screen. Patty doesn't want to answer it, but it seems like it might be an emergency. It's the fifth time she's called in ten minutes. She hasn't left a message. She goes back into the bedroom and tries her best to nudge Kyler awake, only to have her mew and hug a body-size pillow.

"It's your mom. She's called like a million times," Patty says.

"I want a necklace of your hair. Can I have a necklace of your hair?" Kyler runs her fingers through Patty's white-gold softness.

"Should I answer? What should I tell her?"

Kyler clamps her eyelids shut.

Patty only knows the basic outline of Kyler's lie, that they are supposedly on a school-sanctioned trip to Lubbock to check out Texas Tech. She knows they are supposed to stay until Tuesday. But how does she have Kyler's phone, and where is Kyler? She hears the ringtone again from the living room.

"What should I tell her?" Patty asks. She wants to be good in the story, to say the right thing. "This is definitely a text-message situation."

Kyler says, "Tell her I love these butthole pills. I feel like a marshmallow in hot cocoa. The way it gets puffy and softy and disolvey."

"I think it's really something this time. She called a million times."

"Where does she get these wonderful things?"

"I'm just going to let it ring then."

"Where do they live?"

"The Superstore."

"In the heaven aisle?"

"The pharmacy. You've got to have a prescription."

"Awwwwwwww, this shit makes me want to drown in a bubble bath."

10.
Turtle, Turtle,
Gopher, Dollar Sign

12:34 P.M.

"HOW MANY TIMES CAN THEY ASK YOU TO MAKE IT THINNER OR thicker?" Efren asks. He's just sliced meat for "The German Bitch," a notoriously demanding customer who seems to take sexual pleasure in demanding that the deli associates slice her turkey pastrami the thickness of wet toilet paper.

"The German Bitch, bro. You did it. You're totally initiated now," Bobby says, wiping the slicers down.

"What's the code for the bean salad?" Efren asks.

"Three-one-one. It's taped under the scale."

"That's how the German people are in all of the movies I see," Efren says.

"I hate Germans, bro," Bobby says. "I'm a quarter Jewish."

"They can tell you to make it thinner and thicker all those times?" Efren asks, stabbing a meat thermometer into a rotisserie chicken.

"As many times as they want," Bobby says. "People care exactly how thick their meat is. And you got to be polite and smile no matter what. You never know when a customer is an undercover QPR."

"What's QPR?"

"Quality Personnel Recruiter. They're Broken Arrow guys who come in dressed as customers. They might be a shithead to see how you react. If you do real good, they might give you a three-level promotion right on the spot. If you can't handle yourself, you could get fired. I got this idea that The German Bitch is like queen of the QPRs. Like if I eat enough of her shit, one day that bitch will make me president of the Superstore."

"Is that real?" Efren asks.

"I don't know. I have things like that I think to myself all the time so I don't go crazy on the customers with a box cutter."

"It's amazing how serious some of the people feel about the thickness of the meat," Efren says.

"Most of them don't have good jobs like we do. The thickness of their meat might be the only little power they feel all day."

"What do I do with this?" Efren asks, holding the pile of inadequately thin turkey pastrami.

"Eat it. We can't sell it if we don't know what it tastes like," Bobby says.

"I'm not hungry," Efren says. He glances at the black camera bubble above the deli station and says, "If a manager tells me I can eat some, I will eat some," for the benefit of the hidden microphones.

Bobby grabs several slices from Efren's hand and stuffs them into his mouth.

"You're not a Cowboys fan are you?" Efren asks.

"Fuck no! Raiders! You should see my fucking house. The couch and the chairs and the coffee table and the lamps and the rug: every fuck ing thing is silver and black. Who's your team?"

"I don't have a favorite team," Efren says, agitating the cold salads in the front display cooler and checking it off of the list. "My favorite team is hating the Cowboys."

"I'm so glad they didn't send me a chick to work mornings with. Do you ever watch that show *X-treem*? Man, they show this like fucking guy getting dragged by a train by a really broken leg and this goofy voice comes on that says like, 'Whoa Mr., you better buy a ticket.' And like slide whistle sound effects. Do you ever see that shit?" Bobby asks.

"I never seen that one. I have seven girls." His daughters generally dislike accident shows, except for Rosa, who thinks they're hilarious.

"I got two girls, man. I know how it is. Do you ever see *The View*?"

"No," Efren says: a lie. He throws a nine-pound ham in the large, gray trash can.

"*Ellen*? You can tell me, bro. You ain't got to lie. I got girls too. I watch *Oprah, Dr Phil, Project Runway*, all that shit. When I grew up my dad ruled the remote control, but I don't want to be like him for a lot of reasons. Do you ever see *Fear Factor*?"

"Yeah."

"Have you seen the shit they eat: like hog vomit and raw horse cock and maggots? I could do that shit, bro. I'll eat anything, man. Will power. Do you know how I stopped smoking crack? I just stopped."

"I used to do anything for money when I lived in Juárez. Do you know what I'm saying? All I want to do now is live like a sheep for as long as possible."

"Did you have a white tiger on a chain and a bunch of hot chicas by your pool and shit like that?"

"I wasn't like that. If the organization I worked for was the Superstore, I would have been an Assistant Servant/Leader."

"I bet they paid better. And you didn't have to take shit from customers."

"I'll take all the shit they have as long as they don't shoot at me. This job is better."

"I'd close my eyes and eat a raw horse cock for ten thousand dollars," Bobby says, laughing. "Will power. Same to heights and scorpions. *Fear Factor* makes Guantanamo Bay look like Girl Scout camp. I would rule that fucking shit. When they need someone to crawl inside the garbage chute to kick down a clog, they call me. I'll do whatever the fuck. Time to make the salads." Bobby opens the box of Readypack Salads. "Each Cobb salad gets a half a egg, ten cubes of ham, and one scoop of bacon bits. The croutons come in their own little pack here so they don't sog. And also this packet of ranch. Close the plastic box and that's it, man. It's done. Shoot it with the date gun. Bam!"

1:10 P.M.

Inside the log cabin RV, Cal's body has been freshly iced and Dolly is sweating. She wonders if Cal has started to stink yet. Maybe he already reeks. Maybe she's just used to the smell, the way a heavy smoker can smell everything but her cigarette.

She puts on a bra and a dry T-shirt with a sand dollar embossed on the front, applies her perfume liberally, grabs her purse, and pushes the button to activate the stairs.

. . .

Amberlee can no longer smell the six unfixed pugs living in her house. She drips eye drops in between her slightly parted eyelids. *The Simpsons* is playing just over the white noise of her house: a dozen lazy dogs snorting like static. In the summer she makes her bed on the couch, under the evaporative cooler. The burns have cauterized the sweat glands over eighty percent of her body. The sweat seeps out of the flack jacket–shaped section of porous skin on her torso. The oldest of her pugs, Martha, a small brown dog with a patch of white on her chin, curls up on her chest. A cocktail of pain killers and the gentle vibration of Martha's snort puts Amberlee to sleep.

. . .

Josiah's screams are formless and piercing, like a yawn through an amplifier.

Wilma signs, "What?" with flustered hands. She learned sign language almost as soon as her grandson was diagnosed, but at two years old, most of Josiah's signs are still informal. He sucks his cheeks in and parts his pursed lips like a gasping fish, a sign for momma's breast.

Wilma hasn't slept in almost fifty hours. Her son, Wes, Josiah's father, is sequestered at a clinic off of Interstate 10. He's been making his money lately by participating in clinical studies as a professional lab rat. This time it's an experimental antianxiety medication that requires he be under constant supervision for four days. Josiah's mother, Laurie, and her milk-heavy chichis are hostessing at the Red Lobster, and Wilma's husband, Tony, is working in the lumber department at Home Depot.

She stares down into the pot, waiting for bubbles. She lifts the pot to check the coil. It hasn't even started to glow. Josiah's sounds are more plaintive than angry now. *Strange how that boy can get so much across with sounds. He never heard anyone whine, but he sure knows how. It must be way down in there.* Wilma sighs and begins to cry a little. The coil under the pot is just starting to glow, and she feels a fleeting urge to touch her tongue to it. Her knees are locked and she is holding herself up with the counter. "Look at my face and read my lips: sleeeep motherfucker."

Josiah makes a disturbing bleating sound and grabs at his grandma's pockets.

Wilma imagines cutting his tongue out with a paring knife. She tussles his hair and brushes his cheek lovingly with the side of her index finger.

The water begins to bubble. She submerges the rubber nipple, sucks the last dregs of watered-down Dr Pepper out of her disposable cup, and thinks, *Burn away, germs. Nobody gives a fuck about invisible life.* Her grandson has tight ringlets of glossy black hair, skin like burgundy and cream, and a heart-shaped face with fat, dimpled cheeks. *Use that shit, baby. Use everything you got.*

Wilma wads up the comforter along the headboard so that she can sleep semireclined. Her pit bull, Daisy, curls up at her feet. Josiah makes a soft pillow of his grandma's armpit meat and feeds himself from a bottle. Light from the street bounces off of the tinfoil covering the windows and into the dark room, projecting passing cars onto the ceiling. Josiah watches them matter-of-factly.

"Stay still, baby. Take a nap with Granny." Josiah releases the rubber nipple and emits a sustained, monotone groan: the sound of someone stretching a very sore muscle. It seems to Wilma that noise of one sort or another is always coming out of Josiah. Like a constant and unconscious frequency. She wishes she were deaf. What would be best would be hearing that she could turn on and off at will, but at this point she would settle for completely deaf. She puts in the movie *Monsters, Inc.* and turns off the sound. Josiah's seen this movie forty-six times, and the friendly colors usually put him to sleep, but not this time. He jumps off the bed and crawls under the bedskirt. Wilma feels him kicking the bottom of the mattress.

"Okay then. Just stay in the room," Wilma says. *Who am I talking to?* she thinks as she dozes off on the thumping mattress.

• • •

Ron is trying to think up a reason to walk through Cold Dairy now that he has had an uncomfortable talk with Claudia about their situation over lunch. He wants to clear some proverbial air, to show her his cool professional self—the self that isn't embarrassed, that can joke around and be lighthearted and not creepy.

"How are the new organics moving?" Ron asks.

"Like freaking crazy," Claudia says.

"Do you know we actually lose money on each one of those we sell?"

"That doesn't seem smart."

"It's actually incredibly smart. It's about cornering that upper-middle-class organic milk/whole-grain demo. They come in for milk and buy a hundred other things. Things with a slightly higher markup. We believe in statement pricing at the Superstore."

"What if they only buy the milk?" Claudia asks.

Ron laughs and says, "Nobody comes in the Superstore and only buys milk."

"I come in sometimes and only buy milk."

"Really?"

"You don't believe me?"

"You go into the Superstore for milk and buy just milk?"

"I have. Often."

"Well, you're one of the special ones."

"Aw, you're a special one too, Ron."

"Please, don't do this to me."

"Do what?"

"Sorry," says Ron. *It's like baking a pie for someone and then they don't even comment on it. They don't compliment the deliciousness of the pie. They don't even compliment the gesture if the pie's no good. They don't say anything. It is that times fifty million when you email a girl a picture of your dick and she never responds. The silence is really deafening, as they say.*

• • •

When Wilma opens her eyes she realizes that some unspecified amount of time has passed. The tendrils of light shining through the tin foil are pointed at slightly different angles. The digital monsters in the movie have ventured into the real world. The nightstand drawer—a drawer that Tony and Wilma refer to as "The Fantasy Drawer"—has been pulled out of its slot, its pornographic contents strewn about the bedroom. Her grandson is trying to wrestle her anniversary dildo away from Daisy.

"Give me that!" She raises the dildo like a rolled-up newspaper and sends Daisy scampering under the bed. "How did you open this drawer up?" It's a very weak lock, she realizes now, just a flimsy metal tab that folds back under the particleboard. All he would have had to do was pull down on the drawer as he opened it.

"Aren't you tired?" Wilma asks desperately. She examines her dildo, the anniversary present from Tony. Daisy has bitten deep into its aqua blue flesh. The head is hanging on like a loose tooth. It has so many sweet, good times attached to it that she can't bring herself to throw it away.

A corner of the holiday issue of *Hustler* is poking out from under the dresser. Next to it is what looks like a remote control, but is upon further inspection a twenty-two-caliber pistol. *Tony! I'm going to kill that motherfucker.* She imagines Josiah on the carpet with a hole in his fat little cheek and his eyes rolled back into his head. Her breaths are coming too fast. Josiah is crying. She shuffles into the kitchen with the pistol tucked in her underwear. Everything is starting to look like a dream. *They can't leave you with me like this. Just because I'm home during the days. I work at night. When am I supposed to sleep?*

She opens a bottle of NyQuil, pours some into Josiah's sippy cup, and mixes it with off-brand Sprite from the Superstore. Josiah tastes medicine and dribbles the concoction down his chin onto the collar of his Bob the Builder T-shirt.

Wilma adds a heap of sugar and dilutes it with more generic Sprite. *What else can I do? I can't sing this deaf little nigger a lullaby.*

• • •

Burt is waiting for the hot biscuit light. Loose skin is draped over his bones like a drenched bathrobe. He brings a bite of enchilada to his lips and wishes he could swallow it. There's a deep, sharp pain where the surgical band pinches his gut. He studies two shadows intersecting over the oversize dish and the mounds of buffet offerings. *There's no shadows in the Superstore. The lights shine right through everything.* In all the

Superstore memories stored in his head—the beet-red faces of crying children, the beautiful girls, the countless hours of stocking, cleaning and ringing up—did anything ever cast a shadow?

He searches his memory and finds no shadows under the hats of the people Rucho sent to buy ammo, and none under the boxes as he placed them on the shelves. *The lady and the shotgun shells.* When Burt attaches words, the image comes into focus: her stout legs protruding from bloused jean shorts, a floppy sun hat, a face like an anvil stuffed with cotton, a lazy eye. *Was there a shadow?* He remembers the way she cocked her neck and raised her voice when she declared she'd "shoot any son of a bitch that comes in my RV." *There must have been a shadow under that sun hat.* According to Burt's digital watch, there are twenty-six minutes left on his lunch break. *How can I spend it here?* His memories are like unfinished paintings, there for him to go into with his fine brushes. He could create the shadows if he liked, but he has to know for sure.

He goes into the restroom, hunches over a toilet, closes his eyes, opens his mouth very wide, and imagines a particularly disturbing bowel movement his childhood dog, Rex, left on the lawn. It was crawling with worms. This works every time.

• • •

When Dolly sees the price of a gas can at the gas station, she briefly considers walking back under the highway to the Superstore, where it will certainly be cheaper. But it's hot outside, and she's worried she might reek of something that no amount of perfume can conceal. There are so many people at the Superstore, so many noses. It's like a small town inside of a medium town. *A gas can in a gas station. I'm the epitome of a captive consumer.*

"And give me a lottery ticket," Dolly says to the clerk. She figures that her husband's passing might have caused some cosmic tilt that needs to be righted. She scratches it off while the people wait in line behind her.

Turtle

Turtle

Gopher

Dollar sign

"Then give me a pack of Chesterfields."

"I don't even know if they make those anymore."

"I haven't smoked a cigarette in thirty years."

"Well, what do you want instead?"

"I don't know. Those red ones."

When the clerk warns her not to smoke around the gas, she wonders if it's because she's a woman.

* * *

"Hold up. Hold the fuck up. Are you telling me that a six-foot party sub is actually six individual one-foot party subs?"

"Yes, sir. I'm very sorry, sir. That is what I'm telling you," Bobby says.

"But I didn't order six one-foot sandwiches. I ordered one six-foot sandwich."

"I'm sorry, we don't serve one complete six-foot sandwich."

"But that's what I ordered. That's what we agreed to. Now I have to go to my wife's kid's birthday party with six one-foot sandwiches?"

"I'm very sorry."

"I'm going to look like a fucking loser."

"I'm sorry, boss," Bobby says. "We don't have six-foot-long bread. We don't have an oven that's shaped that way."

"But that's what you sold me over the phone."

"It makes it easier to just serve it by the foot," Bobby says.

"That's not what by the foot means. You buy twenty feet of cable, the cable is all connected. You buy six feet of fabric, it's all gonna be one piece. You see what I'm saying? I'm not trying to be a jerk. I know you just work here. I'm sorry."

"We should have made that clear over the phone. I'll talk to a manager about getting that cleared up in our advertising, but I doubt he does anything about it. I'll tell you what I can do, boss. Stroke of genius. I'll take it into the back, and I'll cut away the end pieces on the middle sandwiches and fit it all together. I'll cobble together the cardboard with tape. It'll look like it was just precut. Is that okay?"

"Then it won't be six foot."

"Not quite, but I doubt the kids will measure it. I'll wrap up the end pieces for you separate."

"I guess that will work."

When Efren follows Bobby to the back through the double doors, he finds him mopping his armpits with the french bread.

"I don't know how you deal with the assholes like that," Efren says.

Bobby wipes his hand under his balls and then all over the sandwich. He says, "Most of the time people just need to be apologized to."

• • •

Burt is struck by his own lightness, the relatively easy way he is able to maneuver. He circumvents an old man toting an oxygen tank and remembers a time at the Deming Golden Corral–four years and three hundred pounds ago—when he bumped into three people at once on his way to the hot biscuit light. A woman actually shuddered: physically and audibly. A child dropped her ice cream sundae and cried. He said excuse me a thousand times. He can't remember if he added that part about the kid and the ice cream or not, a little postproduction humiliation. It doesn't matter much. If his subconscious decided to add it to his memory, there must be something true about it.

The biscuits are as smooth as river stones. They're something between rolls and biscuits, actually: smooth like a roll, dense like a biscuit. And hot. A young girl with a face like a new penny nudges her little sister and points at Burt, who is juggling a biscuit between his hands and making an O shape with his lips. They laugh. He smiles. *If you were my girls, I'd wait till these biscuits were perfectly warm, and I'd hold them to your cheeks, just to be silly.* The girls smile back at him.

He brings a magazine with him most places so that he'll have something to do. He's self-conscious about eating alone. Before the gastric bypass surgery, when he weighed over five hundred pounds, he could feel people get sadder when they looked at him. They resented him for making them sad, and he felt that too. He felt their resentment manifest into disgust and scorn. *Ninety percent of hunting is staring. For as long as it takes. Noticing every rustle.* He wipes a spot of gravy off of an article on loading your own shotgun shells. After 9/11 he bought a copy of every magazine he could find. For some reason he couldn't name, he found it incredibly important to preserve the *Sports Illustrated* and the *Cosmopolitan* and the *Us Weekly* and the *Spread Eagle Granny* tributes to the victims and heroes of the attacks. He has hundreds of them sealed in plastic and locked away in a storage unit. *Empires grow and die. And it's usually a violent death.* He feels ready for it. Not eager for it the way some of his gun club friends seem to be, but ready for it. He has the firepower, the canned goods, the potassium iodide tablets, and the bottled water.

He is comforted by the volume of food available at a place like the Golden Corral, and frustrated by the gastric bypass band constricting the opening of his stomach. He can feel it down in there pinching. Nobody told him he'd be able to feel it. *Look at this guy. Dipped the ladle into the blue cheese seven times. It's like the mountain of bacon shards and croutons has erupted a blue cheese volcano. Imagine if he burped on you? With that blue cheese and processed bacon breath at a distance and velocity that makes your bangs twitch and scalds your face with a moderate heat.* Burt pukes it all up in one vessel-popping heave. He doesn't even have to stick his finger down his throat anymore. The chemical scenter in the Golden Corral bathroom releases a well-timed *pssssst*, infusing the air with the scent of cinnamon rolls.

I'll tell you another reason I love this place: you never have to wait for your food. You just pick up a plate and start eating again.

1:24 P.M.

Now she's the one who can't sleep.

Wilma uses duct tape to patch the tinfoil covering her windows. She tears off a small strip and covers a beam of light that is shining up into her sleeping grandson's nose.

She drinks her fourth capful of the nighttime cough medicine, but it only makes her more bored. She considers waking Josiah up and taking him for a walk around the trailer park. *I'll never get his little ass back to sleep. This could be my only chance. NyQuil. That was a one-time desperation thing. I was so tired. Am so tired. Anita forgot her grandbaby in the car with the windows up. June in the Superstore parking lot. When*

she got back the poor baby had ripped all his fine little baby hair out.
You're not the worst grandmother in the world.

• • •

Loneliness is so much more bearable with familiar noise: two churning
air-conditioning units, a small television, a rustling ice maker. Dolly
puts on another sweatshirt, this one lavender with a cartoonish lighthouse and the phrase "See Fort Myers" printed on the front. She
smokes her first cigarette in thirty years and tries not to think about
the fact that she hasn't heard Cal speak since she was touched by the
holy woman. She's afraid she'll jinx it, or that the very act of thinking
about not thinking about it will make her think about it. Part of her
wants Cal to talk to her again, even if it means she's crazy. She imagines
what he would say if he were here, but it is very clear that it is her
imagination and not his voice that says, "Sugarsnap, come lay yourself
all on me."

None of the two hundred channels beamed into the RV from space
can take her mind off of what is happening, but searching through them
helps. Oprah says it's not our fault; a TV judge rules in favor of the man
with the hail-damaged car; two well-preserved, middle-aged people soak
in two separate bathtubs on the beach at sunset, their arms slung lazily
between them like telephone wire.

On the couch beside her, the corpse's mouth is open. Something is
most definitely draining out of the log cabin RV and into that gaping hole.

1:31 P.M.

Mustard Grandma has fallen asleep in an erect position, her head resting
against the wall. Keith draws another sketch of her in the Gods of Chaos
Manifesto. This time he can stare all he wants, but the drawing is somehow less exact.

Stacy enters, red and tender, eating soup. When she sits next to
Keith, he closes the book. "Why don't you ever let me see anything anymore? When you were little, every drawing was for me."

"This isn't the kind of stuff you put on the fridge."

"I grew up in the nineties, kid. I know how cool it is to be depressed. I'll call Dr. Lapid in the morning and make you another appointment."

"I won't take the pills."

"Do you think we should track Kyler's phone? Can we do that? Who should I call? Is there an app?"

"I don't know."

"I'm sorry. I know you're doing your best, honey. Nobody knows what to do or how to talk."

One woman in a group of mourners keeps repeating, "She just came in for the flu. This doesn't feel real. Why doesn't this feel real? Does this feel real to any of you?" Keith hasn't been able to look hard enough to draw their faces, but he's done several loose sketches of their somber postures.

"The doctor wants to talk, and I want you to be there with me," says Stacy.

"Why?"

"To ask questions. All the good ones you can think of."

"Just tell me what to ask. I'll screw up," Keith says.

"Have you prayed?"

"Mom."

"It's more important than anything these doctors can do. Don't just bow your head and say the words. You can really talk to Jesus. He's your best friend whether you know it or not."

Behind them, in the recesses of the hospital, is the sound of hustle: urgent voices, chirping wheels, the sound of doors opening and closing in haste.

"We might have some tough decisions to make soon," Stacy says.

"I'm not making any decisions," Keith says. "I'm only sixteen."

"Now you're *only* sixteen."

"I don't want to."

"Do you think anybody ever wants to?"

"You haven't let me make a choice my entire life. Now I'm supposed to decide this? No way. I decide what you decide. That's what I decide."

"Just take some quiet time to think about it, honey."

"I don't want to think about it."

When his mother leaves, Keith opens his laptop. Strangers across the world want to be his friend. He's so sharp in the chat rooms. He uses the word "variant" instead of different. And he says pithy things that always get plenty of lols and capital LOLs, like how cool he thinks the word "bombastic" is, and how honored he is every time he's called it. He goes by "The Omniscient Narrator" online, and his place of birth is listed as "alternate dimension."

• • •

Dolly knew that one can of gas wouldn't last forever, but she thought it would last longer than this, through the night maybe, at least until Maggie arrived. After all, she wasn't going anywhere. How much gas could sitting still require?

The log cabin RV is dark and hot and silent. Without the drones of air conditioning and television, the sounds of her own rushing blood and nagging breaths are overwhelming Dolly. She is waiting for the police to arrive, and return calls from her brother, Scott, and the coroner's office.

She opens the dark refrigerator. She removes a brick of sharp cheddar cheese and cuts a thumb-size slice right through the plastic. The little bit of milk in the jug is still okay to drink. There's just enough for her coffee the way she likes it. But all this food—the whipped cream, the onion dip, the half a pound of maple ham she just bought—is going to waste. She folds the kitchen table down from the wall and sets the food on it: buttermilk, a tub of Country Crock, preshredded iceberg lettuce, half a breakfast burrito, a deep tub of sour cream, orange juice, a brand-new tube of turkey sausage. *It'll all be bad soon.* She puts the piece of cheese on a saltine. She briefly considers opening the door to the parking lot and giving the food away. After all, people are walking into the Superstore to pay money for these very items. Some of them, like the sour cream, haven't even been opened, still have their tamper-indicating pop tops and protective plastic rings. And she certainly can't eat all of it, even as sad as she is. *Is that a crazy thing to do?* she thinks. *They'd probably haul me off somewhere.*

Dolly is startled by a knock at the door and surprisingly kind face. "Good afternoon, ma'am. I'm Bill Bean from the police department. This is my partner Karen. We're here to check up on you."

"Can you hold your badges up to the window, please?" Dolly asks.

"Sure. Your brother, Scott, called us, ma'am. May we come in?"

"Sure. Come on in. Are you hungry? The power is off, and I got all this food going to waste. Sandwich? Omelette. The stove runs on propane. It still works."

"We're fine, ma'am. Thank you."

"There he is. Obviously."

"We're going to have to ask you a couple of questions, just as a formality."

"I understand. It's crazy. It's a crazy thing to do. I'm not sure how to explain myself. I wanted to call my daughter first, but I couldn't. Do you understand? I knew it was crazy all along. I just kept doing it. I was just trying to keep him cold till my daughter got here. Then I swear I was going to call. She's on her way. I just needed a little more time with him."

"We'll get you someone nice to talk to."

"Do you think I could ask you all something kind of strange?"

"Sure."

"Does it stink in here?"

2:00 P.M.

Bobby and Efren work together wordlessly, sorting through the meat pieces, rotating them in the transparent cooler, throwing away, in total, three hundred and eighty pounds of pig and turkey and cow that have been rendered, processed, and packaged.

Efren is a man who has always felt very grateful to have beans and fat to eat. He has been hungry and watched his seven daughters be hungry. Throwing away all that food fills him with a shimmery joy he cannot rationalize or justify.

11.
Oh, Come all Ye Bold and Thoughtless Men

2:10 P.M.

LESTER BRIM CALLS BETTY AND RON INTO WHAT THE SERVANT /Leaders refer to as The Real Office (TRO for short), a very tidy maintenance closet across from the security office. The meetings held in the Personnel Office (PO for short) are essentially public. Associates shuffle in and out to take CBLs and pick up paychecks, then carry bits of information out into the store like ants.

"Ken Provost is in the air, and we're on the itinerary," Lester Brim says.

"I told you. Didn't I tell you," Ron says. He has a promotion-worthy idea he can only tell to Mr. Ken himself. It's an idea that he believes will change everything about the way the store processes pallets. By his crude calculations, his idea will save the Superstore eleven cents on every pallet processed, which could mean millions of dollars a year.

Betty, who gladly takes any opportunity to get off her feet, sits on a bucket of spackling paste. Ron tells himself not to look inside her skirt, then looks inside her skirt and thinks, *Goddamnit! It's going to take a lot of pornography and elbow grease to scrub that out.*

Betty imagines what Ron's hide would look like separated from his body and what his body would look like separated from his hide. As an amateur taxidermist, she is able to conjure a vivid image.

"We're prepared for this," Lester says. "'Each opportunity to fail is an opportunity to succeed in disguise,' chapter thirteen, *My American Way*."

"It's a good day for him to come," Betty says. "We got good, consistent lane volume. Wait times are in the acceptable range. We're well stocked. Very few sellouts. Our endcaps are flying out of the store. Those fluorescent towels: wait till he hears how many of those we sold this week."

"Send home ten percent," Lester says. "I want him to see us pushing it."

"We need to do what we're already doing and do it better," Ron says. "We need to spin more chickens. Free samples, maybe."

"Free samples are a Sunday thing," Betty says. "He'll know we're putting on a show."

"I just wish it was more alive out there," Lester says. "It seems kind of sterile. Like people are out there doing their jobs and people are out there buying their groceries and their dry goods, but nobody is enjoying themselves. I want this store bustling. I want families talking about Little League and young newlyweds shopping to outfit their first little newlywed houses. Cute old couples that still hold hands, war veterans in those mesh war veteran caps, people shopping for picnics and family trips to the lake. I want it to be like the last scene of A-freaking Christmas Carol. Send Amphetamine Bobby home. That creepy new cart pusher with the grandma glasses and tattoos on his head. Anybody who looks like they just got out of jail has to go. And I want some white people working here today. And I don't want to be the only black person. We need to demonstrate diversity. It looks bad if all the associates are Mexican. And I know how this sounds, but I can't figure out how else to say it. Is that girl with the burned face working?"

"She just got back from her lunch break," Betty says.

"Say no more," Ron says. "I'll send her home."

"I feel terrible," Lester says. "But we just can't have that today. We got to have the perfect atmosphere today. That intangible thing. That feeling you get when you come inside. Like you're walking into this bounty, and you can have any of it. And everything is going to be all right. She smirches that."

"There's no need to feel bad," Betty says. "It's disturbing, no doubt about it."

"Target wouldn't have hired her," Ron says.

"That sounded terrible, didn't it? She doesn't bother me. It's other people. The customers. Ken Provost. I'm sure they wouldn't dare to say anything. But . . ." Lester indulges in his only nervous habit: clicking the very tips of his gleaming right canines together very very gently. "It's just that feeling. That bustling, happy, comfortable bounty. How can you have a good feeling when you're looking at a woman with a face like a fetus? I didn't mean that to sound mean. I think fetuses are just as precious as real babies."

"You're only thinking about the store," Betty says.

"It is different. She's disturbing to look at," Ron says. "It's not like someone in a wheelchair, or that happy retarded boy, Jayson C."

"Is Jay-C working today?" Lester asks.

"We called him in like you asked," Ron says.

"Good," Lester says.

Betty says, "As long as we're being pragmatic, he doesn't do much for our man-hour/man-output ratio. You've already sent home ten percent of my team."

"Do we have any more like Jayson?" Lester asks.

"None happy-looking like him," Ron says.

"I'm sorry. Am I missing something? We're cutting our labor cost to the bone here. We need our most productive workers," Betty says.

"Ken Provost knows his name," Lester says. "Every time he comes he calls him by name, talks to him for a while. Asks him a bunch of questions and pretends to take him real seriously."

"Then let me keep Amphetamine Bobby. He's my best worker."

"Fine," Lester says. "We got to kick butt out there. I mean the fry grease is clean, the chickens are spinning, the spill stations are equipped, hot and cold holding logs up to date, and all the shelves are conditioned. And atmosphere. Broken Arrow has a hair up their ass about atmosphere. Remind everybody of the ten-foot rule. They probably haven't heard about it since orientation. Tell them it's especially important today. Let it be known, if I see anyone walk within ten feet of a guest without a friendly gesture and the offer of assistance, I'm coaching their butts up. Smile, wave, not just to Ken Provost, but the guests. Don't spend all your attention on him and forget the guests. Remember, he's watching you perform. So make it bustle."

"Shouldn't we keep a few more people on?" Betty asks.

"That's exactly what we don't do," Lester says. "You got to stop thinking like a manager if you ever want to be a boss. The manager is just looking at the store running smoothly, short lines, stocked shelves, happy customers. A boss is looking at the whole machine, all its little moving parts: margins, overhead, costs, how much you can get out of the people you got. Anybody can do it with enough people on hand. If Ken Provost walks through that door today, I'm going to blow his darn socks off. Maybe I'll get called up to corporate. Maybe one of you guys will get my job."

"Good P.M.A.," Ron says. "'You gotta believe it before you can do it,' page one hundred and forty-two. One of my favorite passages."

"Good," Lester says. "Don't be afraid to quote that when he gets here."

Betty says, "I like, 'Why dream when you can do?' page two hundred and ninety-one."

"Mr. Gene had such a way of writing, you know," Lester says. "He said everything so clean and understandable."

"What should we tell the associates?" Betty asks.

"Don't tell them anything," Lester says. "They already know something big is up. We've got them cleaning the grease traps and polishing glass doors."

"When do you think he's coming?"

"My hunch: five o'clock rush."

• • •

"I'm like the Bruce Lee of fucking, bro. I make that pussy gush." Bobby is emptying the old fry grease into a large, gray trash can. The overwhelming smell of cholesterol. An opalescent gleam to the surface of it. "Something big is up."

"Are we getting FLOWed?" Efren asks.

"Bigger."

"How do you know?"

"They never make us change the fry oil on a Saturday."

Bobby and Efren wheel the grease-filled garbage can to the large, black holding tank in the back of the store.

Bobby submerges the vacuum's hose and presses the red button. The holding tank begins to suck at the sludge. "I don't just fuck 'em, bro. I ruin 'em."

Betty rounds the corner and tells Bobby to kick a clog down the garbage chute without breaking stride.

"I'm going to make you love me, with your big fine ass," Bobby says when Betty is out of earshot.

• • •

Claudia is standing by the clock, waiting for the last digit to turn to a seven before she swipes her badge.

"Headed home?" Ron asks.

"Yeah."

"Cool. Listen, might not want to go so fast."

"What do you mean?"

"Just might want to stick around."

"Why?"

"Something cool might happen, you know. Some once-in-a-lifetime opportunity," Ron says. It's as if his terror is a gushing wound, and his face is an insufficient amount of gauze. He laughs. "Why do you look so worried? It's something good. That's all I can say."

"My feet hurt," Claudia says.

"If you knew what it was, you definitely would want to stay."

"I've got to see a man about a horse."

"I think you may have the wrong idea. I just think if you knew. If I could just tell you. Come with me."

"Where are you going?"

"The maintenance closet."

"I'm not going into the maintenance closet with you."

"No. Look. That's not the idea. That's the completely wrong idea. That's where the S/Ls go when we want to talk in private. Ken Provost is coming to town. I wasn't supposed to say anything."

"Who?"

"The CEO of the Superstore. The boss of everybody. It would be a good thing to meet him. For your career. I could probably make that happen. He'd love you. What did you think I was talking about?"

"I had no idea. Tire pressure? Caprese salads? Hologram Tupac at the convention center? I gotta get home."

"This is *the* Superstore Executive."

"When is he even coming?"

"We don't know. We're not even supposed to know that he's coming."

"I repeat: my fucking feet hurt."

• • •

The live feed of Ron and Claudia talking is up on the monitor in the Loss Prevention Office.

"I would drink her bath water," Glen says.

"She's okay," Quentin says. "Kind of fat."

"She's just how I like them."

"Then you like them kind of fat."

"Hell, I'm kind of fat. You're kind of fat too, buddy, I hate to tell you," Glen says.

"I'm kind of fat. You're fat," Quentin says.

"I'm fat where it counts. Ask your mother."

"What do you think they're talking about?" Quentin asks. "Do you think Ron's trying to fuck her?"

"Oh sure, but that's not what they're talking about."

"What are they talking about?"

"Ken Provost is coming today. That's the president of the Superstore," Glen says.

"I know who Ken Provost is," Quentin says. "Is that what they're saying?"

"Yup."

"How can you tell? Can you read lips?"

"No. I can hear them."

"There are microphones? I knew it."

"No, just shut up and listen. Camera forty-four is pointed right on the other side of this door."

• • •

"Everybody is running around like crazy," Claudia says. "They're just not sure why."

"You should stick around and meet him," Ron says. "He could make you the boss of this whole place on the spot if he felt like it."

"I've got my hours for the week. If I go over again, I'll get coached up."

"Maybe you could clock out and come back and do some shopping."

"Push a cart around the store until he gets here?"

"Think of your career. This is one of the most powerful men in the world. He goes fishing with Dick Cheney," Ron says.

"I'm going home."

"I just want you to know that that thing with the Mustang I rented for you . . . It was a real thing. I mean, that's not like a thing I do or that I've ever done before. That's not like a thing I read about in *Maxim* or something."

"I told you how sweet it was. God, how many thank yous do you need?"

"Listen. I have a proposition for you."

"Ron..."

"God. No. Not like that. But it is kind of awkward. That message I sent you. The one we talked about over breakfast. The one you supposedly didn't see. I'll pay you fifty bucks if I can watch you delete it."

"Why? What's so important about it?"

"You're still playing dumb? I expressed some things in it that I wish I hadn't."

"You don't have to worry about that, Ron. We both had feelings. We didn't even do anything. If you really want me to, I'll delete it as soon as I get home. I won't even read it."

"I'll give you fifty dollars if I can watch you delete it right now."

The way she looks at him, it makes him want to die. She is so clearly toying with him, and he is so goddamn helpless against it. *Maybe she can't help it either,* he thinks. *Can't help but make me love her. Maybe it's not just for fun.* "I'll give you a hundred," he says.

"I'm not taking your money."

"It must be nice to be so pretty and have people falling in love with you all the time," Ron says. "You're going to miss that when you get old."

• • •

"Look at all these associates running around like Jesus is coming in to buy pizza rolls," Glen says

"He's the CEO of the Superstore. He's one of the most powerful men in the whole fucking country," Quentin says.

"What do you think? He's going to walk in, see you, and immediately decide that you should be running this place?"

"I heard he flies commercial."

"These fucking Broken Arrow guys… They don't want us to know how much money they're making for a reason."

* * *

Jayson follows Ron's beckoning hand into the maintenance closet. He is offended by the overwhelming scent of paper and industrial cleaner. Jayson's olfactory senses are by far his keenest. He can only see with the aid of very thick glasses, and he can barely hear with the help of two hearing aids.

"I just brought you in here to see how you're doing," whispers Ron.

"Okay." Jayson says. It's his go-to phrase when the mouth he's looking at stops moving. The expression on Ron's face makes Jayson worry, makes him glad he can't hear, makes him want out of the maintenance closet, makes him smile even harder.

"Your friend, Mr. Ken, is coming in today. Do you remember him?" Ron asks.

"Okay."

"He remembers you. He talks about you all the time. That's the reason he's coming here: to talk to you. How do you like working here?"

"Okay," Jayson says.

"Do you like working here?" Ron nods yes slightly.

"Yes."

"Good."

"How much would you say you like working here?"

"What?"

"I said how much would you say you like working here?"

"Okay."

"I can't really raise my voice very high in here, buddy. Can you hear me?"

"Okay."

"Would you say you like working here a whole bunch?" Ron asks, nodding.

"Yes."

"I really love working here. I, personally, think it's fantastic. I get to meet new people every day. I get to help them with their problems. I get to be a part of this great big Superstore family! I'm on the best team in the world. In the world, like the real word, Jayson, this Superstore is like the Harlem Globetrotters, except that when they do their tricks they're dead fucking serious and nobody laughs."

Jayson laughs at the word "fuck." He says, "The Harlem Globe Trotters are my favorite team."

"That's right! I remembered that about you from that time we talked," Ron says. "And we're the best store in the world, just the same."

"The best."

"Yes! I wouldn't want any other job in the world. I love it. I'm in love with it. I can't stop thinking about it. It keeps me awake at night. I am always thinking about what is best for it. Sometimes I stand in the very center of the store, aisle 34b, and think about how I couldn't possibly get any more inside of it if I tried. Would you say it is good to work here?"

"Yes! I love it!" Jayson says.

"Shhh. That's great. That's more like it. Why do you love it?"

"I love it when Claudia helps me use the trash compactor and kisses my cheek."

"Don't let your heart gush all over her. Nobody can be trusted with that kind of power. Do you want to see something?" Ron cues up two pictures on his cell, one is a bathroom mirror selfie of Claudia in a blouse with a plunging neckline, and the other is a photo of her new tattoo.

Jayson grabs at his penis through his pants.

"God, you're so happy. Really beautiful. Not in a homo way at all." Tears swell in Ron's ducts but do not fall. "I'm going to take care of you."

Jayson laughs with his mouth wide open.

"You want to hear something embarrassing about me? Since we're friends now. Well, it's not too embarrassing. I'm not going to tell you I have genital warts or anything. Not that I have genital warts. A guy with genital warts is obviously not going to go around making jokes about genital warts."

"Okay."

"How old are you?"

"Twenty-eight."

"I bet a lot of people talk to you like you're a little kid. Does that ever get annoying?"

"Yes!"

"Shhhh. I bet you seen some stuff. I know you're not a little kid."

"I've seen the Internet."

Ron laughs. He's been trying to match the exuberance of Jayson's smile, but his cheeks are getting sore. "My name's not really Ron. It's Richard. Rich mostly. When I just started climbing up the Superstore flowcart, there was already a Richard that worked here. And there was already a guy that went by Rich. There already was a Richie, and a Rick. I probably wouldn't have gone by "Dick," even if I had the option, but it was a moot point. Dick Jones already had the name. I lobbied for Ricardo, but they said they would rather give the name to a Mexican American. So I asked Richard Gutierrez if he might consider going by Ricardo so that I could go by Richard, but he didn't like the idea and actually got a little offended. I tried to get them to let me go by Rico, but when I told them, they just laughed. So it's Ron now at work, Rich at home. Who cares, right? Not a big deal. Ron sounds more like Rich than Ricardo does anyway."

"I've seen a million vaginas," Jayson says.

Ron exits the store through the automatic doors and finds Bicho sweating in the parking lot. "Hot today," he says.

"Yep," Bicho says. "The rain only makes it thicker."

"How would you like to go home early?"

"I need the hours," Bicho says.

"How would you like to make some extra money?"

"What do I have to do?"

"Let's start the conversation this way—what would you do for a hundred dollars?" Ron asks.

"Nothing gay," Bicho says.

"What would you do for two hundred dollars?"

"Pretty much anything," Bicho says.

"Good. I have a serious thing I need done, and I need to know your price point."

"What?"

"Claudia is your cousin, right? I need you to talk to her. I need you to bring me her cell phone. All the passwords."

"No. That shit won't happen."

"What will it take to make it happen?"

3:19 P.M.

Ken Provost is darn impressed with Davis Toddich: a small, fit man of thirty-two with an avian face and a short, precise haircut. *He carries the gravity of his job in his posture,* thinks Ken. He spent the jet's ascent quizzing Davis on his résumé: college wrestler, Big Ten (how no cauliflower ear?), Fellowship of Christian Athletes, Sigma Chi, country music fan, computer systems and security expert. He was even able to recall it all without sounding too proud of himself. His sensible suit, clean and well cut, doesn't seem to wrinkle, even after extended airplane sitting.

Ken considers himself to be an especially bad wearer of suits. When he sits down, his shirt blouses in an unflattering way and sometimes the tail falls out all together. When he stands up, the suit looks like it's been wadded at the bottom of a hamper full of wet towels. He adjusts himself with constant vigilance. His hair, his collar, the tuck of his shirt. He changes suits three times a day to keep up the impression that he is a civilized human being, that he isn't homeless. He does this with the help of Dale, the Personal Assistant napping two rows behind. Dale is known for his large and omnipresent attaché case, which he never seems to open. There has been much wild speculation about its contents among the Superstore Home Office folk: live bait for impromptu fishing purposes, Revolutionary War–era dueling muskets, a thermonuclear device. The actual contents of that attaché case, two carefully folded, moderately priced suits exactly like the one Ken Provost is wearing, is a very closely guarded secret. It's a very un-Superstore thing to do, change your suit three times a day—which is to say it's a very un-Mr. Gene thing to do. It's nothing like the Gene Jr. tanning bed scandal of '92, or the Randy Tisdale poetry endeavor, but it is weird, the kind of thing you would hear one of those Hollywood stars doing, someone too big for his britches. Whenever Dale is given the signal (the phrase "cost bubble") he sequesters Ken to a private changing area, ostensibly to share some extremely pressing and private new information from Broken Arrow.

Davis Toddich is employed by the U.S. government in a unique intelligence capacity. His post was created shortly after the attacks of September 11, 2001, when corporate infrastructure was designated a legitimate terrorist target. He has been assigned to Ken Provost and the Superstore, but Ken would like to hire Davis away from the government as a full-time Superstore associate. He has a lot of use for a man like him, a man of deep focus who seems to notice everything, every ticking pulse, twitching hand, drop of sweat, and dilated pupil. *He noticed when I changed suits,* thinks Ken. *And he knew not to say a word.* It was the second look he gave him, a discreet bounce of the eyeballs up and down his person. Ken considers offering Davis a job near the head of the S.L.I.C.E division. *How much is he worth?* Ken notices a lump on Davis' right ankle. Davis gives him a look that is the same as a wink. *And he gets to carry a gun on commercial flights, that's so cool.*

The DC-10 quivers inside an air pocket. A drunk, middle-aged man in an ill-fitting track suit bothers the young woman next to him with stories of his college football heroics. A young child screams, his hands covering his popping ears. His mother instructs him to hold his nose, close his mouth, and blow.

"Do you like the corporate jet?" Ken asks.

"Do you always travel this way?" Davis asks.

"When we're trying to prove a point."

"What's the point?"

"You've flown with a lot of CEOs in your line of work. How many of them had you flying coach and changing planes three times?"

"None."

Ken says, "Diet Coke, please," to the unfriendly flight attendant. "Obviously, we could afford a private jet with fine wood trim and gold fixtures and the like. Heck, we could afford our own air force. But our customers would have to pay for it whenever they buy a gallon of milk or a bag of Doritos. And if our prices go up, our customers go away, and we're no longer the most profitable company in the world. We can't afford the fleet of gold-trimmed corporate jets any more. It's a whatchamacallit—that book."

Catch 22, thinks Davis, but he doesn't say it. He says, "There's a real genius to its simplicity."

"I know what you're thinking, 'What good is it being the CEO of the largest, richest company in the world if you have to fly coach,'" Ken says. "Right?"

"I wasn't thinking that at all," Davis says.

"It's a statement about what matters, about humility. It's a different culture here. I know a lot of Ivy League CEO types who think we're nuts or some kind of cult because we don't have giant oak boardroom tables, or skyscrapers, or Christmas parties with ice sculptures. But it's about something else here. We believe in something. It's not about pomp. We hate pomp. It's about service. The higher up in this company you go, the more people you serve. I am the servant to two million plus of my Associate Partners. And I'm not a servant to them collectively as some kind of amorphous blob. I'm a servant to each of them on an individual basis."

"Clearly you've been blessed."

"Sure, there's plenty of wealth generated. I'm talking about real wealth. Wealth that's not about yachts and silk suits and Italian sports cars with diamonds on the tires. Wealth that's not about spending money like some first-round draft pick. I don't like to say how much I give to the Lord's service, but let's just say it's astronomical."

"Remember the Lord your God, for it is he who gives you the power to get wealth."

"The boy knows his Deuteronomy. The Old Testament is full of sound financial advice. As far as I'm concerned, it's the best book ever written on the subject. How do you define success, Davis? Two words or less."

"I'll say 'passion' and 'security.'"

"Mine are 'constant' and 'struggle.'"

"You're building an unprecedented portfolio. Mortgage, home finance, real estate, pharmaceuticals, health care. Taking over the world must be a constant struggle."

"We don't want to take over the world, Davis. We don't want to take anything. We want to give. We want to give and give."

The captain's voice over the intercom instructs them to put their seats upright, buckle up, and prepare for descent.

"How much money do you make, Davis? My guess is close to six figures with a heck of a benefits package. Was that rude?"

"Not at all. You're in the ballpark. My wife's got some family money. We've made some investments that worked out well. We've got some of our money in your company actually. It's done well for us."

"Take your money out of everything and put it all into us. I'm not kidding. If you do this right now, you don't have to go down with them. Take it out of the bank. Put it all into us, or commodities. Gold. Put it into something you can touch. When it hits the fan soon, we're going to be one of the few left floating."

"Why are you telling me this?"

"I want you to be on board with us."

"New Mexico, huh," Davis says, as the jet begins the approach. Jagged, dramatic mountains slope into neighborhoods of perfectly square, flat-roofed houses. From above, it looks like an endless, dusty keyboard. "New Mexico is beautiful."

"Too brown for me." Ken slurps his Diet Coke and watches the blurred desert floor transform into defined tangles of brush as they descend.

3:39 P.M.

"Give me your cell phone," Bicho says.

"Fuck you," Claudia says. "You aren't using my phone for shady shit."

"Mine's dead."

"Use your own goddamn phone. You're not getting me in trouble."

"I need to make a call."

"Ernesto is going to be here soon. Use his phone." Claudia eats pizza rolls in bed, with her head propped up on two pillows to get a better look at the TV. The smoke from the dirty pipe smells like nail polish remover.

"Come on. I'm thinking of upgrading to one of these."

"It does the things they all do, now."

"I want to see how fast it is."

"Here, motherfucker. Jesus." She's flipping through the channels faster now.

Bicho is holding the phone in his hand. He never thought it would go this far. There is no plan left. The plan has run out of road at the edge of a cliff.

"Give me your passwords."

"You can have these pizza rolls. They're scalding hot and and then ice cold. There's only like a ten-minute window when they're edible." Claudia walks to the bathroom, closes and locks the door. *My fucking phone! Stay in here until he leaves.*

"Claudia?"

No, go out there. That little bitch isn't going to do this to me.

"I just need the passwords."

"I'm shitting."

"Just, come on."

"That's the password."

"It's not working."

"Try I'm shitting in your mouth. With a dollar sign for the s."

"Don't make me."

"Bicho baby dick 89. All one word. An at sign for the a."

"Give me the password."

Claudia grabs the small, sharp grooming scissors off the sink. Her first thought is *Eyes*, but she would have to get past his glasses.

"Does Lencho want my phone? Tell him I haven't been talking to other men. Give me my phone. Let me text him that I love him."

"No. What are you talking about?"

"Why do you want my password?"

"Someone else wants it."

"Who?"

"Ron."

"Fuck him."

"He's going to pay me a lot of money."

"He's not going to pay you shit."

"Then I'll be his problem."

She hears the door open and prays that it's Ernesto.

"Conejito, sit your fat ass on the bed."

"Hotdog salad."

"Find me a bobby pin, Conejito."

"Why?"

"Hotdog salad!"

"How do you spell salad?" Bicho asks.

"Why is she in the bathroom?" Conejito asks.

"Get out of here you fat fuck," Claudia yells through the door.

Conejito walks onto the balcony and down the stairs. He steps over the construction tape and onto the cement where the pool used to be. He sits on a lawn chair embedded into the cement at a strange angle. It leans far to the left, and forces him to cock his head to the right in a way that makes his neck sore. He scoops up the pebbles and concrete chunks around him and tries to break the glass on a toaster oven embedded a few feet away.

4:12 P.M.

Ron is back at home, where his name is Rich, drinking a Diet Coke and dousing the smoldering ashes of his daughter's dollhouse with the hose.

He's not planning on staying long, just long enough to give his daughter her present and make sure that the regrettable image is deleted from every corner of his hard drive. He realizes the futility of this. Once he pushed send, there was no taking it back. It's not a concrete thing that he can find and destroy anymore; it exists now as coded energy. With a couple of clicks, she could send it to everyone he knows. She could ruin his family. At least he wasn't stupid enough to put his face in the image. With the dollhouse gone he can deny it was him. There are only five women in the world who could positively identify his penis.

His wife, April, returns from work with Addy and a bucket of chicken. He quickly shovels the wet ashes from the fire pit into a garbage bag and tosses it over the cinderblock fence that separates his yard from the desert.

Addy sits on his foot and wraps her arms around his ankle.

"Come on kid. I got a surprise for you," he says, walking in giant looping steps to the driveway while his daughter squeals.

He opens the back of the SUV and removes a giant box with a picture of a pink mansion on the front and a small, clear box containing plastic people. "I'll help you put it together when I get home."

"Let's put it together now," Addy says, clapping.

"Daddy's got to go back to work."

"What are you doing home?" April asks.

"I forgot something."

"Daddy, what will I do while I wait?"

Ron hands her the box of toy people and says, "I want you to tell me a story about each of them when I get home."

"This one is Rodney," Addy says. "He's a foot doctor."

"What if he rides a unicorn? Maybe the unicorn raps."

"He rides the same kind of lawnmower as you, and his wife, Rudy, is a dental hygienist."

"What's wrong with this kid?"

His daughter is dazed by the comment, and his wife leads her inside. *April will wring the sobbing out of her. She'll sit on the bed and tell her, 'Daddy didn't mean that. Daddy is stressed. He loves you.' She'll stroke her hair and nuzzle her cheek until it's an unforgettable hurt. And it would have been fine. It would a gone right over her head and out of her memory.*

12.
Here We Are,
Safe in America

4:35 P.M.

"I T HAPPENED IN IRAQ," AMBERLEE SAYS. "BUT I WASN'T A SOLDIER. I was working for a private contractor in what they called nutritional logistics, basically running chow halls, navigating the shady requisition orders, making sure the soldiers had enough to eat. I know I wasn't taking Mount Suribachi or anything, but..."

"You should be proud of your scars," Lester says. "Everyone who was over there is a hero in my book. Especially if you got hurt."

"Well the soldiers, you know. They're the heroes. They're the ones fighting."

"Nonsense. It's about risk and bravery."

"Well, I don't know."

"I do. Here we are, safe in America. Because of heroes like you. People who put themselves in harm's way for their country."

"We had just passed a field of kids playing soccer. A huge game. There had to have been thirty players on each team. I saw her holding a jug full of pink fluid and it didn't register. Even when she threw it in the Humvee it didn't register. It didn't register until the fire started. I don't like to talk about it, actually. I remember every second of it vividly, exactly how it felt. My body was fused to the seat. I'm going to stop talking about it now."

"I'm sorry," Lester says.

"It's just that when something hurts that bad, remembering it hurts a little too."

"Why don't you stick around for a while," Lester says.

"You mean I don't get to go home early?" Amberlee asks.

"Not while I'm Store Servant/Leader."

"One last thing I'll say about it all is that I feel lucky. When I tell people I feel lucky, they don't believe me. But that's only because they didn't see the other person in the Humvee, the man who died in a very ugly way. He suffered a lot, but not for very long. They pretend to believe me, but I can tell the difference. I notice the lines in people's faces more now that all mine are gone. The way they give everything away. I can tell you're uncomfortable."

"Not at all."

"Well, you asked."

4:41 P.M.

Bicho takes off all of his clothes and puts them in the washing machine. He adds twice as much detergent as usual. A pink froth skim forms in the swishing wash water. He stands naked in front of the open closet door with a bloody penis and stares into the darkness through lenses that augment his pupils to the size of mass-produced sandwich cookies. Plastic bins filled with psychotropic mushroom cultures are stacked from the floor to the ceiling. He removes the lid from the bin, snaps off another fresh cap and stem, and tries to swallow without chewing, only to hack it back up on his palm.

He's disgusted by mushrooms. The word *fungus* has as much to do with it as the texture. He rinses the chewed-up mushroom off in the bathroom sink, chops it into tiny bits, and then cuts those tiny bits into even tinier bits, until there is not a mushroom particle left large enough to cut in half. He sprinkles the mulch into a very thick peanut butter, chocolate syrup, and white bread sandwich.

4:44 P.M.

Lester says, "Mr. Ken or no Mr. Ken, that woman is a hero, and she's staying right here until Mr. Ken gets here to see her."

Betty sits on the spackle again. Ron peeks inside her skirt again, and she makes a spectacle of crossing her legs very tightly.

"Two TRO meetings in one afternoon. The CEO must be coming to town or something," Ron says, chuckling.

"Do you know where she got those burns?" Lester asks. "Iraq."

"Wow," Ron says.

"Serving our country. My grandfather fought in Korea. I'm not going to be the kind of person that sends her home because she's hard to look at. That's not what the Superstore is about."

"I'm with you, sir," Betty says.

"Me too," Ron says.

"If they want to discriminate against wounded Iraq veterans, they got another thing coming," Lester says. "And I'll tell you something. If any customers come to me to complain about someone who looks like her working the register, I'll say, 'That woman got those burns in Iraq, protecting America.' What could they say?"

"Mr. Ken's going to love it," Ron says. "Heroism. It's that intangible thing you were looking for."

"But how will he know she got burned in Iraq and not just some grease fire?" Betty asks.

"We throw her a party. An appreciation party," Lester says. "I've already put the Cake Ladies on it. If Ken Provost comes while we happen to be throwing one of our differently abled war hero associates an appreciation party, then so be it."

"And something else," Lester says. "She feels lucky. I've never felt lucky a day in my life. I've always felt like I scratched for everything I got. We all just go along in our own worlds, you know. Take our blessings and our safe lives for granted. I need something like that to come along and give me some perspective. Not dying, or someone close to me dying, or getting burned up, or disfigured, or cancer, or crippled or anything, but something."

4:58 P.M.

Bicho is overcome with a free-floating and urgent curiosity about every-thing. He contemplates the divine agriculture on the back of his hand: a field of wispy, transparent hairs. He stares into a burning light bulb. The computer. The television. His cell phone/video camera/regular camera/calendar/calculator/Internet browser/pedometer/MP3 player/flashlight. He feels like a man from another time, sent from the distant past into new and terrifying wonders.

Bicho turns his eyes away from the lightbulb and smears his palms into his sockets. When he removes his hands, San Malverde is there, hov-ering majestic. His hair is as black as the inside of a coffin buried six feet under the ground, and it is combed straight back on his head. What Bicho is struck most by is the way he looks nothing at all like the shrine. The shrine face is smooth and generic, with a black mustache and heavy glaze. The features seem very stock, as if the sculptor was thinking, "this is what a nose looks like; this what an ear looks like; this is what a mouth looks like," rather than this is what this particular person's very specific face looks like. It makes sense. There are no known photos of San Malverde. His very existence is a subject of debate. The face he is looking at right now is most definitely El Rey de Sinaloa. It is the face of a man who has worked outside most of his life. The lines in his face were carved by the weather. The vision is slightly plump, an indication of some newfound ease. And there is nothing dandy about his personal presentation. He doesn't wear a fancy white suit of clothes or crocodile boots. He doesn't have to. Because he glows. He fucking glows purple-orange light like a beacon.

Bicho is scared of hell. It is as real a place to him as Italy, or New Jersey, or any place in the world he has heard about but never seen. And he knows exactly what it's like from his dreams. He will be impaled on a spike that enters through his anus and exits someplace in his upper chest. It will be hot, of course, and shards of glass will blow in the wind like dust. The fear of this place serves as a kind of conscience.

He prays furiously until the words all turn into one very long word. He prays to San Malverde and the Virgin of Guadalupe, asking them to pray on his behalf. When he closes his eyes, he sees hell. The impaled souls, their skins encrusted with bloody shards of glass, whimper and beg for water.

In the past Bicho had confessed his sins to Padre Limón, and, according to the teachings of the Catholic Church, he was clean again. But he did terrible things to her. How much of it would he have to tell? Could he just say that he lost control of himself? The only truth is that they were all alone, and she was so beautiful that she made everything else in his life seem less than worthless.

Padre Limón does not ask questions in the confessional. But if he only tells part of it, can he ever be absolved of all of it? Would he have to tell about the sick things? Because the thing about the sick things was, he really didn't want to do them. Or, rather, he really *did* want to do them. He wanted to do them so badly that there was no choice, only resisting and succumbing. But he also wanted very badly to be the kind of person who didn't want to do sick things.

How many rosaries? Bicho takes a small-caliber pistol out of the drawer and shoots himself through the left palm. In the brief calm before the pain, while the adrenaline is still doing its thing, he mutters the word "estigma." He stares into the wound and he sees the other side.

13.
Bloody Cake

5:34 P.M.

W*HY DO I ALWAYS WIND UP DOING EVERYTHING?* WONDERS BETTY as she paints the banner. *Does a cock and a set of balls make you physically incapable of decorating?* She's expected to decorate and arrange the food: day-old doughnuts and sub-sandwiches, a few irregular bags of potato chips and some two liters of Superstore-brand soda. It shouldn't be too much trouble. But she's worried about the apparel section of the store. The new girl, Tiffany, seems incapable of doing even the smallest things right, and now, this very second, she is zoning the shelves unsupervised. When Betty is done with the party preparations, she's going to have to rezone the entire section herself before he gets here. And the worrisome thing, the truly maddening thing, is that she has no idea what time that will be. It could be in ten seconds or it could be in ten hours. All she knows is that at 10:00 a.m. it was confirmed that Ken Provost was in a commercial jet hurtling in their direction.

"You spelled 'appreciation' wrong," Flaco says. He is enjoying a free sprinkled doughnut before his shift starts.

5:49 P.M.

Betty moves to a corner of the breakroom where very little English is spoken or understood. She lowers her voice to say, "There's something shady about Flaco. I don't trust anyone on the night shift."

"You know he scored off the charts on the Superstore Cognitive Aptitude Test," Lester says.

"Those tests don't mean anything. I got a cousin with a hundred and eighty IQ. He fixes copy machines." Betty has jammed another "p" into appreciation and is now cutting up foot-long sub-sandwiches into three-inch pieces. "I make way more money than him."

The three cake decorators make a grand entrance. They set the cake in the middle of a large, round table and stand proudly around it. The associates in the breakroom continue eating and drinking and talking about health problems until the decorator with meringue hair announces, "We've got the cake. No cutting till she sees it."

A small crowd forms and lauds the cake. The young decorator with chocolate-colored freckles dotting her chubby, cookie-colored cheeks is struggling to restrain a prideful smile.

The crowd of associates parts for Betty as she approaches. It is the most dramatic edible thing she has ever seen in her life by far. The desert floor is alive with coconut brush and jelly bean cacti. A mountain has been carved out of leftover sheet cake and given three dimensions by a skilled artist with an airbrush. There is a blackened hole in the center of the cake and a charred Humvee leading a convoy of tanks and semitrucks. Multiple casualties are strewn about the roadside. "It's better than on that show," Betty says. "God help the president and all the men over there dying. We don't think about them enough."

"It's totally better than that show," someone says.

"It kicks that show's ass," someone else says.

"Don't say ass," Betty says.

"You can say ass on TV now," someone says.

"But it does. It kicks that show's ass," Betty says.

"What did you use for blood?" someone asks.

"I can't wait till she takes the first piece," the cake decorator with meringue hair says.

6:01 P.M.

Bicho leaves a message on Ernesto's voice mail:

"I got a idea for a TV show. Mira güey: all the people on the show got their own spinoff TV shows. Like everyone. Like the person on the TV show that serves the important person on the TV show their coffee gets their own spinoff where there are a whole different set of characters around him. And all of those characters, even the ones that don't matter, even the ones that sit in the background and pretend to eat dinner, they all got their own spinoff shows too. And everything happens, good and bad and funny and sad. And it just goes out like that forever, until you run out of actors and channels. Until the people become the actors and the actors become the people. Until it's all that's on all the time. You got to remember this because I don't know if I will because I'm high on Lalo's fungus.

"I shot my hand. I'm getting blood on everything I touch.

"I'm gonna make a bunch of cheddar and get my ranfla tricked out all sick."

6:03 P.M.

"Open your eyes," Lester says. "The cacti are jelly beans."

Amberlee is inside of the plastic Humvee on the sheet cake, and she is inside a real Humvee in Iraq. Her skin is fused to both seats. Sergeant Delonte Washington is spilling out onto the sand and the frosting. He is calling for his mother.

"This is a hero appreciation party," Lester says. "For all you've done for us. The country. For all you've sacrificed."

"Why are you doing this?" Amberlee asks.

"Because we appreciate you," Lester says.

Betty asks, "You want some cake, hon?"

"Let's not cut it just yet," Lester says.

"Why?" the cake decorator with meringue hair asks.

"Let's wait for you know who to see this magnificent thing," Lester says.

"We don't know when that's going to be," Betty says.

"The ladies worked so hard at this. I just want a few more people to be able to see it," Lester says.

Several people take pictures of the cake with their cell phones.

"Someone very special might be coming in today," Lester says. "I'd like him to get a look at it before we cut it. But of course it's Amberlee's cake, so if she wants to cut it she can."

"Who's coming?" Burt asks. He is on his second fifteen. He needs to fill his surgically altered stomach with sugar to get him through the last twenty minutes of his shift, and he's tired of stale doughnuts.

"Mr. Ken is coming," Glen says.

"That's not who's coming," Ron says.

"That's what everyone is saying."

"Everyone is wrong," Ron says.

"That doesn't mean we shouldn't prepare as if he were coming," says Lester.

"It's him."

"Not necessarily," Lester says.

"Then who are we waiting for?"

"Can't say," Lester says.

"When is he coming?"

"Don't know," Lester says.

"His name was Delante." Amberlee's hands are shaking.

"I know, it's pretty realistic," Lester says.

6:09 P.M.

When she finally returns to the apparel department, the look on Betty's face sends the associates scrambling for something to do.

A customer walks past Tiffany, who is folding a stack of blue jeans with forty-six-inch waists.

"Tiffany, what's the ten-foot rule?" Betty asks.

"If a customer comes within ten feet of you, you say, 'Hi, can I be of assistance.'"

"That's right. We really try to drill that in."

"Did I miss somebody?"

"Yeah, that person."

"She was more than ten feet away."

"Do you have any idea how far away ten feet is?" Betty steps off ten large paces. "That ten-foot rule is in full effect today. Understand?" She walks back up to Tiffany's ear to say, "And what did I tell you about re-stocking items from the dressing room?"

"I don't know how to use the computer gun yet," Tiffany says.

"What specific thing don't you understand about rezoning with the computer gun?" Betty asks.

"I guess I don't understand any of it," Tiffany says.

"Any of it?"

"Some of it. Nobody ever taught me."

"Didn't you take the CBL on the computer gun?"

"Yeah."

"And you passed it?"

"Yeah. It was easy."

"Well then what do you understand? Let's start with that."

"I understand that the computer gun is a wireless device that con-stantly updates the store's inventory. I know that it sends information to managers and the corporate office that tells them what products to order and where the company is experiencing waste and shrink. I know that computer gun knows every price in the store, every item in the store, and every internal cost, down to the last minute of labor and the last penny."

"Then what the heck don't you understand?"

"What buttons to push."

"My God, you're that kind of idiot," Betty says.

6:20 P.M.

Finally home, Stacy thinks as she changes her tampon for the first time in eighteen hours. The grime in her crevices is beginning to itch. She would like to take a very hot shower, but her raw skin can only bear luke-warm water. The loofah rolls her dead skin into tiny balls that are easily sprayed away. Her brain is wired for worry. All she can think about is her daughter's violent death until she sets the shower head on pulse and holds it to her clitoris. She imagines Dat painting her clitoris with a tiny finger-nail brush that he dips in his own saliva. She adjusts the shower head to a light, steady stream to better accommodate her fantasy. *The only function a shower head should have is to clean. Jesus, this must be exactly what it's for.* The intruding image of her unconscious husband lying in a hospital bed takes all of the joy out of it.

She applies a thick layer of aloe lotion to the parts of herself she can reach and examines her face through the steam. She turns on the heat lamp and quickly turns it back off after a glimpse of herself in its harsh light.

The doorbell rings.

She yells, "Just a minute" to whoever is on the front porch and wraps her red hair in a bright green towel because she hates the way it looks when it's wet.

The screen in the corner of her mind is blank. It sits on a particleboard TV stand in the corner of a small, off-white room with brown carpet. This is the way it is before it hits her: bleak and still, until all four walls are populated by a 360-degree projection of a police officer standing on her front porch, delivering the terrible news. In the room of her mind, she looks up to see the sky projected on the roof and down to see the whitewashed planks of the porch projected onto the carpet. She calls for Keith. When he doesn't answer, she steels herself to look out the window. *Jesus, hold my hand. If it's a cop car, she's dead.* The relief is as beautiful and intoxicating as any narcotic. It bursts inside of her and pools someplace in her guts. It's the St. Vinny truck. She made the appointment last week and promptly forgot about it. *Jesus, please forgive me for giving all this stuff to the Catholics. They're the only ones that will pick up after five.*

• • •

Norwegian Black Metal is shooting up a wire that splits and connects directly into each ear. Keith doesn't think twice about walking into the office to retrieve the digital camera, not until the smell hits him. He contemplates the rust-colored stain on the creamy office carpet. *This is formative. This is so fucking formative.* The smell of singed polypropylene fibers is giving him a headache.

Keith disconnects the computer chord from the charred surge protector and plugs it straight into the wall. When he pushes the power button, the computer whirrs for a couple of seconds and then starts into its regular sequence of loading screens. *Fucking amazing*. The desktop is up. Keith checks his page again. They send their encouragements and their affections, and he registers them.

He rubs the tips of his fingers together. There's something sticky on the keyboard. When he closes his page, he notices the thumbnail-sized image of a woman's disconnected head fellating a man's disconnected penis. He feels the stickiness of the keyboard on his fingertips and runs in full stride to the bathroom to wash his hands under very hot water.

• • •

She stands at the mouth of the open garage and directs the men from St. Vincent de Paul. For Stacy, the purging has always been at least as satisfying as the binging. As a teenager she took pleasure in stuffing herself with ice cream and chips and grilled cheese sandwiches cooked in butter, but she always appreciated the deep satisfaction of seeing it all come back up again, of being free of it. She feels lighter with each plastic bin the men load into the truck. And it is in these moments that she can reassure herself that she is not crazy, not like the compulsive hoarders on *Oprah*, who save their old cat litter in plastic bins and have to navigate through narrow corridors carved into stacks of old newspapers and toppling towers of Styrofoam.

"Take it all," she says. "Leave the ping-pong table. Heck, take the ping-pong table." *Jesus, let all this stuff get to people who need it.* She imagines the ping-pong table in a boys' home: dark-skinned, street-wise boys paddling the ball back and forth with wholesome smiles on their faces.

"When we're done you're gonna be able to park a car in here again," the large man wearing a Velcro back support says. "Maybe even two."

"My husband's in the hospital. I want to surprise him when he gets home. He's been at me to get this crap out of here for months."

"Should we take the Soloflex?" the large man in the back support asks.

"Yes, please. I've been hanging clothes on it for two years. I appreciate you guys coming so late. This is the first I've left the hospital since it happened."

"We pick up till eight," the smaller man says.

"He was electrocuted." If they're not going to ask, she's going to tell them.

"I hope he's okay," the large man in the Velcro back brace says.

"Oh, he'll be fine." Stacy smiles and believes her own words for approximately three perfect seconds.

She has focused all of her worry on her daughter. Why won't she call back? She would feel so much better if she could hear her voice. The longer Kyler is gone, the more worried Stacy becomes. The more worried she becomes, the more stubborn and spectacular and violent the images on the screen become. What is on the screen now is beyond describing, beyond any horror movie she has ever seen in terms of vulgarity, and gore, and general disturbance. But it's easier to watch than something more plausible, like her daughter dead in a mangled car, or dead of an undetected heart defect like her seemingly healthy nephew, Brett. She tries to call her daughter again and is sent straight to voice mail. "Where are you? Your brother is no help at all. I need to hear your voice, or I'm going to lose my mind."

* * *

The Suburban's black leather interior requires full-blast air conditioning to maintain a bearable temperature. The outside is as clean as a scalpel and the inside is clutter free. Right now it is parked and running in the parking lot of a Shorty's convenience store.

"Drink your Red Bull," Patty says from the driver's seat. She tips the bottom of the can until a trickle drops from the corner of Kyler's mouth onto her teal blouse. "You had that shirt on yesterday."

"My whole body is made out of static."

"Your parents..."

"I feel like clothes right out of the dryer."

"Oh my God, there's blood on your shirt."

"Oh no. This is my seventeenth favorite shirt."

"A bloody fingerprint. You can't wear that."

"It's my baby's blood."

"Don't say that."

"I'm made out of lint. Don't blow on me or I'll disintegrate."

"Are you sure you're not too messed up to talk to your mom?"

"My dad's in the hospital. All I have to do is cry real hard."

"I'm going in to buy you a new shirt."

"At the gas station?"

"Well, we don't have time to go shopping, Kyler."

"Then I want to pick it out."

They exit the seventy-six-degree SUV into the ninety-four-degree parking lot. An old man holds the door and tips his Dallas Cowboys cap for them.

"This one!" Kyler says, pointing at a T-shirt with a howling coyote superimposed over a dream catcher. "This one is hilarious."

"Just get this one," Patty says, holding up a plain, blue T-shirt with a hefty pocket in the front.

"No, I'm getting this one. It's hilarious."

"It's an extra large."

"It's the only size."

"Your mom will know you're messed up if you come in wearing a shirt with a howling wolf on it."

"This shirt makes me feel something."

"Fine, whatever. At least it doesn't have any blood on it."

Patty pays for the shirt with Kyler's credit card. She leads Kyler into the bathroom and tries to pull the shirt over her languid arms.

"What are you doing?"

"Put this on."

"I'm not putting that on."

"You picked it out."

"No, I don't want to wear it now. You wear it. I'll wear your shirt."

Poor thing, thinks Patty as she puts on the ridiculous shirt. She doesn't want to bring up the fact that God is obviously punishing Kyler. Her miscarriage. Her father being electrocuted. The father that she promised to stay pure for. He might as well have been struck by lightning. It might as well have rained frogs. She is already forming this all into a cautionary anecdote in her head: the tragic story of an anonymous teenaged friend of hers who had premarital sex with disastrous consequences. If she ever has a daughter, she will hear this story on repeat until it reaches mythic proportions.

When they walk out of the bathroom wearing different shirts, the old man in the cap says something in Spanish to the cashier that makes her laugh.

When they get back to the black SUV, the seats are already very hot. Patty pulls the oversize coyote howling in a dream catcher shirt down between her thighs and the black leather.

Kyler sits with her bare thighs on the scorching leather. It doesn't seem to bother her at all. She says, "Why does everything happen all at once?"

"Everything that happens in this world is God trying to talk to us," Patty says.

"I'm afraid."

"It's too late in the day to be this hot."

"I'm afraid that I'll look at my dad lying there in the hospital bed and I won't even be able to cry." The fear of not being able to cry makes Kyler cry in huffing, spewing fashion.

7:11 P.M.

Earlier, Ken Provost took a salad bowl to the sundae bar and filled it with serrated ropes of soft-serve chocolate ice cream. He topped it with everything but raisins: sprinkles, chocolate chips, peanut butter chips, nuts, coconut flakes, gummy bears, whipped cream, and five maraschino cherries. He is watching most of it melt. "I'm too full to go anywhere tonight. Let's go to the store tomorrow morning. Meet at five a.m. in the lobby."

"Where are we staying?" Davis asks.

"Comfort Inn. Dale and me are bunking in 217. You get the odd room: 244."

Dale notices that Ken's Diet Coke is empty and finishes his own promptly. "Do you want me to get you a refill while I'm up, Mr. Ken?"

"Only if you happen to be getting up to get yourself a refill, Dale."

"I was just on my way up there."

"Thank you, Dale."

"No problem."

"My eyes were bigger than my stomach," Mr. Ken says to Davis. "I guess I went a little nuts. Good Lord, I'm stuffed. I think I'm just going to video chat with my grandkids and fall asleep."

"How many do you have?" Davis asks.

"Seven," Mr. Ken says. "So far." He shows Davis the pictures on his cellular device.

"Those are some bona fide cute grandkids."

"You a family man?"

Davis shows Mr. Ken the latest pictures of Jack and Sarah on his cellular device.

"Little Wolverine fans, eh."

"You've got to indoctrinate them early. They only like everything you like for so long."

"Here's Abigail in her Sooners gear," Mr. Ken says, pulling up the picture on his touch screen.

"I've got to say, it takes a lot to make an OU cheerleading outfit look good in my opinion, but she really pulls it off."

"I do all this for them."

"I know what you mean."

"I'm a very very rich man. I'm not trying to pretend I'm not. I know this trip must seem downright miserly to you, but this company was built on humility as much as anything else."

"Please, I'm not too big for my britches," Davis says.

"Good, you read Mr. Gene's book," Mr. Ken says.

"Are you kidding? I broke the spine."

"You know, when Sears was dominating the retail market they took the customers' money and built themselves a giant tower, tallest in the world at the time. Who do you think paid for that tower? A bunch of customers who didn't want or need a tower, who were just trying to buy a socket wrench or a bra or a bedspread. So Mr. Gene came along and gave all that money back to the customers. He cut cost to the bone in every possible way. You ever heard of the Superstore Tower?"

"No." Davis sops up the brown gravy on his plate with a golden biscuit.

"Our home office is made out of particleboard. We eat at Arby's and Denny's and the Golden Corral. We share hotel rooms when gender appropriate. That mentality has to be consistent, and it has to come from the top. I am a very very wealthy man. The people who love me never have to worry about anything. But there are no gold fixtures or chandeliers. There are no Rolls-Royces in the driveway. I take my own trash to the curb on the rare occasion I'm home to do it. I just don't need all the pomp. I hate pomp. Mr. Gene taught us to hate the pomp, and that has made all the difference." Mr. Ken drapes his napkin over his melting sundae and leaves a three-dollar tip under the napkin dispenser. "I don't like to talk about it. But I've fed a lot of hungry children. Put roofs over a lot of people's heads."

"Service."

"I think you get it, son. How'd you like your dinner?"

"Good. Thank you very much. I haven't been to a Golden Corral in a long time. When I was in high school, all the wrestlers used to come here to eat and throw up."

Mr. Ken chuckles. "There's a lot of money in mass cafeteria-style food retail as long as the cost of food stays practically nothing. We got a lot to do with that, fighting for our customers. You hear these lefties whine about us bullying around corporations like Heinz and Tyson and Nabisco and Tropicana into lowering their prices. Since when is fighting corporations on behalf of the customers a bad thing? I'm not ashamed to say that we fight hard for the customer. I'm not ashamed to say we fight like heck for them: gouge eyes and kick in the nuts when we have to. Do you have any idea how far we reach? So far beyond the stores, son. We never talk about how we make the sausage. We just put it on the table."

"You're preaching to the choir, sir."

"Would you like to work for us, Davis?"

"In what capacity?"

"Let's just say choir boy."

. . .

"I've got to go home and feed my dogs," Amberlee says.

"Before you have any of your cake?" Lester asks. "You know who should be here anytime."

"I'm about to go into overtime," Amberlee says.

"I clocked you out forty-five minutes ago," Betty says. "This is a party."

Ron says, "Let's get some pictures of you and the cake before you leave. For you know who. We'll keep a piece in the freezer for you."

"I don't know if I can," Amberlee says.

"Let's get some pictures of you and the cake," Lester says.

"I don't like having my picture taken," Amberlee says.

"They'll be a nice remembrance of the party we worked so hard to throw you," Lester says.

"Then take a picture of the cake. You don't need me in it," Amberlee says.

"Nonsense. You look beautiful," Lester says.

"Please don't say that," Amberlee says.

"It's true. Let's all get in the picture with the cake," Lester says.

"No," Amberlee says. "I like all the pictures of me to be pictures from before it happened."

"Don't be shy," Ron says.

"It's bad enough there are mirrors. I'm very serious now if you can't read my face."

"Come on. Just one picture." The Servant/Leaders hand Cruz their cell phones and crowd around Amberlee and the cake. They hold their smiles while she struggles with the technology.

"I'm staring at myself," Cruz says.

"Push the arrow in the corner," Lester says.

"I think I'm shooting a video now."

The skin on Amberlee's face is drum-tight and inscrutable. In her old face, they would have registered her anger. They would have seen a woman summoning all of her self-control to keep from slamming her fist in the dead center of the cake.

"Cruz, give it to someone who has used an iPhone before."

14.
Or I Could Poop on Your Chest

7:29 P.M.

"SO, IT'S A ZOMBIE MOVIE?" QUENTIN ASKS.

"No," Glen says. "They're not zombies. They're brainwashed by an alien pretending to be God."

"So it's an alien movie?"

"Why do people have to reduce everything to one word?"

Glen and Quentin are in the cramped Loss Prevention Office reviewing eight hours of security camera footage at three times the normal speed.

"Has one of your scripts ever got made?" Quentin asks.

"It's hard when you're not somebody's nephew," Glen says.

"When you win the Oscar, will you thank me in your speech?"

"Fuck you."

"What?"

"I understand the reality of the situation. I'm not some asshole."

"Why don't you to move to Hollywood? Hustle it around town. Bend yourself over some producer's desk."

"I know that it'll only exist in my head. But I can watch it there."

"Who's your new boyfriend?" Ron asks, wedging his gut into the cramped Loss Prevention Office. "He's a big one. I bet you get all lost in his arms."

"He's the new LPO Don't worry, baby. You're still my favorite,"

Glen says. He's not a fan of this brand of humor, but he acceded to it two years ago semiwittingly when Ron told him that he looked sexy in a hairnet. Glen could have done several things to end it right then and there, but he replied, "Thanks, I wore it just for you." And from that moment on he was an official member of the society of male Superstore associates who prove their heterosexuality by describing fictional homosexual encounters in vivid, vulgar detail.

"Did you know that Glen likes the ol' Cleveland Steamer? He likes the heat," Ron says, exhaling hot air into his palm and rubbing it on Glen's chest.

"When I worked as a C.O., this fag ate his shit like chocolate pudding," Quentin says.

"Wow!" Glen says. "Way to crank it up five notches. We were just having a friendly conversation about consenting adults shitting on each others' chests and you had to go and tell me that? I can't unhear that."

"He was trying to get himself transferred to the psych ward."

"So he ate shit to *fake* being crazy? That seems, I don't know, crazier," Glen says.

"You got to be careful with the words you use here, Quentin," Ron says. "You can't go around saying that word. If the wrong person hears you say the B-word, or the N-word, or either one of the F-words, you could get fired on the spot."

"Sorry. I messed up like that already once," Quentin says.

"That's okay. I'm not the wrong person. No fucking bitches are gonna tell me who I can't call a faggot," Ron says.

"You seem giddy," Glen says. "Did you win Justin Timberlake tickets on the radio?"

"Adrenaline, my friend. Excitement. The best drug."

"What are you still doing here?" Glen asks.

"Shopping," Ron says, rattling the small box of spaghetti in his left hand as evidence.

"So you're off the clock?" Glen asks.

"I'm on salary, bitch," Ron says.

"They still make you clock in when you're officially working."

"Like I said, I'm shopping."

"Why would Mr. Ken come on third shift?" Glen asks. "There are hardly any customers."

"I don't know. A lot happens at night," Ron says. "That's when the store essentially sucks the air back into its lungs. If I ran the whole company, I might want to see that."

"So are you just going to shop all night?" Quentin asks.

"The way I feel right now, I can shop for this fucking box of spaghetti 'til September if I have to."

"Wow, you really want to meet this guy," Quentin says. "He must be pretty hot."

"How tall are you?" Ron asks Quentin.

"Six-eight."

"Did you play basketball?"

"Not really. I mean, I've played basketball before, mostly in gym class."

"But you're so dang tall." Having grown up small and fat, Ron Barns never made it past the B squad, but he is sure that if he had turned out to be six-eight he would have worked harder, been great, not wasted it.

"To be honest, I didn't like the game much."

"Why the heck not?"

"I don't know. I guess people were always trying so hard to make me like it."

"Of course they were. Do you know how much basketball players make?" If God had let Ron grow to six foot eight inches, he's sure he would have woken up before dawn and shot five hundred free throws. He would have maintained his regimen in the face of gale force winds whipping park benches around the court. He would have worn those goofy strength and conditioning shoes with the platform toes everywhere, to prom and to church. He would have been the kind of guy who buys his mother a big house and a staff to take care of it, a live-in nurse and all the medicine she needs. He looks down at his own doughy body. "I bet you get asked that a lot."

"It's okay," Quentin says.

"Fuckin' A. If I was born with a fourteen-inch schlong, I'd be a porno star," Ron says.

"A gay porno star," Glen says.

"Shut up. This is serious. God only gives you so much. And you don't get to choose what it is. You shouldn't waste it. It's a sin to waste it."

"Well, it's too late now," Quentin says.

"How old are you?" Ron asks.

"Twenty-nine," Quentin says.

"Yeah, I guess it is. Still, it's a shame though."

"What?"

"That you're six foot eight and this is all you are," Ron says.

Glen laughs.

"I guess you two supersleuths didn't notice the ambulance and the County Coroner van out there a while ago. Monitor six-D," Ron says.

"We've got a lot of store to watch. Parking lot is last priority," Glen says.

"Did someone get stabbed again?" Quentin asks.

"Some old snow bird died in his RV," Ron says. "The cop said his widow lost her marbles. She was in that log cabin RV out there, keeping his body cold with bags of ice and evaporative coolers."

"Do you want us to investigate?" Quentin asks.

"Who the fuck do you think you are, Jim Rockford?" Ron asks. "I think that falls out of the Loss Prevention jurisdiction. His wife is still parked out there. Tell her she can stay as long as she likes. RVs are big customers. And bring 'em some flowers and a condolence card. Write it off on the Good Will Account."

"Why don't you do it?" Glen asks.

"I just can't look at anything sad right now. It will suck all this energy right out of me," Ron says.

"What kind of flowers?" Quentin asks.

"Whatever kind we're getting ready to throw away," Ron says.

• • •

The sun is falling behind the mountains. Or, rather, the earth is turning the Superstore away from the sun, which makes the sun seem as if it's falling. The result is spectacular light over the parking lot, where Dolly sits with a common amazement: *everything is still going: falling and rising, growing and dying.* "I'm not sure how much gas we have left."

"God, it reeks of Febreze in here," Megan says. "It took them long enough to come and get him." She is sitting in the RV's driver seat because it faces forward, away from the couch her father died on, and away from her mother, who is lying on it, flipping aimlessly through the two hundred channels that beam into the RV from space.

"It wasn't exactly an emergency," Dolly says.

"Somebody is dead, what do you call that?"

"The exact opposite of an emergency."

"Mom, why do you have shotgun shells? "

"It's a long story."

"You don't even have a shotgun. Do you have a shotgun? You hate guns."

In the marmalade shimmer, it could almost be a real log cabin parked someplace beautiful. And maybe not even parked at all, maybe just built right into the ground. Megan studies the interior as if, for the first time, she might notice some gore she had been blocking out: her father's hair pasted to the fake logs. To have sat there with her cup of herbal tea and her *OK!* magazine and not noticed the skull fragments in her mother's hair. And for the cops and the coroners not to have noticed when they took the body away. But upon further inspection, she concludes that all of the blood in the RV is stored safely inside of her skin and inside of her mother's.

"I was in the Superstore and your father was dead. I needed a gun."

"You weren't going to hurt yourself."

"God no! I was going to do the exact opposite."

Protect herself—hurt someone else—"What's going on?"

"Your father is dead, Babybear. I'm scared. It's nothing more interesting than that. Now, we've got some unpleasant phone calls to make. I think hot toddies will make them not as awful."

There is a knock at the door. Megan opens it without peeking out.

Does she just open the door for anyone? thinks Dolly. The first wave that washes over her is an angry fear regarding her daughter's carelessness, her stupidity. *Does she do this at home? In Phoenix!* Her daughter's belief that people are essentially good makes Dolly worry. *I guess I'm just supposed to carry all the worry in the world around for her.*

The second wave is a tsunami of panic that washes every thought from her brain, down to the prime neurosignals that tell her lungs to inhale and her heart to beat. She stands petrified next to the knife drawer. The same very tall man who was following her around the store earlier, who apparently wears his razor sunglasses inside and at night, is standing face-to-face with her daughter: her feet on the third step of the RV, his on the blacktop. She forgot to load the gun. She's not even sure how. Dolly feels like the shells on the counter, useless without the apparatus, the spark.

"Please accept the Superstore's official condolences. And there's no hurry to leave the lot." He hands Megan a dozen slightly peaked long-stemmed roses. "I'm sorry. Roses are ridiculous. Our manager is retarded."

"No, no. They're my favorite. Thank you. I feel like a beauty queen, not like my dad just died," Megan says.

"Who are you?" Dolly asks. "Why are you here? Why are you following me?"

"Quentin Dowell. I'm sorry. I work here. I just don't wear a uniform. I'm a Loss Prevention Associate."

"Then why are you out here bringing us roses?"

"That's a great question. I'm new, actually. Here's my name tag." The letters Q-U-E-N-T-I-N are spelled on the plastic badge in two rows of stickers. He tells her, "I'm sorry for your loss. These flowers are from the Superstore. They're for you too."

"Neither one of us knows how to drive this thing," Megan says.

"I love the log cabin motif you got going on in here. It's freaking awesome."

"Thank you," Megan says. "If my dad were here, he'd give you the grand tour."

"He stays outside," Dolly says.

Megan gives him a soft look and thinks about how nice it might be to have someone sweet and tall and dumb for a while. She wonders how the fact that her mother is obviously terrified of this man has impacted her inexplicable attraction. *He also brought me roses*, thinks Megan.

Too fat for me, thinks Quentin. "I gotta get back to the store," he says.

8:00 P.M.

Wilma hates that fucking clock radio: some newscaster blurting through the alarm, the satanic red glow of its digital numbers. She hates it when she's awake to see it all turn. For hours she has been tossing and turning, looking up at the clock every few minutes, hoping that she's managed to doze off while young Josiah sleeps like a stone beside her.

Josiah is so still and quiet that she immediately looks to his belly and is relieved to find it rising and falling. She wakes him gently, with a tender tap tap tap on the scalp.

On Saturday nights Wilma has to drop the car off at Red Lobster because Laurie never knows when her shift will be cut. Then she has to sit with Josiah in the Red Lobster lobby waiting for Cruz, who is always late and full of excuses. And while Wilma's waiting, all she'll be able to think about are all the things around the house that absolutely must get done: the cleaning and poop scooping and laundry. *Wes gets home from the clinicals tomorrow with enough money to keep the lights on. He makes everything easier.* A few months ago, when he tested the antidepressant BH3-448, he came home puffy and, for the first time in his life, depressed. He stopped brushing his teeth and sleeping, and the cells in his brain that used to automatically zip his zipper back up seem permanently damaged.

Why can't they test that shit on animals? she thinks.

The sun has set. She can feel it, even behind the tinfoil and duct-tape-covered windows.

8:14 P.M.

Stacy and Keith walk back through the hospital's automatic doors, into the muted paint. They pass the cafeteria on the way to the elevators. Keith sees Cide the Suffix sitting alone in front of a dry bagel and a cup of black coffee, crying. *Why are some women only pretty when they cry? Is it something in them or something in me?*

"Do you know that person?" Stacy asks.

"She's in my Spanish class. I should go say something," Keith says.

"I need you up there with me."

"I'll be right up."

The hospital cafeteria has transformed itself into a contemporary coffee shop, with its cheap, angular furniture and its modern-art wallpaper. "Thanks for coming," Keith says, sitting down at her table. "How did you hear?"

Cide the Suffix looks up from her coffee, tears carrying black lines down her cheeks and asks, "What the fuck are you doing here?"

"What do you mean? My dad is in intensive care. What are you doing here?"

"That sucks. What's wrong with him?"

"He was electrocuted."

"How?"

"I don't know—he was just lying there. Why are you here? What's wrong?"

"Nothing."

"You just happened to be here in the hospital cafeteria?"

"As much as you can happen to be anywhere."

Keith buys a coffee from the dispenser. He wants to add lots of milk and sugar, but it seems cooler to drink his coffee black. "My sister is sleeping off a narcotic hangover remedy, but my mother is convinced she's dead in a ditch."

"No she's not. She's here."

"What?"

"She got here an hour ago. She's with that ugly blond girl they all hang around for some reason."

"Patty?"

"You should see the T-shirt Patty's wearing. That bitch does have amazing hair though. Like a pony in a fucking dream," Cide the Suffix says. "How's your coffee, Keith?"

"Are we going to do the names thing or not? Because I'm not calling you Cide the Suffix if you're not calling me The Omniscient Narrator."

"I can't call you that when you're dressed like a normo," Cide the Suffix says.

"Sorry, I haven't had time to paint my fucking face. It's been crazy," Keith says.

"You might as well have frosted hair."

"You pretend to be deep, but you're just a thin layer of freak makeup," Keith says. He sips his bitter coffee and wishes it was Pepsi.

"How deep is the paint on the canvas, the ink on the page? You want to go to the Pancake Alley with me and Daemon Dog later?"

"I couldn't want out of this fucking hospital more if it was on fire. But it might be a while before I can sneak away."

"It's okay. We'll be there late."

"You mean you really didn't know my dad was in the hospital?"

"No."

"Then what are you doing here?"

"I come here when I feel like crying in public. Nobody bothers you. They figure you got a reason."

"Why would anyone ever want to cry in public?"

"Oh my god, you should try it. It's so fucking great."

"So, what are you crying about?"

"Nothing. Just crying like exercising or taking a shit."

"You can't cry about nothing."

"I only cry about nothing. If they let you smoke in here, this place would be perfect."

8:49 P.M.

Ron is sitting at the same table that he and Claudia sat at this morning, dipping his nuggets and sucking his Diet Coke. He still sees her there, with her parenthetical eyebrows and outlined lips, nibbling her straw. Her keen and beautiful face keeps him awake at night. He projects it onto the ceiling while April snores beside him and fills the covers with farts. Often, when he saw Claudia in person, he was disappointed. He could look her in the face and tell himself that he was not in love with her, that she was not especially lovely. But as soon as she was out of sight, the resin she left behind would haunt him.

"Hey, cutie," Octavio says.

"Hey, cocksucker," Ron says.

"What's wrong, cum dumpster? Something got you down?"

"Just... Long day."

"Jaw sore from sucking all those cocks?"

"Yeah, my jaw's sore."

"I thought you would want to kiss me or at least stick your tongue in my ass or something. I haven't seen you since you got moved to days," Octavio says.

Ron says, "Oh baby, don't... Listen, can we just not do this fag schtick right now? I'm trying not to think about something."

"Schtick? You don't love me anymore? If you don't love me anymore, papi, I kill myself."

"Don't worry, you're still my number one bitch."

"Seriously bro, what are you still doing here?"

"Officially: shopping."

"What are you really still doing here?"

"Waiting."

"For who?"

"Can't say."

"When are they going to get here?"

"Don't know."

Octavio says, "Pobrecito. Would pooping on my chest cheer you up at all?"

Ron sighs and takes a long drink of soda.

"Or I could poop on your chest?"

9:04 P.M.

Kyler is emitting intense, guttural groans and letting snot run from her nose to her mouth like a child. The tears are coming so fast that everything before her looks like a movie projected onto thick steam.

"He's going to be all right, sweetheart," Stacy says as she strokes her daughter's back. The machine injects air into Larry's lungs. Kyler's breaths get choppy. For a moment Stacy worries that her daughter might actually cry herself to death. A nurse brings her a paper bag and tells her to cover her nose and her mouth with it.

Jesus, help my children, prays Stacy. *Their lives have been so perfect until now. It seems cruel, like releasing a basset hound back into the wild.* Seeing Kyler sob over Larry makes Stacy love him again. It filters out the affair, the apathy, all of the horrible things they have said to each other, and leaves only shimmery memories that play together like a bright chord: him tracing the kids in chalk on the driveway, kissing the back of her neck while she kneads the dough, inside that baby blue tent in the rain. *My love,* thinks Stacy as she blots the beads of sweat forming on her husband's brow.

"I'm sure everything is going to be all right. I'm praying so hard for it," Patty says. She is also crying, though much more modestly than Kyler.

"Why didn't she call back?" Stacy asks.

"She's been like this since she heard." Patty figured she would be the one to have to answer all the questions, but she hadn't planned on doing it in the ridiculous shirt she is wearing. It makes her feel like a white trash cliché. She wants to tell Mrs. Cotton that she's an A student and a virgin. She says, "I know this is an ugly shirt. I just sleep in it because it's super comfortable. I don't usually wear it out."

"It's still got the tag on it."

"Well, you know. I bought it to sleep in when we were at the gas station. I figured we might wind up sleeping in the waiting room."

"Where have you guys been?"

"Lubbock."

"Really?"

"We sat in on a modern art lecture. Saw the football stadium. A laboratory."

"Come to the bathroom with me. You're going to rub lotion on my back."

9:14 P.M.

Amberlee pulls the loop through the knot. Disconnecting the laces sends the relief trickling up her leg. She kicks off the shoes, pulls off the socks, and stares at her two perfect feet. They are light brown and smooth like a flower petal. The scar tissue covering most of her body is smooth like a beach ball. She spreads her perfect toes, curls them, and plucks an errant black hair.

What's left of her ears have once again adjusted to the snorting of the pugs. What's left of her nose has adjusted to their smell. It almost knocked her over when she first got home. She hadn't left the house in the nine days prior to yesterday's orientation. Her mother made it easy by bringing her groceries to the house, and made her feel ridiculous for getting a job at the Superstore, pointing out that she has a degree in civil engineering, speaks Farsi, and has a wealth of other skills that make her suitable for more prestigious employment. If her mother was the kind of person you could explain things to, Amberlee would have tried to explain that she wanted a job that would force her to come face-to-face with a steady stream of people, where she would encounter all the possible re-actions to her disfigurement in an endless onslaught for thirty-nine hours a week. She imagined that the job might sharpen her ability to put people at ease, that after working as a cashier at the Superstore she could do anything. But after today, she has decided never to go back. She swallows three large pills, changes into sweatpants and an old T-shirt, and wonders how many days it will be until she can summon the energy to change out of them. The large, flat-screen TV glows and mumbles in the background. She opens her laptop and plugs into her second life, where she is a slutty fairy, and has built her virtual house out of platinum and stained glass.

15.
Shimmer and Dust

10:20 P.M.

T HE YOUNG DJ WEARS HIS DALLAS COWBOYS CAP COCKED TO THE left and smokes a grape cigar with a plastic tip while he spins records in the corner of the dust yard. The music is a percussive wind blowing out of giant speakers. Some nod rhythmically or jangle their bodies a little to the music, but nobody dances. They form various huddles of various sizes and shapes and drink beer from blue plastic cups.

Conejito likes it when he gets a foamy cup of keg beer. *If somebody had a gun to my head and forced me to drink pee, I'd want it to be as frothy as possible,* he thinks. Root beer floats are his favorite: the creamy, perfect suds. He pretends to like the taste of beer but is so disgusted by it that he tongues the bloody crevice under his loose tooth just so he can taste something else between sips. Conejito is not sure how to act, so he acts as much like Lalo as he possibly can. He shrugs his shoulders behind his neck like a cobra and tries to emulate Lalo's sense of serene alert.

He joins the huddle at the far corner of the yard. Even standing in the dust, their shoes are all an iridescent white. The same names and words are written on their bodies in the same looping hand. They all wear blue, most of it Dallas Cowboys merchandise. All have the same buzzed heads and the same dangling colito, except for Caro, the only girl in the circle, and a few homies whose day jobs make it impractical. It's not a requirement. There is no uniform or explicit dress code. They just are this: hair or no hair, Roy Williams jersey or button-up shirt. Conejito feels swaddled and safe inside the sameness.

Lalo constitutes the middle of the huddle, wherever he is standing. His head is bullet shaped with hair so thick it seems less like hair than black moss growing far down his forehead, dangerously close to engulfing his eyebrows. Right now he is sitting on the back of a weathered yard couch. Nobody sits on the threadbare cushions, which are covering two modified shotguns. In the back of the couch, behind a flap of orange tweed, there are twenty-three blunts prerolled in grape cigar skins.

Lalo lights and distributes two of the blunts around the huddle, one to the right and one to the left. Each of them hits it in a similar manner, curling their hands up and hiding it behind their wrists, but their exhales are all different. Conejito decides that Steve is the best at it. He lets a thick cloud of smoke fall out of his mouth a little, then sucks it back in again like a reverse explosion. When Lalo is finished with the smoke he lets it rise out of his open mouth like steam. Hector presses his lips together and tries to blow the smoke in a stream as sharp as a squirt gun's. Every exhale for Caro is a painful cough. There is no ceremony to it at all for Ernesto, who just blows it out of his mouth like a silent fart.

Both blunts reach Conejito at the same time.

"Caught in the cipher, little homey," Ernesto says.

Young Conejito's eyes are bloodier than the bloody eyes around him. He hits both blunts at the same time. The huddle laughs and cheers when he coughs. At five foot ten, two hundred and fifteen pounds, it's easy to forget he's twelve years old. The new tattoos inked into the digits of his right hand make it even easier.

"You get new ink, güey?" Lalo asks.

"Yeah," Conejito says. "A couple."

"Did Scooby hook you up?"

"Yeah, I got me some sick shit on my chest too." Conejito stretches the neck of his Roy Williams jersey out to show his tattoo off instead of lifting it up because that's all Ernesto would need to start in on his man boobs—what Ernesto calls his moobs.

"Five-seven-five?" Lalo asks.

"They changed the area code," Conejito says, trying to figure out a way to unstretch his collar.

"What?"

"They changed the area code. All of New Mexico isn't five-o-five no more."

"Well, I didn't change the fucking area code. We're five-o-five for life, little homey," Lalo says.

"But our phones are all five-seven-five now," Conejito says.

"My phone isn't any bullshit five-seven-five," Lalo says.

"Yea, güey," Ernesto says. "Watch. Call my phone."

"My shit is still five-o-five, yo. I got that Sprint. That shit goes through Albuquerque," Steve says.

"Well, fuck it. We'll all get Sprint phones then. Problem solved," Lalo says.

"But the area code is changed," Ernesto says. "Southern New Mexico is five-seven-five now. All of New Mexico couldn't be five-o-five. Too many people with too many phone numbers."

"Those pinche norteños got five-o-five now?" Lalo asks.

"Yeah," Ernesto says.

"When did this happen?"

"A couple of weeks ago."

"Fuck me. I've been calling people. I didn't have to dial a different area code."

"The old numbers will work for another six months."

"Fuck! How could this happen? Was there a vote?" Lalo asks.

"No," Ernesto says.

"What the fuck? What the fuck am I supposed to do with this?" Lalo asks, lifting his shirt to show the prominent 5-0-5 arched across his belly.

"They'll know we're old school," Ernesto says, showing off the 5-0-5 down the back of his arm.

"It seems like this kind of shit is always happening to us," Lalo says despondently, and everybody except Conejito knows exactly what he means.

"I'm going to get me a little seven inside the zero," Steve says.

"There you go, Steve. Now we're problem solving," Ernesto says. "Don't get sad, big homey."

"Hey. Check out my new shit Scooby did," Steve says, lifting up his shirt and pulling back a clear plastic bandage.

"Star Trek?"

"Love that nigga, Dr. Spock," Steve says.

"Pinche mayatero," Lalo says.

10:39 P.M.

The breakroom is empty, except for Fatima, who is throwing away food. The Tupperware without a date on it goes right in the trash. She learned her lesson about opening Tupperware she had a bad feeling about when she was cleaning houses in Dallas and opened a container so foul that it got her and the children in the house sick. She's not sure why she was fired—if it was because she opened the container, because she allowed it to rot, or because she blessed the smallest child when he began to vomit. The boss lady's Spanish was as bad as Fatima's English.

When she lifts her head out of the refrigerator again, Flaco Baca is behind her. Fatima suppresses her first instinct, which is to run away at a full sprint, and smiles. She sees the history of his blood through his skin: poor cannabis farm hands in Zacatecas, hunched and brown in an iridescent field surrounded by steel-colored mountains. She wonders why it is that those at the very beginning, harvesting the crop, and those at the very end, on the streets handing and taking, are the only ones who don't make any money. It's all in the middle. The more in the middle they are, the more money they stand to make, and the whole world seems to be clamoring to get as far inside of the middle as possible. She sees Flaco's father pick up a gun and make a name for himself. She sees him die violently as a twenty-five-year-old man. She sees his widow, Flaco's mother, taking their seven children over the border to live with her brother and clean hotel rooms in El Paso until she marries an honest house framer who saves enough money to buy a tow truck. Soon they have enough to buy a rollback and an impound lot. She runs the dispatch and keeps the books. She sees Flaco as a young boy, bookish and sensitive, loving everything too much—scared of the lot dogs who only want to lick him.

"Cómo está?" Flaco asks.

"Good," Fatima says.

"Habla ingles?"

"Poquito."

"Bueno, welcome to the Superstore. My name is Flaco, and I'm the third-shift Servant/Leader in Charge. I'm here to make sure you love your new job. If you ever have any problems, come to me first."

"Thank you," Fatima says. She thinks about how strange it is here in America, the way they pretend to care about you. And the way you're expected to pretend too, to like your job, to love your job. In Guatemala the power dynamics are definitive and occasionally bloody. You might have to spend your childhood stitching soccer balls and painting rosy cheeks on dolls, as she did, but you don't have to pretend to like it. The people in charge couldn't care less.

"How do you like working here so far?" Flaco asks.

"Good," Fatima says.

"Good," he says.

Fatima isn't always in thrall to her own visions. Sometimes they're wrong. She could, she knows, be completely wrong about Flaco's family history. Maybe her own prejudice against Mexicans has seeped through. Maybe she just added the drugs and violence to make it more dramatic, to entertain herself. She knows that the visions say much more about her than they do about history. She's not one to believe what she conjures in her mind over what she sees with her eyes. Sometimes her mind tells her that virgins don't have babies; it tells her that people don't come back from the dead; it tells her that a clever magician could have pulled off a lot of the so-called miracles in the Bible and that whatever really happened happened a long time ago, so who can know. But then she remembers what she saw as a child. It was like holding a fishbowl up between her eyes and the brightest-imaginable sun. And a woman inside of the light dance: The Virgin Mother. When she spoke, they felt like fetuses inside her womb. She has seen God with her own eyes, and she pities every person in the world who hasn't.

• • •

When Bicho arrives at the party he isn't wearing a shirt, and his pudgy, illustrated torso is smeared with blood. He isn't wearing shoes either, just very dusty socks covered in goatheads. Most noticeably absent are his glasses. Without them he is legally blind and his eyes are the size of fingerprints. Blood-soaked toilet paper rolls have been fastened to both sides of his left hand with duct tape. He says, "San Malverde came in a shiny black light. He said that we are all going to hell, and that there are different kinds of hell. Different levels. I'm going to the worst level. I'm going to go on the spike. But some of the hells aren't so bad. In some of the hells you don't even know you're in hell. They feel like real life."

"What the fuck happened to you?" Lalo asks.

"Yo camine desde mi casa, por el desierto," Bicho says.

"Pero there's no desert between here and your house, güey. You live on Espina," Ernesto says.

"No hay nada que desierto entre mi casa y aqui," Bicho says.

"Damn, this fool is all fucked up on something," Steve says.

"What happened to your hand?" Lalo asks. "Your pupils are like hubcaps."

"La espina de Jesus me perforo!"

"What the fuck are you talking about?"

"Me castigas por las morbosidades!"

Conejito hates it when they speak Spanish. He doesn't understand. Right now, when his craziest cousin has shown up to the party half naked and covered in blood, he has never been more interested in what someone has to say. *Was he shot? Who shot him? Did he shoot back? Is someone dead? Who's dead? Are we going to war? Am I really going to kill somebody? Am I really going to do that?*

"Soy malvado, mi familia. Tengo que ser parado y tengo que ser perdonado," Bicho says.

• • •

Fatima is dazzled by the elaborate cake sitting unmolested on the round table. She even admires the plastic cover that has been fashioned out of several standard plastic cake covers. She thinks of Elvia's seven-year-old body lying in repose at the altar. It laid there incorrupt under glass for seven days before it was buried. The people said she had the odor of sanctity, which smelled to Fatima like flowers and orange soda. Every day the people agreed that she seemed to be sleeping, and from the look on her face having the most wonderful dream. But over the span of those days Fatima noticed Elvia's makeup getting thicker and thicker and the smell of more and more incense burning around her body.

Fatima begins to weep for the fallen plastic soldier next to the black crater in the middle of the cake. He is missing both feet and the plastic stand they were attached to. She imagines the fear in the hearts of the plastic soldiers in the plastic Humvee. She believes that it is the meringue-haired cake lady's masterpiece. The desert mountain is a miracle: the coconut brush and the complicated organic shape of it. She removes the plastic cover with extreme care and thinks, *Esto deve ser lo que dios siente cuando ve la tierra abajo.*

She cuts a small piece from the corner and eats it fast with her fingers. She is able to replace the plastic dome and walk away before the footsteps in the hallway reach the breakroom.

11:03 P.M.

The city of Las Cruces is oldest at its center: a compact neighborhood of mud houses built in Mexico and swallowed by America in the Treaty of Guadalupe Hidalgo. Like a cross-sectioned tree, the layers of old bark form concentric rings: a neighborhood built in the 1840s surrounded by a neighborhood built in the 1860s, surrounded by neighborhoods built in the 1890s, 1920s—on out to the cookie-cutter subdivisions and chain restaurants sprouting up at the rim. The old bark that is Motel Boulevard seems to have died some time during the late nineteen seventies. It's hemmed in by a dilapidated fix-a-flat shop, a forgotten roller skating rink, and motels: buildings in various states of disrepair with long-lost corporate logos. The Pancake Alley lies between Sand Castle Estates and New Meridian. It's a squat, square building with a stripe of windows and a sleek neon sign. The Gods of Chaos are gathered at the back corner booth. Vita fills their cups with coffee. She doesn't like that they smoke cigarettes, and so many of them, but she'd rather they do it here, where she can keep an eye on them.

Daemon Dog says, "You're lucky. Your mom is the nicest lady."

Cide the Suffix asks, "What do you mean by that?"

The Omniscient Narrator kisses the white coffee cup with his black lips. When his coffee cup is full of black lipstick prints, he kisses Daemon

Dog's coffee cup and Cide the Suffix's coffee cup, filling them with black lip prints. "Festooned."

"What?" Daemon Dog asks.

"It's a word I like. This coffee cup is festooned with black kisses."

"What's it mean?" Daemon Dog asks.

"A chain or garland of flowers, leaves or ribbons. Or to adorn with decoration."

"We should put that word in our manifesto," Daemon Dog says.

The manifesto is still in its formative phase, but they have a thesis: the center is evil. Which is to say that anything mainstream and normative is evil. Lawns are evil. Church is evil. The Boy Scouts of America are evil. Most music. John Mayer and all the people who love him are a certain kid of dumb, plastic evil. Most television is evil. *Friends* and *Home Improvement* reruns are considered especially evil, to be watched and savored for their juicy evil nectars. Strangely, *American Idol* is not evil, as long as you watch for the right reason, the only justifiable reason being to feed like a vampire on the crushed and the humiliated, to joke about where they'll wash up after the show spits them out: as a fluffer in porno films, or as a foul smell in some hot aluminum trailer. The kids who form a prayer circle for the troops around the flagpole each morning are pure evil. Teachers are evil. Golf shirts are evil. The color khaki is evil. Nike is evil. Reebok is evil. Adidas is evil. The Gap is evil. Hollister is evil. Abercrombie and Fitch is evil. It is unspeakably evil to wear these labels across a tee or sweatshirt, or stretched across a carefully worn baseball cap with a carefully bowed bill. Any clothing line started by a rap star is evil. Those plastic, ventilated gardening shoes are evil. Flip-flops in all ways shapes and forms are evil. High school football games are evil. School spirit is evil. Pep rallies are evil. The Superstore and its hokey-nostagic-bullshit-bumpkin persona is the epicenter and the deepest darkest pit of evil. When Cide the Suffix declared iPods evil, the Omniscient Narrator smashed his with a hammer.

"The world is festooned with worthless people," Daemon Dog says.

"That's not how you use it," The Omniscient Narrator says.

"How come you guys never write down what I say?"

"The world isn't festooned with worthless people. It's lousy with them." Cide the Suffix runs two fingers through the pond of excess syrup on Daemon Dog's plate and uses it to twist a lock of her blue-green hair into a spike.

The Omniscient Narrator writes this down. He turns the quotes into lightning bolts with his pen.

"Maybe we're evil," Daemon Dog says. "Maybe all that stuff is good like they say it is. Maybe good just sucks."

The Omniscient Narrator writes down "Maybe good just sucks" in large gothic letters at the bottom of the inside cover. Daemon Dog is pleased. The size, placement, and form of the actual letters is of great importance in *The Gods of Chaos Manifesto*. Certain phrases hang like billboards. Some phrases are written in ultratiny letters with a very sharp pencil. Some are placed in thought or word bubbles over cartoons. Some phrases are written in a cryptic, jagged scrawl that is especially difficult for anyone over thirty to read. It all means something, right down to the font.

"Write my name after that one," Daemon Dog says. The Omniscient Narrator imagines foam dice falling out of his mouth every time he speaks.

"We're not writing names by anything," The Omniscient Narrator says.

"Bullshit," Daemon Dog says. "I want them to know I said that shit."

The Omniscient Narrator says, "Who's 'them?' What do you think, someone is going to carve this shit under a statue of you? A million people have had every idea you've ever had. And way before the wretched day you were born."

"It's all of us. Anonymous," Cide the Suffix says. "It's so fucking lame to want to be famous like every other lame-ass motherfucker in the world."

"I just want you to write my name by that one," Daemon Dog says.

"Fine. If you want to be like that. It's totally generic. I don't even know why the fuck I wrote it down." The Omniscient Narrator writes "Ishmael Gomez" under the quote in almost microscopic letters.

"No. Write Daemon Dog, Keith—you asshole."

"Are we really going to do this name thing or what?" Keith asks.

"Of course we are," Cide the Suffix says.

"I guess it is kind of gay," Ish says. "And hard to say. Hey, Omniscient Narrator, you want to go to the mall and get some nachos?"

"It's too pretentious, even for us," Keith says.

"Well, I'm not married to it," Brenda says.

Vita brings a pot of coffee and a plate of gravy fries. "Those truckers hardly touched 'em," Vita says.

Ish drags a fry through the congealed gravy like an oar through a scummy pond.

"Thank you, Mrs. Vargas," Keith says.

"My name is Vita. What the fuck is wrong with you?"

"Thanks," Keith says.

"How's your dad? You heard anything yet?" Vita asks.

"No," Keith says. "He still hasn't woken up."

She passes a gentle hand over Keith's hair and leaves to make her coffee rounds on sore feet.

"Your mom is the shit, Brenda. Bringing us gravy fries and shit," Ish says.

"Yeah, she's really doing you a big favor." Brenda thinks, *Next time I make myself puke, this is what I'm going to picture in my head.* She asks Keith, "What'll you do if your dad dies?"

"What the fuck is wrong with you? He's going to be fine," Ish says.

"I don't know," Keith says.

"If you started dressing like you are now in public, people would say it was because you're sad that your dad died," Brenda says. "They wouldn't know you've been like some gothic superhero, dressing up at night for almost a year. Would that bother you? That would bother the fuck out of me: people thinking they know exactly why I'm doing what I'm doing. Or would it finally give you an excuse to act the way you feel? Would it be the opposite?"

"Goths are lame as fuck. I'm my own thing," Keith says.

"Whatever," Brenda says. "Are you going to come out with the day walkers now, throw away your stupid baseball caps, sit with me and Ish at lunch?"

"Do you think people think they know why you do what you do?" Keith asks them both.

"No. I think that, more often than not, they wonder," Brenda says.

"I think you cut yourself because you were raped," Ish says.

Brenda glares at Ish and warns Keith: "Don't you write that down, motherfucker."

"Who gives a fuck," Ish says. "Let them think what they want. People think I'm doing everything because I'm gay: I dye my hair pink because I'm gay; I do Pilates because I'm gay; I make my own birthday cards because I'm gay; I drink peach iced tea because I'm gay."

"I don't think that. I think you do Pilates because you're fat," Brenda says.

"Is this because I said you were raped? I thought this poetry group was about cutting through the bullshit. I thought we could say anything as long as it was honest. I thought we agreed on that."

"You are fat," Brenda says.

"What's wrong with you?" Ish asks. "Why do you always go right to the rawest nerve?"

"Being honest isn't always pretty," Brenda says.

"You're being a fucking bitch," Ish says.

"The only reason we hang out with you is because you're gay," Brenda says. "That's the only cool thing about you. You're crying because you're gay."

"Fuck you," Ish says.

"Do we have to do this tonight?" Keith asks.

"Sorry, Keith, almost forgot your dad was maybe dying over here and all," Brenda says.

"What's wrong with you?" Ish asks. "His dad is going to be fine."

"I said 'maybe dying,' which is only true. When my grandma was in the hospital, I hated the way people talked to me. That scared me the most: everyone telling me that it was going to be all right, treating me like a figurine. It made me think that nothing was ever going to be all right.'"

"He *is* going to be fine," Ish says.

"Nobody knows what's going to happen," Keith says.

"That's my point," Brenda says. "I hope he's fine. I didn't say I didn't hope he was fine."

"It's just good to be out of the hospital and to not have to be, you know—so visibly sad. I mean I was sad, but, you know, I never felt like I was sad enough or like I looked sad enough. Not like my sister, who was crying so hard she could barely breathe. I never felt like I was sad for exactly the right reasons, either, if that makes sense. I never felt like I was scared of the right things. I just had this overwhelming sense that there was some right way to be and that I was doing it all wrong."

"Wow, that's deep—you should put that in your manifesto," Brenda says. "And while you're at it you should make up a punctuation mark for sarcasm."

"You should be nicer to us," Ish says. "We're the only ones who can stand to be around you."

11:31 P.M.

"I left her there," Bicho says. "There were still sounds coming out of her."

" "

"Yes, I do realize that I'm fucked up on magic mushrooms."

" "

"Yes, I know that does have something to do with what I'm seeing and what I'm saying."

"?"

"I realize that. But that doesn't make any of this unreal. Do you understand that?"

" "

"Your real is your real. My real is my real."

" "

"It will still be real in twelve hours. Now will still be here in twelve hours. It will be right here, where it is."

"?"

"I'm talking about the hells. I'm talking about the vision. He wears regular boots. He works hard. You can see it in his hands. And it wasn't like a TV show at all. There was no music. And everything was in colors I've never seen before. And he doesn't have a halo or nothing but he fucking glows holy colors. Holy light lives on a different spectrum. When you see a color in life, what you see is a reflection. Every color of light is absorbed inside that blue hat except blue. The blue is what's reflected. Your hat is really every color except blue. Holy light comes from God and reflects colors we don't even know about yet."

"?"

"I seen the God colors. Not mixing up already-known colors, but all-new primary colors no alive person's never seen before."

"?"

"I don't have the power to re-create or describe them."

11:42 P.M.

"I forgot what it was like sleeping by myself. I don't like it," Dolly says. "I need a puppy right now. Does the Superstore sell puppies?"

"No, thank God! Not any more," Megan says.

"Goddamn. The only thing in the world I want."

"Do you know what kind of horror that could lead to: the Superstore in the puppy business. The conscience of the customer is the only thing stopping them from opening puppy factories in the Northern Mariana Islands, injecting the females with Superstore brand-dog sperm, grinding up the defective puppies to feed to the fish."

"Still. I could sure go for one."

The kettle blows. Dolly wrings the last drippings of the last lemon into her decaffeinated tea. She adds two plops of good whiskey along with a generous flow of honey from a plastic bear. "No more lemons," she says.

Megan downs what's left of her tepid hot toddy. "You sit here long enough, you start to feel like you're in a real log cabin. Then you open up the window expecting to see some big Montana lake and it's this goddamn parking lot."

"Don't get me started on this thing. I'm selling it as soon as we get back to Kansas. You want another toddy?"

"I can't drink this shit without lemons," Megan says.

"So let's go get some. The lemons are just a parking lot away. They're open all night."

"I don't shop at the Superstore."

"Why not?"

"Are you kidding. They're the biggest culprit in the world. They're the ones that manufactured this whole clamoring American throw-away monster. And you should see what they do to the tropical fish they sell."

"Everything is bad if you look at it hard enough. Are you going to make your mother walk across the parking lot alone at night?"

With the push of a button, metal stairs extend from the side of the log cabin RV. Megan steadies her mother as she waddles down, bracing the floppy woven hat to her head against a desert gust.

* * *

The sudden gust of wind has the DJ scrambling to cover his gear and get it into the car. Nothing fucks with high-end audio equipment like dust and sand.

They have Bicho cleaned up and in the back bedroom, and he won't stop speaking in Spanish. All Conejito understands is that he's saying something that nobody should be hearing.

The word from Rucho is that Lencho already knows about Claudia. He knows who is responsible. The police do not. His reaction is anyone's guess. This past weekend one of the cartels executed sixteen teenagers who had gathered together to watch a soccer game on television. Only one of the teenagers could be connected to their dealings. And they are just as apt to torture, to lock you in a cinderblock house and slice your back open with a box cutter.

Lalo puts a gentle hand on Bicho's head and begs him to stop talking. Bicho narrates each of the sick things that he did to Claudia in Spanish. He doesn't overindulge in details, but he doesn't leave anything out. Conejito understands almost none of it. The words he does understand fly like shards.

They put Bicho's jeans, underwear, socks, and the bloody toilet paper rolls into a sturdy garbage bag and tie it with a sturdy knot. He lifts his arms into the air and allows them to put the clean white T-shirt on him. He steps into the blue track pants and the house shoes.

Lalo tells Conejito to throw the bag in the Dumpster behind the Sonic.

Bicho says, "Don't worry. It's only my blood," and doesn't flinch when Lalo pours hydrogen peroxide into the hole in his hand. He has no idea where his glasses are, but he claims to see everything clearly.

Steve challenges him to read a Led Zeppelin poster on the wall and he says, "Fire penis."

"This motherfucker is all tripped out," Steve says.

"I see it all clear," Bicho says.

"You're blind without your glasses," Steve says.

"He found his way here," Conejito says.

Lalo washes the bloody toilet paper away and wraps a clean white T-shirt around Bicho's hand.

"I've got to go to work," says Ernesto. He takes his keys out of his pocket and holds them in his hand to punctuate the point, even though his car is parked two blocks away.

"Now?" Lalo asks. The Marine Corps trained him to deal with trauma and contingencies, and two tours of combat calcified the lessons. His pulse has slowed several ticks.

"I'm going to work," Ernesto says. "I'm going to push the carts in."

• • •

In the sterile hospital restroom, Patty dips her hand in the electric-green aloe lotion and slides it under the back of Stacy's shirt.

"You have amazing hair. Is that an awkward thing to say while you're rubbing lotion on my back?"

"No."

"I bet you get that all the time."

"Kind of. You should see my dad's hair. It's prettier than mine."

"What does your dad do, Patty?"

"He's a security expert for a multimillion-dollar corporation."

"Which one?"

"I'm not allowed to say, actually."

"Does your mom work?"

"I don't know what she does anymore."

"Poor thing. Thank you so much, honey. That feels so much better. I don't know what I was thinking going out in the sun for more than five minutes. I've been a redhead my whole life, you think I would have learned. Kyler's a good kid, but sometimes I worry about her. I know what it's like being your age. Good friends are important. She says you're a good student."

"Four-point-o, so far."

"I wish Kyler could get it together like that. She's perfectly capable. She just needs to study harder. Maybe you could tutor her. I'd pay you, of course."

"You don't have to pay me."

"I saw you at the Crusade-for-Christ meeting. And at the rallies. You care about things bigger than yourself. Most people your age don't."

"You're starting to peel," Patty says, rinsing the gook and dead skin off her hands. "That's good."

"I know you weren't in Lubbock. I know it was Kyler's idea. I should be asking her, but she's so upset."

"I promised her."

"It's not the end of the world telling your mother you're going to be one place and then going to another. I get it. I did it. It's part of being a teenager. I'm not saying I approve. We all transgress. It's just a matter of how we deal with our transgressions. Do we lay them before God? Are we sorry? Do we atone? Or do we continue to lie about them? Pretend they never happened?"

"We were at my house."

"Were your parents home?"

"My grandmother was home the whole time.

"That's not so bad."

"Kyler is going to kill me."

"Don't cry. You did the right thing."

"Tell her I'm sorry."

"It's late, honey. You should go home now."

· · ·

Ron leaves his fourth voice mail message for Troy: "Bro, pick up. Fuck. I got some funny shit to tell you. This chick sent me a picture of her snatch over the Internet and you'll never believe what I sent her back. I took a picture of my dong coming though a dollhouse window. It's fucking hilarious. It looks huge. It's like fucking knocking over the refrigerator and shit. It's like that time Dugger went to the strip club and pretended to be blind so he could feel on all of them. Better than that, but very sensitive in nature. Very important that you don't tell anybody about this. Please erase all the messages I left, including this one, immediately. Call me back. I'd rather tell you in person, over a beer, but I can say it on the phone if I have to. Just call me back, bro. I got to tell you the whole story. It's hilarious. Please. As soon as you get this. This is Ron. From the West Side store."

12:00 A.M.

"The system is rebooting. It's gonna be six minutes before I can do anything," Wilma says. She turns the light at her register off, slides her money drawer closed, turns the key, and braces herself. *Every fucking night,* she thinks. Every night at exactly twelve midnight the SMART system shuts down to reboot, a loading icon stretches across the register screens, the time clocks are inaccessible, and for six minutes nothing is sold. And every night the people in line take it as a personal insult. When she first started on the late shift she would try to explain to the customers that this happened every night at twelve, automatically, but this always led her into exhausting conversations during which she was expected to apologize profusely for something that wasn't her fault. Now if a customer in line demands further explanation, she immediately calls the manager over the intercom. *Apologizing for shit that isn't your fault is the kind of job people wear a tie and get paid good money for.* A mother in her middle teens buying a generic bottle of infant electrolyte formula and a tired man in a dirty work shirt holding a TV dinner and a quart of chocolate milk stand and stare with pathetic indignation. Often, people scold Wilma, remind her that the customers "pay her salary." She understands these people, how anger bounces. Just this morning she cussed at the acne-ravaged girl behind the fast-food counter for putting an egg on her breakfast sandwich. But the way these two people stare at her... *Say something motherfuckers!* thinks Wilma. *Call me a bitch! Demand to speak to the manager! Call me a nigger! At least then I'd be justified when I jumped over this station and beat your ass! Anything but this hot quiet, those eyes. A human being shouldn't have to stand here and get looked at like this.*

• • •

They came in looking for lemons and wound up here, in the Superstore pet aisle, staring at a wall made of fish tanks.

"This is depressing." Dolly watches a candy-blue fish swim in a lethargic ellipse around the murk.

"Oh my God, they've turned on the sucker fish," Megan says. Four flash-colored fish munch on a bulging eye. "It's a little fish tank armageddon."

"I read that fish don't feel pain," Dolly says.

"Bullshit."

When Megan looks deeply sad like this, Dolly will do anything to make her daughter feel even the slightest bit better for even the shortest amount of time. She says, "Let's buy them all, Babybear. I'm serious. We'll set them free in a great big lake. They'll be able to swim all around."

"There must be a few hundred fish here."

"So what, I got a credit card."

"They'll just get eaten up. Or they'll die of shock. The transition from pet aisle to pond must be impossible."

"Maybe not all of them will make it, but we can really save a few. They can really be free. Anything is better than this."

"You're drunk, Mom."

"Don't be like that. Let's do it, Babybear. Let's put 'em all on your father's credit card. Drive 'em to Elephant Butte and set them all free. It'll be a good homage."

"How are we going to drive them? Neither one of us can drive that RV."

"You can. You have two eyes. You're an excellent driver."

"I've had just as many toddies as you have."

"We'll take them first thing in the morning."

"Let's get the hell out of here, Mom. All this makes me want to smash the glass, put everything out of its misery."

Dolly and Megan steady themselves on the cart as it rolls through the Superstore. The fluorescent tubes illuminate the microfibrous hair on their faces.

1:27 A.M.

Efren heats his soup and joins Ernesto at a round table in the smokeless breakroom. He smiles and Ernesto responds with a nod of the head. There is no need for introductions. Their names are clipped to their shirts.

"Did you see the cake?" Efren asks.

"No."

"You should look at it. It's amazing."

Ernesto walks across the room and glances at the cake, then walks back to his fast-food lunch. "Someone took a piece," he says.

Efren stands up to look at the cake. "What kind of person would do that?"

"You're shocked? Don't you know any people?"

"I work with the deli department. Level three. Where do you work?" Efren asks.

"They got me doing everything at night: stocking, bringing the carts in, checking sometimes."

"How long have you been here?"

"Nine months."

"Do you like working here?"

"Are you kidding?"

Efren looks confused.

"It fucking sucks, güey," Ernesto says. "They pay shit. Some manager or customer is always making you feel like a piece of shit. I can't do this anymore. I don't care what I have to do."

Efren blows on a spoonful of soup and Ernesto dips his fries in his milkshake.

"Work is not bad. 'What I have to do' is bad,'" Efren says. "I'm not your father. I'm no better than you are, but I have seen a lot. I am forgiven for a lot. I won't say what I've done. I will say that I am from Juárez, and I know exactly how it is."

"You like working here?" Ernesto asks.

"You can be a boss if you do all of the things right. You can work your way up to something. And nobody shoots at you for it."

"Fuck that mess, güey. They'll hire managers that look like they're from Mexico, but they ain't hiring managers that *sound* like they're from Mexico."

"Americans don't know how to be poor, with the rent-to-own and the rims and the credit cards. It doesn't have to be bad. I have a lot of dead family at home. I have seven very safe daughters here. I am very happy to work and eat and stay alive. You're too young to know how valuable that is. Stay, mi'jo. Work. Get to know God."

"Have you ever known someone who deserved to die?"

"Many. I deserve to die. Thank Jesus we don't get what we deserve."

• • •

Ron and his box of spaghetti are lying down on an uncomfortable bench in the empty auto-maintenance waiting room. His head is propped up by three rolled shammy cloths and he's watching a *Saved by the Bell* rerun, contemplating his semierect penis. *I jacked off to this episode when I was in middle school. The actors are all older than I am. It's not like I'd be jacking off to* Hannah Montana. *But those images aren't eighteen yet. That girl with the teased hair and the oversized sweater is a sophomore at Bayside High School. You're sick. You're sick for even thinking about it.* Ron decides against it, just to be safe. *This would be a great ethical question to post on the Internet under an anonymous name.* The closest Ron's penis has ever gotten to Claudia was inside her in-box. *She needs a man like me.* He believes that Mexican women lose their figures after they give birth, and wants to fill her with babies until her skin is stretched and sagging. He wants to fall asleep with her on a bed made heavy with forty years worth of their mingling dead skin cells. Even with heavy makeup tattooed above her eyes and around her lips, Claudia is a natural beauty. It is sad and profound, so profound that Ron thinks about it when he prays and when he masturbates.

Ron's telephone vibrates and April's face appears on the LCD screen. He mutes the TV before answering. "What are you doing up this late?"

"I can't sleep without you here."

"Do you know who this man is? This man could change our lives if I make the right impression."

"He's not going to come at one thirty in the morning. Why don't you come home and get at least a few hours of sleep so you can be sharp when he gets there."

"He could come at any time."

"Where are you?"

"I'm at the Superstore, honey. I told you."

"Where specifically?"

"On the floor."

"I don't hear anything in the background."

Ron sets his phone to speaker and holds it out the door. A voice over the speaker proclaims a code white in electronics. "I'm in that room where people wait while they get their cars worked on. Nobody ever comes back here after nine."

"Wouldn't it be better to come home and get some rest so you can be at your best tomorrow?"

"We talked about this before I took the job. This S/L stuff isn't nine to five. The whole family has to be on board. You've got to be behind me, honey, if I have any chance at all."

"Stay then."

"I love you. I'll be home soon, but just to shower and change."

"Do you want breakfast?"

"Sure."

"What?"

"Chocolate chip Eggos and hot coffee."

Ron sits up straight on the bench and flips his phone shut when Flaco raps gently on the hatched glass between them.

"Getting your oil changed, Romeo?" Flaco asks.

"Romeo?" Ron asks. Flaco is not a member of the society of male Superstore employees who prove their heterosexuality by acting gay. In fact, he usually seems put off by it. If he were a member, 'Romeo' would not have tickled the hairs on the back of Ron's neck at all. "I was talking to my wife," he says.

"Whatever you say, Tiger."

"I'm shopping," Ron says, rattling a box of spaghetti.

"What are you really doing here?"

"Just seeing how things work at night."

"Never worked a third here?"

"Sure. Now I'm an early-to-bed early-to-rise kind of guy."

"There's a lot to get done at night: stocking, rezoning, recoding, receiving."

"I see that. I was just taking a little break."

"This wouldn't have anything to do with Mr. Ken?"

"It has nothing to do with that."

"Well, don't worry. This place is going to look like a brand-new store tomorrow. Alicia booked them at the Comfort Inn. Mr. Brim is supposed to pick them up and get them here about six. You could still go home and get a few winks in."

Flaco gives Ron a knowing look, the kind that a bad stage actor projects into the cheap seats. When his shift ends, he will go home and make love to his long-time roommate, Chip, comforted and amused by the picture of Ron's penis on his cell phone.

The dread is in Ron's bones now. Troy finally called him back, but he hadn't responded the way he had hoped. He said that sending a chick a picture of your cock over the Internet was the worst thing you could possibly do, unless, like him, you really had something to be proud of. Because it only takes four clicks to send that shit around the planet. And he said that Ron putting his dick in a dollhouse, his daughter's dollhouse, was "twisted." He used that word over and over. He said that it would most certainly be taken the wrong way. And that there was no way a woman could ever possibly see the humor in something like that. He just didn't seem to *get it* at all. It wasn't that he didn't laugh. He laughed all right.

16.
Parallel Scars

2:11 A.M.

WHEN THE SUN IS BEATING DOWN ON THE DESERT, AND THE BLACK-top of the Superstore parking lot is soaked with heat, the cart shift is a job for a mule. At 2:11 a.m. Ernesto can't believe he's getting paid for it. The customers are just barely trickling out of the electric doors and for the first time all night he feels ahead of the metal carts that are colonizing the lot. He even has a couple of minutes to sit in his car and get high before they overtake him.

The sunroof is open. Cool, dry air feels like it's being poured over him by a friendly god, and the jagged mountains' silhouette sits on the I-10 overpass. Ernesto pictures his home: no pool or porch to enjoy the weather, only the cement pathway that wraps around the second story of the motel. In New Mexico, tumbleweeds can blow across desert for days without touching asphalt or cement and yet Ernesto is often trapped inside boxes, sometimes boxes inside of boxes. *Outside,* he thinks, then leans his seat back below the horizon of the windows, loads his pipe, and remembers the juvenile detention center: the smell of ball sweat and bleach in the laundry room, and the lilac smell of the lotion the black kids used to rub the ashes off their skin. Those smells lived inside of the larger wet paint smell of the building itself, where gang signs and profane poetry were engaged in an epic battle with the thin white layers. And it all lived inside the smell of an industrial ranch, which lived inside the smell of a copper smelter.

Ernesto's memories manifest deep in the sinus cavity, behind his eyes. Aluminum. Sweat. Savage, imperceptible pheromones. He sees Bicho on the ground with his forearms over his face—sees himself, in the blue crowd, stomping in his ribs. Uncle Rucho's five-year-old daughter's face was pretty but unnatural after her fifth plastic surgery. The damage from the dog was no longer visible, only the evidence of the repairs. He sees Rucho kicking the dog, trapping jackrabbits and throwing them in the kennel for it to kill. He sees Claudia's hip under the white sheet, smells the piss on Bicho's childhood bed, and remembers teasing him mercilessly. Rucho put nine rounds into the dog and then cried like a baby. *Guilt into anger. Grief into smoke.*

The voice at the top of his brain is a politician that he doesn't trust anymore. It told him he couldn't possibly screw his cousin, but he did one night when they were both very drunk. And it told him that he could kick his father's ass once, which turned out to be a painful miscalculation. He inhales until his fingers begin to twitch and play his pipe like a flute.

The Superstore parking lot is the size of a Revolutionary War battlefield: too little room for men to kill each other with rifled machine guns and tanks, but just enough room for men to kill each other with knuckleball muskets and bayonets. Ernesto's sixteen-year-old Mercedes-Benz is parked in the far corner where the cannons might have been positioned. The twirling yellow lights of the security truck drift towards it. He is good and high. He doesn't notice the lights until they pulse off the CD dangling from his rear-view mirror. He feels soaking wet in the golden light and bone dry seconds later when the CD is cold silver again. *Is that what the water looked like when he walked on it?* he thinks. *Was the sun going down?* He hears a door slam. There's a loaded revolver in the car that will never be fired.

"It's me, the law," Norm says, loping up to the car in his Superstore Security uniform and toasting the window with his flashlight.

"You scared me, fool. It was all quiet." Ernesto unlocks the door for Norm and loads the pipe.

Norm lays his seat back down below the windows, parallel to Ernesto. They don't stare through the open moonroof like a window; they stare at it like a screen. It removes the pressure to talk, even though what's in the frame is not much worth seeing: a strange moon, stars swamped by street lamps.

Norm talks anyway: "I've drove thirty-eight miles today without leaving this parking lot. It's boring, you know. I heard the last guy got to have a radio. But some customer got stabbed in the parking lot, and of course it was the radio's fault." His blowtorch lighter shoots a straight blue flame that dies before he can get a blast through the tube. "I long-haul trucked for eight years. I can drive all day and all night if I'm going somewhere. But driving thirty-eight miles at five miles an hour with no fucking radio reminds me of being back in high school. You know how bored you used to get? Like you would take bolt cutters and cut your fucking pinky finger off if you could just skip time forward until you didn't have to listen to that boring-ass teacher talk anymore, until you finally got to go finger your girlfriend or race cars with your buddies or whatever. At least I can be as loud as I want. Make up songs to myself. Work on my music. First I pin down the tune with these, just, melodic groans. Sometimes I'm in there with the windows rolled up just groaning my head off. It'd be a hell of a lot better if I had a iPod."

"Least you got air conditioning," Ernesto says.

Norm decides to shut up and listen to the trucks rattle the overpass. *I don't want to say the wrong thing, especially if anything is the wrong thing,* he thinks. *This so rare. This place never pays you for doing nothing. They'll pay you for doing something pointless, like driving around the parking lot for seven and a half hours or wiping a clean meat slicer with a dirty rag, but they won't pay you for nothing. If Ernesto doesn't want to talk, I'm certainly not going to be one of those people that blab and blab and ruin one of the few waking moments of peace you get in your life. I'm not my mother for Christ's sake. Always blabbing. Nobody could call that talking, and it certainly isn't discussion of any kind, ever. It's blabbing. Blabbing, blabbering, blathering, blah-blah-blah. Why do useless words disintegrate into the same chunks of sound? Is it universal? Do the Vietnamese say blabbing, or blabbering, or blah-blah-blah to signify rambling that's lost its meaning? Or are the chunks different? Probably. Probably sounds I couldn't make if I tried. Mexicans probably say something different even,* Norm thinks, and considers asking, but changes his mind when he looks over and sees that Ernesto's dick is out and his eyes are closed.

Ernesto asks Norm to unwrap his ponytail and drape the long blond hair over his lap. Here was another thing the politician spewing from the top of Ernesto's brain swore he could never do. He tries to keep his eyes shut, but they keep falling apart. He thinks, *Pretty yellow hair. I'm not a faggot,* then manages to put all words and labels out of his mind again. He puts Norm's wide back and the apple-skin calluses on his palms out of his mind too. All he sees is a cascade of well-conditioned light blond hair bobbing over his lap, and all he feels is a hot mouth and the occasional light scrape of teeth. He lifts his shirt up and rubs the soft hair into his skin. It forms easily broken tangles with his own curly black belly hair and smells like wet flowers. The hair is its own separate thing that could belong to anybody, like a bowling ball or a pair of socks. It could belong to that anchorwoman who he masturbates to every day at six. It might belong to anybody who cares enough to use the very best shampoo and conditioner that money can buy.

Ernesto pinches his eyes closed and rubs his own head, which has been shorn down to a soft burr except for the spindly black colito dangling from the base of his skull. He remembers the smell and feel of Fee Fee, the makeshift vagina his cellmate at the juvenile detention center taught him how to make. It was a comforting thing to be locked in a dark room with, like a teddy bear you could have sex with. When a C.O. found Fee Fee he usually just threw her away, and Ernesto made another. The materials weren't hard to come buy: hand towel, rubber glove, duct tape, add hand lotion to taste. And he just called her Fee Fee like the previous one. It was generic, not any special kind of name. The boy who taught Ernesto how to make Fee Fee called his fake vagina Fee Fee too. Even the boys who named their fake vaginas after girlfriends or celebrities referred to the actual contraption as a fee fee, i.e., 'My fee fee's name is Jennifer Lopez.' During lockup, in the dark with the fee fee, his mind was on Deborah Norville, Roberta Vargas, Juana Castillo, or whichever girl was bent over whichever hood in whichever custom car magazine he happened to be looking at, anything but the fee fee. The goal was transcendence, and now, years later, he does not understand why his mind is doing the opposite, drifting to this crude contraption during real-life sexual encounters. He wills himself to finish and produces a wet-nap from his glove compartment. His mother taught him that you should never pay for things that people give away, or practically give away, like newspapers, umbrellas, Bibles, or wet-naps. "You want another blast, fool?" Ernesto asks.

"You're in a generous mood. I must have done something right," Norm says.

Ernesto reaches into his glove compartment for a small glass tube with a tiny fake flower inside and a cork on either end.

"Why can't I use your bubbler?" Norm asks.

"You know where your mouth has been."

Norm takes the corks off the tube and shoots the small cloth flower through the sunroof like a wad of spitty napkin through a straw. "What the hell is that supposed to mean?"

Ernesto says, "Friends don't fight about what things mean. Women fight about what things mean."

Norm lights the small torch and admires its straight blue flame, as contained and rigid as a nail. *Fire nails.* There is a clink when he imagines it being hammered. He sees them being driven into Jesus' palms, into wood crossbeams—burning houses. *I was Godfuckingzilla once upon a time. The ambassador of horror, kicking the dead gooks over with my boot. Those bloated fish-eyed bodies. The putrid smell. They stopped looking human when you looked at them hard enough. Like statues made out of meat. You don't know what power is until you order a fire strike, kid. You don't know what a conscience is until you…. How strange that this is a pipe, this glass tube with a tiny fake flower inside. It doesn't look like a pipe. My mother doesn't know it's a pipe. I hope my daughter doesn't know it's a pipe. What percentage of the population knows it's a pipe when they see it sold by the register at the gas station? This is a pipe….* Once Norm finally gets around to taking a hit, he feels like the straight blue flame in his hands: energy without mass. His brain crashes like a computer. The words in his head stop. The images and the smells and the feelings that the words create are a figment of his imagination, a figment every bit as real as a memory. The Vietnam War was over before his first pubic hair. All the dead bodies he's ever seen have been carefully prepared and arranged in caskets.

"Stop wasting fuel. That's why your lighters are always getting dead, güey. Quit playing. I gotta get these pinche carts in," Ernesto says.

"Hell, I'll help you. I'm already sweating." Norm exits the car and draws several excited dry breaths from the desert. The carts fit together like disposable cups. Norm imagines that he is a tugboat as he pushes the impressive stack through the parking lot. When he thinks about running the football, his mind slips back into socket. *I'd run more if I had something to run against,* he thinks as he leans his stout body into the carts. *It felt so good to run someone over, and it was even kind of fun to get run over every once in a while by a worthy linebacker. What did they mean by 'push yourself?'* He tries to imagine it, but he is unable to conjure the image. *You can fall. You can pull yourself along I guess. But you can't literally push yourself. Well, I guess you can push yourself up, but you can't push yourself forward. You'd have to be behind yourself.* Sweat drenches Norm's white uniform shirt so thoroughly that the Superstore security badge looks like it's pinned directly to his chest. His long blond hair drips like melting icicles, and now looks to Ernesto more like a professional wrestler's than a female news anchor's. Ernesto is outraged by the fact that the guy who just sucked his dick can push more carts than he can. It makes him feel bright orange like forging iron, and he can't stop stacking grocery carts onto the train he's pushing. His heart pushes the glass through his veins. His long, thin muscles rage against the weight of the carts.

The problem really isn't pushing, it's turning. Norm is short enough to maneuver his body mass under the handle of the first cart, giving him excellent leverage, and he is powerful enough to lift the wheels off the ground. That's the key, lifting or pushing that first cart up hard enough to get the wheels off the ground. If you can't get enough wheels off the ground, you can't turn it.

A long cart train is rolling down a gentle slope at a shiny black SUV, and Ernesto doesn't stand a chance of getting the wheels off the ground.

•   •   •

Every centimeter of Stacy's skin is stinging like a broken tooth. She can't do anything fast enough. Neither can the cashier, who whistles seamlessly through the beginnings of all the Billy Joel songs you can name as she scans. The beeping register is her percussion section.

Stacy is buying a three-pound autobiography of a sitcom star and fifteen bottles of aloe lotion. Just imagining someone rubbing all that lotion into her skin makes her feel two percent better. *Can't you scan one and hit times fifteen?* she thinks. *Can't you just scan the same one fifteen times? They all cost the same. Lord Jesus please help me to be patient.* She considers telling the cashier that she's in a hurry but chews on her nails because she is intimidated by black women with tattoos on their breasts. The tattoo above the cashier's heavy right breast says 'Wes' and her name tag says 'Wilma.' Stacy considers going back for more bottles before she writes the check. To most rational people fifteen bottles would seem like enough, at least, even for the worst of sunburns, but she wants to be basted in aloe, lathered in aloe, until all the pain is gone—and they're on sale ten for ten dollars. Who knows when or if this will ever happen again. She imagines what Larry will say if he wakes from his coma, *'What are you going to do, fill the pool with the stuff?'* or *'I told you to wear sunscreen,'* or *'I didn't tell you to fall asleep in the sun.' He's always telling me what he told me to do or what he didn't tell me to do, Jesus. Stop. Stop. These thoughts are tearing me apart. Jesus, stop them right now. He loves me and I love him. He loves me and I love him. He loves me and I love him. He loves me so I love him. He loves me so I love him. I love him and he loves me and that's all that matters. I love him and I love Kyler and Keith. They all love me too. And of course all this love is nothing next to your love, Jesus. You are the coal mine of love and we can only deliver small portions of it, just enough to heat the souls around us until we go back down for more of your divine love. Scan! Please! I'm burning up here! Forgive me, Lord. Please help me to be patient.*

Stacy is never alone. She hasn't felt alone since Jesus came to live inside her brain six years ago at a Christian rock concert. A young singer with an impeccably groomed five-day beard was serenading Jesus like a lover, just him and his guitar and four fifty-foot screens set up behind him on which an actor playing Jesus was pretending to be beaten and mocked. He was spat upon. Blood flowed into his eyes as he stared serenely into the camera, seemingly into each individual set of eyes in the sixty-thousand-seat stadium while they drove nails into his hands and feet.

Jesus is her confidant and her censure. Before Jesus, her thoughts often horrified her. She might have wished her husband's secretary would get cancer and die. She had no official quarrel at all, no real reason to hate Deb. But Stacy couldn't stop herself from secretly hating her: polite or not, three hundred pounds or not, postmenopausal or not. She was jealous of the easy way she got along with Larry. They had their own language and their own secrets. And she made German chocolate cakes and snickerdoodles for Larry to take home, with real butter and real sugar, like she didn't know or care that she and her daughter, Kyler, were both on diets. Now her hate plays out in silent images that don't register any more significantly than the images on the perennially lit television in Larry's hospital room. Jesus changed the way she thinks the way being at a funeral changes the way we talk.

The last bottle of aloe finally beeps over the scanner. The total button is pushed and the cost is tallied. Stacy signs the check.

"I'm going to need a current phone number and license number on that check please," Wilma says.

"Alrighty," Stacy says. She thinks, *This is nothing. Oh my Jesus, the sunburn you must have had after spending forty days and forty nights in the desert. Wandering.*

"Gotta sunburn?"

"Sure do. Hurts pretty bad. Can't wait to get home." Stacy digs for a driver's license and a pen inside of the large faux-designer purse she purchased at the mercado back when Americans still crossed the border into Juárez. She copies her license number across the top of the check and curses herself for not having it memorized.

"Shoot, I got a sunburn once. Black as I am. My sister moved to the ocean and we went there to see her. I was too scared to go in, so I just sat and read a book with my feet in the water. The waves licked the sunblock off. Shoot. My feet felt like roast beefs."

Wilma bags the last of Stacy's purchases. She winces at the book among the bottles of aloe and asks, "Who the shoot is Paul Reiser?" She is trying to substitute the word "shoot" for more colorful words after two coachings for violating the *Official Associate Discourse Policy Handbook*.

A third coaching would automatically result in a Decision Day, or D-Day, as management likes to call it, the last step before termination.

"He was on that show that was on a few years ago," Stacy says. "It was in the dollar bin. I just wanted anything to read while I wait. It's a lot of pages for the price."

"You'd have to pay me more than I'm getting paid an hour right now to read that book. The book I was reading at the ocean with my feet in the water was about George Washington. It was my son's social studies book. I like to read what they're reading. Did you know he owned slaves? Shoot, he wasn't like that in my history book when I was a kid."

Stacy's brain is making calculations faster than she can perceive them. It is processing every late-night talk show joke and every tactful subject change she has ever heard in order to compose a benign sentence that doesn't sound racist. "That's probably why he's only worth a dollar," is the best she can come up with.

Wilma laughs and says, "Look what a fucking dollar gets you." She keeps the plastic bag between her hand and Paul Reiser's autobiography as if she were handling a piece of warm dog poop.

"My husband is in the hospital. I'm going to make someone rub this all on me the second I get back there," Stacy says.

Wilma's brain is working fast too, even faster than Stacy's. It's trying to figure out how to keep the woman from complaining to the management. She said "fuck," and the lady is wearing a yarn bracelet with W.W.J.D. spelled out on dice-shaped beads. Wilma is pretty sure that this woman's Jesus would complain to the management about her inappropriate language, get her fired and sent back to Wendy's. When she says, "I hope he's okay. Spent a lot of time in the hospital last year before my husband passed," the guilt tumbles and spreads inside her like smoke.

Stacy gets a bubble in her chest that she identifies, falsely, as pity. *This poor woman. Her poor dead husband. My pain is nothing. How did you do it without sunscreen, or aloe, or any of the modern amenities? And forty days without food, you are so great, Lord. I had a Frosty not fifteen minutes ago and I almost bought a bag of Heath bar dots.* When Wilma finally offers the receipt, Stacy hesitates. "I'm going to pray for you. Will you pray for me?"

"That never hurts," Wilma says, and thinks, *If there's a God that hears us pray, he's gonna hear this woman's prayer and know I'm a liar. She's going to smack God in the face for me.* She imagines a tumor spreading its tentacles into her brain, a malignant lump in her breast, the wires that connect her brain to her body fried by a terrible neurological disorder, all the things God can do to you if you piss him off, then she imagines them happening to Wes, and then her grandson, and then to her husband, Tony. *And what if there's no God that hears us pray?* That doesn't seem any good to her either.

As she exits the store, Stacy imagines herself at the funeral parlor. There's a line to console her. Larry's lips are slung over his teeth like a limp rubber band. The lips of the living wag and gape, but no sound comes out. She understands what they are saying without having to hear it. They're remarking about how strong she is. *There would be insurance.* She could spend as much money as she wanted on the black dress and the shoes. Who could say anything to her? In spite of her massive effort to become sad at the thought of her husband dying, a light shines through her face. *Jesus—you may have come to earth and felt pain I can't imagine. I bet crucifixion makes childbirth feel like a foot massage. And you may have even peed and pooped like a man. But you couldn't have been perfect and human at the same time. Human or perfect, Lord. Please forgive me, but you could've only been one or the other.*

The automated doors open and the breeze hits Stacy's blistering skin like a fire hose. Norm, sweaty blond hair falling into his eyes, has Ernesto in a chokehold. A thin, black tail lashes wildly from the base of Ernesto's shorn skull. Norm screams, "Stop struggling!" as he throws him to the ground and shoots pepper spray into his eyes.

"What the fuck!" Stacy yells.

Norm looks up at her to asks, "Ma'am, is this your car?"

The SUV sits like a volcanic rock under the street lamps, not a smudge, nor a water spot, nor a fingerprint to be found. A long train of shopping carts rests against it. Parallel scars stretch along the rear passenger quarter panel.

• • •

If not for the headlights and the tail lights, Ernesto couldn't see a thing through the burning tears. He stops when they stop, goes when they go, and does his best to navigate the drive home from memory. *Four stop-lights, one stop sign. One right turn. Four left turns.* He makes out the fuzzy pink-and-purple lights of the Taco Bell, which mean he is lost for sure. He can't even be sure which of the three Las Cruces locations he is passing.

He follows one set of lights for a while, decides, for no reason at all, that they know where they're going. They lead him to a stripe of lit widows and a sign that he recognizes.

• • •

The stars, each an astronomical fury of energy comparable to the life-giving sun, are dampened by street lamps casting their dryer-lint light over the Pancake Alley. The Gods of Chaos are smoking themselves into a fog in the corner booth. There are black lipstick prints on all the cigarette butts.

Ernesto enters and sits alone on a stool that faces the flat grill. He asks for orange juice and a menu.

"Having breakfast early?" Vita asks.

"Yeah," Ernesto says, downing his juice.

"What is wrong with your eyes? You look like you've been crying blood. Like some bruja put a curse on you." Just looking at Ernesto's eyes makes Vita's own eyes wet. *Compassion is residue,* she thinks as she refills Ernesto's orange juice.

"Pepper spray."

"Pobrecito, that shit looks like it hurts. Do you need a glass of milk to pour in your eyes? But I don't know. I'm not a nurse. But that shit seems like that might feel good."

Ernesto's laugh hisses through his teeth. "I need a job."

Keith smokes and laughs at the black lipstick print on his white coffee cup. Brenda asks, "Mom, can we have another pot of coffee?"

"I'll be right there, mi'ja," Vita says.

Ernesto is only nineteen, but he feels a vast space between himself and the teenagers in the corner. Most of it has to do with the fact that he is not embarrassed by the vest he hasn't bothered to take off, which asks, *How can I be of assistance?* He should be mortified, and just a year ago he would have been. Something has changed forever and he feels the sadness of that in his neck and shoulders. His hands feel numb and dangerous. He calms himself by reading the only words that have ever given him comfort; they are tattooed inside his forearm so that the tops of the letters point towards the tips of his fingers: *Dios te da y Dios te quitó.*

Vita scrapes the crackling grease into the trough with a flat metal spatula. She tells Ernesto, "My cook's car is always breaking down. Do you got a car?"

"Yes."

"Is it in good working order?"

"Yes."

"What kind?"

"Mercedes."

"Wow. Look at you."

"It's an older model, but I keep it in good shape."

"Can you cook an egg?"

"No."

"Are you retarded?"

"No."

"Then I can teach you."

• • •

If Stacy could stop thinking about her sunburn, it would hurt less. She picks at the white rings of dead skin on her arm with a press-on nail and pictures the hog scalder back on the farm. Her daddy dipped the hogs, then peeled their skins off like gloves.

Flaco Baca is the S/LIC (Servant/Leader in Charge) from ten to seven in the morning. Stacy tells him, "I am never shopping here again." He wants to laugh. Rivers of customers flow in and out of the doors so consistently that they will slice canyons into the earth before the Superstore goes out of business. He mulls it over in his head and no matter how he twists the phrases there is no way to explain to this woman how inconsequential she is without sounding rude. But he is sure it would make her feel better. It makes him feel invisible and safe.

"My shirt is sticking to my back! I can't reach where it needs it most!" She puts a third coat of aloe on her arms and neck, then wipes her hands on the faux leather office chair with the dangling price tag.

"The insurance adjuster should be here soon. I told you I would be happy to put the lotion on your back," Flaco says.

"Let me tell you, I'm almost that desperate. You're telling me there's not a woman working here that can do it?"

"I'm sorry. That's against all kinds of codes." He is annoyed by her lecherous implication, and wishes that he could tell her that he is as queer as a football bat.

"I'm a redhead. This is an emergency. Can I ask one of them? Just independently. Someone off the clock. Any woman would do."

"I can call H.O. and ask if it will make you feel better. But they're going to say no. You could ask another customer, I guess. We certainly don't have any jurisdiction over that."

"Are you kidding? I'll look like a nut."

"Do you want to try calling your family again?" Flaco asks.

I could be dead, Jesus. I'm putting a land line back in the house: a sturdy rotary with a loud bell. She thinks about all the nights she has spent anguishing over her kids. When they are out of the house at night, they're all she can think about until they are safely back at home. Her worry takes the form of vignettes playing out worst-case scenarios: Keith shot randomly as part of a gang initiation, Kyler, in a Rohypnol stupor, being led into the back of a windowless van by faceless black men. Yet here *she* is, out by herself just before dawn, and all their cell phones are going straight to voice mail.

"What can I do to make you more comfortable in the interim?" Flaco asks.

"Apparently nothing. So I'm going. I'm not going to sit here and cry in front of you."

"Of course you're free to leave any time. But I should warn you again that I can only assure you that our insurance company will pay for the damage if you wait for the claims adjuster to get here and fill out the report."

"My husband is in the hospital. I'm trying so hard to be patient right now, Jesus."

"We appreciate that very much."

"I wasn't talking to you."

"I'm going to leave you alone for a little while. I'm sure the claims adjuster will be here soon. We're her only client. Do you want a soda, or a cookie, or a piece of fruit or anything? It's on me."

"Bring me back a 30-30 and about a thousand shells."

"We lock the gun cabinets at eleven. State law." *Otherwise, legally, I guess I'd have to sell them to her,* thinks Flaco as he walks out the door.

The fluorescent tubes cast the empty Personnel Office in sick green light. The phrase "stack it high, sell it cheap," bounces around a row of computer monitors, flipping over itself in three dimensions. Stacy moves the chairs aside and kneels at one of the large, round, collapsible, press-board tables. She closes her eyes and considers the hard tile floor part of her penance. *Lord.... Help.... Please take the burning away. Take it down to hell where it belongs. Put your hands on my back. Soothe the terrible burning. Yes! Yes! I can feel them there! Praise be!* Pain transforms into a strong tingling sensation that Stacy associates with miraculous healing.

• • •

A drunk man in a pizza delivery uniform calls out for more coffee between spoonfuls of rubber eggs. Vita tries not to groan when she stands up. Her feet are killing her from her ankles to her toes, but she likes the job because it makes her walk. Her day job is almost completely sedentary. She spends most of her time scooting around the office on a rolling desk chair. At five feet two, two hundred and forty pounds, she understands that if she stops walking because it hurts too much, she may never walk again. She would get fatter and fatter until she couldn't leave the house. Brenda would have to wash her with a rag on a stick.

The Gods of Chaos stand up from the table. "What are you doing?" Vita asks.

"We're going to go do something," Brenda says.

"What?" Vita asks. "Where?"

"I don't know. We're bored."

"Swear to me you won't turn your cell phone off," Vita says.

"Swear," Brenda says.

"Don't just say 'swear,' Brenda. Say *I swear.*"

"*I* swear."

"Don't do, you know... Any of the things that normal teenagers do."

"That's our motto."

• • •

Finally, Norm thinks. *Some real time to work on the music.* He is in his garage with the door closed, trying to turn getting fired into a great country music song. *Maybe the song is to somebody specific. Like I'm singing it to my boss. Or I'm singing it to my wife, trying to explain how I lost my job. It needs a catchy refrain. Like:* What the fuck are we gonna do now? *No, something they'll play on the radio. Maybe I can turn a bit of folksy wisdom into the refrain. They do that a lot.* The phrase 'one in the hand is worth two in the bush' dances to a simple three-chord progression in his head. *No. That shit is shit. I'm not going to be one of those gimmicky assholes. The best country songs are stories. The story is this: guy gets fired for not taking any shit. When the boss fires him he drives over his little Japanese sports car with his giant American truck. Then he's got to go home and tell his wife and holy shit is she pissed off. How the hell am I going to make all this rhyme?* Norm hits an E minor on his acoustic guitar. The chord rings out farther and farther but Norm can't find the first word to the song. *Just let it come. Sit back and relax and it will come. Stop thinking about it. Thinking about it isn't helping at all. Just let it come. You have the talent. The gift is right there. You've always felt it.*

"What are you doing home this early?" Patty is drinking from a half-gallon jug of chocolate milk. Her exposed navel is like a button on a couch pillow.

"Do you want your daddy to sing you a song?"

"I'm tired."

"Maybe I'll write one for you while you sleep."

"If you wake Grandma up she's going to shit egg rolls."

Norm bangs the chords loudly and sings with his eyes clinched shut, "SHE (E) SLEEPS (A m) LIKE (G 7) THE (A m) DEAD (E)."

"You don't care about anybody but yourself."

Norm asks, "Do you really think that, or are you just saying whatever mean thing you can think of?"

"My practice SATs are tomorrow."

"Well excuse me for writing a song in my own house."

"This is Grandma's house."

"I grew up here."

"It's like four in the morning."

"But the inspiration is now, Sweet Pea."

"Don't turn on the motor and kill yourself." She means this as an earnest warning (hadn't he done stupider things while he was drunk?), so she is startled by the sarcastic tone the words take as they leave her mouth. "Seriously, Daddy, you only have to turn the key halfway for the radio to come on."

Norm is sitting in the bed of his compact Toyota truck. Beer cans are scattered around his legs. The scene is less than natural. Earlier he took a few beer cans out of the recycling bin and scattered them around the bed of the truck for effect. He believes the scene will help him write a great country music song. He imagines accepting a Country Music Award for best new artist. With luxuriant golden hair cascading from under his Stetson, and custom boots that make him seem a foot taller, he stares out into the tuxedos and cowboy hats, the dyed blond hair and the bolo ties, and tells the audience *the song just come to me one night while I was sitting in the bed of my old pickup truck with a guitar in my hands and a pile of empty beer cans round my feet. Me and my old lady was fighting about the fact that I'd just lost my job, and well, ladies and gentlemen, the song just come out.*

"How 'bout I write a song about you?" Norm asks.

"If it gets famous, will you buy me a car?" Patty asks.

"You bet."

"What kind of car would you buy me?"

"The safest one they sell."

Patty shakes up the last few gulps of chocolate milk until it looks like chocolate soap suds. She slurps the suds as she walks sock footed down the cool linoleum hallway. She checks the time on her phone, and finds a notice that Kyler has tagged her in a post: the words, "Sweetie, if you're going to be two faced, at least make one of them pretty," are written over the face of Marilyn Monroe. She decides not to guess about what hell will come next. She's watched Kyler destroy people before. She's helped Kyler destroy people by disseminating whatever vicious rumors Kyler decided were true. She decides not to cry about it. Not now. Crying over her complete ruination is too big a job for the night before her practice SATs. She thinks about college, dreadlocks, and reinvention.

Lying in bed, she can still hear her father through the thin wall, brushing the chords lightly with his thumb and singing under his breath. *If he has to sing, four in the morning in the garage is the only place. If anybody I know ever heard him, I would die, I would absolutely freaking die.*

17.
"gods"

WHEN KEITH POINTS THE CELL PHONE AT HIM, ISH FEELS COMpelled to do something worth filming. He speaks in a very bad Australian accent, which is actually much funnier than a good Australian accent, especially mixed with his slow, clumsy voice. "We're now entering health and beauty. We've got to be very quiet. This part of the store is very dangerous. This doohickey here is for pulling out your short and curlies. Very painful stuff. Very dangerous."

Brenda is laughing in a way that she rarely does, without malice or sarcasm.

"This is nail polish remover. The health and beauty section is its natural habitat. It's normally very docile, but when it feels threatened it emits a noxious venom." Ish removes the cap, stabs a hole in the seal with his keys, and breathes deeply. "Suck my poop finger!"

• • •

Their faces. *You stupid bitch,* they say. *You stupid nigger bitch.* They say it with their eyes now. Wilma. So tired. She has passed through the lucid phase of exhaustion into the completely useless phase. Her I.P.H. number is 188. She's tried opaque velvet drapes, aluminum foil over the windows, but even in the pitch black she can't sleep while the sun is up. Her body's connection to night and day is deeper than light and dark.

Normally the nights are relatively quiet, especially the late hours from twelve to five, but you never can tell when a rush is going to hit.

They come out of nowhere, by the droves, drunk single mothers picking up frozen waffles and hot pockets on the way home from the bar, an unfamous punk rock band called The Nobodies buying salty snacks and a cache of energy drinks for the road, nighthawks, and late shifters who are themselves every bit as tired as Wilma.

Wilma begins to cry in the midst of the onslaught. *Get your bitch ass on a register, Goddamnit,* she thinks at the sight of Flaco Baca standing at the greeter station with a pen and small yellow legal pad in hand. Just thirteen months ago he was the second fastest checker in the store. He earned the gold efficiency smock every quarter. *That motherfucker could help plow through this line.*

A customer walks through the automatic doors and immediately retreats back out of them at the sight of two lines stretched into the candy aisle. Flaco writes something on the pad.

Intercom: Attention! Call me Ishmael. Huffing nail polish remover will make you sick, but huffing duster will get you high as fuck. I'm going to test it all out for you. I'll report back later.

•   •   •

It's a small disaster that happens every night: the third-shift stockers arrange the boxes neat and flat on the shelves like the windows of a skyscraper and return the next night to find them blasted apart. They despise the second-shift stockers, who leave the shelves picked to the bone in some sections, disorganized and scattered with toys and boxes of sugary children's cereals, a half-eaten hotdog on a magazine rack, a rotting package of bologna sandwiched in a stack of SpongeBob SquarePants T-shirts. The restocking never stops, but late at night it's more like setting up a line of fallen dominos than sweeping a dirt floor. Even during a rush, the associates outnumber the customers two to one. Shopping carts yield to pallet jacks. Corridos and gangster rap emanate from the stockers' headphones. Box cutters make surgical incisions through cellophane skin into cardboard: deep enough to open the box and shallow enough to spare the merchandise.

Flaco tells the stockers to keep an eye out for three kids dressed like punks, first in Spanish, then in English.

Performance evaluations for third-shift stockers, which can affect

pay raises, promotions, and terminations, are based on a quantitative formula that calculates pallets processed and shelf footage. Their tired eyes
jump from UPC number to UPC number. They don't bother to lift their
heads when they hear what must be three high teenagers giggling and
tumbling through the aisles.

Ish sucks on a thin, red straw attached to a can of compressed air.
It freezes his vocal cords. He speaks into a red phone that carries his ro-
botic voice through the Superstore intercom, "Attention Earthclan: I am
your new leader. Bow down and suck my poop finger!"

. . .

After Dolly and Megan found the lemons they came in for, they wandered
for almost two more hours. By the time they arrive at Wilma's scanning
station, their cart is heaping with DVDs, sodas, pasta, toilet paper, robes,
slippers, and four different brands of snack crackers. They've been waiting in line for thirteen minutes, but they're in no rush to get back to the
RV. The man behind them mutters "God!" in frustration every couple of
minutes. Megan notes the fact that the increments of time between frustrated "Gods" is shrinking. *Soon he'll be saying "God" every couple of
seconds. Then he'll explode.*

When Megan reaches the front of the line and sees Wilma crying,
she thinks, *There must be something wrong with her eyes.* It's a soft cry,
but her hands are too busy scanning items to keep up with wiping the
wet lines off her cheeks.

"Are you okay?" Dolly asks.

"Tired," Wilma says.

"When do they let you go home?"

"Long time. At night like this all I want to do is sleep. Got to watch
my grandbaby during the day while his parents are at work. So I couldn't
sleep, even if I could."

"So when do you sleep?"

"Hardly."

"Do they give you a lunch break."

"One hour."

"Come out to our RV and take a nap. Nobody's gonna be using my
bed. I can't sleep till I get a puppy."

Wilma laughs.

"Seriously."

"Well which one is yours?" Wilma asks, still laughing.

"It looks like a log cabin."

"Really?"

"Oh, honey," Dolly says. "Two more hot toddies and I'll rub your feet."

Wilma smiles.

The cart is for balance. Dolly and Megan each steer a side, gliding it across the parking lot like drunk pallbearers.

"Can you imagine having to stand there checking people out while you cry?" Megan says. "Can you imagine working there? Eight hours a day that's your job. Scanning products, typing in codes for seven dollars an hour while customers berate you. No stopping. It doesn't matter if your dad just died. It doesn't matter if you can't stop crying. I bet her feet are killing her."

"People treat people so bad."

"We should have bought all the tropical fish. We should have actually done that."

"Let's go back right now. We'll set them free in Elephant Butte."

"Aw, screw it." Megan reiterates with a flutter of her left hand.

• • •

Finally, Wilma thinks as she swipes her name tag through the clock. *There must be a god up there who knows exactly how much I can take.* She's got an hour for lunch and she's considering spending it with the two drunk ladies who came through her line and invited her to their RV. Nobody else could even look at her. She cried and scanned their beer and their chips and their fish sticks and their greeting cards and their diapers and they didn't even look at her. What if she actually showed up? They said they'd be up all night. She needs any sleep she can get. Her trailer and her own bed are too far away. Minus the trips to and from, she'd only have about twenty minutes to close her eyes. She plays out the alternative in her head: an hour in the breakroom with Celia talking about her health problems, or someone else's health problems. It seems to Wilma that bad health is all anyone ever talks

about in the breakroom: so and so's bad back, bad heart, cancer re-
lapse, or aching tooth. Right now that's the last thing she wants to
hear.

She walks past pallets of baked beans, Gatorade, and neon towels
on Action Alley, and makes up her mind to visit the ladies in the RV. The
deciding factor is her recollection of a terrifying thought she had earlier
during the rush: *I hope you all die in a terrorist attack.* The thought was
pointed at each and every customer in the store, even the children, especially the children—especially the snot nose who screamed himself
into convulsions over a movie-themed action figure and the parents who
eventually bought it for him. Thoughts like these feel like spider eggs
hatching in her stomach. After tonight's deluge, her stomach is crawling
with baby spiders.

Wilma remembers seeing a sitcom once that insisted that white people have to bring a gift each time they visit each other's houses. The liquor
aisle is not an option. It closes at 12 a.m. in accordance with state law,
and even if she could afford it, she couldn't exactly walk out with a bottle
of booze on her lunch break. She picks up a box of sugar cookies covered
with pink icing and white and yellow sprinkles.

There isn't a soul in line now. Cruz is propping herself up against
the register, trying to relieve some of the pressure in her lower back.

Wilma says, "Have you ever seen a rush like that this time of night?
Just all a sudden everybody and their cousins was in here. I think I might
have had a panic attack. I was crying. My hands was shaking and I thought
I was going to die. Does that mean I had one?"

Cruz swipes the cookies, "I don't get to go on break until you come
back, so hurry up."

There is no mistaking Wilhelmina Hemphill for easy prey as she
walks across the parking lot. Her eyes are peeled and her gait is confident
and aware. Her right hand is stuffed inside her purse, clutching her keys,
but to the outside world she could be clutching something more deadly.
It's a mistake she hopes they make. On the east side of her native Cleveland, carrying yourself like a punk could cost you your Nikes. The lights
in the RV are on. Fake wood like a cabin, just like they said. Wilma hears
voices inside. She peels the ninety-nine-cent sticker off the box of pink
cookies and knocks politely.

"Check first!" Dolly says. "What the hell is wrong with you? Do you do that in Phoenix—open the door without looking? Please tell me you don't do that in Phoenix."

"It's the cashier," Megan says.

"Fantastic! Fix her a drink." Dolly pushes a button on the dash and motorized stairs extend outside the cabin.

It reminds Wilma of a cartoon she saw once. The cat died and a stairway extended from heaven to greet his winged soul. It made Josiah laugh so bright. *Sometime soon, I'm gonna put his name on my body. Real pretty letters. Right over my other titty.* "I brought cookies," she says.

"Marvelous!" Dolly says. "You didn't have to do that. She scarfs down a pink-frosted cookie in three bites, then grabs another and nibbles daintily. "These are wonderful!"

"Wow, it's like a log cabin up in here. Shoot."

"It was more my husband's taste than mine," Dolly says.

"Well..." *Leave it to white people*, thinks Wilma.

"What can I get you to drink?"

"Do you have Dr Pepper?"

"What would you like in that?"

"Ice, please."

"Come on, we won't tell."

"No thank you. I haven't slept in two and a half days. I don't need any booze," Wilma says.

"Come on. I haven't slept in almost twenty hours," Megan says. "And I'm still drinking. And my dad died."

Dolly says, "My husband, Cal, died in his sleep. Our family doesn't usually stay up all night drinking like this."

"He died on that couch you're about to sit on," Megan says. "I just thought you should know. If that freaks you out you can sit at the nook, or the other captain's chair."

"Did he bleed or anything?" Wilma asks.

"No, we're pretty sure it was a heart attack," Megan says.

"Then it doesn't bother me." Wilma sits on the couch. Her feet feel better as soon as she does. She thinks, *I wish I knew these people good enough to take my shoes off.*

"He had been having some issues with his heart for a while. Last week he complained of a strange pain in his shoulder. He was on blood thinners, and Lipitor. I don't know about all these drugs they put you on. There are all these side effects, and if you mix the wrong ones, bad things happen. And you think one's okay and six months later there's some class-action law suit going on because people's kidneys are failing. Medicine is such risky business."

"He ate terribly," Megan says. "The heart can only take so much cheese and dead animal."

"He was one of these people that just won't go to the doctor unless they have blood gushing out of their eyes. He used to say going to the doctor is like going to the mechanic: you go in for one thing and they find six more things wrong with you. I went in for a biopsy two years ago and walked out with a heart murmur and a prescription for Wellbutrin. If you've got insurance, they'll find something else wrong with you."

Wilma resists a fleeting urge to stab her eye out with one of the miniature cocktail swords on the kitchen counter.

"We hiked down to the bottom of the Grand Canyon on my birthday five days ago," Dolly says. "And back up! He was fine. I was the one who almost died of exhaustion."

"You and Daddy hiked all the way down to the bottom of the Grand Canyon?"

"Well, not all the way down," Dolly says. "I'll get the pictures."

"It was all the animal fat, the trans fats, GM foods, hormones. Hormones!" yells Megan. "Kids' heads are getting bigger according to the *New England Journal of Medicine*. I knew it! I've been telling people for five years! Next time you're in there, look at all the kids' heads. They're fucking huge!"

Dolly points and clicks on her laptop with only the vaguest notion of what she's doing. Cal usually handled the computer. "He was lucky to have his health until the end. So many people deal with health problems all their lives. Have you ever seen anyone die of Lou Gehrig disease? Alzheimer's? God, it's horrific. And cystic fibrosis. I had a cousin who had it. Dying in your sleep is a gift from God. Even if it's a little too soon."

Wilma feels like she has trespassed onto private property and been cornered by two attack dogs made of grief and fur and teeth. Her brain is processing frantically, searching desperately for a T-bone steak to distract them. "My son died in Iraq three years ago today. That's why I was crying. That's why I haven't slept." *I'm so sorry, Baby.*

Dolly takes off her hat, wrapping the floppy straw brim around her chest like a blanket. "Oh my God. And listen to us just talking. Oh my God. That is so horrible. It's so unbelievably horrible, I can't imagine. I'm so sorry. God, I'm just so sorry to be rambling and oh my God."

"Those chicken-hawk bastards! Those greedy frat house morons! Those convenient Christians! Those phony fucking cowboys!" Megan is rounding into her fourth stage of drunkenness. In order they are 1) Chummy and affable; 2) The Philosopher; 3) Brazen and combative; 4) Sad and loud; 5) Hungry. "What can I do?" Megan asks.

"Nothing," Wilma says.

"Are you hungry? Do you want to get drunk? Do you want to talk about it?"

"No," Wilma says.

"She doesn't *have* to talk about it," Dolly says.

"Of course she doesn't have to talk about it," Megan says. She is already imagining this encounter as a truly fantastic anecdote. *When I tell it, I won't even mention that she was black.*

There has to be something," Dolly says.

"There's one thing," Wilma says.

"What?" Dolly asks. "Anything."

"The nap."

"Oh my God, of course!" Dolly says, relieved and excited that what she needs is so easy to give. It almost never worked that way with Cal. She was always trying to give him what he didn't want but she knew he needed, like advice, green vegetables, and medication. She rifles through Cal's drawer and hands Wilma a pair of his old sweats and a white T-shirt. Wilma hesitates briefly before removing her Superstore-issue vest and golf shirt. The name "Wes," tattooed on her right breast, doubles in height when she takes her bra off. Blood rushes down into her legs and feet again. Megan pities Wilma for her breasts as much as anything else.

They seem to her like having to carry two full laundry bags around your neck at all times.

"Do you want a wake-up call?" Dolly asks.

"Five twenty. I'm gonna set my cell phone to go off just in case."

"We're so glad to help," Dolly says.

"If I'm putting you all out..."

"Not at all! Not at all! Sleep!" insists Dolly.

"Thank you all so much. I'm so tired." *1,000 thread count. That shit really does make a difference.* Wilma tries not to think about what could be on them. *Cum, blood, urine, drool—I hope it's drool, then urine, then cum, and then blood. Shut up Wilma Hemphill. Go to sleep. You ain't got long.*

"God, she must be tired," whispers Megan. "She won't even get to sleep long enough to have a proper dream."

"Can you imagine?" whispers Dolly. She finds her favorite picture on the laptop, the one she wanted Wilma to see. She contemplates taking it to the bedroom to show to her, *Maybe she has a picture of her son she'll want to show me*, but she thinks better of it when Wilma's snore switches on like a garbage disposal. In the photo Dolly and Cal are standing at the edge of the canyon with layers of sky and sedimentary rock melded together in the background. They stayed four days longer than planned, waiting for a great sky. The preceding sunsets and sunrises had been nice, but Cal believed they could do better. *This is the great thing about RV travel: we got nowhere to be,* he said over and over. In the photo, they're both wearing fanny packs filled with regulating, life-preserving pills with plenty of side effects. *We're so old now.* The feeling reminds Dolly of taking LSD and looking in the mirror when she was twenty. Her long-lost best friend, Katie Durkin, had dared her to do it, to look in the mirror and think about herself getting old, dying. She could only laugh at death, and at the lines of her face as they seemed to deepen in the mirror, as her hair got thinner, her jowls looser. "Look at him," Dolly says. "The Grand Canyon."

"He looks happy," Megan says.

"We have so many blessings to count, Babybear. Let's make sure to have hot coffee waiting for her," Dolly says.

"Breakfast!" Megan says.

"Bacon!" Dolly says.

"Will you two bitches shut the fuck up pretty please?" Wilma asks from the sleeping quarters.

"I like her so much," whispers Megan.

"Me too," whispers Dolly.

• • •

Flaco, Glen, and Quentin are prowling the aisles, looking for the troublemakers.

Ish is wearing a silver spray-paint goatee. His crooked, beige teeth contrast with the sparkling flecks. His face is fat and intelligent looking, but his brain is like a melon rind, sputtering incoherent blurts and incongruous images. He's not terrified to go to school tomorrow. He's not wondering why he was born to exactly the wrong father: a zealot who travels the gun-show circuit distributing pamphlets that proclaim the sovereignty of Texas. He's not remembering the sight of his weeping mother burning the contents of his room on the front lawn: clothes he made himself, drawings, old toys. He doesn't see her chanting prayers in Spanish over the melting plastic trash can. He's not thinking about the fact that he has been sleeping on Vita's couch for eight months, not wondering when he will have a bed again. He's not insulting himself more harshly than his cruelest tormentors. He's not asking himself when the last time he ate a vegetable was.

"Do you think he's okay?" Brenda asks.

"Define okay," Keith says.

"Do you think he's going to die?"

"Tonight?"

Brenda spots Flaco stepping around a pallet stacked high with rubbing alcohol. Even without the blue vest, it's easy to peg him as an employee. His carriage and his tie say manager. The Gods of Chaos move in synchrony and silence around a metal accordion barrier into the greenhouse appendage of the Superstore, which is closed at night and spookily beautiful when the lights are off, like a deep dark forest in a children's book.

Headlights from the parking lot pass through the foliage, weaving a kinetic tapestry of shadows to rival any stained-glass window.

• • •

"Tell me about the gun, Mom," whispers Megan.

"What's a cabin without a musket?" Dolly dumps pancake powder and water into a mixing bowl. She tries to mix it all without a sound by grinding the whisk on the inside of the Pyrex bowl like a mortar in a pestle.

"I got scared when your father was gone. I never wanted to be one of those women, but I guess I am."

"Statistically, you're much more likely to be killed by that gun than any intruder."

"It's a good thing I don't know how to load it. I would have shot that tall man you opened the door for. What if he was a murderer?"

"He had flowers."

"You shouldn't just open the door for strangers, even if they have flowers. Maybe especially if they have flowers. I'm not sleeping until I get a fucking puppy. I'm serious."

"I'm not going to be able to go to sleep until that gun is out of here. I still can't believe you have a fucking gun."

"I'll take it back then. Come with me. We'll get some more honey and some bacon. It was just a momentary panic."

"You can't do that."

"Why?"

"You don't know what it will be used for. What if you take this gun back to the Superstore and it goes on the shelf and then someone else buys it and shoots someone? Or shoots a deer, or a nice duck, or whatever things mean people shoot? We can't take it back. It's a killing machine."

"They'll just buy the next one on the shelf, Babybear. They had a heap of them."

Megan screams under her breath, "Why do we try to save one person with cancer! Someone else is just going to get cancer!"

Dolly puts her finger to her lips and rolls her eyes towards RV's sleeping quarters. She whispers, "Well, what do you want me to do about it, Baby-B? I can't just throw it away. That would be worse. A kid could find it. Or a bad person. A person could find it in the Dumpster, then commit a terrible crime with it while wearing surgical gloves. My prints would be all over it."

"God, what should we do?"

"I'm going to call the police and ask them to come out here and get it," Dolly says.

"What are you going to tell them?"

"We've got a gun and we want to give it to you."

"Very funny."

* * *

Ish uproots a begonia and hits Brenda on the head with the clodded root ball.

"Fuck you, asshole," Brenda says, shaking the dirt from her blue-green hair, laughing and tossing an uprooted geranium back at Ish.

"Try huffing ant spray," Keith says, laughing and pointing the cell phone camera at Ish.

Ish sprays Raid ant killer into a plastic bag and takes several deep breaths.

"Does it get you high?" Brenda asks.

"It does something," Ish says. "My hand is shaking."

"This shit is going to blow up YouTube," Keith says.

Red-and-blue lights race into the parking lot, splashing frantic shadow puppets on the walls of the dark greenhouse. The Gods of Chaos dash through a door that reads "ASSOCIATES ONLY."

* * *

"That's all I needed," says the very tired insurance adjuster, sliding the papers back across the round table. "I don't know why we couldn't have done this over the phone, or at a more reasonable hour."

"Tell Mr. Manager over there," Stacy says, indicating towards Flaco with the finger she had been gnawing the nail off of.

"I didn't make any of these policies."

"I prayed to Jesus to soothe the pain of my terrible sunburn and I believe he did. I believe he put his actual hand on my back."

"Does it feel better?" asks the tired insurance adjuster.

"It's almost gone," Stacy says. Her cell phone finally chimes. It's a text from Kyler that says, "Hes awake he doesn't know who i am where ru :'("

She sees a blip of her son Keith—made up like a zombie—as he sprints past the doorless doorway of the main office. A girl with blue-green hair follows, then a huffing, pink-haired boy.

Flaco chases after them in a pathetic, middle-aged stride.

Stacy decides not to believe her eyes.

18.
Salmon Sunday

4:50 A.M.

FOR ABOUT THREE YEARS AFTER 9/11, SALMON SUNDAY BECAME patriot Sunday. Instead of wearing salmon ties or shirts, Servant/Leaders wore flag ties and flag shirts, sometimes flag buttons, which was just fine with Rich, who feels uncomfortable wearing an effeminate color like pink, even if they call it salmon.

"What's wrong?" April asks, sitting up in bed, watching him get dressed.

"Why'd he have to come on Salmon Sunday?" Rich asks, retying the offending tie.

"You look nice."

"I look like a fairy."

"There's nothing wrong with a man wearing salmon," April says.

"It's pink. Jesus. Calling it 'salmon' just makes it even worse. You don't know how it is with these Broken Arrow guys. These are hunting, fishing, football-boosting guys. These guys don't wear fucking pink. Lester may be the best manager I've ever worked for, but he just can't learn the culture. The flashy suits and the flashy n-word car with ten TVs in it. He actually thinks that shit impresses them. These are guys who make eight figures a year and drive old red pickup trucks. They make a show out of doubling up in hotel rooms and eating fast food."

"Why do you have to wear a pink tie?" April asks.

"It's Lester's thing: color-coordinated managers. He's been doing it for years."

"Your maroon tie could probably pass."

"No, I did that for the first three months of this Salmon Sunday bull-shit. He's on to me."

"Can't you just say you spilled something on your salmon tie?"

"Pink tie!"

"Are you sure you don't have time for even a quick nap? At least some breakfast?"

"No, I need to get right back to the store. When I tell him my idea, God, things are going to change for us. So get ready. It's the big idea, honey. The pallet idea. The one I've been holding back. He's supposed to be there at six, which means he's supposed to be there at five forty. I want to get there twenty minutes early, at five twenty. And I'm going to pick up this retarded kid Mr. Ken loves on the way."

"You seem awful tense is what I'm saying, like a nap might do you some good."

"I like staying up all night every once in a blue moon. It's exhilarating. I feel sharp. I feel good. I feel like my idea is original and special, and like it's going to change everything."

"I'll put the Pop-Tarts in."

"Black men can wear things that white men can't. They can wear pink and not look queer because of Puff Daddy."

"What kind?"

"Frosted cinnamon brown sugar, please!" He clips a name tag that says "Ron," onto his shirt pocket.

5:02 A.M.

In Wilma's dream, the streets are conveyor belts. Inside the still car, she is a passenger carried by the mechanized road. Giant disposable razors, towering bottles of soda, and candy bars the size of city buses loom in front and behind her.

Wilma's cell phone barely has the time to blurt out the first bar of its musical ringtone before she has silenced it.

"Should we wake her up?" Dolly asks.

"Don't you dare," Megan says.

"That didn't seem like a rational alarm turn off to me. That seemed like a half-asleep alarm turn off."

"Maybe she has a snooze."

"That's true."

"I think she knows what she's doing."

"Her pancakes are gonna get cold."

"Can you fry some bacon, just so I can smell it?"

"I had to throw away everything perishable when the power went out."

• • •

Jayson yells, "Yes, it's still dark outside!" as he shuffles out the door. His mother grabs his hand and tells him to work extra hard today. She explains that today is a special day, and that the friend he'll be seeing is a very special man. She thanks Ron for giving him a ride, and Ron tells her that Jayson is one of their best workers, that they'd be lost without him on an important day like today. Jayson beams. Ron barely makes it back to the car before he begins to cry and wish like hell he was retarded.

"Are you okay?" Jayson asks.

"It must not be that bad if you have a mother like that."

"What?"

"What do you like to do when you're not at work?"

"I shoot basketballs and I make sandwiches and I pet the dog."

"That sounds amazing. Mr. Ken is very excited to see you."

"Okay."

"I brought a picture of Mr. Ken so you'll know exactly who he is when you see him."

"Okay."

"This is very important for me, Jayson. I've got an idea so big I can only tell it to Mr. Ken himself. Mr. Brim is always asking for our 'big ideas' in meetings, but I've been holding this one back for two years. It's too important. It's been brewing up there in the old noggin. Marinating. The more I think about it, the simpler it gets. I know exactly what I'm going to say to him. The exact words. I'm not going to tell you, if that's what you're getting at. I see what you're doing. No, I'm not going to tell you."

"Okay."

"It's about how we process the pallets. I'll tell you that much. It will save us millions. Within a year, everyone will be doing things my way."

"Okay," Jayson says.

"Anyway, when we get there, it's important that you tell Mr. Ken how much you really really love working with all of us at the Superstore. Especially me, your friend who gave you a ride today."

"Okay."

"Pretend I'm Mr. Ken."

"Okay.

Ron stops at the red light and shows Jayson the picture of Ken Provost. "This guy."

"Okay."

"It's good to see you again, Jayson. How have you been?"

"Great."

"What's new?"

"I made five baskets in a row."

"That's great!"

"How's working here at the Superstore treating you?"

"I love it!"

"Great."

"What about that Ron Barns?

"He's great! He's my friend!"

"That's great, Jayson. Good job. But he's not going to ask about me, so you're just going to have to say it. We've got a few minutes. Want to drive through and get some breakfast?"

5:16 A.M.

Betty gazes with approval at her apparel section, which she came in early to rezone herself. The fry grease in the deli is clean, and the chickens are spinning in the rotisserie. A rep from Sara Lee is setting up a samples station next to an island cooler. The floors are buffed. The bathrooms are clean. The registers are processing reasonable lines. There are no empties on the shelves. Everything seems to be in order. She couldn't have done it without Bobby, who she had to send home. She just hopes the staff she has on now can maintain it.

Betty texts the words "ALL GOOD" to Lester and Ron and decides to take a fifteen. The early birds are just starting to trickle in. She sees Quentin when she walks through the associates-only doors. "Did you catch those little pricks?" she asks.

"No," he says, and follows her into the break room. "We reviewed the security footage. They didn't steal anything. One of them went around the store huffing whatever he thought would get him high and the others just egged him on I guess."

"What the hell is wrong with teenagers?"

"Should we call the police?"

"Are you kidding me? Mr. Ken will be here any minute."

They notice the missing piece simultaneously: a rich, brown divot in the icing.

"People are assholes," Betty says.

5:30 A.M.

By 5:30 a.m. Lester Brim is dressed in a salmon-colored suit and is on his way to the Superstore with important passengers in tow. Ken Provost, Dale, and Davis Toddich all have their drive-through breakfast sandwiches and coffees in hand. Anyone who has read Mr. Gene's book knows that he suggests planning to be anywhere important at least twenty minutes early. That way you'll only be late in the case of truly catastrophic circumstances. Consequently, official Home Office Superstore Time (H.O.S.T.) is ahead of the rest of the world by twenty minutes. A short Home Office meeting scheduled to start at 10 a.m. might well be over by 9:55.

"This might be the cleanest car I've ever been in," Mr. Ken says. "Is it brand-new?"

"It'll be three years old this August."

"Wow, you've really kept it up. You could perform surgery in here."

"Thank you," Lester says. "I don't usually let people eat in here, but I make a few exceptions."

"I'm sorry," Ken says, wrapping up his sandwich. "That was

thoughtless." Dale and Davis follow his lead and wrap up their breakfast sandwiches.

"Oh no no! Please!" pleads Lester, baring every one of his gleaming teeth. "Eat!"

"No. You worked hard for this truck, Lester. I know the job of a store manager isn't easy. And this is a nice Durango you got here. TVs all over the place. It's good you take pride in it. Our breakfast can wait until we get there."

"No. Really. I really don't care."

"I'm sorry, Lester. I just don't feel right about it, now," Mr. Ken says.

"I was just saying something, you know, the point being that I don't usually have the CEO of the freaking Superstore in my truck, you know. You can eat your breakfast and wipe your hands on the seat for all I care."

"I wouldn't dream of it. Let me tell you something, Lester. I don't see myself as above the rules of this company or the rules of this truck. I am a Servant/Leader and all that that entails. I work *for* every single person in this car. That's how I see it."

"I wasn't trying to say anything like that," Lester says.

"I drive a 1988 flareside pickup with a milkshake stain on the floorboard. I like it because I can strap the buck to the hood and I don't have to worry about the antlers scratching the finish."

"I didn't mean for you all to stop eating. Really. I wish you'd just finish."

"I just wouldn't feel right about it now," Mr. Ken says.

5:35 A.M.

Wilma awakes to the smell of pancakes filling the log cabin recreational vehicle. There is a vase filled with peaked roses and an eyeball floating in a glass of clear liquid resting on the foldout table. The old woman is asleep on the couch and her daughter has dozed off in the captain's chair. Wilma checks the door and is relieved to find it unlocked. She wonders how long she's been sleeping. *I haven't slept in so long. It could have been days.* She opens the drapes, suddenly panicked that she's in some new town a thousand miles away, but she's here in the same parking lot she fell asleep in.

"Don't mind the eyeball. It's glass," Megan says, working a cramp out of her neck.

Wilma takes off Cal's old sweatpants and T-shirt and begins to change back into her work uniform.

"I haven't eaten meat in sixteen years, but I would do some truly degrading things to some bacon right now," Megan says.

"What time is it?"

"Five thirty-nine."

"Jesus Christ."

"We saw you fiddle with your alarm. We thought you hit snooze or something. We thought you knew what you were doing."

"Fuck. I'm done for."

"I'm so sorry."

"It's my own fucking fault."

"You want some coffee, a beer?"

The text on her phone is from Cruz. It says, "were the fuk ru"

"Name your poison."

"Sleep. I'm going home."

"I think I'm going to drive this thing out of here today."

"Are you sure that's a good idea?"

"I'll double up on my ADD medication."

"Tell your mom I said thank you when she wakes up."

"I will. I expect to be halfway to Ruidoso by then."

"Ever driven a log cabin before?"

Megan laughs.

"Thank you for the hospitality," Wilma says.

"Are you on Facebook?"

"Let's not."

19.
Smithereens

"ARE WE GOING TO GO TO WORK NOW?" JAYSON ASKS.

"In a minute," says Ron. "I'd like to time it perfectly. Eat that delicious breakfast sandwich I bought you."

"When are we going to get out of your car and go to work?"

"As soon as we see Lester's pimp truck pull in the lot we're going to start walking. So keep your eyes peeled. It's purple. I've got this all played out in my head, buddy. I'm going to be walking to the store twenty minutes early for work. I just happened to pick you up and give you a ride this morning, my good friend. I just happened to buy you that delicious breakfast sandwich and chocolate milk. And we walk up together like pals right when Mr. Ken happens to be walking up. And I let you guys chat for a minute because I know you're old friends. And you talk about how much you like working here and all the people. And you talk about how all the people here like you, which they do, Jayson, all of us really really do. Especially me. And maybe you could introduce me to your friend Mr. Ken. Maybe you could introduce me as your good or best friend or whatever, and then I could tell him my idea. And God, Jayson, I wish I could tell you my idea. It's so simple. It's going to change the way all the pallets in the world are processed. But just the off chance that you might— through no fault of your own—say it before I got the chance to say it. And I know you wouldn't ever mean to do that, but I can just imagine it. You—through no fault of your own—say this great idea out loud because it's just so great that you can't contain it. And all a sudden it's your idea, and because of your condition, it's like Mr. Gene's angel has spoken through your mouth. And I'm in the background like, 'Hey, that was my idea! We talked about it in the car!' And then I'm the guy trying to take the credit away from a *special* prophet of Mr. Gene. No, that's not going to happen. Do you want to look at the picture again?"

"Who would win, a Tyrannosaurus rex or The Incredible Hulk?" asks Jayson.

"The Hulk is fictional. The writer can make him beat up anything he wants."

"Who would win between a bear and a shark?"

"It depends on the water."

"Why can't you just answer the question?"

5:47 A.M.

Conejito wonders why he's the one driving. He's only twelve and at least as stoned as Lalo and Bicho. Ernesto has let him drive his Mercedes around the library parking lot and up and down the El Paseo strip a couple of times, but he's never been on a highway like this. He yells, "Out of my way, motherfuckers!" and steps on the gas to pass a small convoy of eighteen-wheelers with Superstore logos painted on them.

"Híjole! Slow down! We're not in a hurry," Lalo says.

It is also strange that Lalo is sitting in the back with Bicho, and that nobody is riding shotgun. He wishes that Ernesto was with them, the cautious one, the only person who can talk Lalo out of anything. He once watched him talk Lalo out of running a kid over with a car.

But if Ernesto was here, I wouldn't be driving, Conejito thinks.

"I can't see anything, again," Bicho says. "Not without my glasses. You're just splotches." He turns his tiny eyes to the window. His left hand is wrapped in an old T-shirt drenched in blood, and a black garbage bag has been fastened around it with electrical tape. Conejito is glad that Bicho is in the seat directly behind the driver, so he doesn't have to look at him.

When they pass the Taco Cabana, Lalo asks Bicho if he's hungry. Conejito is disappointed when he answers no. He could go for steak tacos and a large horchata, but he can't speak up without inviting fat jokes.

The highway opens up into four empty lanes. The Franklin Mountains are silhouetted by a radioactive predawn glow. Lalo directs him onto the exit.

"Slow down on the exits, güey," Lalo says. "You're doing good."

Lalo navigates Conejito past the old Asarco plant into a very old neighborhood made of mud, corrugated metal, and broken glass. The streets are empty except for a calico cat and a boy about Conejito's age wearing expensive sneakers and circling the Cash for Gold parking lot on his bike.

Lalo directs Conejito down an alley. When the Cadillac rumbles over the gravel, he is sure he has never had so much fun in his life.

A motor hums and pulls open the corrugated steel gate at the end of the alley.

"What now?" Conejito asks, shifting the car into park.

"If you hear that gate start to close, put it in reverse and gun it," Lalo says.

A young man walks onto the concrete porch wearing a white snakeskin cowboy hat, long silver basketball shorts, and purple crocks. His eyes are red and swollen. On his chest, there is a tuft of black hair between his puffy, brown nipples. He has no tattoos. Four large pit bulls dart out the front door behind him and sniff the car aggressively.

"I can't see," Bicho says.

"You know where we are," Lalo says.

"I can't see!"

"You can see enough."

"What's going to happen to me?"

"You're going to get new glasses."

"Conejito, I'll give you a thousand dollars to drive away as fast as you can," Bicho says.

Lalo meets Conejito's eyes in the rearview mirror.

"Don't look at him," Bicho says. "Look at me!"

Conejito stares out the window at the dogs circling the car.

Bicho says, "When I confessed. When I told you everything. Does that make a difference to God? Let me talk to Claudia. Let me beg."

"What do you want us to tell Concha?" Lalo asks

"Don't tell my mom anything."

"Anything else?"

"Nobody gets my bike. Throw it in the lake." Bicho reaches across himself and opens the car door with his good hand. He lets out a bleating sound when the dogs shove their noses in his crotch. The brown dog puts his front paws on his back and begins to thrust. Bicho shakes him off and starts to cry. Conejito notices for the first time that the man in the snakeskin hat is crying shamelessly, like he is alone. Conejito is terrified of the man's tears, which scream, *Men feel natural shame when they cry in front of other men! But you are not men! You are not even here.*

The man says something to Bicho in Spanish. Conejito doesn't understand what the man says, but the tone of it makes his butt cheeks clench. Bicho walks towards the man, who pushes him inside and slams the door.

Conejito pulls forward, then backs up at a slight angle. He pulls forward and backs up again.

"Jesus Christ. Let's get the fuck out of here," Lalo says.

Conejito pulls forward and backs up again, only managing to rotate the car another twenty degrees towards the mouth of the alley.

"Ándale pues!"

Conejito backs up again and stops six feet before hitting the new chrome-accented pickup truck parked in the driveway.

"You've got room," Lalo says.

"It looks like I'm going to hit it."

"You've got a ton of space. Go!"

Conejito gives it some gas and the car leaps towards the truck. He steps on the brake with both feet and the tires squeak on the pavement. They are still a good two feet away.

"This is fucking embarrassing," Lalo says.

Conejito cuts it hard and idles forward. He is three degrees shy of the turn into the alley. He backs up once more, about eight inches, and finally navigates the car onto the gravel.

Lalo lifts his face out of his hands.

"Why am I driving? What's going on?" Conejito asks.

"God, I'm sorry, kid. There's no way to answer that without making you terrified of your own family."

"What's happening?"

"You ever had your own hundred dollar bill?" Lalo asks.

•   •   •

This very small Loss Prevention Office, with eight monitors covering one wall, feels, to Fatima, like the last place she will ever see. Fatima attributes the dank air to the size of the room and the furious breathing of the men standing in front of her.

"Oh, you're fired. Don't worry about that. I just wish we could put you in fucking jail for what you did!" the giant man in devil glasses says.

"We're going to send your ass back to Guatemala or wherever the fuck!" the fat man says.

"Oh, boy. Are you in for a shitstorm of trouble," the giant says. "How do you say shitstorm in Spanish?"

The fat man yells, "Caca tormenta!"

"Caca tormenta, bitch!"

Fatima turns her head towards to the monitors on the wall. People are pushing carts full of merchandise through the aisles, checking prices, holding hands, picking up toaster ovens and putting them back down.

"She doesn't understand a word we're saying," says the giant.

"You're fucked. We got you on tape, bitch. Show her."

Fatima wonders if, given her age, they will bother to rape her first. Will they kill her here or kill her at the place in the desert where they will bury her. When she was young, the Guerrilla Army of the Poor (Ejército Guerrillero de los Pobres) took women her age and younger into rooms. She was spared, she believes, because she found the will to look them in the eyes.

The giant man in the devil glasses fast forwards through video of Fatima cleaning the breakroom: picking up cans and wrappers, scrubbing out the microwave and throwing away lunches in the refrigerator. He stops on her grainy image standing in front of the cake. "This is where it gets interesting. Did you need a little midnight snack? You don't look like you're starving."

The grainy image of Fatima removes the cake's cover, cuts away the corner with a plastic knife, and eats it with her fingers in two large bites.

"Did you think we made that cake for you?"

"Did you fight in Iraq and get your face burned off?"

"Do you know Ken Provost is on his way right now?"

"You know how long it took them ladies to make that?"

"We had cameras coming. From the paper. To take a picture of it."

"Beautiful," Fatima says.

"Is that all this bitch knows how to say," Quentin says.

"Era demasiado hermosa. No podía controlar mi."

5:55 A.M.

"Tell me, why the monitors behind the headrests in the back seat?" Mr. Ken asks.

"Just, you know, so the people behind me have something to watch at stoplights," Lester says.

Mr. Ken laughs. "It's a fantastic car."

"I think it's inspiring quite honestly, to all the associates at the store," Lester says. "They see this car and they know that hard work and the Superstore got me it. It makes them want to do better, to reach up."

"Fantastic. Dale, do we sell monitors like these?" Ken asks.

"Yes we do," Dale says, surfing the web on his cell.

"What's the lowest price-point?"

"Three forty-nine eighty-nine is the cheapest model right now," Dale says.

"We need to pay attention to what Lester's particular demographic is striving for. We need to put it in reach. Get Mr. He on that."

"Wow," Lester says when he thinks about all of the wheels that he has just witnessed being put into motion: factories and processing plants going up around the world. When he turns into the parking lot, he is horrified to see two police cars parked along the front curb.

"What is this?" Ken asks.

"I'm not sure," Lester says.

Davis Toddich gets off his cell phone and says, "A sexual assault. A bad one. Not at the store, thank God. An associate off the clock. They're asking questions."

"That's horrible," Mr. Ken says.

"They're taking statements. They are particularly interested in talking to Richard Barns."

"Did you call press for a photo op, Dale?"

"Yes, sir," Dale says.

"Well, call it off. Jesus, get us out of here," Ken says.

"Where to?" Lester asks.

"Back to the freaking airport. I definitely don't need my picture taken in front of that scene."

"You came all the way out here. Are you sure you want to go home?" Lester asks. "I'm sure it's nothing. The police will be gone in a few minutes. I don't even know a Richard Barns."

"Dale, get the jet out here," Ken says.

"You should see all the fluorescent beach towels we're moving," Lester says. "Once we moved them to the endcaps, we couldn't keep them on the shelves. And we got this thing where managers wear the same color clothes: different colors on different days of the week. Today is Salmon Sunday."

"How far away from the airport are we?" asks Ken.

"At least fifty minutes," Dale says.

"I'm freaking starving. I'm going to eat this thing." Ken unwraps his breakfast sandwich and takes a bite. Davis and Dale do the same.

5:58 A.M.

Kyler follows her nose to a recovery room choked with flowers. There are no visitors.

"Water, please," Claudia says when she catches Kyler staring.

"I don't work here."

"You can walk, right?"

Kyler walks past a gurgling cooler and follows the blue line to the waiting room. Her brother, Keith, is sleeping with a backpack for a pillow. There is a smudge of white makeup under his ear.

"I'm the only one here," Kyler says.

"It was my turn to disappear."

"Where's mom?"

"It's her turn. Don't be a baby."

6:00 A.M.

"The Cowboys going to win today?" asks the man sitting at the counter, tearing off pieces of tortilla and wrapping them around bites of chorizo and eggs.

Ernesto doesn't care if the Cowboys win or lose, which is to say that he doesn't care whether he lives or dies. He says, "I don't know, boss. I hope so," and scrapes a gummy brown residue off the flat grill into the grease trough.

Vita's feet feel like water balloons, like if she puts any more weight on them they might pop. She lies down on the sticky floor in front of the flat grill and props her feet up on the counter.

"Your feet again?" Ernesto asks.

"They'll be okay when the blood goes down."

Ernesto is getting better at cooking eggs already. A quick confident motion with the spatula and plenty of grease is the key to keeping the yolks inside their membranes.

"Will you take it to him please, the fat guy in the corner?" Vita asks.

"I got my own job to do."

"Just this once."

"I know what will happen. Your feet will start hurting all the time and then I be the cook and the fucking waiter." Ernesto can't stop rubbing his eyes, which are still bloody from pepper spray and painful to leave open for more than five seconds at a time.

Vita scissors her legs back and forth. To Ernesto's horror, he spies a tiny hole in the crotch of her purple stretch pants.

"Please take this over there to the fat guy, just this once."

Ernesto carries the plate toward the fat man. He looks out the windows and watches Conejito park Lalo's blue Cadillac over one of the yellow lines in the parking lot.

Conejito walks through the glass doors and sees Ernesto holding a plate of biscuits and gravy. "I saw your car," Conejito says.

Ernesto delivers the plate to the man in blue, who asks for more coffee.

"What happened to your eyes?" Conejito asks. "They're all bloody."

"Why are you driving Lalo's car?" Ernesto asks.

"You first."

"My job at the Superstore ended with a can of pepper spray."

"You work here now?"

"I guess."

"That was fast."

"Why are you driving Lalo's car?"

"He let me." Conejito wedges into a booth. He spins the dangling tooth with his tongue until it falls out and then spits it onto the table. The taste of blood in his mouth is making him hungry. "Can I still stay with you? Claudia won't be back for a while."

"Of course."

"Take this hundred dollars for rent and groceries and stuff."

Ernesto folds the hundred dollar bill into his pocket. "Do you want something to eat? It's on me."

"Bacon sandwich."

6:40 A.M.

"We'll, maybe they went to the Valley store first," Ron says, gathering the wrappers and the chocolate milk container lying around his car into the fast-food bag.

"Are we going to go to work now?" asks Jayson.

"Yes we are, buddy. But stay by me, okay."

"Okay," Jayson says.

"Let's go clock in."

Ron walks into the store and down Action Alley. He believes Jayson is the one they are staring at, with his toothy, smiling head bobbing next to his. *So rude,* he thinks, and defends Jayson with his gaze, staring down all the gawkers until they look away. When Ron says "good morning" to people, the associates all answer back in strange voices, like they are saying good morning to a lunatic's sock puppet.

Ron and Jayson walk through the Associates Only doors. A small huddle of associates by the time clock disperses. They clock in and find Betty Pulson hunched over a shoebox-size piece of war cake in the break room.

"Where's Mr. Ken?"

"Oh, he won't be coming," says Betty.

"What?"

"He's on his way back to Broken Arrow," says Betty. "Two police officers are waiting to talk to you in the Personnel Office. Claudia Limón is in the hospital. Someone tried to kill her. Oh, and I have a picture of your cock on my cell phone. Good morning, Ron." Betty says. "Good morning to you too, Jayson."

"Who would win, Betty, a bear or a shark?" Jayson asks.

"What kind of bear? What kind of shark?"

"The toughest bear and the toughest shark?"

"Is there water?"

"Yes."

"How much?"

"The shallow end of the pool?"

"Is it saltwater? Sharks need saltwater."

"God damn it," Jayson says.

6:50 A.M.

"I'm sorry, ma'am. The nail salon doesn't open for another ten minutes," Dat says through an accordion cage.

"Oh, I've got other shopping to do," Stacy says. "I was just walking by."

"It's okay. Come in. I'll open up for you." He raises the cage separating the nail salon from the rest of the Superstore and turns on the lights.

"I don't want to get you in trouble."

Dat pours fluid from three large bottles into three large basins. "Where I'm from, when the sun is up you go to work. We're not obsessed with clocks."

"They kept me here for hours waiting for some insurance adjuster. I've just been walking around since then." She wishes so desperately that he had left the metal cage closed and the lights off. To be locked in the dark cage of this nail shop with him. *Jesus, what is wrong with me? If you're not going to save me, just go away and let me have my thoughts at least. Can't I at least want what I want? It's not like I'm asking to have it.*

Dat tries not to gasp when the lady presents her fingers. The nails have been gnawed to their quicks.

"I've been chewing them. My husband is in the hospital."

"Is he going to be all right?"

"Probably not."

"What do you want me to do with these?"

"Just hold them."

.   .   .

The creaking closet door yanks Tony halfway out of a dream about sitting in his bass boat, catching bears like fish. Wilma sits down hard on the bed, and when that doesn't make him open his eyes she lays down facing him and sighs.

"Are you okay?" Tony asks.

"I don't know," Wilma says. "I did some things today that made me sick."

"Okay."

"Wake up, Tony, please."

"I am awake."

"Well, you know how I don't really like people, right?"

"Yeah."

"Open your eyes and look at me, please."

"I hear everything you say."

"I wouldn't say I don't like people. Do you really think that's true?"

"No."

"I was just so fucking tired, baby. I haven't slept in three days. And I start talking to people. I hate talking to people when I'm at work. When it's not even really two people talking at all. I think one of the reasons I'm so fast at what I do is because I don't care about the customers or being friendly. I just want to get through that line. Which is all they want, too. I don't know why I cared about having the highest I.P.H. number. They never paid me any more. I mean it's *something*. It is something. But I hit a serious wall. I was so tired that it was impossible to keep going. But all I could do was keep going. Then I realized sort of all at once that there was no end to the line.

"I told some white ladies that Wes died in Iraq so they would shut up and let me sleep like they said they would. And I told another lady you were dead. I was trying to get her to feel sorry for me because I said fuck by accident and I didn't want her to complain. So I said it. Now she's going to pray for something that isn't true."

"Slow down. How did my death come up?"

"Cruz said she was in Flaco's office for two hours. And I met these drunk white ladies in line and they invited me back to their trailer to take a nap on my lunch break. I overslept by a lot. I never even clocked back in. He's going to fucking fire me."

"Why do you even speak to the customers?"

"Because I'm bored."

"You say how are you fine how are you. Nobody says more than that."

"I don't know what I was fucking saying and I was so fucking bored and tired I started jawing about history and perspective like you know I didn't mean anything by it. She was buying a book and she had a sunburn, and I told her about that fucking terrible sunburn I got at Kee Kee's and the book I was reading. And then I told her that George Washington owned slaves. She looked at me like I was crazy, but all I meant was that the past is always evil because what's evil is always changing. And isn't it interesting how we forgive racists, slave drivers, genocidal forefathers, and kid-fuckers like Socrates. Build fucking monuments after 'em. Put 'em on the money. What will future generations be forced to forgive us for when we're decomposed? When even our fucking bones are dust?"

"Words are like ball bearings," Tony says.

"I know. Shit. He said next time. Do you think your mom can get me a job at the casino?"

"No, you have to be an Indian."

"Fuck. Unplug the phone. I'm just going to show up to work tomorrow like nothing ever happened."

"How did my death come up?"

"Oh, I don't remember. I'm just so glad you're alive. I got this feeling in my stomach like you were really dead after I said it. It was fucking terrible," Wilma says. "I wanted to be dead, too."

"I'm glad you're alive."

"I'm glad you're alive, too."

"Do you want to go to sleep?" Tony asks.

"I can't sleep when the sun is up," Wilma says.

Wilma ties Tony's wrists to the bed posts with her sweaty, raincloud-colored work socks. The bedpost slams the thin wall that separates Tony and Wilma's room from their son's. Familiar knocking wakes Wes up much too early. The pills they fed him at the clinical trials made him sleep twelve hours a day, and they haven't worn off. He opens his sticky eyes and looks at his son, Josiah, lying in a sleeping bag at the foot of his bed. *Lucky boy can't hear a thing,* he thinks. The morning light is making the blue curtains on his side of the trailer glow. He plugs his guitar into his amplifier and turns it all the way up. He plays along with the even tempo of his parents' thumping bedpost while his son sleeps. They are a strange band.

Acknowledgments

Thank you, Mom and Dad, for your encouragement and support. Thank you, Robert Boswell. You have gone so far above your teaching obligations for me, and I have absolutely no hope of ever repaying my debt. I can only strive to engage and challenge my students with similar dedication, generosity, and truth. Thank you, Antonya Nelson and Kevin McIlvoy, and thanks to all my fine teachers: Chris Bachelder, Alexander Parsons, and Richard Yañez.

Thank you, friends who read this book in various stages and offered your feedback and encouragement: Justin Chrestman, Jill Stukenburg, Rus Bradburd, Peggy Chapman, Ricardo Trujillo, and Blasé Drexler. Thank you to Yvette López and R.H.H., with apologies. Thanks, Amy Smith-Muise, for copyediting my book for free. If your family ever needs help moving or digging a stump out of the yard, I'm your man.

Thank you, Eleanor Jackson, my stalwart literary agent. You have worked tirelessly on my behalf for years. I have little hope that the returns on this book can pay you what your time and heartening pep talks are worth. Thank you, Liese Meyer, for finding my book in the clutter and for making it better. Thank you, Mark Krotov and Allyson Rudolph, for your keen eyes and wise advice. Thank you to my publicist, Kait Heacock, and all of the people at Overlook Press who worked to create the book.

Thank you, Terese Mailhot, for your intelligent and honest mind, for putting up with me, and for carrying our child. I love you. Thank you to my child, who does not yet have a name to put into print. Thank you Isaiah Mailhot, for calling me Dad. Thank you, Cathlin Burns, Graysen Burns, and Rory Burns. I would also like to thank my Wal-Mart coworkers, especially Louie, Jaun, Juana, Roberta, and Estevan.